MW01486852

The Wild Adventures of Doc Savage

Please visit www.adventuresinbronze.com for
more information on titles you may have missed.

THE FORGOTTEN REALM
THE DESERT DEMONS
HORROR IN GOLD
THE INFERNAL BUDDHA
DEATH'S DARK DOMAIN
SKULL ISLAND
PHANTOM LAGOON
THE WAR MAKERS
THE ICE GENIUS

(Don't miss another original Doc Savage adventure,
THE PHANTOM LAGOON, coming soon.)

THE MIRACLE MENACE

A DOC SAVAGE ADVENTURE

BY WILL MURRAY & LESTER DENT

WRITING AS KENNETH ROBESON

COVER BY JOE DeVITO

ALTUS PRESS • 2013

First Edition — September 2013

DESIGNED BY
Matthew Moring/Altus Press

SPECIAL THANKS TO
*James Bama, Jerry Birenz, Condé Nast, Jeff Deischer, Norma
Dent, Carol Diaz-Granados of Washington University, St. Louis,
Dafydd Neal Dyar, Elizabeth Engel of The State Historical Society
of Missouri, Bob Gasparini, Mark O. Lambert, Dave McDonnell,
Matthew Moring, Ray Riethmeier, Howard Wright, and last but not
least, the Heirs of Norma Dent—James Valbracht, John Valbracht,
Wayne Valbracht, Shirley Dungan and Doris Leinkuehler.*

COVER ILLUSTRATION COMMISSIONED BY
Bob Gasparini

Like us on Facebook: "The Wild Adventures of Doc Savage"

Printed in the United States of America

Set in Caslon.

For Leonard Leone,
Bantam Books art director

The man who created the Doc Savage banner
logo, gave the Man of Bronze his widow's
peak, and who posed for Ham Brooks on
the back covers of countless paperbacks—
and for the front cover of this novel.

The Miracle Menace

Table of Contents

Prologue

DARKNESS WAS JUST falling when the combination depot-agent-and-telegrapher at the northeast Missouri farming town of La Plata heard his call on the telegraph wire. It was a message. He answered the wire and went ahead and copied it, using his private hunt-and-punch system on the typewriter.

But by the time the agent-telegrapher had translated the message entirely to the yellow blank, a distinctly strange expression came to his features. He leaned back and stared at the missive. He thoughtfully cleaned his front teeth with a fingernail.

"Fat!" he called suddenly.

Fat was the flunky around the railroad station. Fat Smith.

"This is rich, Fat," the agent shouted. "Here's the craziest dang thing you ever heard."

But Fat was not around the depot. He was uptown getting a coke at the place where his girl worked.

The depot telegrapher stuck the carbon copy of the telegram on his filing spindle, which was the usual procedure, since copies of all messages were kept. In this case, it was to have a horrible result.

Then the agent read the telegram again and its contents, which had earlier amazed him, now caused him to laugh. He chortled. "Haw, haw, haw! The daggone thing had me going for a minute! Haw, haw, hee!"

1

The laugh was not very hearty. It was the kind of a laugh some people gave the Wright brothers when they said they could fly, and also it was a little like the laugh others give when they are alone and have to pass a cemetery at night.

THE GREAT GULLIVER
LA PLATA, MISSOURI

That was the address on the telegram.

The telegrapher studied the name, scratched his head, got down the thin telephone book, looked into it, then shook his head. "Maybe it's that Gulliver Greene who went to work out at old Duzzit's filling station," he suggested aloud to himself.

He carried the telegram to the telephone, laid hold of the instrument.

"I'm sorry, but something happened to the line out toward the One-Stop-Duzzit filling station," the telephone operator said. "The wire failed about an hour ago. We think it is broken or something."

The agent hung up, stared again at the telegram, then took a lot of air into his lungs slowly and let it out so swiftly that his lips fluttered. He stood there for some time, probably much stiller than he had stood in a long time.

"Aw, shoot!" he said at last. "Aw, shoot! Such a thing couldn't be true. It's a rib somebody is pulling."

He sealed the telegram in an envelope and carried it out to a taxi driver to deliver. When a telegram could not be telephoned, it was the custom to deliver it by taxi.

"Try that Gulliver feller at old Duzzit's station," he directed. "Though durned if I ever heard him called The Great Gulliver."

The taxi driver departed. This left no one but the agent-telegrapher in the depot, or near it. The agent went back to the delivery window. The queer expression, the funny look, was back on his face. He had no hunch that the incredible was imminent, being no clairvoyant.

The agent, some five minutes later, was called to the delivery window by a very deep voice. He went over and saw no one standing there. He blinked.

"I'm expecting a telegram for The Great Gulliver," a seemingly disembodied voice said.

The agent looked downward through the glass and spied the shortest man he had ever beheld.

Recovering his composure, he said, "Heh? Why, I just sent Bill to deliver that telegram to the One-Stop-Duzzit Filling Station and Auto Camp, on the edge of town."

The short individual scowled. "Do you remember what the message said?"

The station agent's nod was vehement. "Do I! It said that Christopher Columbus is—" He fell silent, swallowed, then added, "I'll get the carbon copy."

The stunted stranger walked swiftly to the left, opened a door, and entered the room with the telegrapher.

Without asking permission, the miniature man got up on a vacant stool. "I reckon you would remember the names mentioned in that?" he asked in his deep-in-a-barrel voice.

"Why, sure I do—"

The knife which the man put in the depot-telegrapher's heart was long and enough like a needle to go in easily. The telegrapher looked down foolishly, his face twisting, his mouth opening. The man reached up, seized the open mouth, crushing the lips in a bunch with his fingers, keeping back all but some small gurgling sounds which nobody heard, until the telegrapher was dead.

The slayer took the carbon copy of the telegram and left.

FAT, the depot flunky, came ambling back a while later from seeing his girl and having a coke. Fat's face was mostly grin and he was whistling, for he had fixed it up for later in the night. Fat entered the station.

But Fat was not in the depot very long. Just long enough to let out one horror-struck bleat. Then he shot out of the door and ran, pale, mouth gaping, throat making small gurgling sounds which he probably did not realize he was making.

He had not noticed that the copy of the strange telegram was missing, too.

Chapter I

THE GREAT GULLIVER

IT WAS *NOT* a good night for a mystery. The contrary, quite, for it was a crisp October evening, cool, bright, with stars, moon and no clouds—a night that was an ideal setting for peace and lovers. Which indicated how deceptive a setting can be.

The tall young man with the cotton-colored hair leaned over a battered desk in the One-Stop-Duzzit filling station, which was a rather unprofitable place of business located near the small town of La Plata in northeast Missouri.

The young man had a pleasant face equipped with myriad freckles, and rather striking green eyes. He also had a mouth that was grimmer than necessary, and just now he was using the mouth to make a series of the vulgar noises often aptly called Bronx cheers.

Object of the freckled young man's scorn was a book, a large black scrapbook of the type in which newspaper clippings are pasted; this lay open on the battered desk.

THE GREAT GULLIVER
!! WORLD'S MOST AMAZING MAGICIAN !!

THIS DECLARATION WAS SET FORTH IN ELEGANT ENGRAVING ON A DISCREET, EXPENSIVE FOLDER. THIS FOLDER WAS OF THE VARIETY USED AS PROGRAMS BY THE VERY HIGHEST PAID ARTISTS AND ENTERTAINERS WHO CHARGE EXORBITANT SUMS FOR PRIVATE PERFORMANCES ON THE YACHTS AND IN THE MANSIONS OF THE EXTREMELY WEALTHY.

"The Great Gulliver!" the young man said derisively, eyeing

the sample of high class advertising. "The palooka!"

He turned a page of the scrapbook, using a hand which was distinctive, not only because of the wiry muscular development. While none of the hand sinews had the heroic proportions of steel bars, they did strikingly resemble wires.

The next page of the scrapbook held a clipping.

HE REALLY IS, TOO!

THE NEWEST AMAZER ON BROADWAY, A LONG, LEAN PIECE OF ABRACADABRA CALLING HIMSELF THE GREAT GULLIVER—REALLY IS. NO KIDDING, HE'S SWELL. FROM NOW HENCE, HE'S OUR PET. AND MIND YOU, WE'VE NEVER HAD A CRUSH ON MAGICIANS. MOREOVER, THIS GREAT GULLIVER—WE REPEAT HE IS THAT WORD—IS SAID TO BE DRAGGING DOWN THREE GRAND A WEEK FOR HIS HOUDINI-WORK.

WHICH PROVES US RIGHT, OR DOES IT?

The publication in which this item had appeared, *Stagechat,* happened to have a very painful reputation among ham actors and vaudeville performers. It was, in the vernacular, a tough baby. Its columns were unusually free with such opinions as bums, lousy and stinko. *Stagechat's* reviewer had once breezily suggested that a nationally known actor, who had just opened a show, should be given a curtain call and permitted to cackle over the egg he had laid.

Having glanced at the *Stagechat* item, the young man in the filling station absently scratched in his ivory hair. Then he reached down and his remarkable looking hand apparently took two copper pennies out of what seemed to be the solid, scarred wood of an old desk. He tossed the two cents on the printed squib about The Great Gulliver.

"Sold, and no bargain at that price, either!" he said critically.

He turned another scrapbook page, uncovering a second bit from *Stagechat.* This said:

OUR HONEY WON'T!

HE'S A BE-PANTED (LONG PANTS) GOLD DIGGER. THAT'S WHAT! THEY DON'T WANT TO PAY THE GREAT GULLIVER

FIVE GRAND A WEEK ON HIS NEW CONTRACT, AND HE, THE COY FELLOW, WON'T TAKE LESS. ISN'T HE GREAT?

THE GREAT GULLIVER IS A HOLDOUT, AND WON'T BE SEEN IN THE NICER ($ $ $) PLACES UNTIL THEY PAY HIS PRICE. WHAT'S MORE, HE HAS GONE OFF SOMEWHERE WHILE THEY THINK IT OVER. HE'S DISAPPEARED—ISN'T HE GREAT?

WE REALLY HOPE HE IS THAT GREAT. WE MISS OUR PET.

The ivory-haired young man retrieved the pennies he had produced from the desk top and dropped them into a pocket of his coveralls which also held four paper dollars. This was Saturday, therefore pay day. The four dollars happened to be the young man's total wages for the week, his worldly cash wealth. This was also the first week he had served for this remuneration. These circumstances accounted for the caustic inventory of his own value, cash and otherwise, which he had been taking.

"You hunted for two weeks before you found this—er—position," he reminded himself soothingly. "Whoever said there was plenty of room at the bottom of the ladder never tried to get a job down there."

He wished mightily that he'd enjoyed himself a little more economically while pulling down big money as a magician. His philosophy had been: by the time you got a gob of it, you're too old to enjoy it, so spend it while you get a kick out of doing so. A lousy enough philosophy, he reflected, and absolutely all wet as witness his present plight for proof.

ARRIVAL of a taxicab outside interrupted further philosophy on his part.

"Gulliver Greene in there?" the taxi driver said loudly.

The young man stepped outside, grinned and admitted, "In person, albeit with his ego slightly frayed."

The taxi driver somewhat resembled a mink peering out of a hole as he sat in his dark car.

"Yeah. Well, I got a telegram for The Great Gulliver. Is that you?"

"Yes," Gull Greene admitted, and added, "Ouch!"

"Huh. You sick?"

"In mind only, but let it go. Let's have the missive you mentioned."

The taxi driver handed over the telegram, then drove off, and it became quiet around the One-Stop-Duzzit, and dark, too, except under the marquee where five electric bulbs, three red and two white, shed light in a discouraged way. Bugs and miller moths kept tumbling in the night air around the light, and trying out the hardness of the bulbs with their heads.

For some time, Gull Greene did nothing but look at the envelope which contained the telegram. His suspense was exquisite, and there was no real reason why he should prolong it. For weeks, he had waited to hear that his contract with a prominent vaudeville chain was to be renewed at his own figure. At the same time, he had writhed in apprehension lest he be informed they were no longer interested. He even hoped they would repeat an offer at his old salary. He'd been much too cocky, he knew now. Furthermore, he had made other mistakes—he'd been extravagant, hadn't saved his money, and had grandstanded once too often when he had walked out in a huff because his salary demands weren't met.

"Three thousand a week!" he gasped, eyeing the telegram which he had not yet dared open. If this wire only said they'd still pay him that! He'd learned his lesson. Any nitwit who would turn down such a sum deserved to wind up filling gas tanks of automobiles at four dollars a week. True, he had worked for years perfecting his magic, and he'd stunned all the professionals at the last meeting of the American Society of Magicians. But so what? Three thousand a week was still—my God, it was a fortune!

Impulsively, he held the telegram above his head in an attitude of divine supplication.

"O have pity on this sinner who has seen the light and let this telegram say they're offering the old salary of three thousand bucks," he requested hopefully. "And remember, even less would be happily considered—"

"Keep thy hands high, my good brother," came solemn advice from behind Gulliver Greene.

GULL promptly did what was spontaneously natural under the circumstances—he jerked his hands down and turned around to stare at the newcomers.

Holdup! he thought.

It wasn't. Not exactly. No guns were in sight—there was only a little man, a man who would probably have to stand on tiptoe to look into Gull's hip pocket. He had a face that had been battered surrounding a mashed-to-one-side nose. The work of fists, Gull imagined.

"Read that telegram yet?" the small man croaked.

"Nope," Gull said thoughtlessly, his mind busy deciding he had never seen the midget before.

"Then hand it over!" the other ordered.

Gull was particularly struck by a deep, mournful quality in the runt's voice because it reminded him of a foxhound named Old Blow who often ran foxes near the filling station at night. Gull had often listened to Old Blow and reflected that the mournful baying was the exact sound he himself felt like making whenever he thought of his own idiocy in turning up his nose at three thousand and holding out for—

"Hand it over, snowball top!" rasped the small man.

The mite's small size and his grim seriousness combined and struck Gull as comical, and he was moved to do something which he later regretted.

"Look," Gull invited.

He held the telegram out at arm's length, plucked up the sleeve of that arm, at the same time showing the hand to draw attention to the fact that there was nothing in the hand but the telegram. He cupped the other hand and poked the folded telegram—not yet opened—into it carefully, then rubbed the two fists together in realistic fashion.

"Hocus-magokus," he said.

He opened both hands and the telegram had vanished.

"Magician, huh?" said the little man.

"Right."

"So'm I."

So that explains the queer way he's acting, Gull thought. He already knew I was a magician. And magicians are balmy coots and always trying some kind of funny business on each other.

"What's your specialty?" Gull asked with the geniality one magician reserves for another.

"This!" the runt snarled.

He hit Gulliver in the belly. He also kicked Gull three or four times simultaneously; Gull was a little hazy about the exact number of times. He found himself on the floor. He got hold of the midget's neck. The pygmy grabbed his elbows, did something with his thumbs and Gull's crazybones.

"Who-o!" Gull said, and pounded away at the toughest little body he had ever felt. They rolled under the table, and Gull began to win.

The small man started baying for help.

Men commenced popping through the door. Five of them entered, all told. They were flashily dressed, ranged from big down to medium size, and all wore vicious, determined expressions. They rushed to the attack.

Gull had good luck with the first one when he kicked with both feet; the victim whooped, sat down. One fellow grabbed Gull's right leg. Six glass fruit jars full of oil on a rack came crashing down, breaking. The fighting men wallowed in the oil and glass.

"Hold 'im!" bawled the midget. "He put that telegram in a pull and it went around to the back of his coat."*

---

* *The "pull" is a device in common use by magicians. It consists of an elastic with a safety pin on one end, a tiny cup or a clamp on the other end. The safety pin is fastened to the vest in the back, up high. One of the magician's hands draws the cup around secretly and it is held*

The runt got his hands up under the back of Gulliver's coat, groped and found the standard magician's pull which Gull had used.

Gull devoted himself exclusively to trying to retain the telegram. He had no idea what the message contained, had even less of a notion of why they wanted it, or who they were. But the unprovoked attack had made him as mad as the proverbial hornet. He felt in the mood to fight them all night rather than give up anything.

The midget freed the message from the pull, but Gull, clutching, got one corner of it. The yellow envelope tore. The small man got most of the telegram, but Gull retained a small portion.

Bounding clear of the mêlée, the broken-nosed runt cast a hurried glance at his part of the telegram. Whatever he read gave him a shock; that was plain. He bayed a violently profane oath, leveled a dwarf arm at Gulliver.

"This bird may know more'n we figured!" he yelled. "We'd better play safe! Hold 'im."

While the others held Gulliver down, the small man drew a knife, a thing with a very long three-edged blade attached to a handle of polished bone.

Gull Green's long body became slack; his eyes pinched shut, then jerked open; tendons slowly stood out on his neck. At one point in the fray he had been face down in the spilled oil, and now drops of the amber stuff moved down his face and into the shallow V of his drawn, closed lips. His eyes seemed to become wider and wider even after there was no possibility of them opening farther, and deep grooves grew at the corners of his mouth as his lips pulled tighter and tighter; the oil filled the groove in his lips and flowed on.

"Hold 'im!" warned the hound-voice midget.

They didn't. The slippery oil over men and floor helped.

---

so the hand and arm conceal elastic and cup from the spectator. After the article is stuffed in the palmed cup, the device is released, permitting the elastic to yank cup and article under the coat. The device is used to vanish cigarettes, handkerchiefs, papers, etc., with weird effect.
—KENNETH ROBESON.

Nobody had ever before tried to kill Gulliver Greene, which helped too. Gull's wild flounce got him free.

Momentum threw him clear, and toward the door. He continued, dived into the filling station. The washroom door gaped open. He pitched through it, banged the door shut, got his feet against it.

Then he reached for the old double-barreled 10-gauge shotgun, which was kept standing in an innocent looking ancient cardboard box behind the washroom. Pointing it at the door, he cocked one barrel and let fly. There was roar, kick, and then a hole the size of his fist in the door.

The midget howled, "Watch that scattergun!" added some profanity, then bellowed, "Didn't anybody bring a gun?"

Apparently no one had.

"We'll have another try at him later!" the small man roared. "Clear out of here before he ruins somebody."

They ran away.

Gull snatched several shotgun shells out of the bottom of the long cardboard box where they were kept, wrenched open the door, and held the gun ready, the other barrel cocked. Once out under the marquee, he located the sound of running feet. It was too dark to see them. He lifted the shotgun, aimed by guess, and pulled the other trigger. He got a small click.

Both barrels of the old weapon had gone off at once the first time, which accounted for the size of the hole in the washroom door.

An instant afterward, he heard an automobile start, and decided it had been parked down the road and was taking the small man and the others away.

GULLIVER GREENE backed inside the filling station, then reloaded the shotgun. He watched the outer darkness intently and listened until the departing car could no longer be heard. Then he became aware of the oil on his lips, in his mouth, and sidled warily, holding the shotgun, to the towel and wiped his face and hands, blotted at his clothing. In hanging the towel on the hook, he got a sidewise glimpse of his face in the mirror over the washbasin.

"Whew!" he said.

The piece of telegram he had retained lay on the washroom floor and he stopped, still watching the outer darkness and listening, on edge from what had just happened.

The fragment of telegram held a few words from what was evidently the last line of the message, although the signature was not included.

—KNOW POSITIVELY THAT CHRISTOPHER CO-LUMBUS IS ALIVE.

Chapter II

THE CRIMINAL COLLEGE

THE GOLD-LETTERED SIGN on the frosted glass door panel read:

ODDITIES

There was nothing more to the gilt legend, no indications of a proprietor or company name, nor what type of oddities was being offered.

Within, a man's voice yelled hoarsely, "Confound it! Let me out of here!"

Rattling of the closed door indicated the man on the other side was trying to get the panel open. But it seemed to be locked.

In the outer room, stenographers ceased clicking typewriter keys. Secretaries, very neat in their Fall frocks, turned and stared. The brunette on the telephone switchboard abruptly stopped speaking and her rouged mouth fell open.

One stenographer had her desk not far from the closed door to the private office. Her job was an unusual one, she thought. It was to type up newspaper cuttings. The subject of these clips varied. But they all possessed one thing in common. They were out of the ordinary.

Just now she was typing up an odd report of a man who had wandered into a newly discovered cavern in Kentucky. The man had gone into the cavern accompanied by his dog. He had not emerged for three days, claiming to have gotten lost in the winding cathedral of a place. Evidently, he was very fond of the dog, because after gathering up his nerve, the man had gone back in after him. Two days later, the dog had come out. Alone. Curious thing, the dog was by then entirely hairless. No trace of the man had been found to date. And no explanation could be offered for the animal's uncanny lack of hair.

Typing up the clipping gave her goose bumps, and the stenog wondered if it was true, or the product of a small-town newspaperman's imagination.

Her employer had told her that these clippings were assembled for various clients. Some were to become fodder for a movie screenwriter's scenarios. Others were mailed to collectors of oddities, who paid for the service. Still others were interested in unusual subjects and requested anything that touched upon those subjects. Newspapers from all over the globe were delivered to the office for the express purpose of being dismembered by clicking scissors.

After several weeks of employment, the stenographer had privately begun to doubt this assertion.

Now a visitor who had minutes before entered the inner office appeared to be locked in.

A water cooler stood near the door to the inner office. Summoning her scant supply of courage, the stenographer shuffled over to the cooler, ostensibly to get a drink, but actually to try to learn what had gotten the visitor so excited.

She had a good idea of what would happen should she be caught eavesdropping. She would be discharged.

Inside a man was shouting. "Now that I see you two, I know exactly what this is all about!"

The stenographer wondered what two the yelling man could be referring to. Only her employer and his visitor held forth behind that closed panel. No one else had entered since the lunch hour.

The upset man continued his harangue. "I am going to tell the authorities what they would never learn otherwise—the name of the person whose brain is behind the whole thing!"

The stenographer heard the telephone receiver clank forcibly on its hook, then caught the faint whirring and clicking of the dial, as the man attempted to call the police.

Came subdued sounds of a scuffle. Then silence. It sounded as if there were three or four men inside, instead of the two she had seen enter.

Upset by what she had overheard, the stenographer withdrew to her desk and the clipping about the missing unfortunate and his hairless dog.

After a time, her employer stuck his head out of the office door, got himself a paper cup which he filled with water. Looking around for signs that the muffled commotion had been overheard, and detecting none, he retreated to his walnut-paneled preserve.

Glancing through the door while it was briefly open, the stenographer saw clearly that no one else was in the room.

Strangely, the shouting man never emerged.

She decided to say nothing about it—was willing to drop the whole thing. As soon as it seemed prudent to do so, she intended to give her formal notice. There was something highly irregular about this nameless clipping service whose only formal name was Oddities.

She moved on to the next clipping. It was considerably less unnerving than the other, merely being a report of a collector living in the Bahamas, who specialized in relics pertaining to the life of the Discoverer of America, Christopher Columbus. Someone had stolen some of these priceless artifacts. The only peculiar aspect of this theft was that the thief was described as bearing a striking resemblance to the Great Navigator himself, who was long in his grave.

If the curious stenographer possessed optics capable of seeing through the ceiling in the fashion of an X-ray machine, she would have had her curiosity partly satisfied. But she would have been even more astounded than she presently was.

FOR directly above, stood the eighty-sixth floor of the tallest skyscraper in Manhattan. It was a place where few ever ventured. This was the headquarters of the fabulous being known to the world as Doc Savage.

The stenographer knew who Doc Savage was. Few in the civilized world did not. Doc was the stuff of hot newspaper copy.

But Doc Savage was not there now. Instead, two men were muscling the late visitor to the Oddities office out of a small secret elevator that connected the lower office with a vast laboratory on the top floor.

This was Doc Savage's scientific laboratory. It was said by learned men to be unique in all the world. That it was probably the most well-equipped experimental laboratory imaginable was evident in its profusion of up-to-date equipment, ranging from glittering chemical apparatus to an industrial furnace.

The two men were a study in contrasts, both physical and sartorial.

One looked as if he had stepped from a fashionable Fifth Avenue men's clothier window display and came to life. His hair was white as snow, as was the long trailing beard that hung loosely from his face.

The other possessed all the outward earmarks of a longshoreman or dock walloper. He was an astonishing individual to whom a capricious mother nature had bequeathed the pleasantly homely face and brutish build of a gorilla. His loud clothes were rumpled and fit him rather badly.

"Unhand me!" the individual they were manhandling shouted. His voice was identical to that of the shouting man formerly trapped within the Oddities office. The one who had tried and failed to call the police.

"Not a chance," said the gorilla-like man in a squeaky voice.

"You are our prisoner," declared the fashionable gent.

"The prisoner of Doc Savage, you mean!"

"Precisely," said he of the white beard.

"I recognize you now. You are the noted lawyer, Ham Brooks."

"That does not matter now, my good man," said Ham Brooks, removing his white beard. It was an articial one. "I only wore this to lull you into a false sense of safety."

"Your accomplice I recognized right off," huffed the other.

"Disguising my anthropoid friend, Monk here, is a waste of time," drawled Ham. "Now, are you coming along voluntarily, or not?"

"Not!"

Powerful hands seized the reluctant one by the shoulders, spun him around. The captive found himself looking into the simian features of the apish one named Monk.

"I can bend crowbars with these mitts," Monk growled. "Imagine how I'd mangle your skinny shoulders."

Monk dug in a thumb that felt like a blunt railroad spike. The other winced painfully.

Ham put in, "Monk, Doc wants him delivered intact."

"Listen, shyster, this fine, upstandin' citizen has been fleecin' widows and orphans out of their life savings and Doc wants it to stop pronto."

"I am guilty of no such thing!" the other said in an injured voice. "This is a canard."

"Doc personally asked us to grab you up," continued Monk. "So you couldn't do any more harm to honest folks just trying to get along in life."

The accused took umbrage. "You cannot prove your charges!"

"Perhaps not in a court of law," admitted Ham the attorney. "But we are not about to turn you over to the authorities."

"Then what—"

"Doc has a special place for people like you," Ham said flatly. "We call it the 'college'."

"I am a graduate of one of the finest institutions for learning in New England! I need no further education from the likes of you two!"

Monk inserted, "Doc says otherwise."

"That's why we lured you to the Oddities office on the pretext that we wished to invest in your worthless holding company," added Ham.

"I am not going anywhere with either of you!" the indignant man insisted.

"I thought you might take that attitude," snapped Ham.

While Monk held the struggling swindler in place, Ham Brooks popped the face of his gold wrist watch and exposed a reservoir of a sticky brown substance resembling common molasses.

He separated his elegant dark cane, revealing it to be a sword cane. The empty barrel he tossed onto a leather chair. Dipping the tip of the lean blade into the exposed reservoir, Ham coated it with the stuff.

Then he placed the tip of it to the right cheek of the protesting prisoner. The man flinched, struggled vainly in Monk's hairy grasp.

Ham flexed one wrist, made a slight nick in the exposed cheek.

Not three seconds passed before the other became a limp burden in Monk's arms.

"We will convey him to our warehouse hangar," said Ham, restoring watch and cane to their original conditions. "Then we will fly to the college with this worthless scoundrel."

Monk shook his head.

"Doc told me to take the new short-range dirigible."

"Won't that be cumbersome?" Ham protested.

"Doc wants the dirigible. It might have something to do with this."

From a pocket of his dilapidated coat, the hairy one pulled a telegram.

"This came to the office downstairs."

Ham read it:

HAVE MYSTERY WORTHY OF YOUR ABILITIES
STOP THERE IS A STRANGE HOUSE IN THE MIS-
SOURI WOODS WEST OF LA PLATA STOP WHEN
APPROACHED, IT VANISHES STOP ALWAYS TO
REAPPEAR LATER STOP NO ONE CAN GET TO
IT STOP HOUSE FORMERLY BELONGED TO DE-
CEASED SCIENTIST.

033

"Who sent this?"

"One of our graduates," said Monk. "He lives out Missouri way."

"Doc's new setup is sure harvesting fruit," Ham declared. "First this scoundrel walks into the eighty-fifth floor information clearing house, now this lead comes from one of the college graduates Doc rehabilitated."

"Let's get him up there, so he can join the cause," said Monk, grinning from ear to ear. His grin almost split his head in two like a melon. Monk had a big mouth.

They left the suite of offices through a reception room that consisted of an inlaid desk of Oriental workmanship, a huge safe built in the last century, and several comfortable leather chairs. This was Doc Savage's formal reception room.

Exiting to the corridor, Monk and Ham—the former carried the insensate captive over one sloping shoulder like a sack of oats—ignored the elevators and instead found a locked door, which they unlocked.

Entering, they accessed a winding staircase and emerged in a round chamber that had been designed for the novel purpose of allowing commercial dirigibles to dock and discharge passengers.

Previous attempts to perfect this maneuver had been disastrous. But Doc Savage, with his unbounded faith in scientific progress, had lately invented a small dirigible which could be docked here. It would never equal—much less rival—the great trans-Atlantic passenger airships, but for exploratory purposes, it nicely suited their needs.

Moreover, it was small enough that should high winds rock it on its mooring, it could withstand considerable midair buffeting.

Coming to the great gallery, Monk deployed a covered gangway. This extended outward accordion fashion, and made contact with the small gondola of the bobbing airship.

Ham went first, balancing carefully. A fearful fall awaited should he pitch out through the lightweight silk sides.

Monk followed, handing the prisoner up. Ham pulled him along by grasping his hair with his hand, while Monk pushed. They were not gentle about it.

When the prisoner had been taken on board, Monk ambled after him, then released the gangplank, which withdrew mechanically.

For a moment, Monk stared out through the open dirigible door.

The massive spire of the great skyline—the tallest in Manhattan—lay beneath them. It was a long drop down.

"Will you kindly close that hatch!" Ham complained.

"I happen to favor the view," Monk returned. "In case I ever get the urge to pitch an ambulance-chasin' shyster down, I want to know how long it will take him to fall."

Ham fumed, went to the controls, which were deceptively simple. There were control wheels and the expected dials and gauges, which allowed instantaneous monitoring of yaw, pitch and altitude.

"I am about to cast off, ready or not," Ham called out.

With a last look, Monk shut the hatch.

Ham had by that time engaged the engines. There were but two. He pulled a lever and an ingenious mechanical claw of a hook—the only thing tethering the small airship to the mooring mast—let go. Its tines were electrically controlled and snapped open in order to release its steel-clawed grasp.

Engines in reverse, the dirigible backed away from the mooring mast. There was little wind, which was a hazard that defeated all past docking attempts.

When they were clear, Ham advanced the throttle and the little airship gave a jump and began bumping along in a northerly direction. It ran very quietly, owing to interior soundproofing.

In very quick order, the upper regions of Manhattan began unreeling beneath them. The sharp splinters of midtown skyscrapers gave way to blocky apartment houses and other less imposing buildings.

Ham Brooks addressed Monk haughtily.

"At least you had the good sense to leave that blasted pig behind this time!" he uttered.

The hairy chemist was studying the forest of buildings below, apparently unhearing. He began whistling a gaudy show tune.

From the rear of the tiny gondola, a familiar squealing came.

Ham started. Looking behind him he expected a certain porker to come bounding into view. None came.

Ham whirled, demanded, "Was that you making that wretched squeal?"

Monk did his level best to look injured. "Do I look like a pig to you?"

"Of course not! But I *do* know you fancy yourself a ventriloquist."

Monk said nothing. His twinkling eyes sought the ceiling. An expression of innocence roosted upon his pleasantly homely features.

Reluctantly, Ham returned to the controls.

Again the piggy squeal came forth.

Snapping his head around, Ham Brooks eyed Monk and the gondola interior by turns.

"That was you! I knew it!"

Monk continued looking innocent. Anyone knowing him

well would conclude it masked the guilty expression of a practical-joking ventriloquist.

Monk was one of a group of six remarkable men. Monk and four of the others were specialists in some particular line. One was an engineer; another a geologist; another a lawyer; and one an electrical wizard. Throughout the world, few could have been found to excel these five individuals in their chosen professions. Incredible enough, however, there was one man who was a greater chemist, a more accomplished engineer, a more learned lawyer, a more renowned geologist and skilled electrical expert than any of the five men. Furthermore, this fabulous personage was just as proficient at countless other professions. So vast was his fund of knowledge that even those associated closely with this astounding man were continually awed by his tremendous feats.

That unique individual was the leader of the group to which Monk belonged—Doc Savage. Man of Miracles, archangel of science, Doc was a being about whom much was written, much more was rumored, but little was definitely known.

Imaginative newspapermen had taken to regaling readers with the notion that Doc was a spiritual descendant of Sir Galahad, the knight who went around rescuing persons in distress. There was something to be said for that analogy. For the Man of Bronze, as he was most often called, subscribed to the theory that when a good deed needed doing, and wickedness punished, it was best to right the wrong rather than to wait to see how it all came out—which is how the average citizen often regarded trouble not his or her own.

Doc Savage came fully equipped to right wrongs and punish evildoers. He had been raised from the cradle for such a noble purpose.

TWO hours later, they came to the wilderness section of upstate New York. The area was utterly devoid of habitation for miles around.

Below, they spied a cluster of grim graystone buildings set at the base of a mountainous area. This was surrounded by several zones bounded by high woven-wire fences. The outer fence was topped by razor wire. Six feet separated it from the next fence in the concentrated series of fences. There were traps in these zones. The final fence, the innermost one, was electrified.

The traps and the electricity were controlled by persons in a hunting-style log lodge which sat off in one corner.

There were other defenses. Sections of earthen loam were mounted on rolling tracks. When withdrawn, they disclosed concrete pits housing anti-aircraft batteries.

The public knew nothing of these devices. No one was able to enter who was not authorized to do so. The place was a secret.

Any hunter who chanced to stray close to the arrangement of buildings would understand why it was so well-protected. For on the outer fence were posted large signs, several facing each point of the compass. These read:

WARNING
GERM RESEARCH INSTITUTION
—YOU MAY CATCH A DISEASE—
KEEP OUT

The signs looked new and freshly painted. They were. All of the institution was. For this was Doc Savage's Crime College. Although it had been in operation for several years now, formerly it had been concealed behind the false front of the hillside, and was entirely a subterranean affair.

But the fantastic progress of the secret enterprise had forced Doc Savage to move it out into the open, under the guise of a scientific research laboratory. Which it was, actually.

It was here that Doc Savage consigned malefactors whom he captured in the course of his adventures. In these austere confines, they were submitted to a singular course of rehabilitation.

First, their brains were operated upon by surgeons trained in the delicate process. This accomplished two things. It wiped out all memory of their past criminal lives, eradicating their memories even going back to earliest childhood. In the course of this, a gland Doc had discovered to be defective in those who were criminally disposed was operated upon and corrected.

This, too, served to eradicate all tendencies toward crime.

Once the prisoners recovered from this process, they were given new names and set upon a course of reeducation, which included good moral reinforcement, and taught a new trade. After that, they were released back into society to take their rightful place.

This would be the fate of the captured swindler they were now conveying to the institution.

There was a small airfield. This and the frequent visitations by private ambulances carrying the prisoners to the secret place were among the reasons for the recent renovations.

"There is no mooring tower," Ham noticed.

"Let me take over," squeaked Monk, shouldering the dapper lawyer aside. "Doc taught me how to moor this pocket Zeppelin when there ain't no tower at hand."

Reversing the engines with a smack of the throttle, the hairy chemist brought the airship to a shuddering stop. It began drifting.

Releasing ballast in the form of a heavy gas, Monk dropped the craft. It settled quietly. To any distant observer, it would look like an Army blimp on maneuvers.

Paying out the grappling hook, Monk snagged trees, then pulled on the guy-wire control, bringing the ship to a bobbing halt.

Ham looked out the windshield and side inspection ports, frowned.

"How the deuce do we get down?" he wondered.

"Ropes," said Monk, kicking open the hatch and throwing out heavy lines suitable for climbing down.

"My clothes will be ruined!" Ham exploded. The wasp-waisted lawyer was fussy about his attire. A legend surrounding his taste in clothes had it that tailors sometimes followed Ham down the street just to see fine garments being worn as they should be worn.

"Or you can jump," Monk suggested amiably.

Ham let Monk go first, and observed the hairy chemist scrambling with the long-armed agility of an orangutan, into the trees, and then to the ground.

He peered around the cabin, seeking an alternative.

There was a parachute, but their present height was insufficient for its safe use.

Finally, the fastidious attorney shinnied down the rope and managed to work his way down to the ground, ripping only a coat sleeve.

When he was on the ground at last, Ham waved his dark cane as if he wanted to thrash Monk about the face with it.

"I have ruined another fine coat because of you!"

"You should start dressin' properly for our little expeditions," Monk told him innocently.

Ham looked up. "How are we going to get our prisoner to the ground?"

"Watch this," said Monk.

Reaching up into a lower branch, the apish chemist grasped the heavy wire that ended in the collapsible grapnel.

With his mighty shoulders heaving, Monk began hauling in the dirigible closer and closer to the ground.

"Why didn't you do that the first time!" Ham flared.

Monk grinned. "I been hankerin' for some exercise. Come to think of it, you could stand some, too."

While Monk held the airship close to the ground, Ham reentered, and pushed the prisoner out unceremoniously.

Releasing the airship, Monk hefted the limp man across one burly shoulder and bore him toward the grim gray buildings.

"I never like visitin' this place," Monk muttered.

"It might do you some good if you were to spend time here, having your monkey brains cleaned out and straightening up your ridiculous baboon behavior!" snapped Ham.

They were within the inner perimeter, within sight of the electrical fence. Towering evergreens dotted the landscape. Many had knotholes. These concealed television cameras that were monitored by technicians in the log lodge.

Certain arrangements of stone, not recognizable except to those familiar with the glyphs comprising the Mayan language, warned of concealed pits and bear-traps that could snag a man's ankles with steely mechanical jaws.

They skirted these, finally coming safely to the main building.

Armed guards met them, and they were permitted to enter.

"Got us another patient," Monk announced.

"Yes," added Ham waspishly. "And Monk has one, too."

A voice that was remarkable in his modulation asked, "Did you bring the telegram?"

It was the unmistakable voice of Doc Savage.

Chapter III

THE FOREBODING

GULLIVER GREENE MOVED over and stood with his back to the one wall of the filling station which had no window. He kept the piece of the telegram in his hands and eyed it several times, chewing his lower lip thoughtfully. Globules of perspiration came out on his face and skidded over the greasy skin. Twice, he shook his head violently.

Gull gave up. There was no way he could make sense out of it. He swung to the telephone, intending to call the town marshal at La Plata and the State Highway Patrol in Macon, the larger town to the south. The mysterious runt and his men had gone in that direction and might be headed off by the police.

The telephone was an old-fashioned country instrument with a crank, and he sensed from the easy way the crank spun that the thing was dead, even before he listened and knew.

He located the flashlight, went outside with it and the shotgun, listened for a while, then followed the telephone wire with a flashlight.

Four poles away, in the direction of town, Gull found the wire down. It had been cut.

While he was wrestling with the two ends of the wire, trying to get them to meet, someone sent a ring into the line, giving him a disquieting shock. After he swore, he jumped the grader ditch onto the road and ran down the pavement.

Half a mile brought him to the nearest neighbor who had a telephone, and while he was loping that distance, four cars passed him with their noise and lights, like rockets traveling backward. The neighbor, an agriculturist who wore overalls and chewed tobacco, offered a remark that, "I heard that old scattergun go off down there a while ago. You see a skunk?"

"A small one and five big ones," Gull said grimly.

"Whillikers! Lots of skunks, eh?"

Gull telephoned the Missouri State Highway Patrol headquarters at Macon and told them exactly what had happened, answered all their questions truthfully.

"That was kind of a queer business," the officer suggested.

"You're telling me!"

"You stick around there," the patrolman directed. "This is a little worse than you thought, I'm afraid. We'll want to question you."

Gull frowned at the telephone, asked quickly, "What do you mean—worse than I thought?"

"Never mind. You just be sure to stay there."

Gull made two thoughtful passes with the receiver before he got it on the hook. He hadn't cared for that last remark.

AFTER hanging up, Gull stood at the telephone, rubbing his jaw absently and wondering just what the officer meant. A possible explanation occurred to him, and it was not cheering—in his newspaper reading, he had gathered the opinion that the police frequently "held the man for questioning," which actually meant that they kept the fellow in jail.

Suppose they suspected The Great Gulliver of something criminal? Suppose they— "This is a little worse than you thought, I'm afraid." The officer had said that. What in the devil did he mean by that? Gull absently grasped a fistful of his oily hair and moved the scalp hide around as if trying to loosen a growing tension.

Then an idea hit him—the telegram! It must have come through the local depot operator, and they kept carbon copies of telegrams, didn't they?

Gull quickly called the depot and asked for the operator, but got someone else who was a word hoarder. Gull requested, "Put the operator on the wire."

"Can't."

"Eh? What do you mean? Where is the operator?"

"Dead."

"What?"

The succinct voice at the depot said, "Dead. Murdered. Knife. Heart."

"But who did it?"

"Question."

"Well then, why was he killed? He was a nice old fellow. What reason was there for anyone harming him?"

"Mystery."

Gull absently strained his ivory hair with his fingers, then asked the man of few words to look for the copy of the telegram. The man was a long time coming back to the phone.

"Nope."

"You made sure it wasn't there?"

"Yep."

"But where would a telegram for me come, if not there?"

"Here."

Gull repeated his earlier gesture of absently combing his cotton-hued hair with his fingers, then wiped the hand on his trousers. His mouth worked around into various thinking shapes, then straightened out grimly when he remembered the unusual three-edged knife the hound-voiced little man had carried.

"Anything peculiar about the wound that killed the telegram operator?" he asked abruptly.

"Three-cornered," said the word-hoarder.

Gull said grimly, "Thanks."

"Sure."

Gull broke the connection and called the State Highway Patrol at Macon for the second time.

He told the Patrol officer, "It seems the telegraph operator at La Plata has been killed by the same fellows who took the telegram from me. It begins to look as if someone tried to get the wire and also dispose of everybody who knew anything about it."

The Patrolman said, "So I figured when you called the first time. How did you come to get the idea?"

"The runt who got most of the telegram from me carried a knife with a three-cornered blade."

"He did, eh? Well, we've already got our cars watching for him and the lads with him. Now you know why we want to question you. And by the way, here's something you might tell me now—your part of the telegram just says that Christopher Columbus is alive?"

"Right."

"That means the discoverer of America?"

Gull frowned, put his mouth close to the transmitter and said, "This doesn't seem to me like a joking matter."

"No? Who said it was? Listen, you stay there. We want to talk to you about this Christopher Columbus, whether he's the discoverer of America or not."

Gull replaced the receiver, nibbled his lower lip, then walked into the other room, muttering vaguely to himself, "Why do things have to happen to me?"

THE NEIGHBOR, the man whose telephone Gull was using, heard this remark but got nothing out of it but puzzlement. Anyway, he had something else on his mind, it appeared, for he shifted his cud of tobacco to one side and aimed expertly at a can half full of ashes which stood beside the heating stove in lieu of a goboon. He cleaned his chin with a hooked finger.

"Me an' the woman been sorta talking," he got around to advising.

Gull nodded, occupied with other thoughts.

"We calculate you're around thirty years old."

"Close," Gull said vaguely.

"Beats all how some gets white-haired a-fore their time, don't it?"

"What? Oh, my hair. Yeah, I got old kind of early." Gull started for the door.

The elderly farmer said quickly, "That Spook is a funny feller, ain't he?"

Gull halted reluctantly. "You mean Drury Davis?"

"Yep. Spook Davis looks just like you, don't he?"

"Just exactly," Gull agreed, trying, out of common courtesy, not to seem too undesirous of talking.

"But for his carroty hair, he might be your twin."

"He isn't," Gull said hastily. "No relative at all. He's just a stooge."

"Stooge. What's a stooge?"

"A stage assistant."

"Drury Davis passed here going to La Plata to the movie earlier tonight, and we talked a while." The old farmer shook his head and made a *tsk-tsk* sound with his tongue.

"That Spook is sure a liar, ain't he?" he added.

Saying heartily, "He certainly is!" Gull managed to escape outside into the darkness.

The Great Gulliver stood for a while in the night, thinking, and the farmer's pothound came and snuffled at his heels, after which a chicken in the hen house made one of the noises a chicken makes on a roost when another fowl pushes it. A few clouds were overheard and more clouds crowded in the east, in front of the moon. It was somewhat darker than it had been.

Gull walked back to the filling station, closed the door to keep out the bugs, and because there seemed nothing else to do, began cleaning up the mess on the floor.

The futile efforts of his mind to create some reason for what had happened caused him to become rather preoccupied; sufficiently so that he did not at once realize a sound he had heard was something clumping against the door.

A disheveled and gory young man pitched in on the floor when the door opened.

THE young man's hair was as red as a burning brick. The re-markable thing about him—in almost every other particular, he looked exactly like Gulliver Greene.

A gash on the newcomer's head had leaked a quantity of crimson and he reeked of whiskey smell. He blinked painfully at Gull.

"It's a lie!" he said distinctly enough.

"Drunk!" Gull said grimly.

"That's what I meant. That's the lie." The prostrate young man groaned deeply. "What you smell is one thing, and what you are looking at is an entirely different matter. What you see is the result of a young man being original."

"Polluted!" Gull stated decisively. "Full to the gills!"

The young man on the floor felt of his head, gasped and relaxed.

"Have you a Bible?" he asked.

"No. I still would not believe you, no matter what oath you took."

"Spook Davis is abused," complained the young man.

Drury "Spook" Davis gathered himself and got carefully to his feet, not moving his head more than he had to. He observed for the first time the oil and broken glass on the floor and the other traces of recent activity.

"You have a spasm in here?" he wanted to know.

Gull passed on the question—it struck him now that Spook Davis' voice did not sound as if he were inebriated.

"What happened to you?" Gull demanded sharply.

"Will you believe me?"

"If I'm having one of my gullible moments. Go ahead."

Spook Davis drew in a breath, shut his eyes, then whistled

painfully. "You know that patch of brush south of here in old Duzzit's cow pasture?"

"Well?"

"You know the path through it, the short cut from here to town, or vice versa?"

"Hurry up! What happened to you?"

"Well, after the movie was over, I took that path to walk back here. Shorter. I was ambling along—"

"Sure you weren't staggering?" intimated Gull.

"Ambling!" Spook fired back. "I'm not tight. I was ambling along and I heard—or rather, I bumped into—somebody. All unexpected, see. I bumped into this character, and the person drew back and there was kind of a hissing noise as if the party didn't know what to think. Then there was a minute when nothing was said, so I thought I'd sort of break the conversational ice. I tried to think up something original, and I finally had it. But I guess it was the wrong thing."

"What was it?"

"I said—'Don't be alarmed, it's only Chris Columbus, looking forward to his new holiday.' Then—*bop!* I got it. Right on the place where they tell me I do my thinking—*say! What ails you!*" This last was prompted by Gull's stunned expression.

"You mentioned Christopher Columbus entirely by chance?"

"Sure."

"Listen!" Gull then explained, in tense, clipped sentences, everything that had happened.

Spook Davis leaned back, supported only by his elbows, and his mouth fell open foolishly and remained that way. He became, after a while, as grim looking as Gull, and the two resembled each other more than ever in physical appearance, although the two were as apart as the poles in character. Gull was serious, ambitious, steady enough, although extravagant with money— however, of the latter he now considered himself well cured. On the other hand, Spook Davis was flighty and came about as near being what is slangily called a "screwball" as anyone could. At only one point, as Spook listened, did he really look frightened—when Gull mentioned the shotgun. Spook paled then. He had a horror of guns.

It was typical of Spook Davis that, even before Gull finished telling what had occurred, the stooge began to recover from his surprise, to dismiss the mystery, to disregard the seriousness of the hound-voiced midget's murdering to get the telegram, as well as his statement that he would dispose of The Great Gulliver later. Spook Davis was like that—fluctuating.

"HONEST to Blackstone, it doesn't make sense!" Spook grinned.

Gulliver did not return the grin. He said, "The Christopher Columbus angle is queer. First, part of the telegram said Christopher Columbus was alive. Then you were attacked when you wisecracked that you were Christopher Columbus looking forward to his new holiday."

"Say, I remember something else!" Spook exploded.

"What?"

"After this unknown party I met hit me, I heard some gibberish about Columbus being alive. *'Columbus alive—thinks he's alive—sure he's alive—hah, hah, hah!'* Crazy stuff like that. It must have been the guy who hit me gibbering. I'm sure I wasn't doing anything but groaning. Whoo! My head!"

Gull said, "Hold still," and examined Spook's head. There was a bruise and a cut, neither likely to prove serious.

"I remember another thing," Spook exclaimed. "Do you know two fellows named Harvell Braggs and Ivan Cass?"

Gull squinted thoughtfully, and couldn't recall them. "No."

Spook Davis elaborated, "This Harvell Braggs must be an awful fat guy, and the other one, Ivan Cass, kind of a grim bird."

"What about them?"

"They were inquiring around town about you, somebody told me," Spook explained. "I guess they'll look you up later. That's all I know. The feller in the restaurant just mentioned it."

Gull probed his memory again, but concluded finally that he had never heard of the two gentlemen, although it was pleasantly possible that they might be theatrical men from New York who had come to sign him up on a new contract—he fervently hoped this to be the case.

"Say, I remember another thing!" Spook barked suddenly.

"Yes?"

"It was a bottle of whiskey that hit me. That's where the smell of demon rum came from."

THE GREAT GULLIVER now applied first-aid bandages and Mercurochrome—there was a kit in the filling station—to Spook's head. It was while he was working on the small wound that his thoughts got into a new channel....

Spook Davis was a fellow who could get into a remarkable number of scrapes. Spook was blessed with what the Irish call the gift of gab. Given the choice of telling truth or falsehood, Spook invariably chose a middle course. He exaggerated, managing both in a convincing way. It was hard to separate fact from fiction in Spook's windy yarning. For a long time, this failing of Spook Davis had puzzled Gull, but for some months he had known what was wrong with his stooge.

Spook Davis was a chronic Machiavelliast. There are people, psychological cases called kleptomaniacs, who cannot help stealing things. They may have plenty of money and not need the things they steal, but they cannot help taking them. With Spook, it wasn't stealing. It was exaggerating.

Added complication was the fact that Spook Davis looked so very like Gull—when he was wearing a wig which he affected when working as an assistant to The Great Gulliver. However, Gull had hired Spook because of this very similarity in appearance. They utilized it in their work as magicians. When properly disguised, the striking resemblance allowed for the astonishing illusion that The Great Gulliver could be in two places at the same time.

They were dressed differently, now, of course, but when in the same attire, it would be almost impossible to tell them apart, a fact which they had used to advantage in performing magic tricks. Gull had but to get into a wooden box on the stage, which was made to appear empty by means of mirrors, and Spook then would appear immediately in the audience to create a striking piece of legerdemain.*

Spook Davis' exaggerating frequently stirred up trouble, from the results of which Gull, his double in appearance, often had to suffer.

Gull abruptly faced Spook Davis.

"So you said, 'Chris Columbus taking a vacation,' just by accident!" he growled.

"Huh? What— No, it was only that the new federal holiday was on my mind."

Gulliver Greene looked blank for a moment.

"Columbus Day," reminded Spook. "October twelfth. The President of the United States himself signed it into law."

Gull made frowning faces, then the light dawned in his emerald green eyes.

"Forgot about that," he mumbled. Then, shaking off his reverie, his ire returned.

"Blast your hide!" Gull grated. "If this mess is something your whoppers have stirred up—"

"Aw, now, Gull, hell! Really, I didn't—honest—I—"

"Remember that blonde hussy down in Tulsa?" Gull rapped.

"I'm telling you I haven't—"

"You promised to marry her! But it was me she sued for breach of promise, and her witnesses identified me as you! You told her you were young Rockefeller!"

Spook Davis wailed, "This is straight, Gull! Honest to Black-

---

* *This trick, astounding to behold, is the signature of one world-famous illusionist. The author, himself an amateur magician, cannot state with certainty how this feat is accomplished. The gag or gimmick employed by The Great Gulliver may not be identical to the other. —KENNETH ROBESON.*

stone. It's straight. I didn't stir this up, and I don't know what it's all about!"

Gull stood back, not entirely convinced. Spook had his more skilled moments, when even Gull could not tell when he was expanding upon the facts. On the other hand—he might be telling the unvarnished truth. He did, occasionally.

"You stick here!" Gull said abruptly.

"I couldn't move."

GULLIVER took the flashlight and the telegram, left the station, crossed the road and swung over a barbed wire fence. He had decided to investigate the route through the brush patch, the short cut to town which Spook Davis had been following when assaulted. The assailant might have left tracks.

After he had reached the brush, Gull foresightedly refrained from showing the flashlight beam, on the long chance that the marauder might still be in the vicinity. He walked carefully, pausing to listen, holding the shotgun ready.

At first, he thought what he heard was a pig in the brush. This grunting sounded like that, a series of short *Unk! Unk!* noises. Gull halted, and was just beginning to recall that pigs usually slept at night when the grunting turned into a voice that said thickly, "Oh, don't—don't—*don't!*"

Gull spiked the flashlight beam through the brush in the direction of the voice sounds, left the illumination on only a moment, then extinguished it, whipped to one side and dropped flat—just in case there might be shooting.

It was very still, and the groaning continued.

Gull ran forward and turned the flashlight on the groaning. He found himself looking at an old man, a huge old moose who must clear nearly seven feet tall when erect and who was as bald as an egg if one discounted the tufts of very black hair which grew out of his ears.

The ancient's wrists and ankles were tied securely with his own shirt.

Chapter IV

THE VANISHING VICTORIAN

THE MAN WHO stepped into view stood taller than any other in the room. He would have out-towered the Biblical giant, Samson, not to mention other fabulous personages noted for their imposing height and physical prowess.

He was Doc Savage. The Twentieth Century had not, and probably would not, produce another like him.

Six feet would catch his height at the eyes. And they were unique eyes. A metallic gold, filled with aureate flakes which caught the light and imparted the eerie sensation of gold dust swirling in suspension. His skin was sun-bronzed and wind-burned. A lifetime of adventuring had wrought that metallic alchemy. A helmet of hair lay close to his scalp, like super-fine coppery wire.

The entire effect of the man was a little unreal, as if an alchemist had wrought a vital human being out of impervious metals.

"It worked like a charm, Doc," Monk said enthusiastically. "Ham here pretended to be an old geezer, and asked the crook to meet us at the new office."

Ham Brooks took up the tale.

"I entered the office by the secret elevator so that the secretarial staff would not realize I was there. When I seized him, Monk came down to help carry our prisoner back to our headquarters."

"No one suspected the subterfuge?"

"Everything transpired behind closed doors," Ham assured him.

Doc nodded. "It was a good test. But we will not use that subterfuge often, lest the nature of the eighty-fifth floor operation become publicly known."

"This idea of yours is a beaut, Doc," Monk said, handing over the prisoner draped across his apish shoulder. The bronze man took the unconscious man in hand as if he weighed no more than a small child. "Scattering graduates of this place all over the country, where they can gather information and send it back to us for investigation, what I mean."

"It is my hope that it will increase the efficiency of our little organization," Doc stated.

The bronze giant was being characteristically modest when he called his organization little. True, there were only five men who worked closely with him. But this criminal-curing college employed guards and other staff, as did the anonymous office that went only by the plain name, Oddities.

The latter was run by the former head of a private detective agency Doc had hired at the beginning of the present business depression, just before it would surely have failed. Doc owned other enterprises, as well. Steamship companies. Passenger airlines. Railroads. Newspapers. Factories. The financial holdings of the amazing bronze man were immense.

This latest expansion, however, was a clandestine one. The general public would never hear of it. Not if Doc Savage could help it.

"Monk, the telegram, please," requested Doc.

A hairy hand pulled out the night letter, proffered it. Doc accepted it with one hand, the other holding the prisoner steady.

Golden orbs scanned the typed letters pasted onto the yellow flimsy, absorbing the report of the mysteriously vanishing house in the Missouri woods.

"This bears investigation."

"We're gettin' close to Halloween, Doc," suggested Monk.

"Could be a prank."

Doc shook his head in a slow negative. "The person who sent this is a trusted graduate of this institution, and currently works as stringer for a newspaper in the city of Kirksville, not far from the site of this unusual dwelling. He would not report a prank."

And on that sound judgment, the bronze giant decided to look into the mystery. For this was part of what he did—investigate the unusual.

"Is that why you wanted us to bring the small dirigible?" asked Ham.

Doc nodded. "It fit the circumstances described in the telegram and it was time the mooring experiment was concluded."

They moved through the building as Doc conveyed the prisoner to a dormitory-style holding room where he could sleep off the effects of the spell Ham inflicted upon him.

They passed a gymnasium, then an empty cafeteria. What looked like a classroom where educational activities were taking place came into view. Every face in those classes could be found on post office walls, and in police mug books across the nation, if not the world. There were a few small-time dictators Doc had harvested in the course of his recent adventures. Everyone wore a crisp white uniform. The staff wore blue.

Everything in this and the other buildings was dedicated to the transformation of common criminals into upright citizens. No criminal who had ever been subjected to this regimen had ever escaped, or gone back to a life of criminality. It was the bronze man's deepest hope that none ever would.

Now the facility was dedicated to turning out future operatives of the bronze man's new information-gathering organization. It was another reason for the expansion of the crime-curing college to several open-air structures. The former mountainside chambers were still in use, but not so much as before, and now only after dark, where such activity would not be noticed. Passing airplanes might observe hidden stone doors rolling open in the gray hillside and this would attract curiosity that a germ research complex would not.

A great deal of thought had been given to the expansion of the Crime College.

Doc Savage conferred with a man who headed the surgical wing of the operation. He gave swift instructions for the new inmate, and with that accomplished, rejoined Monk and Ham.

"Everything is set," he said. "Six months from now our newest student should be fit for release, ready to take his place in decent society."

Ham nodded soberly. "Some such scheme as this should be substituted for our penitentiaries. Why don't you take it up with our government?"

"Our esteemed and opinionated senators would not touch it," Doc explained patiently. "The idea of catching a criminal, cutting his head open and doing something to his brain that he does not wish to be done is entirely too hard-boiled. The editorial writers and the women's clubs would be up in arms."

There was no denying the bronze man's words. Doc knew prisons actually breed crime. But this institution cured it!

"We will head for the Missouri woods in the dirigible," he announced. "Let's roll, brothers."

THERE was a weather front forming over the Adirondack Mountains when Doc Savage got the small airship turned around and pointed west.

The front consisted largely of angry clouds and a stiff wind. This retarded their forward progress some.

Doc Savage had the controls. The compact size of the airship required that it be piloted from a command chair, rather than a standing position, as would be the case on a full-sized commercial dirigible.

Progress was rapid, given the atmospheric conditions. But the airship was no airborne goliath boasting multiple motors. Two were sufficient to push it along, and so the passage took some time. Dusk began falling.

It was a boring succession of hours.

Monk Mayfair passed the time by scrutinizing the ground passing below through a great luminous quartz lens that had been installed in the floor of the gondola. This was on the order of a giant magnifying glass. Combined with an infra-red projecto-receptor searchlight set in the lower hull, it caused the ground to stand out in sharp relief, darkness notwithstanding.

In the aft portion of the gondola, Ham Brooks was perched on a stack of equipment cases, carefully honing the razor sharp edge of his sword cane. From the tip of the blade he had wiped off the sticky brown compound adhering to it. This was a drug, the presence of a slight quantity of which in an open wound would produce instant unconsciousness. Ham's sword cane had merely to inflict a tiny scratch on a foe to drop him senseless.

This explained the fate of the captive back in Doc's headquarters library.

A slight noise drew Ham's eye. Howling rage, he bounded erect.

"You bobtailed baboon!" he bellowed. "You beetle-browed misfit! You hairy mishap of evolution!"

Ham usually addressed Monk in this vein when aroused. Yet Monk was nowhere in sight.

Ham flourished his sword cane and glowered at the creature which had inflamed his rage. This was a pig.

This pig was unique—a homelier specimen of the porker family was probably never created. The animal had a lean body, razor back, and legs as long as a dog's. His ears were phenomenal. They looked big enough to serve as wings.

Just now, the comical aspect of the pig was enhanced by the addition of the white whiskers which Ham had lately worn. The shoat was walking on his rear legs. Wedged between the toes of one forefoot was a small black cane.

Someone had made the pig up as a caricature of Ham in his disguise.

Ham had no trouble guessing who had done it—Monk. The

pig, who was called Habeas Corpus, was Monk's pet.

Habeas Corpus eyed the perturbed Ham. What happened next would have been quite a shock to a superstitious person.

The pig seemed to begin to speak—with a Harvard accent, such as Ham sometimes affected.

"Jolly good detectives old Harvard turns out, eh, topper?" the pig apparently queried.

Ham squawked, and made a wrathy rush for Habeas. The pig had obviously experienced these attacks before. He bounded away with startling agility, losing the white whiskers and the black stick in the process. He darted under a shelf containing ammunition boxes.

Glaring indignantly, Ham looked around for Monk. He knew that Monk was a ventriloquist, and had put the words in the homely porker's mouth.

A squeaky peal of laughter came from behind the door to the washroom. Monk had been unable to contain his mirth any longer.

Ham started purposefully for the source of the glee.

Doc Savage, gigantic man of bronze, turned and said, "Renny should have reported by now."

The bronze man's voice was quiet enough, but Ham came to a sharp halt. Doc was not in the habit of showing excitement. His simple statement portended trouble.

Monk jutted his simian head out of the washroom, saw that Ham was no longer violent, and ambled out, impossibly long arms swinging.

"Let me try and raise the big-fisted freak," he volunteered.

"You should talk!" Ham snapped. "About freaks, that is!"

Renny was Colonel John Renwick, the civil engineer of Doc's group of assistants. He had been in Chicago, and the bronze man had radioed him to fly to Missouri to case the vicinity of the mystery manse in anticipation of their arrival.

The hairy chemist worked the radio for a time and came back

saying, "His plane landed in a government landing field, all right. But he ain't come back for it. Must be still searchin' around."

"Maybe we had better ask the Missouri State Highway Patrol to investigate," Ham suggested.

"Long Tom and Johnny are near," Doc told him. "We will have them look into the thing."

Ham looked slightly surprised. "Where are Long Tom and Johnny?"

"En route to the scene from Toronto."

The bronze man turned over the controls to Monk then switched on the radio microphone. Behind inspection ports, tubes glowed.

"Long Tom—Johnny!" he called into the microphone.

"Johnny speaking," answered a rather scholastic voice from the loudspeaker.

Johnny was William Harper Littlejohn, the long-worded geologist and archeologist of the group. He was addicted to the linguistic equivalent of jawbreakers, which he never inflicted on Doc Savage. Johnny was an individual so tall and thin that it had been said of him that he could take a bath in a rifle barrel—an exaggeration, of course. But not much of one.

Doc gave the location of the landing field, which was a government-operated emergency field in Millard.

"You fellows had better drop up there and see if anything has happened to Renny," he directed. Then he switched off the apparatus.

Hours later, they heard from Long Tom Roberts.

"We found Renny. He's pretty bunged up. Claims a wild Indian tried to scalp him."

"What happened to the Indian?" prompted Doc.

"Renny says he got clean away. But he got Hiawatha's tomahawk away from him, and he's talking about hunting him down and giving him a close haircut with it."

"Tell Renny to hold his horses. We are less than an hour away."

"Right," said Long Tom.

"Anything else?" asked Doc.

"Yeah. Johnny says the tomahawk looks like the ones they used to make in the old days. But it's not old-looking at all."

Doc requested, "Put Johnny on."

A moment later, Johnny came over the loudspeaker.

"Salutations, Doc."

Which was actually a modest greeting for the bony archeologist. He loved his big words, a relic from the days when he occupied the Natural Science chair at a prestigious university.

"Tell me about the tomahawk," Doc requested.

"It looks as if it was made last week. The rawhide thongs show no signs of aging. But to make one like this, you would have to be practically a woods-dwelling Sac or Fox."

"What did he say?" Ham asked, brow puckering.

"Johnny just named two of the tribes who formerly inhabited Missouri and surrounding states," explained Doc.

"Have you investigated the mystery of the disappearing house?" asked Doc into the microphone.

"Not yet. We were too busy hunting down Renny."

"Do so now. We will be there directly."

"Signing off," said Johnny. The loudspeaker went dead.

Ham spoke up. "What do you make of it, Doc?"

"It is very strange," admitted the bronze man.

Monk scratched behind an ear, noticed that Habeas had ventured out into the open and, picking him up, scratched one of the shoat's ludicrously long ears, too.

"Which?" he wondered. "The disappearin' house, or the scalpin' wild Indian?

"Both," said Doc Savage, turning his attention back to the night sky visible through the airship's windshield.

Chapter V

BEAUTY IN BURLAP

THE OLD MAN with the hairy ears was injured—the side of his hairless head had been clubbed with something a time or two. Four of his pockets, two in the pants and two in the coat, held pint whiskey bottles; two of these had the seals unbroken. And there was no reason to doubt that he was gloriously drunk.

Gull frowned, suddenly suspecting that Spook Davis and this old wolf had merely gotten tight together, retreated to this brush patch, and had a drunken fight. Such a possibility would explain this part of the night's events in a satisfactory manner.

The ancient giant began to mumble and Gull switched off the light and bent close to listen to the gibberish.

"Alive—Columbus alive—positive," The old fellow said with unexpected distinctness.

Gull put his teeth together until he could feel the tightness in his jaw muscles. It didn't appear that this part of the mystery was going to be explained merely as a fight between two stews.

Gull said, "Aren't you stretching it a little, dad?" grimly.

He was surprised when the old man heard that and reacted to it by opening his eyes.

"Who're you?" he wanted to know.

There was no reason why he shouldn't be told, Gull decided.

"Gulliver Greene," explained Gull.

"Liar!"

"What makes you think so, dad?"

The old fellow hiccoughed with exactly the same sound as if a dog had barked. He was very drunk, even if he could talk.

"Gulliver dead—they killed him—"

Gull experienced a sensation between his shoulder blades which he didn't particularly care for.

"Why the killing, dad?" he asked tensely.

The old man reared up suddenly and began to mumble, his voice thick and vague, hardly understandable.

"—that dwarf—on my trail—The Great Gulliver'll know whash shush-should—aw, hecksh wizzit—shoo—shouldn't never monkey wish—wish—"

Gull shook him. "Who tied you up?"

"Huh?" He roused slightly. "Mush shaw your light and run."

"What! Someone was here just now?"

"Sush-sure!" He rocked and his eyes closed.

"Where did they go?" Gull demanded.

But the old man made noises which sounded as if an idiot was trying baby talk, then went to sleep.

Gull straightened, held the scattergun tightly, listened, and heard nothing but the alcoholic breathing of the old man at his feet, but did not feel reassured. If there was someone around…. Well, they'd be escaping while he stood there—would be gone before the police arrived.

Gull shoved his jaw forward suddenly, angrily deciding he'd had about enough pushing around for the night. He didn't like being baffled, didn't enthuse over this stuff about people going to kill him—the more he thought about it, the more wrathful he became. He'd grab this prowler. Then he'd knock some explanations out of somebody….

He began to prowl through the brush, searching. The undergrowth was red oaks and was being pastured with sheep, hence the ground was free of weeds and tall grass except for now and then a bunch of buckbrush. Silent progress was not difficult, and he got along excellently until he stepped on something which lunged, emitted a bleat and upset him. A sheep. There were other sheep, a whole brush patch full of them, and they now scattered through the darkness in all directions. They could go, "Baa-a-a!" louder than any sheep Gull had ever heard.

Since there was nothing to be lost, he took out with the sheep, running south, hoping that he sounded like another sheep. He came out of the brush and unexpectedly ran into a barbed wire fence, but had luckily slowed. It was intensely dark due to the thickening clouds.

Gull had hold of the top strand of barbed wire, feeling to learn which way it ran, when it went taut. It had been very slack; now it not only tightened, but moved in a revealing way— someone was climbing over the loose fence not many yards away.

Gull yanked the wire. The other person overbalanced, fell off the fence; a hard fall, from the sound. Rather approving of himself, Gull leveled the shotgun and poked light out of the flash lens.

Then he did not feel so proud of himself because the cinnamon-haired girl on the ground looked as if she might be lifeless.

GULLIVER leaped to the young woman, who lay face down, and turned her over, wondering if the wealth of entrancing cinnamon-hued hair would carry out a promise that the girl would be a knockout. It did, and so satisfactorily that he was distinctly aware of something turning a handspring in his chest.

She was a long girl, possessing a sinewy curvaceousness that was pleasant to behold. It made tiny goosebumps appear on his wiry forearms—prickles that had nothing to do with the freshening October night wind. Her makeup was very subdued, or she wore none; she certainly didn't need it. Her eyes were closed, and a trickle of scarlet crept from one corner of her shapely mouth.

"Whew!" Gull exploded.

Maybe he'd killed her! The fall could have broken her neck.

Gulliver felt exactly as he had the last time he'd dived into the Santa Fe pond for a swim. It was much too late in the year to go swimming; he'd all but froze.

He spoke to her wildly, kneaded her slender wrists. This got no result. He began perspiring. He'd better carry her to the old farmer's house and telephone for a doctor. But dared one move a person with a broken neck? He'd have to go telephone a doctor....

"No, thanks," she said meekly. "You can spare me the doctor."

Gull was so astonished he failed to notice that he had said nothing aloud about any medico.

"Glory be! You're not—"

"I bit my tongue when I fell," she explained faintly, and produced a small white handkerchief. "The fall must have stunned me for a moment." She shut her eyes tightly, apparently waiting for a dizzy feeling to go away.

Gull, deciding that her throaty voice left nothing to be desired, treated himself to a sigh of relief. Then he noticed her shoes—shoes which seemed rather unfitting for such a beauty; they were heavy leather, and they also had brass caps on the toes and brass reinforcing on the moderately high heels. Her frock, he observed, was of some dark homespun stuff, about as plain a garment, in fact, as could be constructed. It appeared to be burlap. Imagine—a burlap dress! The effect was delightful, though. She certainly was a beauty. He decided it was time he told her he was sorry about making her fall....

She seized his arm. "That old man! Did he get away?"

"The one with the hairy ears?"

"That's him!" she gasped.

"He's still tied up. And in a drunken sleep," Gull explained, startled by the young woman's vehemence.

She tried to get up, made a small sound of pain, and sank back.

"Get him!" she ordered.

"Huh?"

She clutched his arm with both hands, shrilled, "Someone is trying to kill us both! You're Gulliver Greene—I've heard you described. I eavesdropped, but I couldn't learn anything about the horrible business except that you were one of those to be killed. That old man knows. I was following him. I knocked him down with a stick and was tying him up when you scared me away. Go get him!"

"But—"

"Go get him before he escapes!" she said, almost raging. "He's the key to this whole thing!"

In her agitation, the girl tried to get up, and did reach her feet, but after two steps in her heavy brass-shod brogans, she swayed dizzily, would have fallen if Gull had not supplied an arm.

"I seem to be dizzy!" she gasped. "Oh—get that old man!"

Gull eyed her. "Who are you?"

"Saint Pete," the girl snapped. "Oh, do go and—"

"Wait for me," Gull grunted. "I'll bring him here."

FRIGHTENED sheep gave Gull an uncomfortable stare as he ran through the red oaks with the flashlight and the shotgun. In the east, there was a faint bumping noise that was probably thunder, but otherwise the night was almost unnaturally quiet and dark—the clouds, packing more tightly overhead, were slowly turning the sky into an infinitely black thing. Gull put the back of a hand against his forehead where the perspiration on his oily skin kept gathering in drops which jiggled down his face with a sensation closely akin to small bugs crawling.

The old man with the hairy ears still slept, blowing great noisy breaths of alcohol fumes. Gull stooped, lifted him, found him surprisingly heavy. Because it was a little difficult to carry a burden through the brush, Gull moved to one side, found the path which was the shortcut, and followed that, using his flashlight clumsily with the hand which also held the old shotgun.

Broken glass on the path stopped him for a moment. A shattered whiskey bottle, the liquid still splattered over the ground and the surrounding bushes. Gull decided this was where Spook Davis had been whacked over the head with a whiskey bottle.

The Great Gulliver staggered on, his thoughts more occupied with the young woman than with the rest of the mess. Saint Pete, as she had called herself, was something unique. He had distinctly liked the warm feeling he got by looking at her exquisite lines.

He reached the fence, moved along it to where he had left the girl, then poked around for some moments with the flashlight before the truth yanked him up rigid, causing his mouth to fall open and the flashlight beam to become motionless, pointing at nothing in particular.

Saint Pete had taken her departure.

Chapter VI

THE WILDEST INDIAN

THE DIRIGIBLE PASSED over the small landing field in Millard, Missouri, a little past midnight and, seeing no activity through the quartz lens, they pushed on toward the spot where the weird house was reputed to stand, somewhat northwest of the town of La Plata.

At this point, Doc Savage had donned a pair of goggles that were thick and complicated, obviously housing intricate apparatus. These enabled him to see what the infra-red searchlights disclosed to the others.

He followed a highway until he came to a dirt turnoff, then tracked that for a while.

Below, forest grew thick. Leaves had begun falling off trees. These should be brown and gold with some scarlet, but in the infra-red light, colors could not be discerned. All was an eerie world of shifting contrasts.

Suddenly, a thin white whisker of light shot up. It was amazingly intense, for all the fact that it was no thicker than a pencil. It might have been composed of hardened light.

A second rod popped into life. Then a third. They waved about like incandescent insect feelers.

"Those are our spring-generator flashlights," called out Monk. "They're directly below."

"Radio them," Doc told Monk.

The hairy chemist flew to the radio set and raised the party below. Each of Doc's men carried small portable radio transceivers. They had a limited range, but were very effective within that range.

"Everyone O.K.?" Monk asked.

"Holy cow!" came a booming voice that could only be Renny Renwick. *"Have I had a night!"*

"It ain't over yet," Monk reminded him.

"First I was set upon by a scalping Indian, and then I saw a house up and disappear when I walked up to it," Renny thumped mournfully.

Doc Savage called over, "Ask Renny to direct us to the house in question."

Monk repeated the request. A rapid exchange followed.

"Renny says it's due south, about a mile and a half up the trail they're on," reported Monk.

A frown flickered in Doc's golden orbs.

"No better road?"

"No. He says the only way to the house is along this path, which ain't wide enough for an automobile."

Doc nodded. "Tell the others to remain where they are for the time being."

Doc Savage gave the throttles a stiff bat, and the tiny airship nudged ahead, dual propellers whirring.

Following the forest trail was easy. It was the only one.

"Looks kinda like the Indian paths of the olden days," Monk muttered, as he watched it unreel beneath his feet in the big quartz lens.

"No doubt it was," said Doc.

Soon, they were upon the site of the mysterious dwelling.

Except that there was no dwelling. There was a clearing all right, and a foundation. It was a slab type of foundation. No cellar hole. The path ran straight toward it and picked up on the other side. There was no sign of any water or electrical hookups.

Doc propelled the dirigible along the path for a quarter mile, just to make certain that were was no other houses in the immediate vicinity.

It was clear that there was none. Any structure would have poked its roof up through the shivering crowns of trees. Still, to be sure, Doc made slow circles around the area.

"Devilish deserted," ventured Ham.

"This is the only spot cleared of woods for miles," Doc agreed.

Turning the airship around, the bronze man made a beeline for the slab foundation and managed to station the dirigible over it by cutting the engines ahead of time and coasting to the spot without power.

This enabled them to hover after a fashion over the slab, although a breeze pushed them about a bit.

"No house at all," said Doc.

Frowning, Ham got on the radio.

"We found the spot, but there's no house there," he declared.

"Didn't I already say that?" Renny returned in his bearish voice.

"But you claimed that you saw it!" Ham demanded.

"I saw the roof outlines. It was a Victorian. One of those rambling old monstrosities garnished with a lot of useless gingerbread and a tower like a wizard's cap."

"You saw the roof, but not the house?"

"I spotted a light in the tower," clarified Renny. *"Shape of a window pane."*

"So what happened?" asked Monk, leaning into the mike.

"I came up the path and saw the gabled parts of the roof," rumbled Renny. *"That was when the scalping party commenced."*

"Who got scalped?" put in Monk, simian features puckering with interest.

"Nobody. The redskin ran into my fist. He didn't like it."

That was possibly the understatement of the century. Renny's fists were quart-sized pails of bone and gristle. Being beaned by a brick was probably a step down in discomfort.

"Describe your assailant," requested Doc Savage.

"He wasn't very big, but he was all wire and muscles. Wore a deerskin breechcloth, and not much else. He sneaked up from behind and tried to take my hair in one hand and slice off the top of my scalp with the other. But I heard a twig snap, and turned just in time to skin my knuckles against his nose."

"He say anything?" asked Doc.

"Yeah. But I couldn't make it out. It was Indian lingo. I scouted around for a time and found that I was pretty close to the house. So I made for it. I couldn't have taken my attention off it for more than a few seconds, while I searched for that Indian. When I laid eyes on the roofline again, it plumb wasn't there."

"Any other phenomena?" asked Doc.

"None. By the time I reached the spot, I came upon the same slab you are looking at now."

"A trick," sniffed Ham. "No doubt the actual home is elsewhere and Renny witnessed some type of clever fakery."

"I dunno," Monk muttered. "Renny's got pretty good eyes and his woodcraft is top-notch. He would be hard to fool."

"A house cannot simply vanish," Ham insisted.

"So where's the other house—the real one?" countered Monk.

Ham Brooks had nothing to offer.

Monk looked to his bronze chief, his homely face a wide question mark.

Doc Savage added nothing further to the argument. Instead, he said, "Let us pick up the others."

ENGAGING the engines, Doc sent the dirigible over the spot where their three remaining comrades were camped.

A blazing pencil light pierced the night. Midges could be seen swirling in its beam, and a solitary moth fluttered around its vortex curiously.

Releasing the grappling hook from its hull receptacle, Doc snagged a sturdy oak tree and winched the craft as close to the ground as the thick trees permitted. He threw open the hatch, dropped out the heavy knotted climbing rope.

One by one, they slipped to the ground, Monk sliding down one-handed, Habeas the pig cradled in his other arm. He made it look easy.

Johnny Littlejohn greeted them. He was distinguished by a shaggy mop of hair and a lapel monocle which he never wore, and which was a handy magnifying glass. He was so tall he seemed to tower seven feet high, but some of that was skeletal illusion.

Renny Renwick was another giant, but his size consisted of mass, like a well-muscled mastodon, minus the shaggy coat. He was the civil engineer of the group, and looked the part. A forbidding expression dragged down his countenance, which was perpetually gloomy of cast. Strangely, this was the towering engineer's way of smiling. At the ends of his wrists hung a pair of fists as large as the wooden mallets seen at carnival side shows for the purpose of displaying a man's strength by ringing a bell.

Last was Long Tom Roberts. In his own way, he looked as unhealthy as skeletal Johnny—but going in the opposite direction. Slender, his complexion resembling a cellar-dwelling mushroom, Long Tom was the smallest of Doc's men. He made up for his lack of stature by packing around a temper which, when unleashed, was as formidable as Monk's hairy arms, or Renny's gigantic fists. Owing to this, the others left Long Tom strictly alone when he was riled. He was the electrical engineer of Doc's group, and the long hours he spent in his windowless cellar workshop explained his expertise and his pale skin alike.

Doc Savage began examining the tomahawk, which he had taken from Johnny the archeologist.

Doc's flake-gold eyes regarded it intently for almost a minute as he turned it over in his metallic hands, hefted it, judging its workmanship as well as its practicality.

The war axe was carved from granite and mounted on a hickory shaft less than two feet long. This was hollow and at the poll was a bowl receptacle for inserting tobacco.

"They would smoke tobacco from the lower end," said Johnny.

Doc nodded. "There is dried blood on the edge," he said.

"Not mine," insisted Renny.

"Maybe someone should part your hair," muttered Monk. "Indians didn't take the entire scalp, just a patch at the top to show that they had beaten a foe. Maybe you got some hair missin'."

Momentarily alarmed, Renny reached up with one big paw and felt of the crown of his skull. He encountered hair that had been smeared down with Pomade. No raw skin or moist spot.

Long face gloomy, Renny took an annoyed swipe at the hairy chemist. "Think you're funny, huh?"

Monk bounced out of the way. "It never hurts to check," he grinned.

Suddenly, a peculiar sound started up in the night.

HAD these Missouri woods harbored a bird combining the clear cry of the giant Roc out of the Arabian Nights with the call of a tiny tropical songster, such a hybrid creature might have authored the sound that filled the night. It was a mellow trilling, amazing to hear. It adhered to no tune, but was possessed of a weirdly haunting melody.

This was a sound Doc Savage made when his emotions were jarred. Sometimes it denoted puzzlement, or surprise, or other strong feelings. Here, it marked a mix of fascinated wonder.

The sound soon ebbed into nothingness.

Ham looked intrigued. "What's say, Doc?"

"This tomahawk is authentic."

"So? A lot of Indian artifacts are."

Doc said, "For this tomahawk to survive into the Twentieth Century in this condition would mean that shortly after manufacture it had been stored in a weatherproof place, unused, for over one hundred years."

"I have never held a finer specimen," inserted Johnny the archeologist. "But I, too, cannot account for its excellent condition."

"Now what?" asked Monk, losing interest in the tomahawk.

"Investigate the vanishing Victorian," replied Doc.

They started off, using their flashlights to illuminate the way. The myriad beams made weird shadows crawl in the underbrush, threw great trees into sharp relief, gave everything the uncanny illusion of moving, as if they were wending their way through an enchanted forest out of a storybook.

"Our lights make us fair targets for trouble," Ham was saying.

Doc Savage offered no comment to that, but his flake-gold eyes roved the ever-shifting trees on either side of the well-worn path, apparently missing little, but also discovering nothing unusual.

When they approached the clearing, they were startled to see a black tower jutting over the treetops that had not been there moments before.

At first, they mistook it for a tall fir tree, silhouetted against the waning moon. But its edge had not the irregular look of an evergreen. And fir trees were not common in these Missouri woods.

"Hey!" shouted Monk. "That looks like that wizard's hat of a roof tower Renny was talkin' about!"

"That's it!" Renny thumped. "Holy cow!"

They quickened their pace. The path was so narrow that in walking bunched together, their elbows kept brushing. Now they stretched out in single file, eager to get there as rapidly as possible.

Came an ear-splitting shriek.

Everyone reached into armpit holsters for their supermachine pistols, powerful yet compact weapons beyond anything in the hands of any nation. Little larger than an automatic, these packed the punch of a Tommy gun. They resembled one in miniature, down to the canister-like drums mounted ahead of the trigger guards. Each pistol was capable of unleashing a frightful storm of lead, but in fact were rarely charged with solid slugs. Instead, the drums contained so-called "mercy" bullets—hollow shells filled with a fast-acting anesthetic solution of the bronze man's invention. He did not believe in slaying his enemies.

All brandished their superfirers, except Doc Savage, who rarely carried a weapon. He preferred not being dependent upon firearms.

As it happened, their attacker had selected Ham for his first victim.

He dropped down from a heavy bough and landed beside the dapper lawyer. The late arrival was compactly muscled, sinewy and wiry to a degree that comes from living out of doors, and off the land.

White rods of light picked him out. His face was a fierce, snarling animal-like thing, the sharp nose mashed where Renny's iron knuckles had popped it. His skull was shaven after the fashion of the Mohawks, sunburned face smeared with thin, greenish lines. A single scalplock sprouted from the top of his head, to which stiff porcupine hair was affixed.

"Holy cow!" howled Renny. "The scalper!"

That was as much as anyone got out.

RENNY lunged forward, and received a faceful of dirt, flung unexpectedly. He brought his monster hands up and began pawing at his eyes.

Next, Ham Brooks yanked the narrow blade out of the barrel of his sword cane. Assuming a stance similar to a fencer, he lunged, inflicting upon the Indian's bare shoulder a minor wound.

Withdrawing, the dapper attorney stood back, saying, "He will be insensate in a mere second or two."

Instead, the brave made a rush for Ham, much to the latter's consternation.

"Didn't you wipe that sticky anesthetic off your blade?" yelled Monk.

"I forgot!" gulped Ham, defensively weaving the air before him with the flashing sword.

Long Tom Roberts slanted in, tripped the Indian, who somehow pulled the puny electrical wizard down with him. They ended up rolling in the dirt, clubbing and howling like two alley cats in a cartoon.

Long Tom managed to extricate himself, while the Indian bounced back on his moccasins.

So far, no one had gotten off a shot. Johnny Littlejohn stood rooted, as if dazed by the spectacle.

The redskin then turned to engage Doc Savage. He must not have realized the size of the mighty bronze man until he was next to him because a look of astonishment whipped across his twisted lineaments.

Doc then had a remarkable two or three minutes.

The arboreal attacker produced a knife of some kind. He ducked to one side, swept in and attempted to run its edge across the back of Doc's right knee in an effort to hamstring him.

Doc Savage drifted out a hand and seized the wrist back of the knife. He twisted, and the blade spilled, struck earth.

The attacker gave out a wild screech, then tried to wrestle the bronze man.

Doc Savage invariably employed scientific methods in his fighting. This assailant did not. The sheer ferocity of his attack was enough to startle even the bronze giant.

The savage cry must have been part of it. He vented another wild war whoop that froze the blood, as it was no doubt intended to do.

For his part, Doc Savage appeared to take too long to size up his foe. Red hands reached for vital points in Doc's anatomy.

Doc batted those hands away with casual slaps. The other again looked startled. Twisting, he next tried to get one foot hooked around one of Doc's ankles in an attempt to throw him to the ground.

Doc disengaged, lifted his fists to block the Indian.

One secret of the bronze man's success was that he never employed more effort than was necessary. Doc believed in expending the minimum force to achieve the maximum result.

That philosophy was being tested now.

Enervated by an almost animal-like reservoir of strength, the redskin assailant refused to go down. His will to win verged on the indomitable.

Doc tripped him. The man stumbled, bounced back on his feet.

Doc reached out and slapped his opponent off his moccasins once more.

The brave looked thoroughly shaken, but was erect before anyone could do anything about it.

It became apparent that the bronze giant was fascinated by his foe. Doc seemed to be holding back, as if he wished to observe the other in action, the better to understand him.

Doc moved in, had a little better luck with a Ju-Jitsu maneuver. The other hit the ground, and hard. He sprang back up, though, before Doc got hold of him again.

The Indian was good. He was better than anyone Doc had encountered for a long time. It was almost never that he had a physical encounter with a man who was his equal.

For the first few seconds, Doc got a pleasant thrill out of fighting the man. Then he began to get another feeling, which wasn't a thrill. At least not a pleasant sort of a sensation.

The feeling that Doc got—and he wasn't very proud of it—was the fear that he was going to get licked at something at which he was among the best.

The brave knew a species of rough Judo. He knew wrestling as per Frank Gotch, Strangler Lewis and the old-timers. He knew it according to the young grunt-and-groan school. He knew below-the-belt tactics.

Taking hold of him was like taking hold of bundles of steel-wire cables covered with a good grade of buckskin. Keeping hold of him was something like trying to hold down a couple of panthers.

Doc lost skin, some hair, nearly lost a tooth, and most of his dignity. He was glad to circle the other warily.

Monk's bellowing voice spoke up and changed everything.

"Want me to hose him down with a few mercy bullets, Doc?" he asked.

The redskin spun toward that voice, startled.

His dark eyes fell upon the simian features of Monk Mayfair. They all but bugged out of his skull. He gave out a scream. Or was it a curse word? Then, somersaulting backward, he disappeared into the woods and their very deep night shadows.

Doc whipped out his own flashlight and, motioning for the others to remain on the dirt path, went off in pursuit.

The bronze man advanced a few paces, ears hunting sounds, and suddenly took to the trees. He raced along creaking and groaning boughs.

But no trace of the other could he find.

Doc used his nostrils, reasoning that the perspiration odors of a half-naked human being would lead him to his quarry. They got him only so far. Then he encountered a dead skunk, evidently freshly slain, and left there to overpower any such tracking.

DISCOURAGED, the bronze man returned to the others.

"You failed to best him," said Ham, looking surprised.

"He is very wily," admitted Doc.

"What did you make of him, Doc? He looked like the genuine article."

"He spoke like one, too," admitted Doc. "When he saw Monk he yelled a word that meant, roughly, 'evil spirit.'"

The bronze man's knowledge of language was so deep it

included most Native American tongues still spoken to this day.

Ham almost doubled over with laughter. "You mean the sight of this homely ape's ugly face frightened him away!"

"Maybe he saw my mitts and figgered I could pound him flat into his moccasins," countered the hairy chemist.

"What do you make of it, Doc?" wondered Long Tom.

Before the bronze man could reply, Johnny Littlejohn gave out a bleat of surprise.

Pointing high with his flash beam, he said, "A phantasmagorical imponderability!"

All eyes followed his quivering beam.

The roof tower that so resembled a wizard's cap of old was no longer there!

"Vanished!" Long Tom exploded.

They ran toward the sight.

This time they were not attacked.

Reaching the clearing, they came upon the area they had spotted from the air. There was a poured concrete foundation sitting in a cleared space. That was all.

No sign of any roof or house. Not a stick of wood or siding. The nearby trees were astir, as if shivering at what they alone had witnessed. No breeze troubled them. There was just a shivering and shaking amid the leaves.

Doc's eerie trilling came anew—an uncanny accompaniment to the leafy orchestra. But he said nothing.

Using his pocket torch, which he widened to a ray by twisting the lens, the bronze giant made a reconnoiter of the foundation.

"Our moccasin-clad friend has been here. His tracks come and go."

Renny remarked, "Looks like he's been visiting this place pretty often. There are tracks over tracks."

"Perhaps there is more than one Indian hereabouts," Ham offered.

Doc Savage shook his head. "No," he said quietly. "The same man. The detailing and size of the moccasin prints make that clear."

They rummaged around for almost an hour but discovered no further clue to what happened to the vanished house. Or, at least, to its roof. For that was all that anyone had seen of the supposed structure.

Deciding to return to their dirigible, they set off.

Not half a mile away, Monk Mayfair happened to look back, as if still trying to puzzle out the mystery.

"Blazes!" he exclaimed.

All heads turned.

There, clearly outlined in the spectral moonlight behind them, was the conical roof tower that was so evocative of a wizard's cap. It looked as solid as a church steeple.

A wind seemed to have sprung up, for the leaves in the trees began rustling as if full of creeping vipers. Yet they felt no wind on their faces.

Chapter VII

COLUMBUS AND THE SAINTS

WHEN THE GREAT GULLIVER walked into the One-Stop-Duzzit filling station carrying the old Goliath with the hairy ears piggy-back, Spook Davis reared to his feet, made an awful face, grabbed his head with both hands and sat down again.

"Oo-o-o, my head!" he groaned. "Say, what's that you've collected?"

At that point, the old one with the hirsute ears mumbled in his alcoholic sleep.

"Sha fact," he hiccoughed. "Chris Columbus ish alive."

Spook Davis yelped, rose out of his chair, cried out again terribly and fell back holding his head with one hand and stabbing the other in the direction of the old giant.

"That's who hit me!" he yelled. "I know that voice!"

Gull said nothing, but carried the old man into the little room that held the air compressor and sat him on the concrete floor, after which he straightened and stretched until his arm and back muscles had relaxed somewhat from the strain of carrying the ancient giant. Then, searching the elderly titan, he collected the four whiskey bottles, but nothing else.

Spook Davis came shuffling into the compressor room carrying a tire-changing tool.

"I'm gonna wake that old moose up with this and ask him some questions!" Spook hefted the tire iron grimly. "I've been made a sucker out of and it gripes me."

Gull said, "You're not by yourself," disgustedly.

"Eh? Who made a sucker out of you?"

"A woman."

"That ain't so bad. It's the ordained province of woman to make a sucker out of man. Especially if she's a pretty woman."

"This one was divine!" Gull said feelingly.

"Eh?"

"She was glorious!"

Spook blinked. "Huh?"

"Darn her!" Gull exploded.

He told Spook Davis about her, doing very good justice to her physical charms. He added his conviction that the young woman had not been weak from her fall at all; she had pulled a fast one and sent him after the old man to give herself a chance to escape; he did not spare himself for his gullibility in being taken in, in fact he swore at some length about it.

They drew a bucketful of water—they had to get it from the pump outside—and poured it in varying quantities over the old giant with the result that, if anything, he slept the more soundly. Spook insisted on giving the hard, bare skull of the subject a few experimental raps with the tire tool, but that was no more effective than the water.

Spook Davis squinted at Gull. "This make any sense to you yet?"

"Not any." Gull went over and grimly stood the shotgun against the large, elderly iron safe wherein old man Duzzit, who owned this filling station, kept his cash, then he got a broom and finished sweeping up the shattered oil jars broken in the earlier fight; an operation which had nothing to do with the digging he was giving his memory in an effort to unearth something illuminating.

"Look!" Spook Davis juggled his tire iron. "I've got me an idea."

Gull stopped sweeping. "Better let it out of its strange surroundings."

"Caustic, eh?" Spook grinned. "Look, you've got one relative alive, ain't you?"

"Uncle Box Daniels," Gull admitted.

"Just the other day, you wrote Uncle Box a letter asking if he knew of anything that looked like a job for us, didn't you? Now look—maybe that's why we're in this mess."

Gull went on sweeping. He'd thought of Uncle Box Daniels, but he happened to be a relative he'd never met, as well as his only living relative. He'd heard Uncle Box was a so-called mind-reader, working chautauqua, carnivals and the like. He did not see how that could have any connection with this. Still, he couldn't see how he had any connection with the thing himself.

"Customer!" Spook said abruptly.

A LARGE motor van had driven up beside the gas pump. The vehicle was painted the unprepossessing color of gray Missouri mud, and seemed to be loaded with the large tents of the variety used by carnivals and the more prosperous evangelists, because a few poles were protruding from the rear, and an extra roll of grimy looking canvas was tied to the endgate.

Gull and Spook Davis swapped looks.

"Tents!" Spook breathed. "Boy, should I have been a crystal gazer! Your Uncle Box Daniels deals in tents!"

Gull hurriedly closed the door on the slumbering old giant with the furry ears. Then he stepped outside, accompanied by Spook Davis.

THE SILENT SAINTS
Apostles of the One True Spiritual Way

It said this on the sides of the truck.

Three men got out of the cab. They were plain looking men with peaceful expressions, and all three were attired in garments of dark homespun cloth. They wore coarse shirts, buttoned at the neck, but no neckties; their shoes were heavy and plain.

"We are in need of gasoline, my good brothers," one of them explained slowly. "And we are also afflicted with a right rear tire which has a slow leak."

Spook took the gas hose off its hook and began putting reddish gasoline into the tank, which was situated under the cab seat; Gull walked to the air hose, picked it up and attended to the tire.

The air hose slipped. Escaping air made a loud spitting noise, as Gull remembered something. These Silent Saints wore heavy garments of rough burlap, and so had the girl who had said her name was Saint Pete.

One of the plainly dressed Silent Saints was about to enter the filling station, probably for a drink of water. He got a whiff of Spook Davis and promptly stopped. Spook still reeked of whiskey, and he also looked as if he might be well oiled.

The Saint assumed a holier-than-thou expression and said, "My brother, it is the weakness of the flesh only that makes us err. Your soul, I know, finds your present condition most repugnant."

"I don't know about my soul," Spook said, teetering over to peer into the gas tank. "But my stomach is beginning to resent it."

The Saint pulled a paper folder from his burlap coat and presented it.

"What's this?" Spook wanted to know.

"A written gem, my brother," intoned the Saint. "You must read it, for printed there is the kernel of that superb thesis so little understood by this benighted and sinful world. Namely, that the soul is the subconscious guidance of mortal destiny, the power that takes us poor human sheep by the hand and guides us around all pitfalls."

Spook grunted, "I don't get this. What are you guys, anyway?"

"We are the Silent Saints, apostles of the one true spiritual way," the other explained.

"Sure. It says that on the truck."

"If your sinful soul craves more knowledge of us, we have our *Complete Super-Giant Summary of the True Path of the Silent Saints*. It is in book form, which we sell for one dollar to cover the cost of printing."

Spook grinned. "Another racket, eh?"

"Your poor brain, sinfully robbed of its true right by the alcoholic demon, knows not what the evil in your body moves you to utter, my brother."

Spook, looking indignant, gritted, "Listen, my brother, if you think—"

"Tush, tush," said the Silent Saint mildly. "We are the faith of peace, dwelling nine months out of the year close to the soil in the Promised Land, and for three months of the year traveling to the corners of the nation with our proselytizing units, spreading the true path."

IN the west, a streak of lightning bounded along the horizon after which there was a rather resounding grunt of thunder, promise of an approaching rainstorm, which probably accounted for some of the unnatural stillness of the night.

Gulliver Greene lounged against the tailboard of the truck, listening to the lecture which Spook Davis was receiving, and also watching for a chance to ask one of the Saints privately if he knew a Saint Pete, an inquiry which Gull believed was justified in view of the fact that the girl had worn dark burlap clothing such as these men wore.

Spook Davis said, very solemnly, "Thank you, my brother, for your good words. Now I am going to tell you something that I have never breathed to a living soul. Would you believe it, but once my soul left me entirely."

He was off, exaggerating.

Spook continued, "Yes, my good brother, for a whole year, I was without any soul. It left my earthly body, and I, the part of me that is physical, remained in a trance—"

Gull noted one of the Saints on the other side of the truck

and started around the rear to speak to the fellow privately.

Both chance and man's natural curiosity caused Gull to glance into the van. He yanked it open, then stood on tiptoe and stared.

Enough light from the filling station marquee entered the van to show the contents—canvas, bundles, folding chairs, some planks, a throne-like chair, and a man sitting in the chair with a canvas strap around his chest and knotted in front, holding him to the chair. A lap robe lay across his knees.

The strange man had a thin, ascetic face, a high forehead and a firmly lean mouth. He wore his hair long—almost as long as a woman's tresses. His eyes were open, and were remarkable eyes, being dark, fixed and staring as if sightless. This queer individual was very pale, skin like a waxen dummy.

Gull squinted, for it struck him there was something familiar about the strange, trance-like figure sitting there. The face, it must be. But where had he seen it—where—?

"It's Christopher Columbus!"

The whisper rushing into Gull's ear lifted him almost off the ground, brought him around. He found himself looking into the staring eyes of the old giant with the hairy ears, sampling his powerful breath. The old fellow must have climbed out of the compressor room window—the window had been open, but Gull hadn't expected the old soak to awaken—and circled around, keeping out of sight.

"Columbus!" The old man pointed at the trance-like figure in the van. "Great Columbus!"

Gull looked into the truck again, then put his hand on his head, half expecting to find his ivory hair on end. The man in the van familiar? Of course! He had seen his picture a thousand times! It was in all the history books—at least a picture of Christopher Columbus was in the books—and this man looked exactly like that picture!

When Gull turned to where the old man with the hirsute ears had been standing, the old fellow was gone.

Chapter VIII

MIDNIGHT MIRACLE

ONCE MORE, DOC SAVAGE'S melodious trilling came forth. It had a hollow quality this time, as if its individual notes were devoid of certainty. They wandered about the air, as if seeking a melody to embody, yet ebbed away before they could become organized.

"This is nuts!" Monk howled. He began stamping around in frustrated circles. "This can't be!"

"Jove!" breathed Ham, twisting his elegant cane in his manicured hands. He unjointed it as if wishing to use its sharp point on something or someone. But no appropriate object of wrath presented itself.

Renny, Johnny and Long Tom just stared as if not believing their eyes.

It was weird, uncanny to behold. Even in the moonlight, the Victorian roof stood out distinctly. It was sheathed in what appeared to be slate, so the conical structure looked as substantial as anthracite coal.

They trained their flashlights upon it, and the beams quested about, seeking answers.

Presently, a lone bat whirred into view and circled the tower several times, finally alighting. It could be seen that it wriggled into a chink high up.

Ham sniffed, "Bally thing is actually a belfry."

Doc Savage had his pocket telescope out and was studying the tower roof.

"It appears so," he decided after a time.

"Could it be a shell, strung between trees by guy wires?" ventured Renny, who had been appraising the situation with an engineer's trained eye.

"Or a tricky balloon, filled with helium," suggested Long Tom.

"It is not responding to the wind," said Doc. "If it were not anchored to something solid, it would betray its instability. And no bat would dare nest in an unstable shell."

"Let's turn back and get to the bottom of this!" proclaimed Ham.

Doc Savage hesitated.

"Every time we have approached, the dwelling seemed to vanish," he advised. "That is the report from our operative as well."

"Only to reappear after we depart," agreed Long Tom, tugging at one sail-like ear.

Doc Savage seemed to make a sudden decision. "You men take up positions where you can observe the house clearly."

"What are you gonna do, Doc?" asked Monk.

But the bronze man did not reply. He had vanished into the woods, seeming to melt into the clotted darkness beyond their flash rays.

Moments later, they heard the throaty whirring of the dirigible's twin motors and they realized that Doc Savage had reclaimed his tiny airship.

Not long after, he floated past their heads at a height safely over the spiky tree line, but not very high above that.

The dirigible slid along a-pace, then Doc cut the motors. They fell quiet. A spectral silence fell over the forest. Somewhere an owl hooted, as if questioning the sudden stillness.

When the airship reached the black tower, Doc dropped the grappling hook. He snagged the tower on his first pass, arresting the airship over the dwelling—if there was an actual dwelling. They could only discern the slate roof.

A moment later, Doc Savage was dropping down the wire. He landed on a projecting gable. Three bats poked dark, curious heads out of the eaves, seemed to peer about, and winged off into the night, squeaking.

Eyes sharp, nerves on edge, they watched expectantly.

For a very long time, nothing seemed to happen.

Inspired by past experience, they did not remove their gazes from the linked airship and roof. Slowly, they drew closer.

Then, while their eyes were resting upon the rambling roof-line, the silhouette vanished.

Nothing audible came to their ears. One moment a stark silhouette broke the tree line, and then next, it was gone!

Again, the leaves in the trees commenced rustling as if stirred by some power that was not the wind. For no breeze blew.

They let out pent breaths. With them came a series of ex-postulations.

"Blazes!"

"Jove!"

"Holy cow!"

"I'll be superamalgamated!"

"Damn!"

The last to speak was Long Tom Roberts. His voice was an anguished whisper.

"Doc!" he moaned. "Where did he go?"

There was no sensible answer to the question.

WHEN Doc's men had gotten their paralyzed mental pro-cesses going again, they rushed to the spot, pushing boughs and branches aside in their mad haste.

Arriving, they all but collided with the slab foundation that did not support any structure.

Monk laid a hand on it. It was cool to the touch. He said so.

"What does that prove, you ape?" snapped Ham.

"I dunno," Monk admitted. "But it must mean something."

"It's a cool night," said Long Tom.

Johnny seemed to be the one who demonstrated the most calmness and presence of mind. He circled the slab, using his monocle magnifier, which he habitually wore affixed to one lapel of his perpetually ill-fitting suit.

"Fundament is constitutionally a hydrological matrix of aggregate, plus *opus caementicium,*" he pronounced.

"Say that again in English," requested Renny.

"This foundation consists of poured concrete."

"Anybody can see that," Monk returned. "Tell us something we don't already know."

"It is modern. The roof we discerned belongs to a Victorian home of the last century. They were built on stone foundations."

"Ergo?" prompted Ham.

"Ergo, the hallucinatory habitation had to have been relocated from another fundament—foundation to you."

They looked around.

Renny said, "How? The only road in or out is fit for a mule, at most."

Johnny fingered his monocle thoughtfully.

"It is unlikely that it was disassembled and relocated on this spot," he mused. "Wooden homes are not like European castles which can be broken down into their component stones and transported for reassembly."

"So we're back to where we started," complained Monk. "Nowhere!"

Ham Brooks was gazing upward, dark eyes concerned

"Our dirigible is drifting away," he observed with worry.

Monk decided to do something about that.

Selecting a tall tree, he took off his shoes and socks and began to climb it like a great long-armed baboon. His arboreal agility would do credit to a squirrel.

Reaching the top, the homely chemist roosted there and

searched for the trailing grappling hook. He transfixed it with the beam of his pocket flash.

It was dangling out of reach. As Monk watched, it moved away.

Gathering his burly body, Monk launched himself off a branch and caught the guy wire.

With a jar, the dirigible dropped several feet. Then it continued its lazy drifting, the apish chemist holding on.

Hand over hand, Monk ascended the line until he came within reach of the dangling climbing rope.

Monk began swinging side to side, building up bodily momentum. Now he brought to mind a Neanderthal man in action.

"That hairy gossoon is certain to get his neck broken!" howled Ham. For a moment, he forgot himself. Fear for his friend's safety was written all over his patrician features.

Soon, Monk was swinging like a human pendulum. This brought him closer and closer to the trailing rope. One hairy arm reached out, seized it.

At the apex of one swing, he transferred as neatly as if he had been doing it all of his life.

Again, the airship jarred downward, then righted itself. It seemed to roll along its longitudinal axis, like a barrel in water.

When it settled down, Monk made the climb to the open hatch and took control of the airship. The engines engaged, propellers whirling. Monk sent the craft spiraling around.

Neighboring trees began roiling and tossing their crowns this way and that, as the prop wash troubled them.

Venting gaseous ballast, Monk brought it low enough to snag a tree branch and reeled the line in. That accomplished, the airship was made fast.

Dropping down the rope, the homely chemist reached the anchoring trees and worked his way back to solid ground.

"Nice work, you caveman," Renny commented.

Monk smacked his hands dry of bark. "We ain't solved the

main puzzle yet."

"See anything of a roof anywhere up there?" Long Tom asked, grasping at straws.

"Naw, there ain't none."

That left them to wander about in annoyed and worried circles, seeking any sign of the missing Victorian dwelling and their absent leader, Doc Savage.

As men are wont to do when they lose keys or wallets, they covered the same ground over and over, their confounded faces expressing fresh perplexity each time doing so failed to turn up any sign or solution to the mystery.

At last Johnny Littlejohn spoke the obvious.

"All that is left for us to do is temporize."

"Wait for what, may I ask?" scoffed Ham.

"The house has disappeared and reappeared twice in a single evening," Johnny pointed out in a precise tone of voice. "It may be only a matter of time before it again returns to its foundation."

"Are you being serious?" Ham demanded.

Johnny eyed him with thin tolerance. "Have you a better course of action to suggest?"

Ham thought about that and finally admitted, "I have not."

They sat down on the rough-textured slab to wait.

The night wore on. The moonlight made cobweb patterns among the trees. A great horned owl hooted now and again. Furtive bats flung themselves from tree to tree.

There came a small grumble of thunder to the east, but it sounded very far away.

"I wonder where Geronimo got to?" Monk asked during one protracted silence.

"That interrogative query is the opposite of my intellectual curiosity," Johnny ruminated.

"Opposite—how?" asked Renny.

"I have been pondering whence the aborigine originated."

Johnny produced from his clothing the rude flint knife plucked from the Indian's fist by Doc Savage. He passed it around for inspection.

"Looks like something out of the history books," said Monk at last.

"That is what worries me," said Johnny. But he would not elaborate on why that should be.

They returned to their pensive waiting and worrying. They were men of action, scrappers who had first joined forces during the Great War, years ago. They did not enjoy the oppressive mental state in which the present situation had placed them. Like a mental fog, inaction weighed on them.

At length, Ham Brooks stood up, a peculiar expression twisting his handsome features.

"I just thought of something," he said in a queer tone.

"What is it?"

"What if that house reappears on this very spot?"

"Well, that's what we're all hopin' for, ain't it?" countered Monk, scratching the long ears of his pet pig, Habeas, cradled in his arms.

"Yes. But we are sitting on its foundation. If it returns, what will happen to us?"

At that realization, they all stood up.

With an alacrity not evident in their postures before this point, they retreated to the edge of the clearing and sat upon tree stumps left over from the days when the space had been cleared.

It was well that they did so.

FOR just around dawn, with the dust of lack of sleep clogging their eyes, the Victorian home reappeared on its foundation. They realized this when the forest began stirring. Although there was no wind, leaves rustled and boughs creaked.

To a man they turned to face the breeze.

And there was the ornate monstrosity of a house, looking as substantial as any tree.

Their expressions varied. Monk's eyes popped. Ham Brooks grabbed his chin and seemed to want to pull it off. Long Tom's jaw fell open. Surprise caused Renny's big fists to open like mouths. Johnny had been twirling his monocle in one long finger. He dropped it, seemed not to notice.

Renny was the only one who spoke.

His "Holy cow!" caused roosting bats to flee their holes.

The group stared at the house for what seemed the longest interval of their lives. They stood rooted in their shoes, unmoving. No one blinked.

Long Tom asked, "Do we barge right in?"

"Haste begets many things," murmured Johnny. "Regret is one of them."

They took in the structural lines of the place. Other than its ornamentation, it was unremarkable. The siding was a dismal maroon, rather suggestive of old blood. Gingerbread had been painted in somber black, now faded by sunlight and passing of time.

There was a railed porch. It swept around two sides. They happened to have taken up waiting positions facing the front of the eerie dwelling.

The front door was a shade of dried mustard. It was shut. There was no door knocker.

Soon it opened and out stepped a familiar figure. One they knew well.

Monk was the first to call out his name.

"Doc!"

Doc Savage stepped out onto the porch and looked about as if not certain where he was.

Seeing his men, an expression akin to relief crossed his metallic features.

He stepped off the porch and approached them.

Only when he began drawing near did they notice the hue of his face. The deep, healthy bronze tint that exotic climes had given his skin had faded to something like a ghost's pallor. The bronze man wore a shocked expression upon his regular features. The golden flakes of his eyes looked stark, as if petrified.

Doc came to a stiff halt before them. His mouth parted. It was fully a minute before he uttered any word of explanation, and even then it was but a single sentence.

"I have apparently traveled through time," Doc Savage said in a tone of voice that suggested he doubted his own pronouncement.

Chapter IX

FAT MAN AND FRIEND

THE GIANT ANCIENT had gone galloping off into the night—he stumbled in the darkness and made some noise. Instantly, Gull was after him, running with long-legged determination. He started to shout, decided it wouldn't do any good, and put on more speed. For a drunken man, the oldster made good time.

Gull, coming up behind, tripped him. The old man staggered, fell down, saying, *"Oops!"* foolishly. Gull fell upon him. The ancient gathered Gull in a rib-cracking bear hug, revealing some astounding strength. They fought, went over and over, mashing weeds, and Gull got a scissors hold, then an armlock.

"Behave!" Gull advised.

He heard the big van motor start, looked, saw it moving out of the filling station; they must have paid Spook for the gas, and were departing.

Gull tried to yell at the van to stop, but the old man got hold of his throat, and after they had fought some more, and the intoxicated old gentleman was subdued, the truck had gone down the road.

Giving permission both vocally and with the toe of his shoe, Gull escorted the old giant back to the filling station.

He was greeted by a flash of lightning and a bumping report of thunder. The storm which had been approaching all night was now very close.

"I thought grandpa was asleep!" Spook exploded in astonishment.

Gull propelled the ancient into the station, floored him in the washroom, and called, "Get me two of those long fan belts and we'll cut them and tie his hands and feet," to Spook Davis.

While they did this, Spook complained that old Duzzit, the filling station owner, would make Gull pay for the ruined fan belts, but his grumbling died when he got a good look at Gull's face.

"Hey, you look like you'd seen a ghost!"

Gull said, "A ghost would have been a treat," grimly.

"Huh?"

"Christopher Columbus was in that van," Gull advised shortly.

Spook Davis opened and shut his mouth, closed one eye and scrutinized Gull closely with the other, then absently scratched his chest, bent and picked up the shirt with which the old giant had been tied earlier, and untied the knots which the prisoner had loosened enough to slip free. Finally he said, "You wouldn't be nuts, maybe?"

The old man shook his head contrarily, "Go waysh. I'm mad ash yoush fellers."

Spook said, "I'll bet that tire iron would sober him up. Holy Houdini, I never saw such an unpredictable stew."

An automobile, a large sedan with two yellow spotlights, rolled into the filling station and stopped beside the gasoline pumps. Gull thought at first that the State Highway Patrolmen had arrived, then realized they didn't drive four-thousand-dollar limousines, and directed Spook Davis to go and take care of the customers.

Spook came back at once. "Two guys, and they want to talk to you."

"Me?"

"Sure. Remember I told you earlier that two fellows were inquiring around La Plata about you? Well, I think this is the same two. One of them is a trifle overweight, and the other one looks as if you could crack rocks with him."

THE DOME light of the sedan was glowing.

Gull came to the front of the car and looked in at an individual who was an ambulatory pile of balloons. His head was a balloon. His jaw was mostly chins—rolls of them. His paunch was another balloon. When he moved, the balloons seemed to want to fall over, but they didn't. The skunk-colored hair atop his round head might have been a wig slapped carelessly on his dome. Even his ears looked fatty.

He said, all in one bombastic rumble, "I am Harvell Braggs, and I take it for granted you are Gulliver Greene, and you are also known as The Great Gulliver, and may I introduce my companion here, Ivan Cass."

Ivan Cass was a lean man with piercing black eyes, a mouth so lipless that it became practically invisible when he closed it, and his face, as Spook Davis had intimated generally, looked hard enough to crack rocks with.

"Delighted, I'm sure," Ivan Cass said, who didn't sound as if he was. He had an ugly way of driving words through his clenched teeth.

Gull asked, "You wanted to see me?"

Harvell Braggs said, "I won't beat around the bush, as the fellow says, and will start out by telling you I happen to be a collector of Christopher Columbus antiques, and since I have financial means, my collection is, or was, excellent, containing a genuine Columbus sword, a blunderbuss that looks as if it were constructed only last year, some of his clothing, and other pieces of the equipment carried when the great navigator discovered America."

He got another breath.

"But Christopher Columbus came and stole most of my collection, and now—"

"What?" Gull yelled.

"Well, it is an idiotic statement to make, but the thief did look very much like Christopher Columbus. You see, I'm a Columbus authority, and familiar with his picture, and I got a fair look at the thief, and he also spoke to me in the strange stilted language of that day—he spoke English, by the way—and he assured me he was Columbus, likewise assuring me he would kill me with an ancient blunderbuss he was carrying if I interfered with him, so I naturally did not interfere."

Gull shouted suddenly, violently. "What kind of a run-around is this? Talk sense to me! I've got enough of this damned foolishness!"

Harvell Braggs said earnestly, "I am telling you the facts, and I wish to add that later I received an anonymous note telling me a young man named Gulliver Greene, also known as The Great Gulliver, a magician, could recover my stolen Columbus relics for me, and—"

"You got a nerve accusing me!" Gull shouted.

"Not accusing, no, but nevertheless the anonymous note— anonymous means unsigned, you know—told me you knew a great deal about the Columbus relics."

The intimation that he didn't know what the word anonymous meant did not help Gull's temper, and he opened his mouth to express himself on that point, and probably on several others.

But Spook Davis came galloping out of the filling station.

"We've got it!" Spook exploded. "We've got it!"

GULL said angrily, "We've sure got something!" and scowled at the two men in the car; then at Spook Davis. "What ails you?"

"I was right!" Spook howled.

"All right," Gull groaned. "Don't mix me up any more. Talk sense."

"Your relative!"

"Eh?"

"The big moose with the hair in his ears is your Uncle Box Daniels!" barked Spook. "He told me so! He's willing to talk now! He says he was coming to you for help and advice. He says he wants to tell you the whole story."

The hard-faced Ivan Cass got out of the limousine.

"Here's where I come in," Cass said. "I don't know what this is about, but old Box Daniels notified me to come here and serve as his bodyguard. He said he was coming to see Gulliver Greene, his nephew, and that somebody might try to stop him, might even kill him if they could. Well, I'm here to protect him."

Box Daniels was hardly in need of protection, because he lay on his back under the open compressor room window with his right temple caved in. Like a black island in the puddle that had leaked from the temple lay the weapon which had taken old Box's life.

Gull, staring at the weapon, knew it for one of the heavy, brass-bound shoes which the disturbing girl, Saint Pete, had been wearing.

Chapter X

BIG NECK

DOC SAVAGE TOOK a moment to compose himself. This in itself was highly unusual. The bronze giant had been schooled to conceal all outward emotional display. This had been a part of his rigorous training, the scientific system that made him a virtual superman.

Doc put out his arms and made of his fists two blocks of bronze. He stared at them as if exerting a supreme effort of will to make his fingers flex into the shapes of fists.

He did so with studied purpose, as if attempting to contain an inner excitement.

For a moment, the bronze man did not seem to know what to do with himself. So without warning, he launched into a portion of the two-hour routine of exercises that had been his habit since very, very young.

These were responsible for his tremendous muscular development and astounding mental powers.

This was the physical regimen. Doc removed his shirt and thus stripped to the upper waist, went into a run of calisthenics that included pitting his fabulous muscles against one another. Muscles formerly in repose now sprang forth like bundled wire and cables, as if straining to emerge from skin resembling flexible bronze.

When he was done, some fifteen minutes later, a thin sheen of perspiration bathed his upper torso, making their metallic aspect all the more distinct. His flake-gold eyes, which had been whirling violently, now settled down to their customary eerie currents and eddies.

Quietly, Doc Savage donned his shirt and faced the others.

"How long was I away?" he asked quietly.

Monk spoke up. "About three hours."

Doc nodded. "Two hours and fifty minutes passed by my watch."

"Where were you?" asked Ham curiously.

"Where I was, it was broad daylight, a little past the noon hour," answered the bronze man in an odd tone.

Doc's men looked to one another. Sunrise was creeping up above the bushy tree line.

Johnny popped a question. "How can that be?"

Instead of answering directly, Doc Savage rapped, "It is imperative that we locate Big Neck."

"Who?"

"The Indian brave who attempted to scalp Renny. He is called Big Neck and must be returned to his people."

"Who are his people?" asked Ham.

"It is too dangerous to allow him to run loose in the present time," said Doc, as if he had not heard the question.

They set off back to the anchored dirigible, reasoning that it would provide the best vantage point from which to conduct their woodland search.

At Doc's direction, they walked along with their machine pistols firmly in hand, held at the ready should they sight their quarry.

"It would be best to bring him down with mercy bullets at our first opportunity," Doc advised. "Capturing him might prove difficult."

"But how the deuce did you learn his name?" questioned Ham Brooks, walking along with his sword cane in one hand and intricate superfirer in the other.

Instead of replying directly, Doc Savage began telling a story.

"The last battle between white and red men that occurred in this area took place in July of 1829," he said steadily.

Johnny nodded. "It was lost ignominiously by the palefaces."

Doc went on. "A hunting party of Iowan Indians known as the Big Necks because that was the name of their chief, came into the Chariton area west of here, near a settlement known as the Cabins. Here the Indians' dogs attacked the settler's pigs and killed a few of them. The Indians ate the pigs."

Monk looked down at Habeas Corpus totting along beside him and suddenly gathered him up in one arm protectively.

"The next day," continued Doc, "three white settlers—Isaac Gross, John Crain and Jim Myers—called on the camp to make a complaint about the lost hogs and ordered the Iowans out of the area. Big Neck refused to comply with their demands. He also stated that if anyone wanted to start something, be at it. The three white men took to their heels. They fled south to Randolph County, some seventy miles away, where they stirred up a scare.

"About forty volunteers got together under the command of Captain William Trammell to chase the Big Necks back to Iowa. They made a fast march, forty-four miles in two days, to reach the Indian camp.

"There was an argument, and at first it seemed Big Neck was willing to go back to Iowa without a rumpus. However, the talk got loud, both red men and white made a show of waving guns and loading flintlocks—until a gun went off by mistake. Jim Myers thought he had been shot, and killed an Indian. With a war-whoop, the Big Necks tied into the settlers. The white men's horses stampeded. Several threw their riders. The whites took to their heels."

"I remember this account," interrupted Johnny. "Three settlers were killed—James Owenby, Frayer Myers, and a poor devil named William Wynn, who was wounded and carried for a short distance by friends, then tossed aside to be scalped and burned at the stake."

"Nothing of the sort happened to him," Doc related.

"How do you know that? There is only one account of the Big Neck War. I have read the same document that you are recalling from memory."

"Because I came upon William Wynn, who was dying of his wounds. I could not save him, so I buried him."

A long silence greeted that remarkable statement. The sounds of the forest along the dirt path, the leaf rustling and the calling of waking birds in trees, were all that filled their ears.

"What does the record say about Big Neck?" asked Monk after a suitable interval.

"Big Neck, alarmed by the fuss he had stirred up, went back to Iowa and was not heard from again."

"Wondered what happened to him?" muttered Monk.

"History," Doc Savage said thoughtfully, "may not record his fate because it has yet to be decided."

Another thick silence followed.

AT length, they reached the blimp-sized dirigible.

Because he felt a need to work off some of the nervous excitement he felt, and not because it was necessary, the bronze giant vaulted into the trees and reached the leafy crown. Amid the changing leaves, he was hard to discern, the browns and gold blending with his clothes, which ran to khaki and tan.

Reaching out, Doc snared the guy wire and, bracing himself, hauled the dirigible down, using only the Herculean thews that nature and a life of intensive, physical conditioning had bestowed upon him.

Soon, the open hatch was hovering at teepee level.

"One at a time," Doc called down.

And so, one by one, they climbed the knotted rope and worked their way to the hatch. Ham went first.

The minute he disappeared from sight, the dapper lawyer gave out a violent yell and there was a thrashing commotion followed by a few lusty whacks of Ham's cane.

"What's goin' on?" Monk bellowed up.

Out of the hatch flew a solitary bat, wings beating like the Devil himself.

"Bat took up a roost in the gondola," Ham called down. "I have chased away the beggar."

"Great goblins!" said Johnny. "A fitting omen for a Hall016een of a night."

The others took their turns climbing; finally Doc Savage swung on board.

Six men—especially six who weighed as much as they did— made the airship hang logy and sluggish in the air. It bogged down somewhat.

"The projecto-receptor lens won't be of any help, now that it's light," Long Tom ventured.

"We have other means," said Doc Savage, taking the controls.

They cast off in the usual manner, reeling in the grapple and climbing rope, and began a careful orbit of the patch of woods on the west side of the Chariton River.

Doc Savage turned the controls over to Long Tom Roberts and brought a pair of binoculars of excellent quality to his ever-active eyes.

Through them, he scanned the surrounding terrain. It was tough work. The brave had worn deerskins and this, along with his sun-cured hide, enabled him to blend into the autumnal forest to a degree that smacked of magic.

In time, their patience paid off.

Along the banks of the Chariton, Doc Savage spied a wisp of white smoke. It was climbing skyward.

"Camp fire!" squeaked Monk.

"Possibly someone cooking his breakfast trout," Doc suggested. Reaching over, he killed the engines and allowed the airship to loaf along. Fortunately, there were few crosscurrents of air and so there was little deviation from the course he set.

Riding along in an airship is a sometimes uncanny experience, especially when not under power. The ride is smooth, silent and serene. Floating on a cloud may be the closest equivalent—if men could ride clouds, that is.

In time, they came to a place where they could see the river bank.

Crouching over a fire, a small figure in buckskins was holding a speared fish over the flames. He turned the stick around, so as to cook the fish evenly, and from time to time pulled off bits of flesh with his fingers.

"That's our boy!" said Monk.

The Indian brave may have been an expert hunter and tracker, but while he looked about from time to time to see if he was being observed, it still did not occur to him to look upward.

He had no inkling that an airship was stealing silently upon his camp.

AFTER observing the man for some time, Doc Savage switched on the loudspeaker and microphone hook-up that allowed him to call down commands to a ground crew during landing.

He spoke a language none of them understood.

The camping Indian looked startled. His head twisted around, his dark eyes darting this way and that way. It still never crossed his mind to him to look up.

Using the man's native tongue, Doc Savage suggested that he do so.

The Indian craned his thick neck about, seeking the source of the voice. He soon found it.

Even from a distance, the expression on his well-cured face could be read. It was a twisting, wide-mouthed horror.

Taking up his stick, he threw it at the airship, steaming trout and all. The only result was that he lost his meal.

Doc called out something else.

"You *puck-achee!*" the Indian called back loud enough to be heard.

"What did he say?" asked Ham.

"Scram," said Johnny Littlejohn dryly.

"He wants us to go away," agreed Doc Savage.

"That ain't likely to happen," snorted Monk. "Ain't that right, Habeas?"

The porker grunted boisterously in response.

Mention of Habeas gave Ham Brooks an idea. "Perhaps we should offer him that infernal pig as a gift to entice him into surrendering."

"Nothin' doin'," said Monk, grabbing up Habeas.

To everyone's surprise, Doc Savage said, "That is a very good idea."

Taking the homely shoat from Monk's hairy hands, Doc Savage held the pig up to the windscreen and displayed him.

Then he spoke.

Curling his lips, the Indian retorted in a way that indicated displeasure.

"What'd he say?" asked Monk.

Doc replied, "He said that the pig is too scrawny for eating."

Doc Savage returned the insult with another short remark.

"I just told him that Habeas is a better meal than a lost trout," explained Doc.

That seemed to impress the Iowan brave. He sat down and folded his arms as if daring them to drop the pig at his feet.

"I will tell him to expect the pig momentarily," said Doc.

Another gobbling exchange took place and Doc ordered the airship dropped as close to the ground as practical.

It was soon floating over the burbling river, within a few feet of land.

"He thinks we are cloud men," Johnny said, after listening to the Indian talk loudly for a time.

Handing Habeas to Monk, Doc Savage said, "Drop him into the water."

Monk's small eyes got round. "But Habeas will get—"

"Do it."

Reluctantly, Monk complied. The homely chemist dangled the scrawny porker by one ear, then let him drop. His wide face hung slack.

Habeas landed in the stream with a noisy splash and was soon swimming for shore. His beady eyes took one look at the deerskin-clad native wading out to capture him and changed his mind. Reversing his course, he made for the opposite shore.

The Iowan rushed out to grab him.

Doc Savage pried a machine pistol from Monk's fist and set it to fire single shots. Sighting through the open hatch, he trained the spiky muzzle on the advancing man in the deerskins.

Doc fired once. The report was modest. A single brass cartridge about the size of a penny jumped out of the receiver.

The splashing Indian flew backward and began floundering in the water. His struggles were brief. He sank. Disturbed water regathered over his shaven skull.

Doc plunged in, lest the man drown.

Reaching him, Doc lifted his head from under water and dragged him to shore, where the bronze man laid him out. The Indian did not move, except to breathe.

The others brought the airship nosing over and several dropped off, except Long Tom who held onto the controls as Monk went splashing after Habeas.

After gathering him up, Monk worked his way back to shore.

Doc Savage had the Indian he called Big Neck stretched out on the pebbled dirt and was examining his deerskin outfit, testing the stitching and quality of hide.

The Indian wore good moccasins. Everything about his apparel seemed of recent manufacture.

"This material is too fresh to be authentic," Ham decided after fingering it.

"All clothes were new once," said Doc cryptically.

Once his examination was complete, Doc Savage lifted the

brave's eyelids and saw that the man would be out for at least an hour.

"What do we do with him?" rumbled Renny.

"Take him on board the dirigible." Doc supplied.

This was easily accomplished. Long Tom threw out the knotted climbing rope and Monk and Renny—the two largest save Doc Savage himself—hauled the airship toward the ground.

Doc simply picked up the insensate Indian and handed him over to Renny, who had climbed into the gondola hatch.

They got aboard and cast off. The airship rose sluggishly, now weighed down by a seventh passenger. But before very many minutes passed, it had achieved a comfortable altitude.

Reclaiming the control station, Doc Savage powered up and booted the rudder about until the airship was droning on a dead reckoning course for the Victorian dwelling that possessed all the proper properties of a traditional haunted house.

"I don't like the fact that we're headed back to that spook house," Monk Mayfair ventured.

The facial expressions of some of the others suggested that this was no minority opinion.

Curiously, Johnny Littlejohn wore an intrigued, if not excited, expression on his scholarly mien. He was not much of a man for smiling, but his lean mouth was fighting a grin of anticipation. He appeared quite eager to investigate the curious old dwelling.

Chapter XI

THE CURIOUS CASS

GULLIVER GREENE THREW his arms across the door leading to the back room of the filling station, blocking the door, keeping the other three—Spook Davis, Harvell Braggs and Ivan Cass—from entering the room where the murdered old man sprawled.

"What the dickens!" Spook Davis yelled indignantly. "You gone wacky?"

"Leave it for the police!" Gull said tightly.

"Is he dead?" Spook blurted. "We hardly got a look!"

Gull seemed a little taller, and his muscles, never especially bulky, were tight and stood out with the prominence of wires in his neck and wrists. Some of the hearty color had faded under his tan, but the absolute snow whiteness of his hair still made it contrast almost weirdly with his piercing green eyes. The approaching rainstorm thumped and rumbled in the western night, and he listened to it, thinking how appropriate the sound was, then turned his head to look at old Box Daniels.

Dead old Box Daniels wore a pair of enormous old-fashioned button shoes, cheap trousers, a cotton undershirt. He lay on his side with his bald head far back and his mouth and eyes straining open wider than it seemed possible they could have become. The blow which crushed his temple had also mangled the tip of his large ear on that side and the crimson leakage had filled the ear, turned his bald head all red, and puddled on the floor. Saint Pete's plain, brass-reinforced shoe lay in the red lake.

"Look for whoever killed him!" Gulliver barked suddenly.

He wrenched the door shut, ran outside with the others. He had the flashlight in his hip pocket, and he poked its white beam into the darkness. Harvell Braggs, the enormously fat man, had a flashlight in his car, and he got it, and the hard-faced Ivan Cass produced an unexpected gun—a compact dark revolver—from a hideout under his armpit.

"The murderer has gotta be close!" Spook Davis wailed. "The old man was alive when I came out to tell you he was ready to tell us his story."

Spook Davis, pale and shaking, ogled Ivan Cass' gun with fixated horror—more shaken by sight of the gun than by the bald old man's unexpected murder. Spook had a helpless fear of guns.

Gull got the double-barreled shotgun which was kept at the filling station as bandit protection, and joined the others in searching the surrounding night. The thunder kept whooping in the west, and there was beginning to be a little lightning, although the night remained unnaturally still, as it does before storms in Missouri. Behind the filling station was a pasture thick with clumps of buckbrush, a few small red oak trees, and in front of the filling station ran U.S. Highway 63, a concrete slab, but no cars had passed for some time. Across the road was a cornfield, the corn just about high enough to hide anyone who ran doubled over. The lightning got brighter and brighter and thunder louder as they hunted.

They returned to the filling station finally, defeated.

IVAN CASS started to go into the back room where the body lay. Gull got in front of him, blocking him, and said grimly, "The police won't like having their clues messed up."

Cass put out his jaw and tightened his lips; his crow-black eyes smoldered.

"I'm a private detective!" he said. "Read this."

He drew a telegram from a coat pocket and held it so Gulliver could read:

IVANHOE CASS
CASS DETECTIVE AGENCY
ST. LOUIS

IN A JAM STOP LEARNED SOMETHING BY AC-
CIDENT AND IT MAY BE THE DEATH OF ME
STOP AM GOING TO SEE MY NEPHEW THE
GREAT GULLIVER AT LA PLATA MISSOURI STOP
MEET ME THERE ACT AS BODYGUARD.
                                        BOX DANIELS

Ivan Cass said, "That's why I'm here. Why was old Box
Daniels coming to see you?"

Gull said grimly, "It's a mystery to me."

Gull watched Cass fold the telegram and put it back in his
pocket, but the rock-hard face of the man was inscrutable and
told him nothing, gave no indication of whether Cass believed
Gulliver was entirely mystified by all that had happened. Gull
slowly strained his ivory hair with his fingers, then wheeled and
stared at Harvell Braggs with questioning intentness.

Harvell Braggs said hastily, "Young man, I hope you don't
retain for a moment the misapprehension that I—"

"I wonder what the police will think of your story about how
you came to be here," Gulliver put in grimly.

Braggs' shrug pushed his many chins up almost around his
full-lipped cherubic mouth which contained a cigar.

"Fantastic or not, young man, it is my story, and I stick to it,
and I repeat now that I am simply a collector of Christopher
Columbus antiques whose collection was stolen by a strange
being who looked like he was Columbus and who insisted he
was the genuine Columbus, and I will also add that I am going
to tell the police that I am here because of an anonymous note
which said—"

"Where's the note?" demanded Gull.

Evidently, this was Harvell Bragg's usual bombastic method
of speech—he liked to use sentences as big as he was.

Braggs peered at Gull, absently removed his chewed cigar,

tossed it away, and drew another one out of a pocket and stuck it in his mouth. Then, without speaking, he produced a scrap of paper.

BRAGGS:
SEE GULLIVER GREENE, WHO IS ALSO KNOWN AS THE GREAT GULLIVER, ABOUT YOUR CO-LUMBUS STUFF THAT WAS TAKEN.

This was printed in pencil, rather expertly, although the letters were very small. He did not recognize the handwriting, but that meant nothing. He had never received a note from his Uncle Box before this day.

"Satisfied?" Braggs asked, speaking a short sentence for once.

Gull walked out slowly and stood for a bit under the lighted marquee, then began to work the iron lever which pumped pink gasoline up into the glass bowls of the station pumps. He watched, without really perceiving it, the gasoline surge and bubble behind the glass.

The world had turned black; lightning cracked and gushed split seconds of red noonday.

Despite this impressive display, not a drop of rain had yet fallen.

Some aspects of this thing were clear—poor old Box Daniels, the relative whom Gull had never seen before tonight, had learned something that endangered his life, and had tried to reach Gull for help, but had been killed. But why hadn't Box Daniels gone to the police? He'd sent Gull the telegram, which must have been important, because the small man with the hound-voice had seized it, even killed the local telegraph operator to keep its contents unknown. It followed, Gull decided, that the devilish midget had also slain old Box here a few minutes ago and, being small, had escaped in the night.... But Saint Pete's shoe lay in there by the body, the murder weapon, obviously.

Gull moistened his lips; they had become suddenly dry. He felt heavy, compressed inside. For the exquisite girl, Saint Pete, had not impressed him anything but favorably during his few moments with her after he had found her trying to seize old Box—as she had said, so that she might make him tell her what he knew. Gull made an abrupt, grim mouth. In all this puzzled mess, it stood out in his mind that the girl had been frightened, anxious, and honest in her desire to question Box Daniels. He'd believed her. True, she'd fled, but that was understandable because she had been frightened....

"Look here!" Cass yelled.

He'd evidently found a knife behind the filling station safe, a long knife with a three-edged blade.

"It's got a woman's fingerprints on it!" Cass shouted.

GULLIVER GREENE looked at the knife with rigid intentness—it was the blade wielded by the small man with the hound-dog vocal cords, the weapon which had probably slain the telegraph operator. How had it gotten behind the safe? Planted, of course. And with a woman's tapered fingerprints on it....

Nature squirted the heavens full of lightning flare and cataclysmic noise, showing all their strained faces, quaking the air about them, beating against their eardrums. Gull, when his lungs began feeling very strange, realized he had stopped breathing, and he drew in breath with a slow, determined rush.

They paid him no attention when he sauntered back outside. He whipped around to the murder room window. He reached in, got Saint Pete's heavy, brass-bound shoe, the armored heel of which had caved in Box Daniels' temple.

He ran a few yards, bounded across the grader ditch, crossed the highway, and was in the cornfield, dusted off his hands, and hurried back to the filling station. He entered casually.

"I think something just happened outside," he said.

Harvell Braggs and Ivan Cass sprang out under the marquee. Spook Davis did not go with him, but stood staring at Gull Greene.

Gull picked up the knife with the triangular blade and carefully wiped all fingerprints off the hilt, then pitched the knife out the office window, where it made a soft sound striking wood. He looked at Spook Davis.

"Mum's the word," he said.

"She must be quite a number," Spook Davis said dryly.

"Who?"

"Don't kid me, old socks. I think you're ertsnay to cover up for her. But I'll also say that sink or swim, in the clink or out, I still follow Thursday as far as you're concerned. I'm your man Friday, in other words."

Gull did not say anything, did not show any emotion except by a slight loosening of the muscle knots at the rear of the jaws, and a small upward warp of the ends of his mouth.

A FEW minutes later, two Missouri State Highway Patrolmen got out of their car and came into the station. They were neat, brown-clad, their leather polished, their metal shiny, and they strode in at once to look at the body.

"No murder weapon," one said, after a preliminary look around.

"The hell—!" Cass closed his thin lips on his bark of surprise.

Gull, in the background, waited tensely, but Ivan Cass did not say anything more, and Gull felt more disturbed than if Cass had spoken, knowing that Cass had seen Saint Pete's shoe lying there beside the body. Then he caught a slight nod from Cass. They drew outside.

"My impulsive young friend," Cass grated, "do you want some advice?"

"No," Gulliver said frankly.

"Murder is murder and nothing to be to trifled around with," Cass said harshly. "You're sticking your nose into something you don't know anything about. If you did know what it is, you'd probably start running and wouldn't stop. Now the best thing you can do is sit on your hands, keep that blab of yours shut, and hope you won't wind up getting hung for two murders."

He sounded deadly serious.

Cass wheeled. Gull grabbed for him. Cass twisted away and walked off. Gull, aching to take his neck and wring some information out of him, was deterred by the presence of the two Highway Patrolmen, and also by the fact that his worst fears had turned out to be well grounded—Cass knew he had hidden that shoe.

Ivan Cass and Harvell Braggs went and sat in the latter's sleek, expensive limousine. Gull aimed his ears in their direction, and soon realized they were talking heatedly. The two Patrolmen continued their investigation; with their powerful flashlights they began examining the filling station surroundings.

"It looks like you're sliding into the wildcat nest," Spook Davis said, drifting past Gulliver.

Gull didn't care for it. To Spook, he hissed, "Don't worry, You'll be in it with me before long."

"How come?"

"You'll start lying to these cops. They'll get you."

Gulliver said this to scare Spook. His stooge hadn't done anything—yet. Gull hoped the scare would deter him. Heaven knows, they had enough trouble already.

Spook Davis had a frothy temperament, and he also had the flexibility of a grass blade—when the sun shone, he erected and waved happily, but when storm winds came, he flattened readily into the mud of despair. Just now, he was waving; no wind happened to be blowing, and because the clouds of menace were not touching him, he was a little too careless of their presence.

When the police began questioning Gull, it actually relieved his mind, the mental activity of answering their questions drawing his thoughts from speculation about what Cass intended to do. Gull had no idea of withdrawing from the affair—although he still couldn't see where there was anything to withdraw from. Cass must know that; the question was, what course would he take? This ran through Gull's mind as he told the fantastic story of the night's happenings to the two officers, who, as they listened, became more and more doubtful, more and more bewildered.

"Christopher Columbus!" one cop said, and snorted skeptically. "Buddy, this is too wonderful! Maybe there's truth here somewhere that ain't out."

Cass—he had left Braggs—came to the door, looked at Gull malevolently, then said, "Cops, I'll show you things."

He did. He showed them Saint Pete's shoe which Gulliver had buried with the impulsive idea of keeping suspicion from the entrancing girl. A long stick had been shoved down in the soft cornfield earth to pry up the shoe.

"Blood on it," an officer said. "It's the murder—" he scowled at Cass. "How'd you find it?"

Cass shrugged his crow-like shoulders. He pointed at Gull. "Saw him bury it."

By now Gull knew he'd done a foolish thing when he removed the shoe and wiped off the fingerprints. Whew! That girl had certainly had an effect on him! He stood for a moment, conscious of the grimness of the police, trying to sell himself on the idea that the girl after all might have slain old Box Daniels. No dice, though; she wasn't that kind. And he felt better.

Just then a Highway Patrolman yelled. He was pointing his flashlight up in a maple tree. He climbed the tree. When he came down, he held a knife which had been sticking in a limb up in the leafy crown. He examined it.

"It's the knife that murdered the depot agent!" he barked.

"Sure?" yelled the other officer.

"Look at this tri-cornered blade! The depot agent's wound showed he'd been stabbed with this kind of a blade. And these kind of knives aren't plentiful. This is the first one I ever saw."

Ivan Cass, a few moments later, made profane mention of the feminine fingerprints which had disappeared from the knife hilt.

Gull gulped. He believed he had every reason to gulp, and he became sure of it when one officer reached out abruptly and said, "Shake hands, pal."

Gulliver knew the gag, but if he did not fall for it, they might get rough. So he shook hands, and the patrolman jerked him off balance and briskly snapped something cold and metallic back of his hands.

The handcuffs on Gulliver's wrists looked rather new.

"Now look here!" Gull exploded feebly.

"That's what we're going to do," returned the officer. "We are going to look into everything thoroughly—including you."

"Am I arrested?"

"Just anchored for the time being."

Chapter XII

MEN IN THE DAWN

DAWN HAD FULLY arrived by the time the unlovely Victorian house hove into view. The sky was full of fleeing crows, and there were clouds on the horizon. Heavy, lead-colored ones. Such air as came into the cabin through ventilation inlets possessed that clammy sensation of impending rain.

They were free-ballooning now, Doc Savage having throttled the two engines back to stillness.

"This overgrown blimp sure handles sweet, don't it, Doc?" suggested Monk.

The bronze man seemed preoccupied. It was his habit not to answer questions he did not wish to, but in this instance he seemed oblivious to anything other than the task at hand.

Once more Doc had his binoculars out and was scrutinizing the forest below. He searched intently, seemed to find nothing of interest, and addressed Monk, "Climb down to the ground and walk toward the house by the approach path," he directed.

"You want to see if it up and disappears? Is that it?"

"Exactly," said Doc.

The hairy chemist popped the hatch and swung out in a fashion that might do credit to an ape man, if such a fanciful creature ever existed in real life.

"He belongs in a jungle picture," sniffed Ham. At the same time, his sharp gaze tracked the homely chemist all the way to the ground.

Monk accomplished this with simian ease. As if out for a

Sunday stroll, he ambled up the dirt path in the direction of the uncanny dwelling.

Doc Savage kept his intent eyes upon the ornately ugly dwelling. All of them did.

It fascinated. In the rising sun, it seemed to smolder rather redly. The black gingerbread hung from its roof and porch eaves like funeral crepe. Whoever painted it originally, had very dubious taste.

When Monk was within sight of the roof, the house evaporated.

There was no transition between the sight of the apparent solid structure and its vanishment. It simply ceased to occupy its former spot. All that remained was the bare slab foundation.

Monk's excited *"Ye-e-eow!"* came clearly to their ears.

Doc reached for the radio microphone and raised Monk on the latter's pocket transceiver.

"Monk. Remain where you are. I will join you directly."

Renny took the controls this time and Doc Savage slid down the rope, knot by knot. He didn't need them for purchase, so great was the corded power of his metallic digits. But to slide down would be impossible, with the handholds in the way.

Ham came scampering down, uninvited. His curiosity had evidently been aroused.

Doc joined Monk at the spot on the narrow woodland trail where he had last seen the hideous house standing there.

"It's gone," gulped Monk. The look on his face was priceless. Perplexity seemed to crawl up it and then down again, like a nervous spider.

Doc Savage abruptly left the trail, began beating the woods, eyes ranging alertly. Monk followed. Ham soon joined them, using his cane to bat aside blocking foliage.

"What are we searching for?" he asked Monk.

"Beats me," admitted the homely chemist. His twinkling eyes, so deeply sunk into the pits of gristle that marked them, were scouring the woods.

Doc Savage found what he sought, and stopped.

Monk and Ham came up and their questing gaze went to the spot where Doc was silently pointing.

A small device was attached to a tree, low to the ground. In the black housing was installed a lens. It was pointing toward the Victorian home of uncanny and almost sentient behavior.

"Photo-electric eye!" breathed Monk.

Ham said, "Jove! What is it doing out here?"

"Designed to actuate a relay whenever an approaching intruder intercepted the beam of light falling on the photocell," explained Doc Savage.

Ham frowned. "But what does it do?"

"Don't you get it?" Monk said suddenly. "It makes the house disappear!"

"Don't be absurd, you hairy mistake," fumed Ham. "How could an electric relay cause an entire house to vanish into thin air?"

"We all saw the house vanish, didn't we?" returned Monk, "Well, something had to cause that, didn't it?"

Ham had no reply to that. Not because he wasn't considering one. Waspish retorts were his stock in trade. But whatever stinging barb his agile brain was in the act of formulating was forever lost because a man stepped out of the woods and pointed a double-barrel shotgun at them. The ends looked big enough to jump into.

Doc detected the stranger's approach. Normally, he would have become aware of this before anyone could get the proverbial drop on him, but his state of mind still seemed queer. He was plainly not quite himself.

"This is private property," the man ground out.

They heard him before they got a clear look at him.

The shotgun-wielder was an average man in every way a man could be average except one. His hands and face were coated with a white confection that looked like someone had smeared his skin with greasepaint and then applied ordinary baking powder.

"I say," drawled Ham. "Rather early for Halloween."

"What is your business here?" the man demanded, pointing the immensely black barrels at them.

"We might ask the same of you," flung back Ham, pointing with his cane.

"I own this patch of land, if you must know. I intend to build a house out here."

"On that slab yonder?" inquired Doc.

The man started slightly. He restrained himself. "Sure," he admitted. "What of it? It's private property, which makes it my private business. Now clear out!"

The shotgun man waited to see the reaction his harsh threat would produce. His fingers were held carefully outside of the trigger guard. Evidently, they were hair triggers.

Doc Savage noticed this. His arresting golden eyes flicked upward, seized the other man's gaze, and held it.

"I possess credentials you might be interested to see," Doc offered evenly.

"I don't care if you—"

The shotgun man never finished his sentence.

Weirdly, those compelling orbs seemed to swallow his attention. He never saw the bronze giant move. There was only a puff of air that stirred his unruly hair.

Stepping back suddenly, the man became aware that his hands were stinging. He directed his attention at his smarting fingers.

What he beheld caused him to blink dumbly. For his hands were numb claws that no longer held his weapon.

The stunned assailant started. His shotgun was now in Doc Savage's metallic hands. The big bronze man had captured it before the flour-faced one could comprehend what was happening.

The other blinked like a camera shutter that couldn't quit. His jaw slowly sagged until its point touched the knot of his simple tie. He had been disarmed by a man to whom the menace of a double-barreled shotgun was a negligible thing!

DOC SAVAGE, having retreated to his original position, calmly broke open the double-barreled weapon and removed the shells. He pocketed both, then gave a casual upward toss that caused the shotgun to leap into a nearby oak tree and lodge high up amid its branches. It would take some considerable effort to retrieve it.

Doc eyed the flummoxed man.

"How is it you are planning to build a cabin on a slab already occupied by a Victorian house?" he inquired.

Again the man started. He tried to cover it up.

"What house?" he asked belligerently.

"The one that was there a few moments ago," Doc supplied.

"Mister, I poured that slab of concrete with my bare hands. There won't be anything gonna sit on it until I plant it there."

"I see," said Doc Savage, aureate eyes whirling steadily.

Hairy Monk started walking around the man, looking him up and down.

"What's with the Halloween getup?" he asked at last.

"I sunburn easily," sneered the man.

"Rather late in the year to worry about that," Ham offered.

The man's manner became testy. "First you tell me I'm too early for Halloween. Now it's too late to burn. You birds give me a sharp pain. And I repeat that you are standing on private property, sticking your citified noses into business that is not yours."

"What is your name?" asked Doc.

The other hesitated.

"If this is your property, as you claim," pressed Doc Savage, "then there is no reason to not identify yourself."

"Wes Snow," said the man at last.

"Live around here?" asked Doc.

"In these general parts," the other admitted.

"Your trade?"

"What's my work got to do with anything? Who are you birds anyhow?"

Ham said coolly, "You are speaking to Doc Savage, fellow."

"Doc Savage!" the man squawked. He gave the impression of going pale under his greasepaint and flour mask.

"Heard of him, ain't you?" taunted Monk.

The man who called himself Wes Snow nodded vigorously. "Big city trouble-buster," he said thickly. "They call you the Man of Bronze. And I plainly can see why."

Suddenly Snow lifted his voice, "Hey, Pap! Zeke! That's Doc Savage's blimp over yonder!"

Monk and Ham cranked their faces around, attempting to learn to whom the man named Wes Snow was directing his call.

There was no answered response—at least, not in words.

A shotgun whanged once and then again, and a spurt of flame and gunsmoke seemed to go straight up not far away.

It must have been filled with buckshot because it peppered one side of the gasbag of the small dirigible so thoroughly that immediately it began deflating.

Doc Savage had taken the precaution of armoring the control gondola as much as would permit the airship to navigate. But the gasbag was another matter. Its lightweight skin could not be protected from small-arms fire without compromising its ability to remain aloft under differing atmospheric conditions.

"Blazes!" Monk bellowed. "He got our airship!"

Doc Savage lunged forward in the middle of the thundering of the shotgun. Sensing his chance, Wes Snow attempted to bolt. Ham's fist clipped out, connected, dropped the disarmed man. The latter collapsed on his feet—knocked out.

"Watch him," Doc instructed Ham.

With Monk following hard on his heels, the bronze giant pitched in the direction of the echoing shotgun blasts.

Doc's sense of hearing verged on being unerring. He flashed through the trees, came upon the shotgun man as he was in the act of reloading. Those tiny sounds had drawn Doc.

The shotgun was of the hinged type. The shotgun man got one firecracker-red shell into the breech, saw the bronze giant descending upon him, and hastily snapped his weapon back into a unit.

Raising the muzzles, he took hasty aim.

Doc Savage wore a bulletproof undervest. In fact, he was mailed from neck to knees with a kind of union suit of light flexible chainmesh alloy.

But his head was not protected. Throwing up his hands to protect his features would have resulted in the destruction of his fingers, at best, and might not have preserved his life.

When the shotgun man squeezed down on one trigger, Doc Savage pitched to one side.

Monk Mayfair, following directly behind, was not so fortunate.

The man unloaded one barrel at the hairy chemist, putting the shot charge in Monk's middle, just under the ribcage.

Monk wrapped long hairy arms over his stomach area and tilted forward and backward, but did not go off his feet. He swayed there, face almost buried in his chest. A long groan emerged from someplace deep inside of him.

Doc Savage went against the man with the shotgun. Doc got hold of him by the front of his flannel hunting jacket and knocked him against a tree so hard that the man bounced off it in a weirdly rubbery way, falling to the forest floor.

Monk's loud groan was a deep, horrible thing and it brought Ham Brooks running from his guard post, waving his sword cane in one lifted hand.

"Monk! Monk!"

He came upon Monk, who was almost doubled over, and clutching his middle.

"You're shot!" Ham screeched. He moved toward the hairy chemist solicitously.

Monk groaned again, "Get away from me, you!"

Ham stopped, stared. "You're *not* shot?"

"Sure I'm shot." Monk fell to coughing. "I'm shot right in the belly—and my bulletproof vest doesn't have the stiffening ribs under it. I left the stiff undervest off. I think all my ribs are broke, blast you!"

Ham looked relieved. He glanced at the fellow who had shot Monk.

"Who is he?"

Before they could examine the man, their attention flew to the dirigible, which was fast sinking to the ground.

For the latest member of Doc Savage's fleet of aerial conveyances was coming to an ignominious landing.

The craft settled along the nest of tree crowns and draped itself there, looking forlorn and pitiful as it slowly deflated. The gondola banged about as it struck high branches, but the cabin maintained its structural integrity.

Soon the knotted rope was lowered and Doc's men came sliding down like firemen down a firehouse pole. All but their prisoner, the one the bronze man had called "Big Neck."

Renny was the first to arrive at the scene. He took in the unconscious shotgun man, and Monk, who had decided to sit down.

"Who is this lunk?" the big-fisted engineer wanted to know.

Doc Savage told him, "He is with a man named Wes Snow who claims to own this property."

Renny grunted, "So why did he shoot at us?"

"Evidently he thought that we were trespassers."

"Maybe he'll be relieved that no one got seriously hurt," Renny suggested hopefully. "Once he finds out who we are."

"Oh, won't he?" Monk gasped. "He didn't fool around long about trying it."

Ham said, "There is another man. Wes Snow. He's disguised."

Renny peered about. "That makes it different. Where is he?"

Ham looked stricken. "I was guarding him," he croaked.

"Was?"

The resplendent barrister turned around and fled back to his post, heels kicking up dirt.

Ham's voice came bouncing back, greatly relieved. "Still here. Out cold."

"What happened to him?" Renny wanted to know.

"His jaw encountered my fist."

"Nothing to worry about then," thumped Renny, looking up at the forlorn sight that was the deflated dirigible.

"Should we go and fetch that red-handed scalper out of the cabin?"

"He will keep," advised Doc Savage.

The others trotted up, brandishing supermachine pistols, and went searching for enemies. Finding none, Johnny and Long Tom holstered their weapons.

"We are in a fix," suggested Long Tom querulously.

Renny said, "It isn't that long a walk to a highway. From there we can get a ride to our planes back at the airfield."

"First," Doc Savage said, "we will await the return of the house that vanishes every time a photo-electric cell is tripped."

Explanations were made as they went back to the man with the flour face.

But when they reached the spot, he was no longer there!

Ham Brooks lay supine in the shade of an elm tree. Elms were the most plentiful tree growth in this section of forest, although there were oaks and even maple trees.

There was a lump the size of a robin's egg forming on his forehead.

"Looks like he got whacked on the head by his own cane,"

Long Tom observed.

They conducted a search for the assailant and the missing man with the pancake-floured face. There was no doubt in their minds that he had taken advantage of Ham's temporary absence, and ambushing him suddenly, ripped his cane from his hand for the purpose of braining the dapper lawyer with its heavy gold knob of a head.

The search took quite some time. Doc Savage had the most luck.

He trailed the man carrying the insensate Wes Snow to the bank of the river. Deeply indented footprints told that tale. There, the tracks ended.

There were signs that a canoe had been beached there. A third man had been guarding it, by the look of footprints in the soft mud of the riverbank.

Doc offered, "Explains how they came up on us unheard. By water."

There was no point in trailing any farther. On foot, they would be no match for a canoe being paddled downstream.

When they gathered back at the spot where the shotgun man had been laid low, they discovered a new problem.

He was dead. From the look of him, his neck had been broken while he lay oblivious. His head was sitting on his shoulders so crookedly that it made them feel uneasy to look upon the angle at which it hung askew.

There was a circular patch at the exact top of his head, red and raw.

Renny blurted, "Holy cow! Scalped!"

Chapter XIII

GUILTY!

ONE OF THE Highway Patrolmen left the filling station with the three-edged knife, was gone about half an hour, during which thunder gave many great whooping laughs in the night sky, inappropriately enough. Gulliver waited, but he entertained no hopes; the officer had not said where he was going, but hadn't needed to—Gull knew he was taking the knife down to compare it with the wound of the slain telegraph operator. Nor was he wrong, for the cop returned with the information that the telegrapher, slain so that the text of Box Daniels's telegram concerning Christopher Columbus would remain a secret, had evidently been killed with this knife. Gull was informed he would be placed in jail without delay.

The returning officer picked up the heavy death shoe and tried the heel in the depression of the murdered man's temple. It fit.

"This shoe was definitely used to kill him," the officer decided.

These fellows, Gull thought grimly, work faster than machine guns. The quickness of their operations, the efficiency that it betokened, did not cheer Gulliver. Bad business to try to fool these fellows with tricks such as burying murder weapons!

"The wildcats got you," Spook Davis told Gull.

An officer growled, "What do you mean by that?"

"Don't mind me," said Spook. "I'm just quaint."

The policeman stabbed a finger at Gull. "You're under arrest on suspicion of slaying the telegraph operator and Box Daniels, then bringing the murder knife back here and sticking it up a tree, thinking it wouldn't be found. Also, of burying this shoe, with which Daniels was slain. What have you got to say for yourself?"

"Whew!" was all Gull could manage.

"Don't you think you want to confess?"

"What I want is a lawyer," Gull said gravely.

"What you need is a genuine magician to get you out of this," said the cop. "The only good a lawyer will do you is maybe make out your will."

It would be hard to find a lawyer who would wax enthusiastic over a client who only had four dollars and two cents to his name, Gull thought. He had never looked at a blacker future.

Lightning glared and thunder continually whacked over Old Duzzit's filling station. Ivan Cass loitered nearby. His stony face kept its cold expressionlessness; he offered no commentary. Harvell Braggs had remained in his limousine, complaining of his feet.

Spook Davis stood at one side, alternately opening his mouth and scratching his head. As his agitation grew, he began to resemble a man who was holding a deadly cobra by the neck and wondering how to let go.

"Oh God, I don't know wha-what to duh-do!" he wailed suddenly. "If—if—you policemen would only protect muh-me!"

The cops stared at him. So did Gull.

Spook shook and flopped his mouth open and shut.

"Huh—huh—he'll kuk-kill me if I talk!" Spook moaned.

A cop roared, "What are you talking about?"

"The green-haired man!" Spook gulped.

"*Who?*"

"The murderer," Spook emphasized.

The officers stared at him with pop-eyed attention. "You—know—the—killer?"

"A green-haired man," Spook said excitedly. "I saw him!

Knocked Box Daniels in the head, he did! Discovered me watching him. Threatened to kuk-kill me if I told anything. I've buh-been—afraid!"

A State Highway Patrolman scratched his head. "I'll be damned," he said.

"I can prove it," Spook declared solemnly.

With this, he went to the filing station safe, turned the knob, made the combination work, and opened the safe—to Gull's astonishment. Gull didn't know the combination of old Duzz-it's rusty safe himself, was surprised that Spook Davis knew it. But Spook often knew things no one expected him to know.

Out came a green wig.

"See," said Spook. "I got the killer's wig."

GULLIVER teetered on his heels, seeing complications coming. The strange chartreuse hairpiece felt like a finger of suspicion pointed directly at him. Since Gull's hair had gone white the year before, the unfortunate consequence of habitually using special greasepaint for stage purposes, he had transformed a liability into a spectacular addition to his magician's act by dyeing his snowy crowning glory the exact hue of spinach for his performances, giving him a unique trademark. The Great Gulliver, the Magic Genie with the Green Hair, was how one New York critic had ballyhooed him.

They would not know that in La Plata, Missouri. But an investigation would bring out this unique fact.

Spook Davis meant well with this stuff—this exaggerating. That's what it was, of course, although it had deceived Gull for a moment. Spook Davis was a skilled prevaricator, and it was natural that he should resort to such an insane ruse in an emergency. For Spook was the victim of a strange psychological condition. Some people are kleptomaniacs and cannot help stealing things, but with Spook it was telling whoppers. As for that green wig, it was part of a disguise which Spook wore when working as Gull's stage assistant during the illusion where The

Great Gulliver got into a steamer trunk on the stage, which was then made to appear empty by means of mirrors, while an instant later Gull appeared in the audience. This was affected by the simple ruse of Spook, and not Gull, appearing in the audience, Gull really being still in the stage trunk. This stunt invariably brought down the house. Gull thought of all this in a rambling way as he waited for the worst to happen.

The officers passed the wig back and forth between them, holding it gingerly by the hair as if it were a skunk hide still retaining some of the aroma characteristic of polecat hides. While they considered, the sky became noisier with approaching storm.

It was obvious to Gull that Spook had produced the wig from one of his pockets via sleight of hand, but the patrolmen never suspected that, so slickly was it accomplished.

"You want to be protected from this killer?" an officer asked.

"You bet!" Spook said, ill-advisedly.

"Then we'll put you in jail too," another officer said helpfully. "The town of La Plata has reason to be proud of their jail. It is a very substantial little jail."

Spook Davis's mouth fell open and he couldn't seem to get it closed. Ivan Cass, who had been staring at them intently, shook his head and sucked at his lips.

Spook was handcuffed and placed beside Gull. Spook now wore an injured expression.

"How do *you* like it in the wildcat den?" Gull asked.

"To you," Spook said gloomily, "the fruit of the pecan tree, and many of them."

The Great Gulliver found himself resisting a strong impulse to determine just how much force would be needed to kick in his stooge's ribs. Then fate arrived. Fate in the person of one known as Tonky Duzzit, who was short, wore gum boots and overalls the year round. And who carried the reputation of being the toughest old scamp in Macon County; he owned the One-Stop-Duzzit filling station, which made him Gull's employer.

Tonky Duzzit glared at Gull, opened his mouth….

"I quit," Gull said.

Old Tonky Duzzit made it unanimous by going ahead and telling Gulliver he was fired.

One of the patrolmen added with grim humor that Gull and his pal were taking a little vacation with expenses paid. And in the midst of that, Gull emitted a piercing yell.

He pointed out into the thundering night, using both handcuffed hands to do so.

"Look!" he yelled. *"The green-haired man!"*

The officers spun, "Where?" Lightning glare washed them.

Spook began bellowing, and scampered forward, stabbing his arms ahead, shouting, "I told you I saw a green-haired man! There he is! Look! There!"

An officer ran forward, seized Spook, restraining him; everyone was changing positions, craning necks and trying to see the marauder. This went on for a few moments, with the lightning winking mighty red eyes noisily.

Then two patrolmen discovered that Gulliver Greene had taken his departure into the very black night.

"He's gone!" a cop bawled wrathfully. The handcuffs that had been encircling his wrists now reposed—open and empty—atop the office safe. "Picked!" he guessed, correctly, as it seemed obvious.

"Hunt for him!" an officer ordered violently. "He can't just walk off from us like that!"

"That trick," Spook Davis said triumphantly, "is known to conjurors as misdirection."

Ivan Cass came over and knocked Spook senseless with his fist.

In the confusion, no one noticed that the office safe door, which had been ajar, was now firmly closed. Nor did the excited officers possess the presence of mind to peer inside for a huddled man. Only a contortionist could fit inside the small space.

Besides, Spook Davis had earlier worked himself into position so that he stood in front of the safe door, concealing its condition from view.

THE TWO patrolmen hunted Gulliver Greene for half an hour. Then nine more policemen arrived in three patrol cars, and they all hunted an hour longer. Two farmers who were fox hunters were routed out of bed, their foxhounds borrowed, but the animals refused to trail anything but foxes as good foxhounds should. Disgusted, their faces long, the patrolmen returned to their cars and stood a while discussing ways and means, not only of catching Gulliver Greene, but of keeping the newspapers from printing the story of how ridiculous had been the ruse by which he escaped.

Spook Davis, back among the living, remarked, "You don't need to feel so put out. Of course it was an old trick, but you must remember The Great Gulliver and myself—especially The Great Gulliver—are two of the fanciest escape artists since—"

"Gr-r-r-r!" growled a cop.

They loaded Spook Davis into a car and headed him for the La Plata jail, after first confiscating the bent hairpin they noticed dropping out of his mouth for lockpicking purposes.

IVAN CASS and ponderous Harvell Braggs got into their limousine and also drove into town, where they registered at the small hotel, getting separate rooms.

Ivan Cass did not stay in his room long, saying instead that he was going for a walk. His route took him to a vacant lot on the edge of town, near the highway, and to a dull gray trailer which was parked in this lot. He knocked twice, coughed, knocked once, then entered the trailer, sat down at the compact table, poured himself a drink from a square bottle, and lifting the glass, scowled at the other men in the trailer.

"To a bunch of prize goops!" he said.

"Sure, rub it in," said the hound-voiced little man across the table, scowling back. The other men in the trailer—men of normal or better than normal size—also scowled. There were five of these.

"You apes," Cass said. "That damned magician queered the frame we laid on the girl to draw attention from you. What do you think of that?"

The small man blinked. "Devil he did!"

"You runt," Cass said. "You killed the telegraph agent, and you killed Box Daniels. But did you do anything about Gulliver Greene, the one guy who can mess us up? No, you didn't have a gun. And he didn't wait for that knife. He only saw the knife, that's all, and recognized it was the same one that fixed the telegrapher. You do love to use those funny-shaped knives, don't you?"

The little man leaned back, lifted one end of his upper lip and showed an eyetooth. He shook one small sleeve and another three-edged knife appeared. He waved it about, made it spin a bit, after which the dagger disappeared up his opposite sleeve.

"Of course you sold your bill of goods, master mind?" he asked casually.

Cass nodded. "They think I'm a private detective. As such, I didn't get to dispose of the magician. But I did stop him from covering for the girl. In fact, I think the law now wants him for what you did."

"Where is he?"

"Loose."

The small man frowned. "How come?"

"He's pretty good."

The other snorted. "Gulliver Greene the magician, filling tanks with gasoline for four dollars a week and board, and you say he's pretty good."

"Know why he's doing that? I'll tell you. He's holding out for five thousand dollars a week in New York City. They've offered him three thousand. I'll repeat that—they've offered him three thousand. They'll pay him five, and he knows it, so he's taking a hideout vacation until they come across with a contract. That's the guy old Box Daniels ran to for protection and help. That's the one Daniels hoped would rescue Columbus from us, my sawed-off numbskull. That's also the guy who is running around loose somewhere, sharpening his little hatchet for us."

Ivan Cass' hand shook enough to clatter the bottle against the glass as he poured himself more liquor, and his breathing was audible in the intervals of dead quiet between the great concussions of thunder in the night sky. One of the men got up, not saying anything, and opened a locker and took out a revolver, broke it to examine the breech for cartridges, then dropped it in his coat pocket.

"What do we do about it, know-so-much?" the runt asked viciously.

Lightning ran across the sky, making a reedy crackling that was audible a fractional moment before the thump of its thunder, and the thunder trailed off in the clouds above, seemed to start up again with renewed violence, and gradually trailed off again, leaving the unnatural pre-storm stillness.

"Gull Greene doesn't know we grabbed Saint Pete," Ivan Cass related. "He's a bit puzzled about how we got her shoe, to use on Box Daniels."

"Um-m," said the little man sourly.

"We've got to clear out of here, pennywits," Cass added.

The runt glowered silently.

"Old Box Daniels is dead, and nobody else really knows what the truth is. Small thanks to you, sawed-off-and-stupid."

The little man showed all his tiny teeth fiercely.

Cass said, "I hie me now to the local bastille. Where I shall put a bullet in Spook Davis, just on the chance that he might be able to alibi The Great Gulliver on the murder of the telegrapher. Every little bit helps, eh, little baboon?"

He got up.

The little man got up on his seat, so that they stood almost face to face.

The two of them shook hands and grinned at each other and slapped each other on the back with the greatest of friendship, after which Ivan Cass eased out into the night and departed. The hound-voiced midget sat back in his chair, still grinning, and assured his men that Ivanhoe Cass was a great guy, the salt of the earth.

About this time, Gull Greene was crawling out from under the dull gray trailer, a location from which, between thumps of thunder, he had been able to hear just about everything that had been said.

Chapter XIV

THE REVERSION

AFTER EXAMINING THE scalped man and finding no identification, Doc Savage made a low sound in his throat perilously like disgust.

"Big Neck must be recaptured without delay."

They began to search the dirt floor of the forest for tracks. They found plenty.

"Moccasin prints for certain," Johnny muttered, after applying his magnifier to them.

Monk Mayfair suddenly squeaked, "Hey, where's Habeas!"

"Wasn't he with you?" Ham demanded.

"Sure. When I got shot. The blast must've scared him off!"

"You don't suppose that Big Neck made off with him," suggested Long Tom, looking about sharply.

Monk seemed to forget about his bruised anatomy. He vented a howl and suddenly charged in the direction where the moccasin prints paraded.

The others hastily followed.

Doc Savage overhauled the hairy chemist, arrested him with iron fingers, cautioned, "We do not want to warn him."

"Speak for yourself," growled Monk. "If that bull-necked nature boy so much as bruises Habeas, I'll peel his scalp from his skull and feed it to him. I'll twist his fingers off, one at a time. Then I'll come down on him so hard, his moccasin tops will be up around his chin!"

Seeing the way of it, Doc Savage released Monk.

THEY found their quarry in amazingly quick time.

Doc Savage spied him first. Big Neck was running at a dog trot. Tucked under one arm was the squealing porker with long wing-like ears and feet more appropriate for a hunting dog.

Monk squawled anew. His flat feet propelled him forward with ungainly speed. At intervals, he stooped and used his hands to propel himself along, anthropoid-fashion. The apish chemist's arms were almost as long as his legs.

Big Neck—if that was indeed his name—peered over his shoulder and began to look alarmed. He picked up his brisk pace.

That did not help as much as he wished because, before long, the Indian prudently dropped the pig and redoubled his efforts. He was fleet. His pounding legs made excellent time.

But when he saw that he could not outrun his pursuers, Big Neck did a bold thing.

The brave stopped, spun about, and went into a crouch, similar to that of a wrestler facing an opponent.

Doc Savage reached him first. He began speaking in the man's own lingo.

Big Neck spat back words that didn't need to be translated. There would be no surrendering.

Doc switched to the Mayan language, the tongue they had learned long ago in the course of their first great adventure together, and gave his men rapid instructions that couldn't be understood by the Indian.

Carefully, they surrounded Big Neck. Monk had scooped up Habeas, and was reassuring him. Otherwise, his wide face seemed to reflect a kind of gorilla ferocity.

Seeing Monk's animal-like expressions, Big Neck began backing away. Evidently, he feared no ordinary man, but Monk's simian physiognomy brought from his lips a growled word that Doc Savage translated for them.

"He thinks Monk is some kind of forest spirit. A bear man."

Ham Brooks found that funny for some reason. He began laughing.

The Indian assumed that the laughter was directed at him, and took umbrage.

Ham became a casualty almost at once. His trust in his sword cane proved to be his undoing. While he was fiddling with the thing, attempting to unsheathe it, the Indian closed with him, picked the sword cane out of his hands, and bent it nearly double over Ham's head and left shoulder. Fortunately, the blade was not out of its barrel, so Ham was not cut. But he shifted backward, stood with his back pressed to a tree, dazed enough that he would have fallen except for the trunk.

Big Neck suddenly found himself facing Doc.

Doc Savage was a man with many unusual qualities, and most of these unique abilities or traits were the result of his being placed in the hands of scientists when he was a small child, and who kept up the training into manhood. Many scientists had contributed to this training.

Among those had been experts in Judo, Ju-Jitsu and other exotic fighting skills. These experts had taught the bronze man to turn a foe's ferocity against him.

Doc simply stood there.

The Indian lunged, hands clutching for the bronze giant.

The next thing Big Neck knew, he was flat on his back, a strange expression twisting his painted face. This bewilderment did not last long.

Springing to his feet, he came again. This time Doc tripped him. The Indian went sliding on his face, ending up with a mouthful of rich Missouri loam.

Spitting it out, the murderous redskin went into a crouch and attempted to butt Doc Savage in the manner of a charging bull.

The bronze giant surprised his foe. Bracing his feet wide apart, Doc stood his ground. As part of his training, the bronze man had learned to stiffen his abdominal muscles, allowing boxers in training to use his midriff as a punching bag.

The result was that Big Neck's skull bounced off Doc Savage's heavily-muscled abdomen. He reeled backward, holding his head in his hands, looking as if he had collided with an oak tree.

The Indian stamped around in small circles, evidently attempting to shake off his concussion. His eyes became strange, as if seeing stars.

Monk remarked, "Looks like Geronimo has had enough."

That observation proved premature. Wildly, Big Neck shook his head, and that seemed to clear his dazed senses. Growling, he turned to face the bronze warrior who had so far defied his skills.

And then it dawned on Doc that the other was somewhat unscientific in his approach to fighting. The Indian liked to rage and snarl as if making noise was sufficient to overpower a foe. Perhaps at certain times, it was. For he was very good at making faces and issuing forth cries calculated to intimidate an opponent. Unfortunately for him, he relied a little too much on it.

Too, the brave may not be accustomed to man-to-man combat without benefit of a knife or tomahawk.

Doc moved in, and had a little better luck. The other hit the forest floor, and hard. He was back up, though, before Doc got hold of him again.

Monk shouted encouragement. "Knock 'im flat, Doc!"

Monk's normally squeaky voice had become a howling battle roar. This caused Big Neck to swing his head about, eyes growing fearsome and fearful at the same time.

Doc Savage made his move then.

Seizing the man by his most prominent feature—his neck—the bronze giant found nerves and dug in his steely fingers. While the Indian squirmed and struggled mightily, unable to see what was happening, Doc kneaded flesh, found nerve centers and induced a disabling paralysis that caused the brave to cease his floundering struggles.

Doc held him long enough to be certain that his fierce foe was out of action, then stopped, letting Big Neck fall onto the ground. One bronze shoulder ached. The wily brave had attempted to pull that arm out of its socket at one point in the match.

"Well, that's that," decided Monk.

Then he noticed Ham Brooks, leaning against a tree with his damaged sword cane at his feet.

The dapper lawyer did not look like a man who had any fight left in him.

"Did you bring a spare cane, shyster?" asked Monk.

Ham Brooks simply mouthed his No. He looked as crestfallen as his sharp features could manage.

"That will teach you to laugh at your betters," Monk snorted.

They did not have to go far to find the others. Renny and Long Tom and Johnny came trotting up to them, all but out of breath.

"That durn house," puffed Renny.

"It's back!" exclaimed Long Tom.

"Supermalagorgeous!" finished Johnny. He was grinning again.

Chapter XV

THE HOUDINI

THE JAIL OF the town of La Plata looked as solid as a concrete block, and consisted of one cell, into which Spook Davis was pitched. There had been some delay about his incarceration—the State Highway Patrolman had kept him out in front of the jail in their car while they asked him numerous questions, a catechism which they ornamented with precise and writhing details of just how capital punishment worked in the State of Missouri.

Spook Davis, an unstable soul at best, was wet with sweat when they pitched him into jail, slammed the door and went away, carrying off his handcuffs. It was very dark in the cell.

The night sky was making more and more light and noise, but as yet not a drop of rain had fallen. And Spook Davis soon grew conscious of the darkness, of his aloneness in difficulty, and it depressed him—depressed him terribly. His was a changable emotional makeup; his enjoyments bounded among the pinnacles and his intervals of gloom shot him to the depths. When low, he always remembered with profound remorse the different windies he had told lately, and invariably made a firm resolve to tell no more. At such times, he was prone to address an imaginary individual he called his personal devil.

"Devil," Spook now said sourly. "This is a fine thing you've done to me. Here you've got me mixed up in some kind of an infernal mystery and two murders and nobody knows what more. Why can't you lay off a guy once?"

"This is nothing," said a voice. "Wait until I really begin to put it on you!"

Spook Davis' heart nearly failed; like most people who know they have psychological complexes, he'd always been afraid he'd go insane. He had spoken to his imaginary devil; it had replied. He was crazy!

"Great Blackstone!" Spook gulped.

"Sh-h-h," said the voice. "I'd just as soon the whole town didn't know I was in here with you."

Lightning flared and thunder grumbled, disclosing that Spook was not alone.

"Gull!" Spook choked. "Whew! Gull! Why—what—Shades of Houdini!"

"This seemed a good place to hide out," Gull explained from a corner of the tiny space. "And the cops couldn't see the open door from where they were talking to you."

Spook Davis, trying to recover his wits, made sounds similar to those of an old hen trying to assemble her chicks, but finally got himself together.

"A fine idea!" he sneered. "You saved them all the trouble of catching you. We're locked in here."

The Great Gulliver found himself suppressing an urge to strangle his startled stooge.

"Of all the times to pick to tell one of your lies!" Gull gritted.

"Aw—I was tryin' to help you," Spook mumbled downheartedly. "How'd I know they'd arrest me as a material witness. I thought they'd turn you loose and all would be very spiffy."

"That was your own wig you gave them!" Gull groaned. "That wig we use so that people will not know you look almost exactly like me."

"I know. The wig cost us forty dollars when we bought it."

"The whole story about a green-haired man was a lie!"

"It was a good one, though." Spook sighed disgustedly. "But not quite good enough."

Gulliver said grimly, "We're going to be the worms that turned. So far, everybody and his dog has pushed us around. We're going to change that."

"The idea is that we are now going to push people around?"

"To the best of our ability."

Spook Davis groaned, "At least we've got an opportunity to start off in a big way—all we have to do is get out of this jail."

"Easy."

"Oh, sure!"

"I've got the key," Gulliver explained.

REACHING through the bars, fitting the key in the lock did not prove difficult, after which they looked around cautiously for anyone who might observe them, and seeing no one, Spook mumbled that it was a good thing they rolled up the sidewalks here at eight o'clock, sounding as he made the remark as if his mind was very much on other things. The sky roared and glared above, and in the darkness that followed, they dashed across the street and into an alley beside the local telephone office.

"How'd you get that key?" Spook breathed.

"Hocus-pocus," Gulliver said. "Be quiet."

"Be nice—how come the key?"

"Two weeks ago, a fellow got to bragging how Houdini could escape from jails," Gull explained. "Just so Houdini wouldn't have anything on me, I immediately filched the jail key, made a duplicate and hid it in the jail. The idea was to inveigle that Houdini fan into a bet sometime and make us some easy money."

Which was perfectly clear, and quite sensible in view of the fact that The Great Gulliver made his livelihood with just such legerdemain, as Spook freely admitted. "But who are we gonna push around first?"

"Ivan Cass," Gull said.

"But we haven't got him."

"We'll have to remedy that."

They repaired, with fitting caution, down an alley and through back yards, in a rough circle. End of their nocturnal progress found them posted a few blocks up from the jail. The sky roared and glared above them.

"You seem a lot more cheerful," Spook observed. "What in thunder in this mess can you see to be cheerful about?"

"Sh-h-h," Gull breathed. "We're waiting for Cass. I've finally hit a line on this thing."

"You know what it's all about?"

"Not by a long shot. But I know that Box Daniels found out something, was shut up by being killed. I know Saint Pete is a prisoner of Cass and that hound-voiced runt. And I have good reason to believe that Christopher Columbus is the key to it all."

Gulliver continued, whispering, until he had made Spook Davis acquainted with how he had fled straight from the filling station to watch the arrival of Harvell Braggs and Cass, a simple act because it was a small town. Watching Cass' hotel, Gulliver had seen the man leave, followed him to the trailer. Gull showed an excellent memory in repeating almost verbatim to Spook what had been said inside the trailer.

"You think they're mixed up in this?" Spook asked.

"Cass admitted as much," Gull growled. "He gave the idea the thing back of this mystery is pretty big."

"What about the loquacious leviathan?"

"Harvell Braggs? How he fits in I can't fathom."

"Which puts him even with us," Spook lamented.

An alley-prowling dog approached them and sniffed, but fled when Gulliver hissed, after which they moved over and crawled under an elderly telephone lineman's truck which was parked in the alley; from this point they could watch the vicinity of the jail across the street.

"We take Cass," Gulliver explained. "My guess is he can tell us the whereabouts of Saint Pete and Christopher Columbus, and maybe more."

Ivan Cass appeared, striding down the street with long confident steps, and turned in at the jail, where he was lost to sight. When he reappeared, very shortly afterward, he was in a stone-faced hurry.

Gulliver heard a clicking sound beside him—Spook Davis's teeth chattering, which was probably the result of it having occurred to Spook that he had missed death at the hands of Cass by a narrow margin. He was terrified; a moment before he had been elated. Gull gripped Spook's arm, put on pressure, twisted, and the teeth-clicking stopped.

Cass got well up the street. They followed him, decided he was heading toward the gray trailer. Gull had been afraid he would hunt up the police to learn why Spook Davis was not in jail. Gull veered left, running, urging Spook along; they would circle and arrive at the trailer ahead of Cass, he whispered hastily.

Lightning went *rr-r-rip!* and added, *whoom!* The bolt split a tree in the little La Plata park, and they heard the parts of the tree come crashing down. In the west, there was abrupt tumult as if many cattle ran through a brush patch.

"Suh-sounds like a gosling drowner!" Spook Davis puffed as he ran.

IN front of the beer place down by the theatre, a man was cranking up an awning in expectation of the coming storm. The streets looked very wide, very empty, and on the south side of the square which contained the town park, they were building a new post office with WPA money; the piles of bricks and the cement mixers stood out irregularly in the sky glow. Gull swung in that direction, stuck a brick in each trouser pocket, carried two more in his hands, and Spook Davis did the same, muttering that he preferred these Irish daisies to guns any day of the week.

They ran six blocks more, and Gulliver got behind a large maple tree.

"We drop anchor here," he said.

"Eh?"

"The vacant lot and trailer are just down the street. Cass will pass here."

Spook hefted his brick. "Let me have the first kiss, huh?"

The cattle-through-the-brush sound came out of the west and upon the town, a breath at first, rather warm. The trees fluffed themselves, branches swaying, and a few loose leaves began to run across lawns and sidewalks and collide gently with their ankles.

"He oughta be coming along by now," Spook complained.

Wind pushed against their faces, mussed their hair—they wore no hats—and shook their clothing and got into their mouths. The wind was still unnaturally warm. Gulliver waited, brick ready, watching the street, mentally voting thanks to the local city fathers who had a squabble with the public utility supplying electricity to the town, and in retaliation, had discontinued all streetlights. It was very dark between lightning flashes.

"What's keeping him?" Spook muttered.

Dust was boiling like fog in the light from the window of a home far down the street. Then, so abruptly that they almost shivered, the wind became cold, and stronger.

"There!" Gull said suddenly. "Two of them!"

Spook murmured, "Stopped and picked up one of his pals, probably."

Gulliver, waiting, grew gradually more aware of the brick in his hands, of its smooth hard weight, of its sharp edges. His thoughts, leaping, recognized the murderous possibilities of this thing as a weapon with which to strike a man's skull. He began to feel doubt, a chilly kind of doubt, brought on by the knowledge that he had never knocked a man senseless, had no idea how hard one must hit to get results and not kill....

"Take the one on the inside," he breathed tardily.

Feet scuffed the walk over the wind, and there was no lightning flash as two figures came even with the trees and passed, after which Gulliver Greene and Spook Davis stepped out with the bricks.

Gull struck first. It was about like hitting a stump with a brick, he decided. He caught his senseless victim, not to break the fall—to hit again if necessary. But the victim—it must be Ivan Cass—went slack.

"Wands of Thurston! I can't find the other one!"

That was Spook Davis' horrified explosion. The sky rumbled contrarily but did not make lightning. Gulliver remained perfectly still, waiting for an aerial flash. Spook must be doing the same, for there was no sound but the wind and the trees and the convulsing leaves.

Then a small, scared voice gasped a hesitating question.

"What—who—who is it?"

Gull reached out quickly, grabbed feminine garments, jerked, and Saint Pete came toppling down upon him. She made no sound, but struck at him and he seized her hands, which seemed to be bound together at the wrists with a small rope.

Chapter XVI

THE WIZARD'S TOWER

PACKING THE UNCONSCIOUS Big Neck over one shoulder—the one that did not ache—Doc Savage led his men through the Missouri woods back to the rambling and grotesquely garish Victorian dwelling.

The light hitting it made it look a little ethereal, but as they neared it, its innate substantialness became apparent. It was constructed along the lines of the old Queen Anne style, which meant a steeply pitched roof, many angular gables, and a lot of unnecessary ornamentation. The siding appeared to be cedar shakes, arranged in irregular patterns and smeared with a dark maroon paint reminiscent of beet juice. The unusual color scheme was of the type that caused houses like this to be dubbed "painted ladies."

Abruptly, Doc halted, signaling for the others to do the same.

"We do not want it to disappear again," he explained.

Setting Big Neck on the ground, the bronze man looked about. He spied a tree that he seemed to favor and said, "Wait here. Do not approach."

Moving quietly, Doc went to the tree and began climbing. He employed a method he had learned during the portion of his youth spent in the South Seas. Removing his belt, the bronze man wrapped it around the smooth bole. Using this as a brace, he walked up the trunk in stages, shifting the belt upward every few feet.

Soon Doc was in the branches, moving along them with the

agility of a russet squirrel, if such rodents weighed in excess of two hundred pounds.

One stout bough brought him to an adjoining tree. Doc launched himself out into space, and landed in the crown of this second tree. Both were maples. Working along, the bronze man got into a position where he could clear the intervening space between his perch and the gabled roof top.

"Tarzan couldn't have done any better," remarked Monk.

Landing on the slate roof, Doc found the cap-like tower and attempted entry. The single window would not open, so he employed the ornate carvings to clamber down, finally reaching the porch, which was also maroon, but appeared festooned with geometrical spiderwebs thanks to the ebony gingerbread ornamentation which hung all around the porch roof.

Going to the front door, Doc tried it cautiously—giving it a push, hesitating momentarily, as if chary of reentering the grotesque and demonstrably unpredictable domicile.

Then Doc entered, vanishing from view.

It was some minutes before he returned to wave his waiting men to come ahead.

"I don't like this," Renny grunted dubiously.

"Yeah, what if—" Long Tom started to say.

"You mean, what if once we're inside the house up and vanishes again?" Monk squeaked.

"That was my drift, yeah," admitted the pale electrical wizard.

"Doc would not call for us unless he had first defeated that problem," snapped Ham Brooks.

Nevertheless, they approached with caution, such as would men infiltrating an enemy fortification.

By the time the group reached the wraparound porch, Doc had withdrawn deep into the interior of the gloomy dwelling.

Not shy around danger, Monk barged in first.

"Hey!" he said, catching himself on the threshold of the entry.

"Watch the step," came the vibrant voice of Doc Savage.

Turning, Monk warned, "You have to step up into this joint."

Renny came next and found that this was true. The entryway was elevated—raised one step.

They shouldered through an unnecessarily narrow foyer and then walked into an octagonal room meant for parlor furnishings.

The room was strange. For one thing, it seemed smaller than it should be. They experienced a distinct claustrophobic sensation. The wallpaper was antiquated, colors faded and yellow as old cotton. There was a decorative strip of floral wallpaper running along the top of the wall, all the way around, of a different pattern than the main wall covering.

After a while, Renny, who understood architecture, boomed, "These durn walls are built too thick."

"What do you mean—too thick?" challenged Monk. "They're just walls, right?"

Johnny Littlejohn had extracted his monocle magnifier and was examining the pattern of the ancient yellowing wallpaper and added, "A thickness of utmost extremity."

"Whatcha mean?" asked Monk.

"Johnny means," inserted Doc Savage, "that the walls are built to the specifications of a concrete blockhouse—nearly two feet deep."

"What the heck for?" wondered Long Tom.

The question hung in the air unanswered.

There were no furnishings. Not a stick of furniture stood anywhere. Victorian homes of that era were usually populated by overstuffed chairs and other heavy appointments. Highboys, china cabinets and the like. This parlor area had none of those. The polished pine floor was scratched and dusty.

Old-fashioned gas fixtures studded the walls, but these appeared to be merely decorative. No gas service out here in the forested wilderness, of course. Just to satisfy his curiosity, Monk tested one, twisting the key and sniffing the opened valve.

"No gas stink," he reported.

Doc led them up the substantial staircase to the second floor. There were only bedrooms, but these too were bare. Up here, pale scabs of loose paint hung from the cracked ceilings, like dead skin from a molting snake.

There was no sign of a habitation. Evidently, the place had been built before indoor plumbing was invented and never renovated to accommodate modern conveniences.

"Ain't no one livin' here," Monk muttered.

"It's just a shell," rumbled Renny, bringing his blocky fists together, as he did when stumped.

"There remains the tower," reminded Doc, who moved along an L-shaped corridor until he found the sturdy staircase to the attic tower.

They ascended carefully. Step risers creaked forlornly.

"Swell joint for a ghost," muttered Monk.

"Why don't you consider moving in?" snapped Ham unkindly. "You would fit right in."

"I got a good mind to lock you in the attic until you grow some sense," Monk growled.

"If you had a good mind," countered Ham, "you would have a forehead instead of those beetling brows."

Their banter trailed off when they stepped through an unlocked door into the tower void.

The interior was a shadowy cone. But it was not empty.

A DEVICE stood in the center of the room. It was a complicated array remindful of nothing they had ever seen. There were moving parts, rather on the order of a gyroscope, mounted on an ornate pedestal of wrought iron. All appeared to be hand-forged by some imaginative artisan in metal. Doc walked around this carefully, circling it twice. From his lips came a vague susurration—his tremulous trilling, pitched very low. It might have been the bronze man's version of a near-silent whistle of intrigue.

"This is the heart of the machine," he said.

"What machine?" asked Long Tom querulously.

"This entire structure," supplied Doc Savage in a steady voice, "is a machine of a type imaginative writers have long speculated over, but which science has never considered feasible to construct."

Ham blinked. "I fail to—"

Then everyone froze into silence. The truth sunk in.

"Are you saying this ramshackle old dump is a time machine!" exploded Monk.

Doc did not reply in words. He simply nodded.

They fell to examining the central mechanism. Much of it suggested interlocking or concentric rings. These were calibrated in some manner. Part of it was clearly electrical in nature, but other structures involved specially-shaped crystals whose purpose and function was puzzling in the extreme.

"Reminds me of a gyroscope," remarked Long Tom.

"That is one way of putting it," said Doc. "As nearly as I can tell, this is what might be termed a gyroscopic astrolabe."

Monk clucked, "Johnny, translate that, will ya?"

"I fail to follow," the bony archeologist said weakly. "But an astrolabe is a device employed by seafarers in olden times to navigate vast oceans by computation of the stars. This construct is infinitely more complex than a navigator's astrolabe."

"Consider the possibility that a vehicle can be devised to transport a person back into the past," stated Doc. "What other considerations must be taken into account?"

Ham frowned. "How far back in time to travel?"

"That is part of it. But there are other problems. For one, the Earth is spinning in space, and for another, the planet is traveling in a constant orbit around the sun. Even the solar system is in motion. To travel back in time one hundred years into the past would risk materializing in outer space, unanchored and floating helplessly in an airless vacuum."

"Because the Earth itself moves," crowed Ham.

"Exactly," said Doc.

Monk grunted, "The guy who thought this up must have been a daggone genius."

"Constructing a reliable vehicle for temporal displacement is considered impossible," Doc continued. "The inventor of this machine—for this entire house comprises the time displacer—was unquestionably brilliant. He not only solved the essential problem of reversal in time, but also the issues arising from the celestial mechanics of such a journey."

"If this is the brain of the thing," wondered Long Tom, "where are the circuits of the time machine itself?"

"All around us," said Doc Savage. "The entire house is the time machine. The raised floor and thick walls no doubt conceal the essential electronics involved. I had no opportunity to study them. If indeed, such could not be done without gutting the whole structure."

They stood in the weird tower room that from the outside was so reminiscent of a witch's conical cap, studying the mechanical brain of the thing. It was like nothing any of them had ever seen before, which given that the bronze man's tiny band comprised some of the greatest scientific minds of the century, said a great deal.

"So every time we approached this place," Renny remarked, "the house took itself back in time."

Doc nodded. "Triggered by a photoelectric cell, which I have disabled. It was a perfect mechanism to prevent the house from falling into unfriendly hands. Every time someone approached, the mechanism threw the dwelling back to a predetermined year in the past. A timer caused it to reappear later. Anyone encountering the phenomenon, even the most rational of individuals, would be inculcated with superstitious fear."

"Except us, naturally," boasted Monk.

Ham made a sneering sound of disgust.

Johnny looked thoughtful. "Earlier, you said that you had been transported into the past. What happened to you there?"

Doc Savage hesitated. "I would rather that account wait. We

have an urgent mission to accomplish. Big Neck must be brought back to his own time."

"That's simple," said Monk. "We'll lock him in a closet and send the whole works back."

"There is more to the problem than that," advised Doc. "When I was in the past, I met the man who owns this time transporter."

"Holy cow!" boomed Renny. "You mean to say the guy lives in the past?"

"No, he is *trapped* in the past. The unfortunate is being held for ransom by the Big Necks. I promised the Iowans that I would bring back their chief. They, in turn, vowed to release this man."

"What's his name?" asked Long Tom.

"He would not tell me. But that is something we can uncover later. First, two of you will come with me, while the others will remain here to guard the location."

Everyone hesitated—except for Johnny Littlejohn.

"I will gladly volunteer," he said, eyes bright.

Doc looked to the others. They were brave men, willing to court death and danger. But here was the prospect of a journey into the unknown unlike any they had ever faced. It forced them, for once, to consider the risks involved. Feet shuffled. Eyes searched the ceiling. Ham Brooks fell to examining his mangled sword cane, frowned deeply, and tossed it away with disdain. All this temporizing was an unusual sight.

Various expressions crossed Monk Mayfair's wide, simian features.

"Heck," he said at last, "count me in."

Ham abruptly inserted, "Include me, as well. If that hairy ape is willing, so am I."

"Best to keep this party small," said Doc. "Three will have to remain behind."

"Let Monk remain behind," declared Ham. "He would only frighten the Indians."

Grinning, Monk extracted a coin from his hip pocket. "Match you for the privilege," he suggested.

"Heads," Ham said sharply.

Monk gave the nickel a flip with his thumb. It spun and rang in the air. A hairy hand snapped out, and caught it. Monk slapped it onto the back of his other hand, removing the fingers holding it.

"Tails," he crowed.

"Let me see, insect!"

Monk displayed the coin. It was a buffalo nickel. The humped shape of the buffalo showed plainly.

"You have used two-headed coins to trick me in the past," complained Ham. "Let me see the other side."

Grinning, Monk reversed the coin, showing the Indian profile that proved the coin was genuine.

"It is settled," said Doc. "Begin divesting yourselves of any weapons and other items."

Johnny blinked. "Why?"

"We can't risk the possibility of losing modern weapons in the past, where they could fall in the wrong hands and be duplicated. That eventuality could alter the course of history as we know it now."

"Good thinkin'," said Monk, unholstering his supermachine pistol. Johnny followed suit.

Doc Savage did not carry a weapon of his own, but he removed his special equipment vest and began emptying its pockets. Certain items, such as a padded container of fragile glass marbles—actually anesthetic grenades—he kept, since once used, they were no longer effective, and could not be duplicated by the science of the Nineteenth Century.

"Wrist watches as well," reminded Doc. "And modern money."

When it was over, a pile of items sagged in Renny Renwick's huge arms.

Unseen by anyone, Monk palmed his buffalo-head nickel.

He considered it to be his lucky coin, and feared that Ham Brooks would appropriate it out of spite.

"Now we will fetch Big Neck," announced Doc.

THEY found the Iowan where they left him, slumbering on the fading autumn grass, oblivious to all.

Doc Savage lifted him in his great corded arms and bore the limp-limbed brave back into the parlor.

"Do you understand the mechanism well enough to operate it?" asked Johnny.

"I do not," admitted Doc. "But since it is set to go back to a predetermined month and year, it is not necessary that I do so." Turning to Renny, Long Tom and Ham, he said, "Once you three retreat to the forest, I will reengage the so-called magic-eye mechanism. At my signal, you will approach the building. That will trip the electric eye and actuate the time transporter."

Renny and Long Tom looked uneasy.

"This sounds kinda risky," Renny offered.

"It *is* risky. But it must be done. It is as important to retrieve the stranded man from the past as it is to return Big Neck to his tribe."

No one offered any contradictory thought on that score.

Renny rumbled, "I feel like we ought to shake hands in farewell, or something."

"Aw, we'll be back soon enough," snorted Monk. "Heck, we ain't even goin' far."

"Not in geographic terms," agreed Johnny.

"Still," cautioned Ham Brooks, "if something unfortunate befalls you, or you cannot return to the house in time, you will all be marooned back in 1829."

"If we do not return with the house," explained Doc calmly, "simply trip the electric eye repeatedly until we do."

"O.K.," said Long Tom. "But if something does go wrong, it's a long walk back to October, 1937."

"Indubitably so," agreed Johnny. "A walk of some one hundred and eight years in duration."

With that sober assessment hanging in the dim air, Ham Brooks, Long Tom Roberts and Renny Renwick retreated to the porch and walked up the narrow lane through the close-pressing trees.

When the trio reached a point they thought correct, they turned around.

Doc Savage's voice called out, saying, "You may proceed."

Together, they approached the house. There was no sensation of triggering the electric eye, of course. It was impalpable, as well as not visible, being a beam of infra-red light.

The blood-colored Victorian dwelling simply popped out of existence like a soap bubble. They felt a movement of air all around them, as if the surrounding atmosphere were rushing in to fill the sudden vacuum. Leaves rustled briefly. That was all.

Despite the fact that they were psychologically prepared for the phenomenon—at least, they thought they were—audible gasps came from their compressed lips.

"That's that," rumbled Renny.

"You make it sound like they're gone forever," breathed Ham Brooks.

"It will be a calamity if they are," moaned Long Tom, the biggest pessimist of the group, next to Renny.

The pallid electrical wizard stared at the void where the hideous dwelling once stood.

"Anyone see what became of Monk's pig?" he asked after a time.

Ham looked about. "He was here a minute ago." His sharp gaze found the hoof marks of the ungainly shoat in the dirt, followed them with his dark eyes.

"They lead back in the direction of the house," he said.

"You don't suppose..." Renny started to say.

"Habeas could have jumped onto the porch just before the house left our era," Long Tom mused. "The way it wraps around, no one would have noticed."

"If that is the case," muttered Ham, "Monk is going to have his hands full."

Chapter XVII

BEAUTY IN THE DARKNESS

THERE WERE TWO or three sounds made by Spook Davis taking random passes in the darkness with his brick.

"I still can't find anybody!" he gulped.

Gull said, "Relax."

Gulliver Greene sat perfectly still, crowded a little between the girl and senseless Ivan Cass. He did not say anything, being fully dumbfounded. When lightning came, a long lurid brightness, Spook Davis leaned forward, popping his eyes at the girl.

Her deliciously cinnamon-hued hair was fluffy, tousled by the rough handling, and her exquisite lips were drawn thin, her blue eyes wide. She still wore the frock of dark burlap which had the effect of setting off her breathtaking contours.

Spook Davis sighed deeply in the following darkness.

"I don't blame you for hiding that shoe," he told Gull.

"Oh!" Saint Pete said. "It's you two!"

Her voice struck Gull as being as perfect as it had that time when he came upon her trying to capture and question poor old Box Daniels. That reminded him of how, when he had seized her on that occasion out by the filling station, she had gasped for him to rush back and get old Box Daniels, only to disappear when he did so. He decided to start his questions at that point.

"Why did you run off from me earlier in the night?"

She did not answer.

Gull said, "I'll turn you loose."

146

He did this.

"Why did you run off before?" he asked.

Her silence continued.

"Where is Christopher Columbus?" Gull questioned.

Sky fire showed her tightly compressed mouth.

"What is the mystery about Columbus?"

The storm noise seemed to be getting louder.

"Where did I hook into this thing in the first place?"

He waited vainly for a reply.

"She ain't very talkative," Spook Davis said dryly. "That makes her unique among women."

Gulliver put a hand on the girl's arm, held it and found that it quieted a little under his fingers. He retained his grip and with the other hand patted Ivan Cass' clothing, located a lump that was a flashlight, then moved the girl behind the big maple tree—with the tree between themselves and the vacant lot and the trailer. The light on the girl's face showed very wide eyes, paleness, lips that shook each time she could not hold them tightly together.

"Scared," Gulliver decided.

Spook Davis stated firmly, "Young lady, we have no intention of harming you, so you needn't be afraid."

"She's not scared of us." Gull dabbed the flashlight beam on Saint Pete's face again. "Are you?"

She stared into the flash glare and her lips loosened to shape the beginning of a word. The word did not come. She lifted both hands and pushed the wealth of cinnamon hair back from her forehead, then her palms pressed tightly to her temples and remained. As if squeezing a horror within.

"Listen," she said huskily, "I'll tell you something."

Gulliver waited.

"You had no real connection with this in the first place," the girl told him.

"No?"

"Box Daniels got mixed up in it. He tried to extricate himself, and discovered he not only couldn't but that he was to be killed because the rest of them were afraid of him. Box couldn't go to the police because—well, he had his reasons. He thought of you. You were a famous magician. He admired you. So he tried to come to you for help."

"We figured that much already," Gull said. "All but the reason for his not going to the police. Go on. What was Box Daniels mixed up in?"

The girl insisted, "Turn me loose."

THE WIND pushed against them harder and harder. The sky kept exploding as if shotguns were going off. A big drop of rain hit Gull's face like a watery pebble, then another; the drops came faster, got smaller, slowly turning into a wall of water that beat them, filled their pockets and speedily came up around their ankles.

Gull held on to the girl.

"Keep talking."

She leaned close to him, screaming over the storm, "If I am not with Cass' men, they will think I am working with you."

"What's wrong with that?"

"They will believe I've told you what little I have learned."

"Little?"

"And they'll kill Christopher Columbus," the girl shrieked.

Gulliver seized her shoulders, pulled her close to his face.

"What is this Columbus stuff, anyway?" he shouted.

"Let me loose!"

Gulliver roared at Spook Davis, "Where's the rope that was on her wrists?" They had some difficulty locating the rope in the streaming rain, but succeeded, and Gull found it long enough to tie Saint Pete's wrists in one cluster. He propelled her against the maple.

Meantime, Spook Davis searched Ivan Cass. He found a roll

of greenbacks, licked his lips, glanced quickly at Gull and observed Gull had seen the money. Reluctantly, he replaced the roll in Cass' pocket. He shoved his hand under Cass' armpit, jerked it out as if stung, and straightened.

"We ain't learned a heck of a lot so far!" he shouted.

"Get Cass' gun!" Gull directed.

Spook Davis shuddered, reached back into Cass' armpit, and brought out his compact dark revolver. He held it gingerly with thumb and forefinger, and started to throw it away, for he would rather handle a snake than a gun.

Gull seized the weapon and said, "Finish searching him."

Going back to the girl, Gull couched beside her and yelled over the rain, advising her to talk freely. He made rash promises about protecting her from danger. He was saying that they would find Christopher Columbus, if he was in danger, and protect him, too, when Spook Davis stumbled to them in excitement.

"Cass had the rest of old Box Daniels' telegram!"

GULLIVER GREENE and Spook Davis pressed against the tree and jammed their shoulders together to make an ineffective tent in which to inspect the telegram—the message which Ivan Cass and the small man with the big voice had tried to keep unknown by murdering the La Plata depot agent.

It was long.

> IM REALLY JAMMED UP OR I WOULDNT HOLLER HELP TO A NEPHEW I HAVE NEVER SEEN BUT YOU HAPPEN TO BE MY ONLY LIVING RELATIVE AND A BIG SHOT SO HERE GOES STOP I HAVE BEEN A FOOL WITH MY MIND-READING AND GOT IN SOME TERRIBLE DOINGS WITH A MAN NAMED IVAN CASS AND SOME OTHERS STOP THIS IS NOT PLAIN CROOK BUSINESS AS YOU MAY THINK BUT A LOT WORSE AND SO BIG ITLL AMAZE YOU STOP DONT THINK IM CRAZY

STOP I SLIPPED AWAY WHEN CASS AND THE
REST THREATENED ME STOP NOW THEYRE
TRYING TO BURY ME SO I NEED HELP AND AM
COMING TO YOU STOP IN CASE I DONT MAKE IT
YOU BETTER HAVE DOC SAVAGE INVESTIGATE
THE SILENT SAINTS AND THEIR PROMISED
LAND NEAR LAKE OF THE OZARKS STOP UP
TO YOU NOW STOP *I KNOW POSITIVELY THAT
CHRISTOPHER COLUMBUS IS ALIVE.*
UNCLE BOXTON

In reading the telegram, Gulliver Greene supplied the last
seven words from memory. The seven missing in this wire being
the portion of the message which he had torn off while fighting Cass' runt assistant for the missive.

"I'm disgusted," Spook Davis said.

Gulliver felt likewise. The telegram itself explained Ivan Cass'
desperate efforts to apprehend it. The message made it unnecessarily clear that Christopher Columbus was involved. It
implicated the Silent Saints. It mentioned their Promised Land,
located near the Lake of the Ozarks. That part at least was a
new development. It also suggested that they sic the famous
Doc Savage onto the mess. That was perhaps the queerest part
of all. Gulliver Greene, of course, knew who Doc Savage was.
He was a trouble-buster of Herculean proportions. Although
he had never met the famous Man of Bronze, Gull always felt
a strange feeling in the pit of his stomach whenever he saw
Doc's picture in the newspapers. It was as if he had met the
man—although his memory was notably blank in that department. Still, Gull was an admirer of Doc Savage, although he
never liked to talk about it.

But the element still lacking was the thing Gulliver wanted
most to know. Spook voiced it when he muttered:

"But what's the shooting all about, anyway?"

Gulliver said sourly, "You better watch Cass in case he comes
out of it."

"Oh, he won't. I hit him a couple of more times with my brick."

Gulliver sank beside Saint Pete. The roaring violence of the wind was easing. But even more rain was coming down; it rushed against them in clammy strings.

Gulliver held the flash ray briefly on the girl's garments—the dark, plain, coarsely woven cloth. He fingered the fabric speculatively, eyes narrowed, while he blew the rain off his lips and shook his head to get it out of his ears. Definitely burlap.

"You had best forget this and let me go," the girl said unexpectedly. "It is none of your affair."

"No. I'm just the guy who got two murders hung on him. Who are the Silent Saints and what is the Promised Land?"

She gave him silence.

"Who is Christopher Columbus?"

Saint Pete said suddenly, wildly, "You won't believe me! You'll think I'm crazy. But Christopher Columbus is the great navigator who discovered America."

Gull straightened and his back felt bowed and tight not alone because of the beating rain. The rain running over his tall body was like something alive and moving. He winked water out of his eyes and blew it off his lips.

Spook Davis croaked, "Christopher Columbus, the discoverer of America! Listen, who's going crazy around here?"

Gull sank to the girl's side. "Let's have the story."

She did not answer.

Picking up Cass' hat, Gulliver used it to cover the revolver, which he held in one hand. Talking loudly over the storm, he directed Spook Davis to remain with Ivan Cass and Saint Pete and watch them.

"I'm going to corral that little runt and the others," he ended, "then we're all going to be sensible and go to the police."

"If you find Columbus, grab him," Spook Davis suggested wryly. "I'd like to talk to that long-haired zombie."

GULLIVER strode off, hunched against the cold rain, keeping behind the maples. When he had covered a score of paces, there was foot-slapping noise behind him. Then Spook Davis' hand was on his arm.

"The girl says call you back. She's got something to say."

Gull took long running steps back through the dark storm. He collided with one of the maples in his haste, and thereafter had the feeling that his nose was mixing scarlet with the water pouring down his face.

The girl's voice had a strangeness.

"Those are not ordinary men."

Gulliver asked, "Why?" and sounded puzzled.

"They have extrasensory perception."*

"They've got what?"

"Extrasensor—they are mind-readers."

Spook said dryly, "Oh, fan me, mother!"

Gulliver was silent. He put the light on Saint Pete's face, turned it off quickly, not liking the wide-eyed horror he saw.

"Mind-readers," Saint Pete repeated. "Watch them. They can tell what you are thinking, what you know."

The expression on Gull's tanned face must have conveyed his doubt, for the girl seemed to reply to his thoughts.

"You are wrong," she said calmly. "Scientists, many of them at least, agree that the ability does actually exist."

Spook Davis blinked foolishly at the young woman in the burlap frock. The one-way conversation had him puzzled. He opened his mouth....

The amazing girl said, "No, The Great Gulliver is not whispering to me or anything."

Spook started. "Hey! That is exactly what I was gonna ask

---

* *Extrasensory perception is the term applied by scientists to the human ability to fathom with uncanny precision what is in another person's mind. Almost everyone has had the weird experience of writing a friend, and the next day receiving a letter which the friend wrote at the same time. This is extrasensory perception. Some people have only flashes of it; others have, or claim to have it all the time. Science has not yet explained what it is. Like gravity, it is still an enigma. —KENNETH ROBESON.*

you!"

Gull snapped, "Keep your shirt on, Spook."

Spook said, "Whew!" blankly. "Somebody wire Dunninger that his act's been stolen!"

Impatiently, Gull demanded, "What is back of this mess?"

"Have you any idea?" Saint Pete sounded as if she really wanted to know about that.

Gull had no idea; but he did not have to say so.

"I see." The girl seemed relieved. "You'll be amazed when you learn. But if I told you the truth now, you'd think—well, human credulity is controlled subconsciously by retrospection."

"Huh?" Spook Davis grunted. "Use little words. What you just said means as much to me as abracadabra-hocus-pocus-presto-chango."

"Your mind is like your stomach—it often does not like to digest strange food," Saint Pete elaborated.

Spook's "Oh!" showed he still didn't understand.

Gulliver waited for a while before he said, "Go ahead."

"That is all." She closed her eyes tightly in the light which he put on her again. "I hope—wish you luck."

Gull doused his flash. A lightning flash came at just the right moment to show the burlap-clad girl in the middle of a violent shudder.

A little later, Gulliver Greene arose and moved away in the black rain. Spook followed for a short distance. Understanding began to dawn upon his confused thinking.

"That girl!" Spook gasped. "She is—duh-do you realize—she has the power that so few in the world have. *She actually has it!*"

"I feel sorry for her," Gull Greene muttered. "She's so awfully pretty to be insane."

Spook went back. Gulliver continued on toward the vacant lot and trailer, feeling cold and clammy inside and out.

Chapter XVIII

THE ANNIHILATION OF TIME

THEY STOOD IN the center of the empty octagonal parlor, awaiting the unknown.

Doc Savage began speaking. "You may safely expect certain psychological symptoms to occur during the reversion process."

Almost as soon as the bronze man spoke those words, *it* happened.

First, there was an alarming flickering of the house lights, followed by a pins-and-needles prickling on their epidermis. The air became unaccountably thin in their lungs.

"I'll be superamalgamated!" Johnny exclaimed.

Monk began scratching at his hairy forearms arms furiously. "Hey, it itches like murder!"

"That is to be expected," said Doc, calm-voiced.

Suddenly, they went blind. It was not the blindness of utter blackness, such as blind persons experience. Instead a hazy gray veil descended over their vision. This was interspersed with crisscrossing black lines. It was as if something was being projected in front of their retinas.

"Granular grayness," was how Johnny expressed it.

The combined sensations continued for barely a minute. During that unsettling interval, a new sensation took hold. It was a familiar feeling. They had felt it before.

"*Ye-e-o-w!*" howled Monk.

"I feel as if I am dropping into a void," bleated Johnny.

Monk grabbed for something to hold onto—found nothing. Stumbling into a wall, for the first time he became aware of the fact that the walls were humming and vibrating. This had not been audible until he touched the wall. Powerful mechanisms stood behind those walls. That electromagnetism was involved was proven by the way the overhead light fixture began to twist wildly, as if in a storm, pulled by powerful forces emanating from the thick walls. They heard this rather than saw it.

"This is like ridin' our express elevator back at headquarters," gulped Monk.

Indeed, it was. The sensation of dropping continued for what seemed to be several eternities, which, with their vision virtually shut off, was to say the least unnerving.

Monk was saying, "When does this stop?" when it did. Abruptly.

The grayness was gone. In its place was an utter darkness. It was no more comforting. Less.

"What just happened?" Monk howled, looking around, jaw agape.

"We have arrived at our destination," came Doc Savage's very calm voice.

"Why is it dark?"

"The mechanism is set not to return to the exact same segment of time in each instance," explained Doc. "The timer advances after each reversion. I arrived during daylight hours last time. Now it is night, presumably of the same day. But that remains to be seen."

They had no flashlights, so they stood around while their eyes adjusted to the absence of light.

Soon, they saw threads of moonlight among the trees. It was a near-full moon. The lunar lantern had been waning when they left.

Going to the parlor windows, they looked over their surroundings. The forest they had left behind them—or ahead of them as the case might be–was still there. But it was noticeably thinner and the solitary path was more distant. At least, they failed to find it with their eyes.

Doc Savage stepped onto the porch.

Monk followed. He sniffed the air. "Cleaner than in our day."

"We are in the age before automobiles, and far from the industrialized metropolises responsible for modern miasmatic exhalations," reminded Johnny, sliding back into his big-word-ed habit.

Doc retreated inside to take possession of Big Neck, chief of the Iowans.

Doc considered how best to handle the unconscious brave. Moving to a closet, he rummaged around. It was not entirely empty. There were tools, including rope. With his clasp knife, Doc cut this into lengths, and fashioned a slip noose which he placed around Big Neck's thick throat, and then tied the Indian's wrists to the loop. Then he unwound the rope to a length that could be used to pull the man along once he was on foot.

"Afraid he will get away?" asked Johnny.

"In order to make the ransom exchange," Doc explained, "Big Neck must be brought before his people as a captive."

"Makes sense," squeaked Monk.

From another pocket, Doc produced a vial containing a chemical restorative infinitely more potent than the ordinary run of smelling salts. He hesitated to use them, however.

"Best we carry him until we are ready to make a show of it," Doc decided.

Packing Big Neck across his shoulder, the bronze giant carried him out of the house.

There, Monk tasted the air again. "I could get used to this country air."

Doc Savage looked around, golden eyes whirling animatedly.

"We are in the time of our great grandfathers," he breathed.

The thought filled them with a silent, almost spiritual

wonder—until Monk found his tongue.

"Hey, maybe when this is settled, we can hunt them down. I heard some tall tales about mine."

"That would be unwise, if not dangerous," said Doc gravely. "We must accomplish our mission as soon as humanly possible."

Monk peered back at the weird Victorian house. "How long before it goes sailin' back to the Twentieth Century?"

"Three hours. Let's go."

DOC SAVAGE carried Big Neck as if he were hollow, which the muscular Indian was most assuredly not. The Iowan hung limp, empty hands slapping against Doc's rolling form as they progressed.

Moving along the moonlit path, the bronze-skinned Hercules employed his nostrils.

Monk caught the scent, too.

"Cooking fire," he undertoned. "Out now."

Doc nodded, moving in that general direction.

The idea that they were walking through a time long before they were born was uppermost in their minds. Johnny stopped to apply his monocle magnifier to various flora and other items, but discovered nothing more remarkable than a broken flint arrowhead, which he pocketed.

After a while, they understood that they were traversing an ordinary woodland. There was nothing of the incredible about it. They might have been walking a different segment of this same forest in their own time.

But, of course, they were not.

Before long, dawn began creeping. It was a strangely reassuring sight. Darkness, even one split by moonbeams, did nothing positive for their peace of mind.

As the sun rose, fresh woodsmoke could be scented.

"The camp is up," advised Doc Savage.

Stooping, he lowered Big Neck to the ground and again

brought out his smelling salts. These were not the type that could be purchased at any pharmacy, but a quick-acting concoction specially formulated by Doc for unusual situations such as this one.

Uncapping the ampule, he waved the pungent fumes under the Indian's nostrils.

Big Neck started at once. Eyes snapping open, he took in his surroundings.

A few words in his native tongue from Doc Savage failed to quiet him.

Big Neck sprang to his feet.

Doc Savage was ready. He tripped the brave, placed a foot upon the man's heaving chest, and gave the restraining rope a hard yank.

Big Neck saw at once the lay of the land. He was a prisoner. He subsided.

Doc instructed him to stand up.

Big Neck was stubborn. He just lay there, his face a knot of resistance.

So Doc pulled the Iowan to his feet, showing no outward strain.

When the bull-necked brave was up on the soft soles of his moccasins, he glared at Doc Savage. Doc met his regard with one of his own. The impassive cast of his bronze features showed no outward concern.

This more than anything else impressed the Iowan chief.

So when Doc started off, Big Neck followed without further protest.

IT took a while to find the camp. They had to work around and through close-packed trees after they left the meandering path. Bees were buzzing in and out of hollow trees. There were many hives about. The morning sun was stirring them to life.

"I'll be bombinated!" Johnny remarked. "This is the old bee-line!"

Doc Savage nodded. "The ancient trail the pioneers followed, and one of the enticements that drew them to build the settlement called the Cabins, which is not far from here. Honey is plentiful hereabouts."

"Earlier, you intimated that you had walked smack into the Big Neck War," Johnny prompted.

"No, its aftermath. I participated only in that I buried poor William Wynn after he perished of his wounds."

"Remarkable," breathed Johnny, unable to summon up a more elaborate word.

Soon enough, they could see the hazy gray smoke of a camp fire.

Braves were going about their morning business. It appeared that they had caught a raccoon and were skinning it for breakfast. Like Big Neck, they had shaven heads and a single scalplock trailing down the backs of their heads. To these were attached feathers or deer tails as decoration. Deerskin breechcloths and moccasins were their only attire.

Johnny watched this activity avidly, his interest in other eras and people of the past holding him fixed in place.

"Speak any Iowany?" asked Doc.

"Some."

Big Neck listened to this exchange and suddenly filled his lungs. There was no mistaking his intent. He gave out a yell of alarm.

Doc Savage let him finish. Then he added words of his own.

The timbre of the bronze man's voice carried. It seemed to fill the forest.

At the camp, the Indians froze, began looking around. Some reached for tomahawks and war clubs.

One yelled, pointing a finger in their direction.

At that point, Doc Savage stepped out into view, leading Big Neck as if the latter were a recalcitrant mule.

Doc Savage continued his salutations.

"Oho!" he greeted in the Iowany tongue. "I have returned, bringing Big Neck, as I have promised. Produce the white man you hold captive."

The Iowan band were advancing, weapons in hand.

Doc Savage ignored this. He continued to approach, towing his reluctant prisoner.

When the dark eyes of the braves fell on Big Neck, there was consternation.

Big Neck yelled something coarse.

Turning, Doc cuffed the man. Hard. Big Neck was knocked off his feet. Everyone beheld this, saw how lightly Doc had seemed to strike. Yet the muscular Indian chief was knocked for a loop.

It made for good theatre, and caused those readying their weapons to hold off and ponder the power of this mighty bronze colossus.

Finally, a brave stepped forward. He was lean and very sunburned.

"We have the white man," he said.

"Produce him," said Doc.

This was done.

A man was dragged into view, stumbling feet lashed by buffalo-hide rope. He looked thin and famished. There was nothing distinguished about him otherwise. He had a long thin neck with a prominent Adam's apple and his disorderly hair was the color of straw that had been bleached by the summer sun. He seemed dispirited, but said nothing.

"We will parley," said Doc.

THEY assembled around the camp fire in a circle.

The ropes were left shackling Big Neck. Nor was the white man untied. That was the way of it.

Pieces of roasted raccoon were passed around on spilt sticks.

The Iowans ate nervously. The cause of their unease was

Monk Mayfair. Being ignorant of apes and gorillas, they had never seen anything remotely like him.

Fingers pointed. Words were whispered.

"What are they sayin'?" asked Monk.

"They are calling you 'Buffalo Man'," whispered Johnny.

Grinning, Monk produced his nickel, flipped it. It flashed upward and landed on his other palm.

"Monk," warned Doc. "Do not lose that."

"It's only a nickel."

"The year stamped on it says otherwise."

Monk looked. "Says 1932."

"It would not do to leave a 1932 nickel behind in 1829," cautioned Doc.

"Gotcha, Doc."

Monk made a show of displaying the nickel, with its Indian head on one side and standing buffalo on the other. He palmed it, made the coin change hands as if by magic and performed sleights and other mystifying tricks of the magician's trade.

"What are you doing?" Johnny whispered.

"Just showin' them that I really am a Buffalo Man. That ought to impress them."

The Big Necks were duly impressed. Their eyes became very wide.

Doc Savage stood up. He made a speech. It was earnest and went on for a good while. It became clear to Johnny, who translated for Monk, that the big bronze man was recounting the original bargain that had been struck during Doc's previous visit.

A sense of unreality began returning to the proceedings.

They were in the past. Sometime in the Summer of 1829, to be exact about it. It was an awesome realization. Having journeyed so far from familiar settings, return seemed an undeniable impossibility.

Finally, the Iowan sub-chief spoke his piece. His name, he

said, was Red Snake. He dwelled upon his virtues as a warrior, and the honor of his people. A bargain had been made and it would be honored, he declaimed.

It was settled. The sub-chief of the Indians drew forth a skinning knife and cut the rawhide thongs restraining the white man.

Doc made a show of untying his captive and freeing Big Neck, giving the latter a contemptuous kick in the process. This was to impress everyone that the giant bronze man considered the mighty Big Neck to be no personal threat. It was sound psychology.

Big Neck, who had been seated with his head hung in shame all through the convocation, leaped to his feet and looked as if he wanted to prove his prowess to all comers.

Doc Savage calmly reminded him, "A truce is in place."

Big Neck snarled, clenching jaws and fingers.

Monk sprang to his feet and began growling.

This had a remarkable effect upon all. The Big Necks began shrinking from the colossal creature they called Buffalo Man.

"What are you doing?" hissed Johnny.

"I got 'em buffaloed—I think." Monk growled anew, displaying as many of his massive teeth as his wide mouth permitted.

Evidently, the simian chemist was not far off in his estimation, for the Iowans began looking uneasy. Red Snake called for Big Neck to sit down and eat.

Big Neck was having none of it.

Now a volley of upset voices began calling for him to settle down.

Doc Savage let them argue it out.

Finally, Big Neck settled down. Nobody other than he wanted a fight, it seemed.

Big Neck reluctantly returned to his place and jammed pieces of seared coon into his mouth, then decided that Red Snake, the sub-chief who had bargained for his freedom, had enjoyed the limelight long enough. He got up and shoved the man aside, taking his place at the council fire.

That seemed to satisfy Big Neck's injured ego.

A peace pipe was produced. The red catlinite pipe was of the "acorn" type—very short with a big center bowl. Dried tobacco was stuffed into the bowl and ignited. Red Snake took a few puffs, then passed it around.

Ordinarily, Doc Savage did not take tobacco in any form. Under the circumstances, he allowed himself a few puffs. Monk seemed to enjoy his share when the pipe came into his hands. Big Neck took one grudging inhalation, and passed the aromatic calumet to the next man.

The white captive was not invited to partake of the solemn ceremony.

Eventually, the peace pipe found its way back to Red Snake, closing the ceremony.

At that point, Doc Savage stood up and announced, "It is time for us to return to our lodge among the stars."

Big Neck growled, "It would be well that you did so."

It sounded like a threat and probably was one.

With appropriate farewells, Doc Savage took his ransomed captive and turned to go.

No one followed them.

Monk looked over his shoulder a time or two, but saw no signs of pursuit.

All seemed to be concluding well when a commotion stirred in the forest. They wheeled, halted.

OUT of the woods charged a familiar, if unexpected and distressing, sight.

Trotting up on his dog-like legs, fabulous ears outspread, scrawny spinal bumps showing, came Habeas Corpus the pig!

Hard on his heels was a black bear, running on all fours. The bear appeared to be gaining.

"Blazes!" exploded Monk. "How the heck did you get here!"

Doc Savage stepped up, and began pegging some of the glass marbles that contained his special anesthetic gas. One struck the bruin on the tip of his long black snout, where it shattered.

The bear stumbled, actually turned a kind of somersault as it fell asleep in mid-stride, momentum sending it sliding along even after consciousness departed. The creature came to rest on its back, belly heaving as it breathed. It slept soundly.

The anesthetic gas dissipated almost as fast as it had vaporized—a property that kept it from affecting anyone standing away from it.

Squeaking shrilly, Habeas rushed up and sprang into the burly chemist's clamping arms.

Monk demanded, "How is this possible? Did the others follow us?"

"No," said Doc. "Habeas must have rushed the house and gotten as far as the porch when the dwelling removed itself from its foundation. No doubt the shoat's senses were overwhelmed by the ordeal of the trip. He must have come to and followed our scent."

"Well, hog, you're comin' back with us," squeaked Monk.

At that juncture, Big Neck came rushing up and began hectoring them and gesticulating in an accusatory fashion.

"What's he sayin'?" muttered Monk.

Doc replied, "Big Neck is insisting that we must go, but the pig has to stay."

"*What!*"

"Remember that we gave Habeas to him."

"Nothin' doing!" Monk flared.

Big Neck howled wrath. Monk opened his comically wide mouth and showed teeth that would have shamed a bull gorilla. They were very intimidating molars.

"I am afraid," said Doc, "that Big Neck will not take no for an answer."

"Yes," seconded Johnny. "He is very insistent."

"That thick-necked tomahawk tosser will get Habeas over my dead body," growled Monk.

"Settle down," admonished Doc. "Let me handle this."

Doc Savage turned to the others—for by now the other Iowans had trotted up—and made his case.

Big Neck made his in expository language, accompanied by expansive gestures. He pounded his chest for emphasis.

The Iowans, having patiently heard both parties, sided with their chief.

"They are insisting that Habeas remain behind," translated Doc.

"Never!" bellowed Monk.

"It will be war if we do not acquiesce," warned Doc. "Big Neck's pride has been injured. He is spoiling for a fight."

"I ain't doin' it!" yelled Monk, small eyes stricken.

Doc Savage went to Monk and laid a firm hand on one apish shoulder.

"Leave him," he said earnestly. "We will come back for Habeas before anything dire can befall. It is the only sensible recourse we have."

Face flushing, Monk Mayfair reluctantly set Habeas onto the ground.

Under his breath, he hissed, "Shoo. Scat. Or you're breakfast bacon."

Habeas needed no further encouragement. He fled, ears flying outward like pink fleshy wings.

But Big Neck was ready. He flung himself in the direction of Habeas's curled tail and tackled the squealing porker to the ground, much like a halfback throws himself upon the pigskin football.

Howling, Monk leaped up. Doc got in his way, blocking him.

The homely chemist jumped up and down, raging like a Congo gorilla.

In a test of sheer strength, Doc Savage and Monk Mayfair were not equals. But Monk's strength was born of sheer rage and desperation. He was no pushover.

It looked as if the two men were going to have to battle it out.

They circled one another and Doc shifted around to conceal his left hand, which stole into a pocket. Bronze fingers emerged, holding one of the tiny liquid-filled glass balls Doc usually carried. He broke this. Noticing this, Johnny held his breath, as did Doc. Monk did not.

Overcome by the invisible, odorless vapor, Monk abruptly collapsed on his feet.

Johnny murmured, "A calamitous gaseous ambuscade."

Doc Savage bent down and lifted the slumbering chemist off the ground. Monk weighed about two hundred and fifty pounds, much of it muscle, yet the bronze man picked him up without outward strain.

Without a word, he walked off, Johnny guiding the ransomed captive, while Habeas Corpus kicked sharp hooves and fought in vain to free himself from the clutches of his gleeful captor.

Chapter XIX
THE UNEXPECTED COLUMBUS

THE VACANT LOT was flat, and a little lower than its surroundings. The rain had turned it into a lake about ankle deep. Gulliver shuffled through it on hands and knees, a dark shape in the lightning. The rain flogged him. He kept the revolver above the water with one hand, holding Cass' hat around it to keep it as dry as possible, which might be an unnecessary precaution so far as he knew since he had only read somewhere that cartridges sometimes didn't explode after being immersed.

There had been no car attached to the gray trailer when he had followed Ivan Cass to the vehicle. One was hooked to it now. A coupé—small, black, and it was either new or the rain was making it look shiny.

The trailer's color interested him. Gray, a mud gray. Exactly the same hue as the truck driven by the Silent Saints who were carrying the weird individual who resembled the historical Christopher Columbus.

Gull looked for a dog, but there was no dog. Listening in the rain uproar accomplished little, but he kept his eyes open in the lightning flashes. He saw no one.

Windows of the trailer were closed, but splinters of light indicated illumination inside. Gull got close beside it, and found the door. He knocked twice. He coughed. He knocked once again. It was the signal he had heard Cass use. He opened the door and followed the revolver inside.

The small man with the hound-voice and the others sat quite still on folding chairs and at the compact table.

Gulliver thought—now to get their hands up—

They lifted their hands.

Gull stiffened. He hadn't told them... But of course it was the natural thing for them to get their hands up.

He'd make them turn around. The psychological effect of a gun at the back was greater....

They turned around.

Gulliver's eyes narrowed, his lips pulled a little off his teeth, and he felt an absurd tightness up and down his back. They couldn't be reading his mind like that! Gull was a magician, dealing in legerdemain. Creating the impossible, the incredible. But all his effects were mechanical, based on speed, trickery and misdirection, and like most magicians, he held no brief whatever in the genuineness of mediums, clairvoyants, spiritualists, mind-readers, or the rest of that ilk. He did not believe in extrasensory perception.

"Stay like that!" Gulliver ordered grimly.

There should be a rope or a clothes line around the trailer. He roved his green eyes, saw none, but noted a seat-locker, rather large, across the forward end of the trailer. He concluded to back up and open the locker on the chance that....

"There's a rope in that cupboard by your elbow," the hound-voiced little man said.

Gulliver, growing tighter all over, felt as if the water soaking his clothing had become very cold. The impossibility of the evidence occurring before his eyes appalled him, hurtled with stunning force against his smug platform of conviction that all things are of the body and reality. He felt utterly shaken, confounded by the incredible, but growing, conviction that these men were actually receptive to his own thoughts. The structure of facts which he had erected—there had been good motives for the slaying of Box Daniels and the telegraph operator—had been menaced by the impossibility that Christopher Columbus, discoverer of America, was somehow alive, but he thoroughly believed there was a sensible explanation for that, even the grisly one that the girl, Saint Pete, was unbalanced. But this new development threatened to demolish the sanity of things, to scatter and confuse with impossibility.

"Where'd you get that gun?" the hound-voiced midget asked, booming.

It was Cass's gun, of course.

"Cass carried blanks in his gun," the small man yelled triumphantly.

Gulliver glanced down involuntarily at the gun—and a folding chair hit him.

A MAN to the right of the group had thrown the chair. One to the left drew a gun. Spun half around by the chair, Gull saw the gun coming out, saw also other hands stealing for pockets. Gull dived out through the door, whanging it shut behind him.

Whirling, he exploded his gun at the trailer. The sides were thin and let the bullet through. Someone bawled inside. They had rushed toward the door, but the bullet drove them back.

"One of the blanks!" Gull yelled. "Here's some more!"

He put two more bullets into the thin skin of the trailer. His breath came and went with whizzings through his teeth. He felt conscious of the hardness of his muscles, but his mind was detached from all fright for the moment, dulled by the potent drug of intense anger.

Lead came out of the trailer. The shots bumped hollowly inside. The bullets, after they were outside, made about the sounds that a man with pneumonia makes when coughing. Their menace made Gulliver change position, and when he stopped, it occurred to him that if they were really mind-readers, they could tell where he was. Evidently, this was not the case, because only one slug came close.

"Throw them guns out or I'll make a sieve out of that thing!" Gull roared.

Even then, no unusual amount of lead came in his direction. In the trailer, they couldn't locate his voice accurately. He waited. No guns were thrown out. He worked around in front, so his lead would range the length of the trailer, but there was a crash on the side as a window was broken, then the thump of a man hitting the ground. A gun banged from beside the window by which they were leaving. Thunder rumbled, and lightning gushed through the rain. Gull saw the men, fired at them. They shot back.

Gull turned and ran in the darkness. The capture attempt had flopped. The thing to do now was get the girl, Cass and Spook Davis and leave this vicinity.

Gull ran toward where he had left Spook. And rapid footsteps came to meet him. He halted.

"Hold it!"

Spook Davis puffed, "I heard yelling and thought maybe—"

Gun noise thumped and several bullets searched for their voices.

"They're *shooting!*" Spook croaked. "Holy Houdini, I thought it was thunder!" He ran wildly, not back in the direction from which he had come, but off to the right, his thoughts only of getting away from the terror of guns.

The big voice of the little man bawled angrily, ordering his men to rush Gulliver. They did this enthusiastically, shooting, waving the beams of powerful flashlights. Gull retreated, dodging off in the direction Spook Davis had taken.

Then Ivan Cass began to yell, great whooping shouts which carried to the lot where the trailer stood. His men heard him and ran toward him. Gull raced with them. Their flashlights picked him up, and their lead drove him to one side again, kept him from reaching Cass and the girl before they did.

Desperate, Gulliver doubled back and sprinted through the rain and storm noise to the trailer. The door stood open, and he dived through it. He was hunting another gun—he had fired this one five times, and it only held five cartridges.

Inside, the trailer was a surprising wreck. Someone had torn the table from its fastenings, window glass was over the floor, and bullet holes were rimmed with splinters, leaking stuffing out of upholstery. Gulliver was lucky and wrenched open a tall locker beside the door which held a repeating shotgun and a broom. He pulled back the slide a little and a dark blue shell cocked up at him.

Leaving the trailer, he splashed rapidly to the small coupé, opened the door and stood beside it, holding it open, resting the shotgun inside, out of the rain. He used his other hand and located the light switch. He waited. The lights were pointed toward the street, the direction by which Cass and his men would return....

When he heard them, he turned on the lights, made out their dim figures clearly enough to know Saint Pete was not in the lead, then pumped three charges out of the shotgun. The men yelled and cursed and shot, then ran away. He waited for them to return....

They did not come back.

GULLIVER waited beside the coupé for a long time, listening, expecting an attack. The loudness of the storm decreased, and the violence went out of the rain, although it continued to pour down heartily. He saw lights come on in three houses two blocks distant—they were the nearest houses—and the residents looked out of the windows, one of them coming out on his porch. They looked and listened; after the thunder cracked a few times, they went back inside, evidently concluding that was what had made the racket.

Waiting drained from Gull Greene some of the anger that had made him, he thought to himself, go through the gunfight like a veteran. He jammed his back to the car and no longer kept the shotgun inside out of the rain, but held it tight and ready.

When Spook Davis called softly, he all but fired.

"They gug-gone?" Spook wanted to know.

Apparently, they had, for Gull and Spook crouched for many minutes and heard nothing but the rain, and the occasional lightning, distant now, showed nothing. Cass was back with his men, and they had Saint Pete again. Gull made his jaw muscles ache pulling his teeth together. He and Spook Davis were almost back to where they had started.

"We sure had us a streak of luck, didn't we?" Spook muttered.

Gulliver asked, "You hurt anywhere?"

"My heart won't ever be the same again."

Gulliver considered. "Stick here."

"Alone?" Spook gasped. "They may come back!"

Gull moved off into the night, hunting, but he located no one, although he roamed for fully half an hour. He ventured downtown, which was reckless, but saw no sign of Cass, the small man with the big voice, Saint Pete, or the other men, the mind-readers—if they were mind-readers. Sight of a State Highway Patrol car in front of a restaurant robbed the downtown district of its charm. He went back to the lot and the trailer, noting as he approached that things seemed quiet.

Spook Davis was not in sight.

"Spook!" Gull called.

"Come in out of the rain and see what I found in the big locker in the end of this thing," Spook shouted from inside the trailer.

"See what?'

"It may be hard to believe," Spook Davis said, "but Christopher Columbus is in here."

Chapter XX

THE HOUSE TERROR

DURING THE DIFFICULT march, Johnny Littlejohn was interrogating the ransomed white man.

"What is your name, fellow?"

"Herman. Herman Bunderson."

"You are the inventor of the—"

The man shook his head violently. "No. I am not. I merely inherited the house. My grandfather, Method Gibbs, built the Time House, built it in the solitude of the forest and let the woods grow up around it so that civilization would not disturb it. He was a kind of a hermit. He died before he could finish experimenting with it."

"Where do you fit into this picture?" asked Doc.

"I inherited the house, as I said. And with it my grandfather's papers and complete instructions for the operation of the mechanism. I soon realized its potential and decided to use it to turn a profit."

"A reasonable expectation," mused Johnny.

By now Habeas' squawling had abated. Or was the frightened shoat simply too far back in the woods to be heard?

"What if they slaughter him?" asked Johnny of Doc.

"They have just eaten breakfast. Habeas will no doubt be saved for a feast."

"He's on the lean side," Johnny pointed out. "Not much meat to go around."

"Big Neck has been reunited with his warriors," added Doc. "They will have a feast. That gives us a few hours to work things out."

"What happened to him?" Herman Bunderson asked of Doc Savage, indicating insensate Monk Mayfair, draped over one brawny bronze shoulder.

"Anesthetic gas. He will come around soon enough."

Bunderson swallowed, making his prominent Adam's apple bob. "Thank you for coming back for me."

"It was the sensible thing to do," said Doc casually, as if it were a small favor. "Continue with your story."

"It is incredible," warned Bunderson. "You may not believe much of it."

"We are Twentieth Century men walking through Nineteenth Century Missouri," reminded Johnny. "Of course we will believe you."

"There is more to this story than Big Neck. Much more."

"We are very interested in hearing it," encouraged Doc.

Herman Bunderson was silent for a very long time. Then he spoke.

"What if I told you that Christopher Columbus was alive in our time?"

Doc Savage halted. His trilling began, subtle at first, but rising in cadence like agitated cicadas stirring to life. The low, indefinable sound caused Herman Bunderson to inspect his gangling person for inquisitive bees.

Setting down Monk Mayfair, Doc faced Bunderson, his golden eyes becoming very animated.

"Speak plainly," he suggested. His voice was strange, metallic, almost brittle.

"Big Neck was not the first person conveyed from the historic past to the Twentieth Century," Bunderson said flatly.

Johnny Littlejohn became strangely excited, so much so he forgot to formulate any of his amazing jawbreaker words. "Do you mean to tell us that the discoverer of America is alive in our era?"

"I am saying exactly that. I can't prove that the man I speak of is actually Columbus, but I am convinced that he is the famous historical figure."

Turning to Doc, Johnny said, "We must return to our time as quickly as possible. I must meet this man. There are so many unanswered questions—"

Doc Savage cut him off with a wave of his hand.

"There is still the matter of Monk and Habeas."

Johnny got himself composed with difficulty. "Of course. What is your plan?"

"I would awaken Monk, but he would be difficult to control. You remain here, guarding him."

Addressing Herman Bunderson, Doc asked, "How long until the house returns to its own time?"

"When did you arrive?"

Doc glanced at the position of the rising sun. "Two hours ago."

"In that case, you have fifty minutes."

A flicker of concern touched Doc's metallic features.

"Then there is no time to waste," he rapped. "Johnny, if I do not return in time, revive Monk with this"—the bronze man pressed into Johnny's long-fingered hand a vial of his powerful chemical restorative—"then enter the house."

"What about you?"

"Send the house back again," continued Doc, "and I will catch it the next time it appears in this year." He was so matter-of-fact about it that the bronze giant might have been talking about catching a later train.

Johnny nodded. He appeared fidgety—a certain sign that he was uncomfortable with the bronze man's plan. But he said nothing. He trusted Doc Savage implicitly.

Doc then left the forest path and began moving from tree

to tree in a manner that brought to mind a stalking woodland animal. He was soon obscured by the close-packed arboreal trunks.

After Doc was lost from sight, Johnny faced Herman Bunderson. "Tell me more about the man you believe to be Christopher Columbus...."

DOC SAVAGE filtered through the woods on bare feet. He had unlaced his shoes and hung them about his neck by tying the shoelaces together, preferring to move with the greatest stealth.

He found the river and waded in. This way, he left no track.

Wise in the ways of the Iowan tribe—at least, as its lore had come down to the Twentieth Century—the bronze man knew that after breakfast, they would bathe in the nearest body of water.

There were several hereabouts. Bear Creek. Titus Creek. The Chariton River. The latter seemed to be the most profitable place to start.

Wading for a time, Doc scanned the surroundings, sniffing the air constantly. He was as likely to scent a body of Big Necks as spot them from a distance, and he had no appetite to face Iowan arrows.

The bronze man's first surmise proved to be inaccurate. Nowhere along the banks of the creek did he come upon bathing Indians.

When he reached a point upwind of the Big Neck camp, Doc left the water and began moving through the forest. Here hickory and walnut trees seemed most plentiful. They were full of bushy-tailed squirrels, busy making nests.

A few scolded the big bronze man as he passed in their midst, but there was no helping that. Nor much harm in it, either. Squirrels would scold a beaver as readily as a foraging bear. The ruckus would not alarm the camp.

Finally, Doc reached the encampment. He watched from

concealment of a clump of thick buckbrush.

Had this been an Iowan homestead, women would have been left behind to guard the food stores, but Big Neck had led a small hunting party into Missouri, far from their home preserves. So there were no women.

The camp appeared deserted.

Doc stole up, his shoes knocking softly about his neck.

The pig, Habeas, had a distinct odor all his own. Monk the chemist kept him in a mud wallow back in his Wall Street penthouse. The wallow was scented, the better to make Habeas fit for human company.

Doc's sensitive nostrils picked up Habeas' perfumed odor. He moved in that direction, soon came upon the ungainly shoat.

Habeas had been staked to the ground, a rawhide thong looped about one rear leg. He was attempting to chew through it.

Stealing up behind the busy porker, the bronze giant clamped a cabled hand over the porker's long snout to shut off any outcry of surprise.

"Hush, Habeas," he whispered.

Overcome, the pig subsided.

Doc produced his knife, thus freeing the pig.

Cradling Habeas in both arms, Doc retreated to the river.

It had been surprisingly easy to recover the pig. But it was a long swing back to the strange house that moved through time.

Once in the water, Doc surged downstream, his muscular legs churning. The water slowed him down, but he did not wish to risk discovery.

Nor did he have to worry about that.

Far downstream, the bronze man caught the smell of something burning.

Golden eyes sweeping the tree tops, he sought its origin.

Burning wood produces distinctive odors. Dried oak smells a certain way, wet timber another. The smell of a burning house generates an unmistakable tang, partly because along with the wood burns paint, plaster and other man-made substances.

Acrid smoke reaching his lungs was unquestionably that of a burning domicile.

Wasting no time, Doc Savage plunged for the embankment and, pig tucked under one massive arm, raced for the weird old Victorian house.

To his alert ears came war whoops and the sounds of men in contention.

Fixing those sounds, Doc charged in that direction. He broke out of the trees to spy a party of Big Necks sending a sparkling cloud of arrows into the roof and outer walls of the overly ornate dwelling.

On the porch hunkered Johnny, the temporal experimenter, Herman Bunderson, and the unconscious Monk.

Big Neck himself was leading the war party, his scalplock jumping about his shaven skull like an excited thing.

Pointing in the direction of Doc Savage, he let out a howl, followed by a ripping string of words.

Translated, they meant that he had been justified in leading his scout party back to watch the white men depart. Their bronze chief had not been among them. This meant treachery.

The kicking pig in the bronze giant's arms was proof of that charge.

There was no use arguing the point, Doc realized. He had been caught red-handed.

Doc came lunging out of the woods and the Big Necks turned, began loosing ordinary arrows in his specific direction.

Dodging and weaving, Doc Savage avoided the first wave of flint-tipped missiles.

He was forced to retreat a ways, then sweep around, using the more substantial tree trunks for shields. They began collecting quivering arrows. The repetitive sound of their thudding was unpleasant.

The open space between himself and the looming house was

deep. It would be difficult to cross safely under fire, Doc judged.

From the porch, Johnny was calling, "Doc—hurry!"

The bronze man's eyes went to the morning sky. He saw the position of the sun, and instantly calculated the time.

The house was scheduled to lurch forward to the Twentieth Century any moment now.

Big Neck wasn't waiting for that. He had fashioned a firebrand out of a bough of hickory and a bunch of dried grass. With a flint striker, he got it blazing.

Using this, the Iowa chief was lighting the back of the house where those waiting on the porch could not see him.

Doc called out, "Behind you! Torch!"

Hearing this, Johnny looked stricken. His eyes widened. He was frantically waving Doc to come ahead.

Then the burning beet-colored domicile vanished from sight—leaving only a sharp spiral of smoke that behaved as if alive in the inrushing breeze that sought to fill a sudden vacuum.

Soon enough, the curl of smoke melted away like a gray ghost dissolving into eternity.

Chapter XXI

FRIGHTENED FAT MAN

THUNDER GRUNTED WEAKLY in the distance and the last leakage of the rainstorm came splashing down on Gulliver Greene as he stood outside the trailer door, listening and staring toward the nearest houses of the small northeast Missouri farm town of La Plata.

"I tell you we've got that long-haired zombie!" Spook Davis yelled excitedly inside the trailer.

The stormy night held no trace of Ivan Cass or his mind-readers—if they really were mind-readers—led by the little fellow with the big voice. They must have left town, taking Saint Pete, the puzzling redheaded girl who was afraid to tell anything. The little Missouri town slept peacefully in the wet night.

"It's Christopher Columbus, all right!" Spook whooped. "He's sure a zombie, if you ask me."

Gulliver said, "I don't feel ripe for any more crazy stuff."

He was not, for some reason, particularly anxious to climb into the trailer and look. He felt confused by things happening which were apparently impossible. Cass' men seemingly were mind-readers, for it was their mind-reading that had been partially responsible for Gulliver's disaster when he tried to capture them. Gull did not believe in mind-readers. Gulliver Greene—stage name The Great Gulliver—did not believe in mediums, clairvoyants, or crystal gazers; he took no stock at all in numerology, astrology, or palmistry. He was convinced he could duplicate anything they could do with cleverness, just as he made the impossible happen with magical trickery. Anyone who believed such pap was weak in the head.

But Cass' mind-readers had baffled him. And there was Christopher Columbus. Harvell Braggs, the bombastic fat man, insisted his Columbus artifacts had been stolen by a man who was the genuine Christopher Columbus who discovered America. Saint Pete had said likewise. Such stuff was harder to credit than the belief that there might be genuine mind-readers.

Confusing also was his inability as yet to find out just what Ivan Cass and his mind-readers were doing that was so big and profitable that they had slain old Box Daniels to keep him from divulging its nature. Tried to kill Gulliver and Spook, too, merely because they were trying to ferret out the truth. And baffling likewise were the Silent Saints, their so-called Promised Land, and their connection with the affair. The Promised Land was situated near Lake of the Ozarks, in south Missouri. He knew that much, at least, because it said so in poor Box Daniels' telegram which Gulliver had in his pocket.

Gulliver shook his head and said, "Maybe you should be cutting paper dolls, Greene." He got into the trailer, and was tall enough that he had to duck as he did so.

"Meet Christopher Columbus," Spook Davis said dryly.

CHRISTOPHER COLUMBUS lay on the floor. He was dressed in plain coarse dark burlap cloth, and the suit had black buttons and was too big for him. He was a long thing with lots of bones, a thinly ascetic face, a high forehead, a lean and firm mouth. His wealth of brown hair lent a queer quality of antiquity to his quaint appearance. The eyes were brown. Open, fixed and staring. They were weird eyes, or rather, they were in a glassy condition. The entire visage of the man was unpleasantly blood-less, as were his long-fingered hands.

"Uh—hello," Gulliver said tentatively.

The pale man on the floor did not respond with movement

or sound. Except for the stirring of his chest, he looked dead.

"He's not much of a conversationalist," Spook Davis said. "I can't get a peep out of him."

Gulliver thoughtfully strained his white hair with his fingers—the hair seemed to contrast more weirdly than usual with his young, freckled and moderately handsome face and striking green eyes. His soaked clothing clung to his long body, making him seem thin instead of just wirily muscled.

"It's crazy to think this is Christopher Columbus, discoverer of America," he said.

"Pal, I've seen plenty of pictures of Columbus in history books," Spook grunted, "and this staring zombie here sure looks like the genuine article."

"What is wrong with him?"

Spook shrugged. "Search me."

"You didn't hit him with anything?"

"Not me. I just found him in that locker and pulled him out."

The locker, across the forward end of the trailer, was there as a combination seat, bunk and storage space. The lid stood open, and in the locker a cotton comforter and a pillow made a pallet. Gull looked inside it, moved the pillow and comforter, but found nothing and came back to get down on his knees beside Christopher Columbus. He held Columbus' thin wrist, then put it down.

"There's a pulse," he said.

He suddenly grabbed the stringy flesh of Columbus' forearm and pinched it. The pinch must have been painful, but Columbus did not move, did not show in any way that he felt the pain.

"Could be he's fallen into some kind of a spell," Spook offered.

"Spells are for witches," snapped Gull.

"Say!" gasped Spook. "Maybe he's some kind of a living dead man. That would account for him being here about four hundred years after he is supposed to have died."

"Don't make up any ideas like that," Gull advised Spook.

"This thing is dizzy enough as it is."

He stared at Christopher Columbus until he began to have an eerie feeling, an absurd impression that something must be amiss with a mentality—his own—which would for an instant entertain the idea that Christopher Columbus, discoverer of America, might be this fellow—alive four hundred years after his time.

"Hey!" Gull shook Columbus. "Can you hear me? Bat your eyes if you can."

Columbus did not respond.

Gull went through the pockets of the dark burlap suit Columbus wore. They were empty. Gull rolled back the man's eyelids to study the pupils of the silent, motionless figure. He tried the pulse again, then picked up one of the legs and let it fall; it fell as slackly as so much meat on a butcher shop scales.

"Drugged," Gull decided. "That's my guess."

SPOOK DAVIS pulled in a great, shaky breath, wiped his forehead and began to grin ruefully. "Drugged, eh? Boy, this had me going. I was beginning to think he was maybe some kind of a half-alive mummy."

"Where's a rope?" Gull asked.

They had to hunt for the rope, and in the process came across a locker containing several suits of clothing, dark and plain, fashioned of coarse burlap. When they found the rope, a long thin line, Gull tossed turns of it about Christopher Columbus and began tying him securely. Columbus remained as quiet as death, with his deer-hued eyes wide open.

"Why do that?" Spook wanted to know.

"I'm no doctor. He may be faking, instead of drugged. We don't want him running off on us."

Gull returned to the clothing locker. He got out the garments, held them up to the light, exhibiting their plainness, the coarseness of the dark burlap clothing. He glanced at Spook Davis meaningly.

"I get it," grunted Spook. "The Silent Saints wore plain stuff like that."

That was what Gull was thinking. He and Spook Davis had seen three of the Silent Saints in a truck earlier in the night, and the Silent Saints had worn clothing such as this. Christopher Columbus, in the back of the truck at the time, had looked as helpless and trance-like as he seemed now, Gull thought grimly. But now he was here in this trailer, which probably meant that Cass had seized him, as he had seized Saint Pete. And there was a connection between Saint Pete and Christopher Columbus, for Saint Pete had refused to answer Gull's questions, saying that to do so would mean Christopher Columbus would be killed.

"Columbus, here, is wearing another suit made of this gunnysack material," Spook reminded. "Figure that means anything?"

Gull frowned. "The whole crowd of them may belong to the Silent Saints."

They stripped off their wet clothing. Gull Greene's body without clothes was more striking; the distinct presence of each muscle, the symmetrical blending of the whole, would have interested an artist. The legs were not too thin; the stomach was flat, with visible muscles. The body was that of a man under thirty, despite the snow white hair.

They put on the burlap clothing they had found. It was dry. They became, then, exactly alike but for one detail—Spook Davis' hair was not prematurely white, but brick red.

They were looking at each other when Gull Greene seized the shotgun, knocked the door open and pitched outside. He landed on his knees and remained down, listening.

THE RAIN that remained made some sound on the roof and sides of the trailer; the water running off the vehicle and pouring down the gutters of the nearby street was even more noisy. The thunder seemed very far away now, and no lightning of any consequence had happened for some minutes.

Feet made slogging sounds in the soft vacant lot earth as someone tried to ease away in the night—the sound Gulliver had heard inside.

Gull cocked the shotgun. "Hold it!"

There was silence. Gull had transferred the flashlight to this suit, and he got it out, but did not turn it on. It might draw a bullet. He was tense, thinking what fools they had been to remain around the trailer. Cass and his men might come back for Columbus. And the State Highway Patrol still wanted Gull and Spook on suspicion of murdering old Box Daniels and the La Plata telegrapher. The officers might visit the trailer.

An unexcited, rather deep voice spoke.

"Let us trust this situation can be terminated without unpleasant consequences to myself, and explanations satisfactory to all concerned arrived at," the voice said bombastically.

Gull whitened the speaker with the flashlight beam. The fellow was a big cone of flesh topped by unruly black hair, small twinkling eyes and a mouth which contained a bedraggled cigar. His chins flopped down over his collar, and he was using one hand to hold his belt in place over his enormous stomach. He lifted the other hand slowly to shade his eyes from the light.

Gull said, "Anyone else around, Braggs?"

"I sincerely hope not, and I do not think—"

"Come in out of the rain," Gull invited tensely.

Harvell Braggs got into the trailer—the trailer grunted on its springs and swayed. Gull followed, then glanced about quickly, for Christopher Columbus was not in sight.

Spook Davis caught Gulliver's eye, winked, and jerked his thumb slightly at the locker to indicate he had hidden Christopher Columbus in the place where they had found him.

"Young man," said Harvell Braggs. "I am convinced that—" He stopped, blinked his small eyes at each of them in turn. Then he took the cigar out of his mouth.

"Gracious!" he exclaimed. "Which—what—you look just alike, and I must say I never saw such a resemblance, and if you will kindly tell me—"

"Greene." Gulliver pointed at his own chest. "Now shoot your story."

"I am convinced that—"

"How come you are not at your hotel, Braggs?"

"I shall explain that very simply by stating that I became suspicious of my casual acquaintance, Ivan Cass, and watched him. Cass left the hotel, and I followed him, with the result that I witnessed a terrific fight in the night, and became quite frightened, hiding out until a few moments ago before I dared venture close in an effort to find out—"

"Whoa—period." Gulliver frowned at him. "What did you think you would learn?"

"Young man, I have told you my valuable Columbus relics were stolen. I am trying to find them. That, briefly, is the fact."

GULLIVER, deciding to search the enormously fat man, tried to hand the shotgun to Spook Davis, who recoiled wildly and refused to take it, his lips apart and his eyes staring with his fear of firearms. Gull promised profanely, and at some length, to some day tie Spook Davis to a tree and fire off cannons until he was broken of gun-shyness. Then he put the shotgun down, got a butcher knife out of the galley as protection, and smacked his hands over Harvell Braggs' ponderous person. He found no weapons.

Gull opened the seat-locker and pulled Christopher Columbus out.

"Know anything about this fellow?" he asked Braggs.

Harvell Braggs made clopping sounds with his round, full-lipped mouth before he made words come. His eyes seemed to try to leap out of their fleshy sockets.

"That's the man who stole my Columbus antiques!" he yelled. "He's the one! Remember what I told you? He claimed he was Christopher Columbus, discoverer of America!"

Harvell Braggs moved closer to the locker, hitched at his

belt, and stood staring down at Columbus. He shut his eyes tightly for a moment. He grimaced. He used one hand to mash down his thick, skunk-black hair.

"I am a Columbus authority," he said slowly. "And if it were not so utterly incredible, and undoubtedly would make you think I was quite unbalanced mentally, I should say this man here is the genuine Christopher Columbus."

Chapter XXII

PANIC!

DURING THE WAIT for the unlovely Victorian home whose thick walls concealed the mechanical works of a time-traveling machine, Ham Brooks, Renny Renwick and Long Tom Roberts were forced to while away the hours.

Renny and Long Tom took it upon themselves to look into the condition of their damaged dirigible. The airship hung close to the ground, one side peppered with buckshot perforations. It was still buoyant, although barely so.

"Not so bad, after all," Long Tom observed.

Renny nodded. "She'll float once we patch her up."

They climbed into the control gondola, which tilted like a ship's deck in a rough sea. They found the patching kit, and Renny got to work. The gasbag interior was constructed in cells, like a honeycomb. Climbing into an inspection tunnel, Long Tom saw that the damaged cells could be reinflated, once patching was complete.

Ham Brooks stood watch. There being not much to do in the forest, boredom soon set in.

Fidgety due to the loss of his cane, Ham began searching for a length of hickory with which to cut a rough walking stick replacement. It would prove no substitute for the real article with its concealed blade, but the dapper lawyer did not know what to do with his manicured hands without it.

During his perambulations, Ham came upon a rock face with writing on it.

"Jove!" he breathed.

The writing was chiseled deep into granite, and appeared half-familiar. Dirt and erosion of wind and rain had softened the original incisions, so the excited lawyer used his new stick to dig at it until the lines stood out more clearly in the wan light.

Ham scanned the writing once, then again with eyes growing in wonder, and suddenly turned tail, running as fast as he could sprint.

When he arrived back at the slowly inflating airship, Ham was shouting.

"You won't believe it! I can't believe it! But it must be true. I read it with my own—"

Before Ham could get it all out, a sharp gust of air hit him in the face and the atmosphere was suddenly full of heat and smoke and confusion. Startled crows shot out of the trees.

For the blood-colored Victorian monstrosity had returned to its base, back end blazing like a bonfire.

Ham's eyes were aghast.

Then to his immense relief, figures began tumbling off the smoldering wraparound porch.

Ham began counting them. Johnny came first, dragging what appeared to be Monk Mayfair. Then a third man stumbled off. Hope flared in the elegant barrister's heart, but almost immediately died.

The new arrival was no one he recognized.

"Doc! Where is Doc!" called Ham.

Johnny turned, yelled sharply, "Help put out this infernal blaze."

The others had come running up by this time. Seeing the conflagration, they started for the fleeing figures.

Quick-thinking as ever, Ham snapped, "Wait!"

"For what?" demanded Renny, hesitating. "The place to burn down?"

"If we trip the electric eye," Ham warned, "the house will return to the past! That is why."

"So?" flared Long Tom.

Ham shook his hickory stick angrily. "We have to put out that fire before that can happen. Doc is trapped in the past!"

"It's true!" Johnny put in.

Renny grunted. His long face grew stricken. The wisdom of Ham's warning had struck him hard.

While they foundered, physically and mentally, Johnny tried to get everyone organized.

"Find water. We have to save that building!"

Renny groaned like a stricken mastodon. "The nearest water is over a mile away, and we have no buckets!"

The house continued burning, but miraculously, it did not vanish.

"Electric eye mechanism must have malfunctioned, or something," Renny said dully.

Ham was the one to come up with a solution to the blazing calamity.

"Our dirigible! It carries auxiliary water ballast."

The dapper lawyer rushed for the airship, which was floating tethered to a tree, and got the engines going. Renny and Long Tom undid the grappling hook anchor, and the dirigible lifted free, motors moaning.

Ham guided the gasbag until it stood hovering over the roof, which was of slate and therefore not burning. He grasped a lever, releasing a cascade of sheeting water.

It struck the corner that was most fully engulfed and, miracle of miracles, quenched the worst of the greedy flames in one watery swoop.

Rushing up, the others began beating the smoldering siding with their coats.

It took a great deal of furious action, but they got the remaining flames whipped.

STANDING around, eyes dull with shock, faces blackened by soot, they regarded the travesty of a house that had emerged from the past in flames.

Johnny recounted the events leading up to the conflagration. He employed small words so that everyone could follow him.

At the conclusion of the breathless recital, Renny wondered aloud, "Do you reckon the time-defeating gadget still works?"

"I know it does not," declared Ham in a stricken voice. He had hooked a tree and climbed down the line to the ground, leaving the tiny airship moored safely.

"What do you mean?"

Ham pointed back into the woods. "Going for a walk, I found a rock face in which was chiseled a message in stone."

"Go on," invited Long Tom.

"The writing was Mayan."

"The Mayans didn't get this far north," Johnny insisted.

"I know that!" snapped Ham. "The message was from Doc Savage. He said he was stranded in the past."

Silence held them all for a time.

In that interval, Johnny remembered the restorative Doc Savage had given him. He went over to Monk Mayfair, and uncorked the vial beneath his broad, laboring nostrils. The snoring chemist awoke, sat up heavily, and peered around with tiny eyes that blinked dully. He began pawing at them.

"Why are my eyes burnin'?"

Renny advised, "Smoke. The old dump caught fire."

Clambering to his feet, the hairy chemist looked back at the haze-enwrapped Victorian dwelling, and muttered, "I can see that. We're back. Right?"

"Not all of us," Johnny informed him.

"Brace yourself, Monk," Ham said. "Doc is trapped in the past and we don't know if this house is fit to travel."

Monk licked suddenly dry lips. He seemed to want to speak, but his wide mouth only made gulping fish motions. He seemed at a loss for words.

Renny strode up and towered over the unfamiliar man with the long neck and straw-colored hair.

"Are you the bozo that invented this contraption?"

"No," said Herman Bunderson. "I am merely the man who inherited it. I know very little about how the machinery operates, only how to make it run."

Renny gave the man a hard shove. "Well, get in there and give it your best shot."

THE INTERIOR of the Victorian was too smoky to permit habitation for very long. They all pitched in and got the windows open, employing their coats to fan the bad air out. Ventilation helped.

Finally, they worked their way up to the conical tower room, where the gyroscopic portion of the mechanism was housed.

It had not exactly melted, but in places, vacuum tubes were blistered, and charred wires sagged sadly.

"Don't look good," Renny rumbled. He turned to Long Tom. "What do you say?"

The pale electrical wizard began picking through the melted mess, and the look on his face was not encouraging. He inspected the thing for several minutes, then let out a leaky sigh of resignation.

"Some of this stuff might be replaceable, but I don't know about these crystals."

"In other words—" prompted Renny.

"In other words, I'm not sure Doc Savage himself could fix it."

Gloom pervaded the smoky interior. They filed out of the house to get fresh air into their lungs while they considered options.

Herman Bunderson offered a modicum of solace.

"If it is any consideration," he said, "the damaged portion of the device merely governs where in time and space the house lands. The displacement circuitry is built into the flooring and walls. It may not have been damaged."

"Which means what?" asked Monk.

"The house may yet be able to travel through time unimpaired."

"Without the navigational controls to make sure it goes back to 1829," grumbled Long Tom, "what good does that do us?"

"I do not know. But it means the situation is not entirely hopeless."

Ham Brooks had rejoined them by now.

"I think you all should read what Doc Savage carved into the stone," he suggested.

Reluctantly, for there was nothing they could do of immediate usefulness, they followed Ham into the woods.

As they walked along, the dapper lawyer suddenly remembered something.

"What became of Habeas Corpus?"

Monk grunted, "Big Neck probably ate him by now."

"The contrary," countered Johnny. "Doc had rescued Habeas. He was bringing the pig back when the Big Necks set fire to the house."

"Did you hear that, Monk?" asked Ham. "Habeas is alive in the past!"

Monk refused to be comforted. "That means Habeas died probably a hundred years ago—along with Doc Savage."

The chilling thought that their bronze leader had perished almost a century before his own birth stilled their tongues.

When they reached the stone face, they saw what Ham had described.

Mayan carvings. They spelled out a simple message in the bars-and-dots number notation of the ancient people, each number corresponding to a letter in the modern English alphabet, so that the entirety of the message constituted a double code.

"Still alive in December, 1829, 5 months since burning home departed. Carry on without me. Doc."

The signature was etched in English.

Words were unnecessary. But Ham Brooks spoke them anyway.

"This is incontrovertible proof that we were unable to rescue Doc Savage. Otherwise, we would have plucked him out of his predicament before winter had set in."

THE FIVE who had first met up during the World War had been through innumerable perils and travails over the years of their association. Many times in the past, Doc Savage had been declared dead. And each time, a resurrection had appeared impossible.

Yet in every instance, the seemingly-indestructible bronze superman had resurfaced, still alive, often coming to the rescue of his beleaguered aides.

Now, it seemed that no such miracle was in the offing.

Consumed by depression, Doc's men separated, walking in different directions, as if wishing to be alone with their inconsolable thoughts.

Over an hour passed before they rendezvoused back at the still-smoky house that stood at the center of their grief, like some fantastic painted tombstone.

Ham Brooks was the first to speak.

"Doc Savage charged us with carrying on with his great work. I move that we dedicate the remainder of our lives to that cause."

Monk glowered like a gorilla. "We're givin' up on rescuin' Doc. Is that what you're sayin'?"

Long Tom shoved out his jaw. "I intended to take apart that house until I figure out what makes it tick."

Renny squinted at his big fists, as if half disbelieving he owned such freakish appendages.

"How long do you think that'll take?" he rumbled disconsolately.

Long Tom said glumly, "Months. Maybe years. It doesn't matter. I will spend the time."

"In the meanwhile, we have Doc's work to do," suggested Ham.

Johnny put in, "There is an immediate conundrum."

Ham looked at him. "Which is?"

"According to Herman Bunderson, no less a personage than Christopher Columbus is running loose in our present era," he explained.

They gawked at him.

"Try big words," Renny grunted. "Your little ones aren't making sense."

"Bunderson told me part of the story while Doc was searching for Habeas, and Monk was out cold," Johnny said firmly.

They went and collected Herman Bunderson, who had not wandered far.

The man was reluctant to tell his story, but Monk Mayfair took hold of his shirt collar and shook him a time or two, dislodging his reluctance.

"I inherited the house from my grandfather, Method," he began. "With it came a journal that told the story of the construction of the Chronodomus."

"The which?" demanded Renny.

"That was what he called it."

"It is Latin for 'Time House'," supplied Johnny.

Bunderson continued with his story.

"I experimented with the property and discovered that it worked. Then I thought to myself that there must be a way to make money with the discovery. My first thought was to hire it out. There is a man who is a collector of antiques relating to Christopher Columbus. Harvell Braggs is his name. I went to him with my story. Naturally, he scoffed."

"Naturally," said Long Tom dryly.

"Braggs lived in the West Indies, where Columbus made his first landings in the New World. I thought to myself that I could prove my value by going back to the time of Columbus and bringing something forward that would prove my claim. In fact, while scoffing at me, Braggs suggested that I do exactly that. So I set out to prove it to him."

"You personally journeyed back to the time of Columbus!" Johnny exclaimed.

Bunderson nodded. "To Jamaica, to be exact. It was my first serious experiment in time traveling and I found myself in 1503 after the shipwreck of Columbus' fleet, during his fourth voyage to the New World."

"Wait a minute!" snapped Ham. "If you can leap backward in time, but not space, how did you travel to the Caribbean?"

"The house can be set up to arrive at a different location, provided the landing spot is safe and level. I traveled to the Caribbean and located a field that has been unchanged for hundreds of years. So I scheduled the house to reappear in that spot."

They all looked at him, disbelief written on their slack features.

"It worked perfectly," Bunderson continued, "thanks to the mechanical brain that governs the operation of the temporal dislocator. From there, I was able to find the encampment of Christopher Columbus and his shipwrecked men. By night, I stole into the camp and attempted to plunder some items, but I encountered an unexpected obstacle."

"Which was?" demanded Ham.

"I had no idea what Columbus looked like. I could not distinguish him from the others in the encampment, and I did not speak Spanish, or any other language Columbus knew."

Renny thumped gloomily, "After all that, you didn't find a portrait of Columbus to go by?"

Johnny interjected, "There are no authentic depictions of Christopher Columbus. None."

Renny's long perpetually mournful face grew dubious.

"It is true," Bunderson said. "No one alive knows what Columbus actually looked like."

"What about all those pictures in the history books?"

"Paintings executed years after Columbus had passed on, by artists who had never laid eyes upon the Great Navigator in the flesh," supplied Johnny.

"So what happened?" prompted Ham.

"I was spotted. A very imposing man began chasing me, blunderbuss in hand. I fled back to the house, but he followed me in. Just as I was actuating the return to our time, he came bounding up into the tower room. Then we lost all vision as the Chronodomus restored me to the present.

"My sight cleared first," he continued. "Columbus had dropped his weapon. I seized it, ordered him to stand back. He fled the house, plunging into the woods."

A long silence intruded while the full import of Herman Bunderson's words sank in.

"I took his blunderbuss to Harvell Braggs and told my story. He didn't want to believe me, but the weapon convinced him. You see, it was inscribed with the name, *Don Cristóbal Colón,* which was Columbus' Spanish name. So we know that the man was in truth the actual Columbus. Braggs organized a search party, hiring a private detective named Ivan Cass to assist, but they never found him. Columbus appeared to have vanished. When Braggs began pressing me for the location of my grandfather's Chronodomus, I refused to have anything more to do with the matter."

Herman Bunderson shook himself as he sighed. "Braggs paid me off and swore me to secrecy. I took the money and went my own way."

"How long ago was this?" asked Renny.

"Two years ago. I have had no contact with Braggs in the intervening time. In that period, I have been concentrating on going back to the Nineteenth Century. There is a treasure in gold coins that was buried in these woods. It had never been found. My goal was to locate the cache. Unfortunately, during one sojourn, I encountered the Big Necks and was made captive. I tried to explain that I needed to return to my house, and that it would take me to the future. I took them to it, but they refused to release me. However, Chief Big Neck entered the house and while he was rifling it, the structure returned to the Twentieth Century, stranding me in his era, and Big Neck in mine."

"Until Doc Savage stepped in," observed Ham. "It's possibly the most bizarre account I have ever heard—in or out of a court of law. But its truthfulness cannot be gainsaid."

"What flummoxes me," boomed Renny, "is you have a machine that can jump around in history like a grasshopper, and you waste it searching for loot."

"Unquestionably dubious thinking," sniffed Johnny. "Great universities would pay a fortune to have you answer some of history's most compelling questions."

Before the bony archeologist could launch into a dry recitation of such inquiries, Monk asked, "What was the treasure?"

Bunderson told them. "Back in 1832, the friendly Fox Indians made a trip to Saint Louis to get $15,000 in gold due them for selling the La Plata area to the whites. A small war party went to collect the money and, on the way back, was waylaid by the Sac Indians. The Foxes were outnumbered. There was a bloody fight. All the Foxes were killed. However, they managed to hide the gold coins, and the victorious Sac could never find it.

"This occurred on the Chariton River, west of La Plata and somewhat south of here. At least two generations of Fox and Sac Indians returned to this site to search for the gold. There is only one authentic recovery—some boys unearthed about a thousand dollars in 1870."

"Kind of a coincidence that this joint was built close to the treasure," Monk ventured.

"Not at all. My grandfather was very interested in that gold. He built close to it, hoping to locate it, either in this era or a previous one. He was unsuccessful, of course. I have been carrying on his work." There was a trace of pride in the man's tone.

"Because of your blundering about in time," scolded Ham severely, "the world has lost a great and irreplaceable man, Doc

Savage, and one of history's most famous notables is a castaway here in our century."

Herman Bunderson hung his head in undisguised shame. "If I had any idea where Columbus is hiding, I would gladly restore him to his proper era in history."

The five Doc Savage assistants swapped strange glances. No word was spoken. None needed to be. All understood what the bronze man who had led them into countless battles would wish them to do in the present circumstances.

Long Tom spoke up. "I'd better stay here and tinker with the confounded time contraption while the rest of you run down Christopher Columbus."

They began laying plans for their first campaign without Doc Savage. It produced in them a very hollow feeling.

Chapter XXIII

LUCK, AND LEGERDEMAIN

GULLIVER PICKED UP the rope, a part of which he had used to tie Christopher Columbus. No one said anything. Gull handled the rope slowly—it was a heavy rope, evidently kept in the trailer for towing purposes. He tied a knot in the end, then made a noose, which he ran out cowboy fashion.

He flipped the noose over Harvell Braggs' plump pink hands and jerked it tight, holding the lardy man's arms to his sides.

Braggs yelled, "What—you can't—what—?"

"I'm kind of losing my temper," gritted Gull.

"You—you're insane!" Braggs howled.

"I'm afraid of that, too," admitted Gull, "if this keeps up."

Braggs began to struggle. Gull threw extra loops about him. Spook Davis helped. They all fell to the floor and ruined a camp chair, but Braggs was finally tied.

Braggs' flabby suet seemed about to burst out of his skin, "Young man, I'm determined to recover my Columbus collection. Such foolishness as this will not deter me!"

"At least it will keep you from telling the police where they can find me," Gull suggested.

Braggs roared, "Do you two scamps know where my relics can be found?"

"Bang! G-r-r-r! Boo!" barked Spook Davis.

Braggs gulped. "I say now, what provoked—"

"That's all we know about anything," Spook told him. "I

could use more words, but it wouldn't make it any clearer."

Gull lifted Harvell Braggs, grunting, deciding the man must weigh well over three hundred pounds. The fellow felt soft all the way through. He stretched him out on the bunk, then straightened his own dark clothing, which fitted about as well as a gunnysack would have fitted.

Spook squinted at Gull. "Shall we search this bombastic behemoth?"

They searched him. There was a billfold containing currency, which Spook Davis examined with the appreciative remark that here was sure, "folding money, as the feller says." The bills were large. In the pocketbook also were a number of cards from antique dealers in various parts of the United States and one from Madrid, two from Genoa, Italy, which they recalled was the birthplace of Christopher Columbus.

There was also a note, reading:

> BRAGGS:
> SEE GULLIVER GREENE, WHO IS ALSO KNOWN AS THE GREAT GULLIVER, ABOUT YOUR COLUMBUS STUFF THAT WAS TAKEN.

Harvell Braggs had shown this unsigned missive to Gull earlier in the night, explaining that it accounted for his coming to see The Great Gulliver. Why the man should get such a note, Gull couldn't understand.

"As usual, we've learned nothing," Spook complained. "What do we do next?"

Gull studied Spook Davis. "Want to give this mess up and clear out of the country?"

"Now you're talking sense, boss!" Spook declared heartily. "I'm no hero."

He sounded proud of it, rather than ashamed. Gull, recognizing some hardheaded common sense in Spook's behavior, was himself generally cautious about thrusting himself into danger.

"I'm kind of mad," Gull admitted at last.

"Eh?"

"Running wouldn't clear that murder charge against us."

Spook rubbed his jaw. "They couldn't make that stick."

Gull said, "We're going to hunt up the Promised Land of these Silent Saints and see what hatches out."

Spook groaned, "Aw—Holy Joe Dunninger, Gull—"

"You stay back here and watch our bulbous friend and this fellow who discovered America. I'll drive."

Spook Davis lifted his shoulders, and let them fall. "Why the hell don't you tell the truth, Gull?"

"Truth?"

"It's that girl!"

"You guess."

"Ah, rats on this mystery business! Say, are we leaving here, or—"

Gull said grimly, "You ride in here and watch our sleeping prize."

"Me ride—hey! Hey, we're not taking this trailer."

"We'll have to have some way to move the sleeper, so we might as well take trailer, coupé and everything."

"Will wonders never cease," Spook opined.

THE COUPÉ was black, new and efficient. It needed most of the efficiency in getting out of the muddy vacant lot. Gull turned south, drove a while, then hunted for road maps, found one, and from it learned that Lake of the Ozarks was close to a hundred and fifty miles almost directly south.

He felt no great certainty that he was making the right move. Old Box Daniels' telegram had advised that Doc Savage be asked to investigate the Silent Saints and their Promised Land located near Lake of the Ozarks, which indicated something worth looking into. Furthermore, the police were hunting for Gull and Spook in this part of Missouri. And finally, all visible leads in this direction had evaporated with the flight of Cass and his men with the girl.

Gull watched the speedometer absently. Spook Davis had hit the truth in thinking Saint Pete was the real magnet drawing Gull into the affair. The girl was in difficulties. Gull sighed, recalling some of the exquisite features of the young woman. She was, he decided several times over, something worth going to a lot of trouble for.

The trailer rumbled along behind the coupé.

The gasoline gauge showed a tank nearly full, which was just as well, or they would have to draw on Harvell Braggs' large bankroll. Gull and Spook Davis were flatly broke, for the police had taken their slender stake.

The coupé and trailer approached a brightly lighted highway intersection outside the town of Macon, but got through without anything happening. It was still raining a little.

There was a dash clock on the coupé. It said the hour was well past midnight.

Exactly one more hour had elapsed when Gull heard Harvell Braggs's voice bawling from the trailer. He stopped and looked back. It was very dark.

"He fell out!" Bragg's voice roared from the trailer window.

"What—?"

"Spook—fell out of the trailer!"

Apprehension crowded a mass into Gull's throat. He'd been driving fast—anyone who fell out at that speed could hardly escape injury. He pitched out of the cab, ran for the trailer.

He ran into the hard muzzle of the shotgun in the fat hands of Harvell Braggs, who stood in the night beside the trailer.

"Just act sensibly," the huge man advised.

"But Spook—"

"Spook thought I fainted and untied me so I could knock him senseless," said Harvell Braggs happily. "He's still in the trailer."

NOT because it was what he ached to do, but because it seemed the best idea at the moment, Gull lifted his hands. He would have brought a very low price if he sold at his present estimation of himself.

"With Cass' gang, eh?" he accused.

"Not at all," Harvell Braggs corrected hastily. "I have no interest in anything whatever except my precious Columbus items which were stolen."

"Why this act, then?"

"Since you showed no interest in recovering my antiques, I must proceed along those lines myself. I am capturing you, simply because it is necessary. The one I want is Christopher Columbus. I am going to make him tell me where the artifacts are, once he can talk."

Gull said, "So you know he is drugged."

"On the contrary, I do not know anything, but I did surmise as much."

Braggs reached out cautiously, then slapped vigorously at armpits and belt line to make sure no weapons were hidden on Gull's wiry person.

"I must say you are a solidly muscled young man," he stated. "And now if you will kindly lie down—"

Gull lay down. Harvell Braggs reached into the trailer for the rope. By that time, Spook Davis was groaning inside the trailer.

"Get your friend out," Braggs directed. "And tie him securely."

Gull did this, working in silence. Spook Davis awakened in the midst of the binding operation, emitted an ear-splitting yell, which got him an admonishing kick in the ribs from Harvell Braggs. Spook became pale and silent, staring at the huge man's shotgun.

Harvell Braggs himself tied Gull, then tested all the lashings. He picked up Gull and Spook and heaved them into the trailer, showing no great strength despite his enormous size.

"You whalephant!" Spook grated, mixing up his beasts.

Braggs gagged them both, saying, "Politeness is a quality which can be taught by force."

He yanked up his trousers, bent to inspect Christopher Columbus, and slapped Columbus very hard several times with no results. Then, holding onto his belt, he got out of the trailer sidewise and closed the door. He locked the door. A moment later, the trailer was in motion.

Gull rolled over. He could roll. He butted Spook Davis with his head. Spook then took his hands out of the ropes which secured them, doing it as easily as if the ropes had not been tied. He wrenched his gag out, plucked away Gull's gag, and began untying Gull's wrists.

"Good thing that hippowalrus is ignorant of Chinese rope tricks," Spook snorted.*

He untied Gull, chuckling over the break the rotund man had given them in forcing Gull to tie Spook first, giving Gull a chance to employ the trick knot which Spook had freed so easily.

Gull said, "We just lay low now and see where our elephantine friend is going. He locked the door, anyhow, so we couldn't get out without a rumpus."

Gull and Spook Davis had plenty of time to exchange opinions in the three hours of steady driving which followed. About the only thing they decided upon for a certainty was that Harvell Braggs was going on to Lake of the Ozarks. They could tell that by looking out the windows.

Throughout the long drive, Christopher Columbus lay on the floor, moving only when the motion of the trailer threw him about. They untied him, and put a pillow under his head for greater comfort. The lurching of the trailer moved him off the pillow and Gull went over to replace the cushion.

"*Gracias,*" Christopher Columbus said feebly.

---

* *The term, "Chinese Rope Trick" is general, and applied by magicians to knot tricks with ropes. Innumerable are these rope tricks, many revolving around a knot which appears to be solid, but isn't. —KENNETH ROBESON.*

Chapter XXIV
TRAIL TO TROUBLE

THEY LEFT DOC SAVAGE'S pocket dirigible tethered to a tree, should the bronze man return and have need of it, and trudged toward the emergency landing field where Renny's plane was hangared.

During this woodland trek, they encountered a man.

The man was what might have been, in his younger days, styled an "elm peeler" or an "apple knocker." The local term was Chariton tiger—a hillbilly, to most people born outside of Missouri. He was a knobby fellow with the rangy look of a dirt farmer.

He wore a frayed straw hat, farmer's denim overalls and had a sprig of wheat clamped between his pinched lips. One cheek bulged from a plug of tobacco tucked behind it.

"Reckon you-all fellers are out for a stroll," he remarked casually.

"Reckon we are," returned Renny politely.

The man tipped his straw hat in passing and they continued on their way.

Monk happened to glance behind him after the old elm peeler.

The old man was in the process of pulling a long-barreled revolver out of the bib of his overalls.

"*Ye-e-ow!*" Monk warned, yanking his supermachine pistol from its underarm holster.

The oldster spat a chew of tobacco from his mouth and redoubled his efforts to extract his weapon.

Ham waved his arms wildly. He was lost without his sword cane.

Casually, Johnny Littlejohn reached down and retrieved a sizable stone. He wound up and gave it an overhand pitch.

The stone smacked the old man in the forehead and down he went.

Monk growled, "I could have potted him before he got that thing loose."

"An unnecessary expenditure of ordnance," insisted Johnny, rushing to the fallen figure.

"Huh?" squeaked Monk, following him.

Renny thumped, "Johnny said that it would have been a waste of bullets."

The straw-hatted one was not out cold, merely stunned.

Renny placed an oversized boot on the man's scrawny chest and asked a question.

"Name?"

The man merely grunted. So Monk Mayfair reached down and took hold of a sunburned ear. He gave it a twist.

"I've seen Renny reduce a man's ribs to kindling, just by shifting his weight," he said.

The oldster spat out a brown stream of tobacco juice. With it came words.

"Buzz Harlan. They call me Pap—Pappy Buzz."

"Pap!" exploded Monk. "Wasn't that one of the names that flour-faced Wes Snow called before Big Neck scalped his friend?"

"The other was named Zeke," supplied Ham.

"Zeke was a friend of mine," muttered the oldster. "He worked for Mr. Bunderson, along with Wes and me."

"Doin' what?"

"Guarding his property. Keeping city slickers and outlanders clear of it."

Johnny asked, "Did Bunderson explain why?"

"No. Why should he? He inherited the place and it needed looking after whenever he was away."

Johnny frowned. "He was away—or the house was away?"

"House? That house has stood on that spot when most of the trees hereabouts were saplings."

The man sounded insincere, so Renny pressed his Brobding-nagian foot onto the other's sternum by way of expressing his displeasure. Cartilage crackled.

"That Wes Snow told us he poured the foundation only a few months back," Renny remarked.

"Yeah," chimed in Monk. "And when he told us that, the house wasn't there."

"We observed this with our own optics," Johnny added.

The jig was up, so Pap Buzz decided to come clean.

"I don't understand it all, but Mr. Bunderson was working on experiments in that house. Secret experiments. He didn't tell us no more, except that we was to lie our heads off whenever anyone came around asking fool questions."

"Sounds reasonable," rumbled Renny, removing his heavy foot.

Monk employed his long arms to reach down for the bib of Pap Buzz. The hairy chemist made a fist and pulled upwards.

Pap Buzz was suddenly standing on his feet, a purple-green bruise slowly forming on his forehead.

"Bunderson is back at the house," Monk informed him.

"My job and Wes' was to keep folks away, not pry into Mr. Bunderson's doings. If you say he's back, he don't need me barging in."

Renny demanded, "Get many prowlers way out here?"

"Some," Pap Buzz admitted. "We run a few off about a month or so back. They seemed to be looking for something special-like. Maybe they got wind of that ramshackle old house, I don't know. But Mr. Bunderson was powerful concerned about it. Told us to shoot on sight, if folks didn't skedaddle."

"Wonder who they were?" muttered Monk.

Pap Buzz confessed that he did not know, nor did he care. He was just a hired hand. He spat out another stream of tobacco juice by way of ending the conversation.

With that, they let the man go, minus his revolver. His story had sounded reasonable and explained some of the actions of the previous night.

THEY trudged along the shoulder of the blacktop road in the direction of a faint glow which dashed whitely at regular intervals, until they came to a gravel way which arched from the highway, crossed a railroad track, then angled down to the emergency airport. The village of Millard—one store, one filling station, blacksmith shop—was beside the railway tracks only a short distance to the north.

Colored lights edging the government flying field became distinguishable. There were no hangars; only the radio operator's little house and towers. A plane or two a year landed on the field as a rule.

The rotating beacon flung its stab of white periodically.

They claimed Renny's plane. It was intact. They deactivated the alarms that kept it secure from theft, and boarded. They left the smaller aircraft Johnny and Long Tom had flown from Toronto for later recovery.

Ham Brooks got on the radio and began contacting the local authorities.

"I am seeking information on the present whereabouts of an individual named Harvell Braggs, a collector of historical antiquities," he explained.

This led him to a local hotel in the town of La Plata. When he reached the front desk, via radio-telephone, he was told in no uncertain terms, "Mr. Braggs did not return last evening."

"Did he check out?"

"He did not, and his bill remains unpaid," the desk clerk said, with a trace of distaste.

"What does Braggs look like?" asked Ham.

"A pachyderm," replied the other succinctly.

"Say that again," requested Ham.

"Harvell Braggs," clarified the desk clerk, "is the biggest, roundest, talkingest elephant of a human being you or I ever saw teetering on two legs."

"That kinda narrows it down," muttered Monk when Ham reported his findings.

"It does not!" flared Ham. "We have no idea where to find this person."

Johnny Littlejohn was twirling his monocle magnifier by the black ribbon he used to keep it attached to his coat lapel.

"I believe that I have met this man Braggs. At one of my lectures, actually."

"That still will not help us to find him," fumed Ham. "The world is full of fat men."

"Harvell Braggs is not merely fat," retorted Johnny. "He is mountainous."

Ham made flustered sounds of impotent rage. The absence of his sword cane was not helping his nerves, either.

For lack of a better plan, they called around to various State Highway Patrol barracks, asking if anyone had noticed a prodigiously fat man walking or driving around.

It had all the makings of a snipe hunt, but dogged persistence showed in the end that it was not.

"Such a man was seen driving through the rain down in Lake of the Ozarks, asking directions," reported one barracks captain. "Know it?"

Ham said, "I have been to the locality. Thank you."

Getting off the radio telephone, the dapper lawyer suggested, "We might as well fly as drive. It will be faster."

"Fly where?" wondered Monk Mayfair.

"Lake of the Ozarks."

Renny sprang into the control bucket and began warming up the engines.

"Lake of the Ozarks. Wasn't that the spot where we—"

"Yes. And I hope that our troubles this time won't be quite so cataclysmic," complained Ham, racing Monk to one of the few seats the two-engine aircraft boasted. Monk lost. He had to sit on the floor.

By the time Renny had the booming plane in the air, Monk had idly picked apart the neat knots in Ham's shoelaces without the dapper lawyer noticing. He kept a straight face all the way up to two thousand feet. It was not difficult. Awareness of the bronze man's fantastic predicament made his thoughts oppressively morose. Monk and Ham had entertained themselves by bedeviling one another for as long as each had known the other. The going rarely got so tough that the pair forgot their perpetual quarrel. But now, neither had much heart for pranking.

The big pontoon craft did not circle for altitude, but roared away into the cloud-troubled sky, motors a-moan like a banshee in mourning.

Chapter XXV

PROMISED LAND

GULLIVER GREENE SANK back on his heels, then swallowed and got his astonishment down. He called softly, and Spook, who was sharpening a butcher knife grimly, sprang to his side.

"He was drugged, all right," Gull said. "He's coming out of it."

He kneaded Christopher Columbus' wrists, then tried liquor from a square bottle, which was considerably more effective.

"Maybe I can move—in time," Columbus said haltingly.

Spook Davis leaned close to the man. "Who are you? And look, if you say 'Christopher Columbus,' they'll have to put me in the booby hatch."

"I am Don Christopher Columbus," the man said in a thick, slurred voice.

Spook said, "Oo-o-o!" and grabbed fistfuls of his own hair.

"Do not conceive the wrong idea," Christopher Columbus said earnestly. "I am fifty-one years old, not four hundred. I have not been continuously alive since the time of my own era."

"That makes as much sense as the moon being composed of green curd and starfish," Gulliver pointed out.

"Mine is a strange story, I will admit," said Columbus. "In the Year of Our Lord 1503, I was shipwrecked with my men on the island of Santiago, in the West Indies, when I chased a strange man into an even stranger house. The house had not been there the day before. While in this accursed dwelling, I was overcome by a sorcerous spell, which robbed me of my

212

senses, and when it was over, I escaped the house, only to find myself, lost and wandering, in an unfamiliar forest. That forest is not far from here."

"Strange," said Gulliver, "hardly describes that unbelievable yarn."

"It is the truth," said Columbus stiffly. "I am again ship-wrecked, but in another era."

The idea made the muscles creep in Gulliver's long arms.

Spook Davis released his hair. He pulled a folding chair over and sat down on it, braced against the trailer motion. He beat his knees several times with his fists, then said, "Boy! Boy, is this something! Is it! What a whopper! I could eat worms, I'm that impressed."

Christopher Columbus cleared his throat several times, then tried moving his head in different positions. But when he spoke, his voice timbre was still thick and his enunciation difficult to follow.

"It was some kind of narcotic they used on me," he mumbled. "It's wearing off."

"Why did they drug you?" Gull asked intently.

"My curiosity got me that." Columbus rolled his head. "I was taken in by the founder of the Silent Saints—"

"Founder?"

Columbus seemed to try to nod, but couldn't. "The founder started it several years ago, along with some like-minded breth-ren. It was a good idea. Ivan Cass came along with plenty of money. We expanded and started sending our apostles all over the country."

He stopped and his eyes studied them steadily, "Know why I am telling you this?"

"Eh?" Gull said.

"You were involved in this by no wish of your own—but wait, I will tell you the rest. It is simple. I noticed old Box Daniels acting worried. I began checking up on him. I found he had discovered that Ivan Cass and a few others in the Silent Saints organization were engaged in some sinister activity. I confronted them and demanded they leave our brotherhood. Somehow, they divined who I was in actuality. They immediately seized me and drugged me, demanding answers to questions I did not possess. They might have done away with me, but old Box Daniels threatened to go to a nobleman named Doc Savage with the whole story. So they tried to kill old Box, and in desperation, he went to you, but they followed him, eventually murdering him."

Gull leaned closer. "What's Cass pulling?"

Columbus said, "I have not been able to find out. He has only a few men, a dozen or so, in the Silent Saints. They are the wrongdoers. All the other Silent Saints are true missionaries of the one true way of spiritual peace and tranquility."

The trailer jumped about, evidently traversing a rough stretch of road. The boughs of trees began to scrape the roof and occasionally the sides. Spook Davis sprang to a window, looked out and said, "It's about daylight and we're going through a young jungle and a lot of hills."

Gull nodded in the direction of the coupé. "Know this human whale, Harvell Braggs?"

Columbus shut his eyes wearily. "Never beheld the worthy before. And I cannot understand that fanciful story he told others about me stealing my own property from him."

Gull sighed and stood up. He did not consider himself to be psychic, but something in the other man's tone communicated the idea that he was speaking the truth. Gull had had that feeling all during his incredible account. It was preposterous—and deeply disturbing.

"Have you seen my adopted daughter, Petella?" Columbus asked suddenly.

"Who?" Gull demanded.

"Petella van Astor. Her public name is Saint Pete."

SURPRISE and the lurching of the trailer almost took Gulliver Greene off his feet. He did sit down heavily on the twin locker benches which formed part of the table arrangement.

"Now," he said, "we *are* getting places."

Columbus repeated, "Have you seen her?"

"Was she mixed up in this?" Gull countered.

"She would try to find me. She probably would try to find me by trailing the mind-readers in Cass' gang."

Spook Davis said, "Then if she's so nicey-nice, why did she refuse to tell us who you were or where you were—"

Gull got hold of him, shut him up, but it was too late. Columbus was staring, and just a little of the intense horror that must be within him showed on his face.

"Cass got hold of her," Gull told Columbus. "He threatened to kill you if she talked. Anyhow, that's the way it figures out. We saw her, but she wouldn't talk to us."

"Where is she?"

Gull said, "Cass has her," and looked at the floor, the walls, at the tree branches scraping past the windows, anywhere to keep from watching the hurt expression on Columbus' helpless face. The trailer rocked, jerking up on first one side then the other as the wheels ran over rocks. There was more light outside, the red of dawn in the east.

"You young men," Christopher Columbus said slowly, "are taking your lives too cheaply. Cass is a bad man, a very bad man."

Gull studied him. "What are you getting at?"

"A warning. Be careful."

Gull nodded. "Any other advice?"

"If we get separated, go to the Promised Land. You may find Cass there. If not, there is one other place."

"Cass has two hangouts, eh?"

Columbus said, "I am not sure. There is an island in the West Indies, near Hispaniola, which is now called Haiti. This isle is owned by Harvell Braggs. It goes by the name of Satan Cay, due to the treacherousness of its surrounding reefs. I have overheard Ivan Cass talk of visiting a certain island often. I presume that they are one and the same. But this may not be so."

Gulliver rubbed arms and legs, and put Spook Davis at the same task. They fed Columbus more liquor. Gradually, the long-haired man seemed to be recovering the ability to use his limbs.

Outside the little window, the sun continued its rising until the surroundings were hazy with dawn light.

"How come you speak regular American?" demanded Spook.

"As I related, in my time of trial, I was taken in by the Silent Saints—a deserved name if there ever was one," explained Columbus. "They taught me to speak the modern tongue, allowed me to live among them and be useful. My strange accent and manner of speaking was not so unusual around these Godly people. It was a blessing, for which I am, and will always remain, eternally grateful."

As they heard him out, Gulliver and Spook noticed the way the long-haired man enunciated his words possessed an unusual flavor. His accent was peculiar, and the cadence of his delivery was off, in a manner consistent with one to whom English is not the tongue spoken since birth.

"Box Daniels was a mind-reader," Gull said, getting at something that was bothering him.

"Not genuine," Columbus said. "He did not have true extra-sensory perception. He was the carnival type, a faker, if I may be excused for speaking the truth of the dead."

Gull snorted. "All mind-readers are fakes!"

"It is a human tendency to consider impossible that which defeats understanding," Columbus said quietly. "Some of Cass' men are genuine mind-readers. Even my adopted daughter, Saint Pete, has the ability to some extent."

Gull exploded. "Pete—a mind-reader!" His disbelief was in his frown.

"We will not go further into this," Christopher Columbus said somewhat stiffly. "It would be impossible to convince you without a concrete demonstration."

Gull opened his mouth to add that several concrete demonstrations would probably still find him unconvinced, unless he was badly mistaken. But the trailer stopped. Moving quickly, he lifted Columbus and allowed him to peer out of the window at their surroundings. He asked, "Recognize anything around here?"

There was red oak timber outside. Mixed in with this dominant Missouri Ozark country growth were walnut trees, evergreens, and others. Hills surrounded the highway on all sides. On one side of the road—the left—the hills looked down over a shimmering blue surface. Lake of the Ozarks, it must be, the enormous body of water brought into reality by the great engineering feat that was the Bagnell Dam.

"The Promised Land is about a mile to the west," said Christopher Columbus.

HARVELL BRAGGS came back toward the trailer. They could hear him breathing in a way only a fat man could breathe. Gull made gestures, and Spook Davis lay down on the floor and arranged the rope around his wrists to look as if he was still tied. Gull himself lay nearer the door, in a prominent spot, with the rope draped across his ankles, but with his hands behind him, gripping a saucer heaping full of black pepper which they had found in a galley can. This was the plan they had decided upon.

It did not work.

Harvell Braggs arrived at the door, jingled a key, then was very silent—didn't even breathe—and sidled around to the other side of the trailer. He looked in through the broken window. Gull had no idea he was there. Braggs saw the pepper Gull was holding. A surprised gasp escaped him. Gull turned his head and realized what had happened.

"That revolver!" Gull yelled. "Let him have it!"

"No! No!" Spook bawled. "Don't kill him! Give him a chance to surrender!"

Spook did not have any revolver on him.

Harvell Braggs ran around to the front of the trailer and jerked the coupling pin. Either he didn't want a shooting scrape, or he did not care to partake of one armed with a shotgun which would not drive slugs through the side of the trailer with any effectiveness. He waddled rapidly to the coupé and got in.

Gull kicked the trailer door, caved in the veneer lining, but the outer skin held. He told Spook, "The old one-two!" and they hit the door together with their shoulders. It opened and they slammed out onto the ground. At the same time, the front end of the trailer dropped as the coupé started and the coupling came apart.

The coupé gears wailed noisily in low, clashed into second, and Gull and Spook pursued the machine. They gained. Harvell Braggs stuck his shotgun clumsily out of the coupé window. Spook Davis screamed as if he had already been shot and dived for the nearest tree. Gull also took shelter, but without the vocal demonstration.

Harvell Braggs did not fire the shotgun. He drove the coupé rapidly out of their sight and hearing.

GULLIVER said, "He may send the police back after us."

They went back to the trailer, entered and picked up Christopher Columbus and the liquor bottle. Then, as an afterthought, also took a loaf of bread and some boiled ham. Spook Davis, somewhat recovered from the fright the shotgun had given him, thoughtfully stuck a small jar of mustard in his hip pocket.

"Which way to this Promised Land?" Gull asked, and turned around slowly pointing until Christopher Columbus said, "That way."

Moving through the woods, they first tried to cooperate in carrying Columbus. It proved more feasible to take turns carrying him. The brush was very thick, the route steep, mounting sharply up a hill.

Topping a ridge, they saw below them a vast valley crowded the shore line of Lake of the Ozarks. This valley was intensely cultivated, and very green. The blue and the green created a pleasant effect. Corn seemed to be the most prominent crop.

Across the middle of this lush valley ran a paved road. The traffic lanes on this showed as dark streaks of grease, indicating it was a well-traveled road.

Beside the road, on the nearer side of the valley, stood a cluster of long white-washed buildings. Except for their pale hue, they resembled military barracks. There was an impressive revival tent, white in hue so that it resembled a canvas temple. Nearby was a larger structure, an airplane hangar of a thing. It was also white.

Along the road was parked a row of trucks, trailers and small automobiles. All of these were a uniform but unprepossessing gray.

"The Promised Land," Christopher Columbus said.

Gulliver took a breath to ask the first of many questions, changed his mind and said, "Cass has his men scattered among the Silent Saints, eh? Do you know which men are his?"

Christopher Columbus looked miserable with his eyes. "No, I don't."

Gull said, "Then we're asking for it if we go down there and let anybody see us. We'll just hang out in the hills today, and maybe by night you'll be able to walk, and we can get around a little without being seen."

"A good idea," Columbus agreed. "Three will be a crowd down there tonight, too."

"Eh?"

"Each night in the Promised Land we hold the same kind of meeting as those held by the units which we send out all over the country. This is how we bring others into the fold."

"How is that?" asked Gulliver.

"By including mind-reading in the sermon, the better to reach into the soul."

Gull blinked. He whistled without emitting any sound.

In the course of the next hour, Gulliver learned quite a bit about the Silent Saints. First, he was reminded that Box Daniels had himself been a mind-reader, working his pitch in carnivals and chautauquas and on the stage. This, Gull concluded, made them kindred spirits—they had even worked some of the same theaters, although Uncle Box had been there years before Gull.

Box tried turning evangelist, but had proved himself ill-adapted to it. He had done this, Columbus explained, to get away from the carnival atmosphere, of which he was weary. He was bored with the kind of fake mind-reading that mentalists practiced, but had become fascinated by the possibility that the genuine faculty existed naturally in some persons.

"You see," Columbus said earnestly, "two of our brothers were true possessors of extrasensory perception."

There it is again, Gull thought. Mind-reading, even if Columbus was calling it a two-dollar word. He again stated flatly he did not believe there was such a thing. They argued for some time about it, neither convincing the other.

Changing the subject, Gull learned the Silent Saints were meek, righteous souls, living for nine months of the year close to the soil, and spending the rest of their time in traveling units, spreading the doctrine of the one true way. The true way, Gull gathered, was simply the healthy satisfaction and joy of living which came to almost anyone who had sense enough to get plenty of exercise and eat plain food. He was not irreligious, but he did not feel one needed the faith of the Silent Saints, if one had will power enough to live sensibly. The results would be the same.

"Who first suggested sending out these units?" he asked.

"Why—Ivan Cass," Columbus said.

Gull was thinking that over when Spook Davis began hissing like a snake in the top of a tree which he had climbed to watch the valley below.

"Cass just arrived in the Promised Land!" Spook exclaimed.

GULLIVER climbed the tree, but decided he was too far from the Promised Land. He left Spook with Christopher Columbus, and crept down the hill, finally posting himself in a thicket much nearer the cluster of white-washed houses and the pale temple of a meeting tent. The latter, he understood, was the temple in which the Silent Saints held their meetings to convince the public—and no doubt to pass the hat, Gull thought heretically.

Watching, he saw Cass several times. Cass seemed to be merely mingling with the other Silent Saints.

But late in the afternoon, he saw something interesting. A car drove up, a gray machine evidently belonging to the Silent Saints. The three darkly clothed Saints who got out of this vehicle were received with a reception which somehow conveyed that they had been away a long time.

Later, one of the new arrivals casually met Ivan Cass behind one of the white-washed shacks. Something changed hands. The Saint walked away. Ivan Cass took the other direction, pocketing what he had received—apparently an envelope. He went to a large trailer and climbed into it. Cass had been entering and leaving this trailer all afternoon, and Gull marked it as one object to investigate when darkness arrived.

Gull went back to Spook Davis and the enigmatic Columbus.

"Was one of your touring units due to return today?" he asked.

Columbus showed surprise. "Why, how did you know?"

"One of the returned Saints slipped something to Cass on the sly," Gull explained.

Christopher Columbus was improving. They ate the boiled ham and the bread, and used Spook's mustard. And it made them very thirsty.

"I'll be able to walk a little by darkness," Columbus decided.

The drugged quality in his voice had now gone away completely, which allowed his true tones to come to the fore. Although the unusual man spoke perfectly modern English, his fully revealed accent sounded strange and stilted to their ears.

Chapter XXVI

STORM

THEY ENCOUNTERED WEATHER on the way south. A storm front began moving in from the west. Dark thunderhead clouds were forming, seeming to bang together with a sound like small mountains colliding. They looked like mountains, too. Gray, granite ones.

Renny flew the pontoon plane wordlessly. The others were sunk deep in their thoughts. The dismal atmospherics seemed a reflection of their communal gloom.

Doc Savage was stranded in the past. By all reckoning, he was long dead. Their only hope was that Long Tom Roberts could fix the device that had made the Man of Bronze a castaway in time.

The situation was so beyond understanding that they found themselves having to grapple with it mentally. It seemed unreal.

"At least Doc has Habeas to keep him company," Monk said in the middle of his funk.

"If your dratted nuisance pig hadn't followed him back, maybe none of this would have happened." This from Ham Brooks.

Monk glowered as he considered a suitable rejoinder. He decided that silence was best. He was miserable. They were all miserable. It showed on their faces and the strained way they avoided conversation.

Lake of the Ozarks came up under their wings as the sun began setting.

The lake itself lay nestled in the autumnal Missouri Ozarks

like a sprawling blue-gray mirror laid against a profusion of brown and gold foliage. Storm clouds were bunched all about them now.

The sturdy plane began shuddering in the violent air. It was a low-wing all-metal job, streamlined to the ultimate. But it was no air goliath.

A sizzling bolt resembling a devil's pitchfork erupted into view directly ahead, turning the sky into a momentary flash of fire.

Renny shouted, "Holy cow!" and fought the wheel. A booming cannonade followed. The wings vibrated alarmingly.

Rain began smearing the windshield. Renny engaged the wipers, but a fierce wind immediately plucked one away. A moment later, its mate was carried off. The glass swam. Visibility became impossible.

"I'm going to put her down on the lake," Renny decided.

"It's as good a place as any," Monk agreed.

"Or as bad," murmured Ham darkly.

The big-fisted engineer wrestled the control wheel around and gave the rudder abrupt pressure, as he prepared to drag the surface of the lake.

The plane was an amphibian, fortunately. So landing on water would not be a problem. Provided, of course, the turbulent atmosphere did not interfere.

Another boom told them that a thunderbolt had struck somewhere behind them.

Johnny peered out his window, saw a white-hot trident split a tree amid a shower of eye-hurting pyrotechnics.

"Coruscating Olympian pyrotechnics," he gasped.

"No need to translate," Monk grumbled. "Put us down, Renny."

The giant engineer was an expert pilot. He turned on the landing floods and blinked as their backglow impinged upon his eyes.

Commencing his first dragging pass, Renny was startled when a succession of incandescent lightning displays made sizzling spidery cobwebs on either side of him.

"Heck!" he boomed. "I can't see a durn thing. I'm setting us down now."

Pushing the wheel ahead, he smashed the twin pontoons onto the smooth surface of the lake. The craft jarred, bounced, and bounced again.

Cutting the engines, Renny wig-wagged the rudder to kill some of their airspeed. That helped.

Soon, the ship settled in the dark waters, and all was still as a continuous booming erupted all around them.

"Some night," Renny grunted.

Monk went to the hatch and flung it open.

He craned his furry nubbin of a head out and was instantly drenched. "We're pretty far from shore," he remarked.

"You know of a dryer place than in here?" Renny thumped.

Deciding that he did not, Monk slammed the door shut and returned to his spot on the cabin floor.

"Drat!" sniffed Ham, suddenly noticing that his shoe laces had gotten untied.

After he had retied them, Monk left the laces alone. His appetite for pranking had dwindled away. He was thinking of Habeas Corpus, trapped before his time.

Red lightning blazed across the sky, making the cabin interior lurid.

Peering out into the storm, Johnny said, "Disembarkation would invite electrocution."

"If you're sayin' that we'd be sittin' ducks to be struck by lightning," said Monk, "I won't argue the point. Especially if we set out on a raft."

"Might as well grab some shut-eye," said Renny, leaning back in the control bucket. "We're not going anywhere until this storm breaks."

As an opinion, it made perfect sense. As a prognostication, it was far from the mark, however.

NOT an hour passed before there came a knocking at the door.

Monk was sound asleep on the floor when it came. Rousing, he made sleepy eyes at the door. The others were also gathering themselves together.

"Who the heck is that?" demanded Monk.

"Why don't you answer it and see?" snapped Ham.

Scrambling to his feet, the apish chemist said, "Maybe I will," and ambled over.

They had no thought of danger. The situation did not seem to warrant it.

But just to be certain, Monk put his face to the door and lifted his voice.

"Who's knockin'?"

"Missouri State Police," a voice returned.

"Got identification?"

"We can hardly slip our badges under the door, now can we?" the voice returned matter-of-factly. That authoritative tone of voice by itself convinced Monk Mayfair that it was a contingent of state troopers in crash boats looking into the matter of a possible crippled aircraft. They had not obtained permission to land on water.

So when Monk hurled open the door, the bushel of rifle barrels pointing at his homely face took him immediately aback. These jutted up from several bobbing boatloads of armed men. They did not look gratified by the soaking they were getting from relentless rain.

"You are Doc Savage's men?" a voice growled.

"Yeah. What of it?"

"You were expected."

"Yeah? By who? We didn't tell anyone we were comin'."

"Nevertheless, we were informed in advance of your coming."

"Who done that?"

"The individual's initials are E. P.," said the man. "Extrasensory perception to you."

Monk made faces and attempted to discern the features and garb of the men. He saw no badges shining in the dark.

"You ain't Highway Police," Monk decided.

The other grinned in the manner of a skull—without warmth. "Perhaps you, too, possess extrasensory perception. No?"

"No," squeaked Monk, giving the man a shove, and grabbing the door handle in an effort to slam it shut. It was a prudent move. The craft was bulletproof.

Bullets began snapping around his blunt skull, forcing the hairy chemist to duck and spring back, the hatch door unclosed.

The small flood of armed men sprang onto the pontoon and began shouldering into the pitching aircraft.

Ham Brooks had already set himself. He had his superfirer out and used to it hose the hatch, sending stricken men falling back into the water.

More gun muzzles poked in, commenced blatting. Rounds began spanking around the interior, ricocheting off the inner walls, which resisted slugs.

In that storm of wild lead, surrender made perfect sense.

Ham was the first to drop his weapon. He had emptied the drum anyway, so it was momentarily useless.

"If I had my cane, this would have ended differently," he complained.

"But you don't," reminded Monk.

Johnny had the presence of mind to shove open a window and drop his machine pistol into the lake. It would not do to have it fall into criminal hands.

At the controls, Renny considered his options. If the engines were hot, he could gun them and throw everyone off balance. But they were not.

Reluctantly, monster hands upraised, the big-fisted engineer came out of the cockpit, long face almost smiling. Conversely, this meant Renny was miserable.

One by one, they clambered out onto the port wing, where they were searched and prodded into boats. They ranged from motor boats to a couple of lake canoes—all filled with shadowy, soaked-to-the-skin men.

Out on the wing, a thick-bodied man commanded the miserable flotilla. He took possession of Ham's empty supermachine pistol and Renny's unfired one, after the latter was ripped from the big-fisted engineer's underarm holster at gunpoint.

"Where are we going?" Renny rumbled as the boat began making headway.

"You have heard of the Promised Land?"

"Who has not?" countered Ham in a supercilious tone.

"That is our destination this night."

"Holy cow! I don't like the sound of *that*," boomed Renny mournfully.

Chapter XXVII

CONVICTION OF A SKEPTIC

AUTOMOBILES BEGAN ARRIVING in the Promised Land before sunfall. They continued to come in increasing numbers, parked along the road, and the occupants alighted and either entered the big meeting tent or roamed around gawking at the burlap-clad Silent Saints. The Saints in turn circulated in the crowd, selling books which set forth the doctrine of their true faith. These brought a dollar, and they sold quite a few.

Gulliver Greene, Spook Davis and Christopher Columbus decided it was safe to approach the Promised Land. And did so. Gull had inquired closely into the nature of the services to be held in the tent. He was intrigued. It appealed to his showman nature, and also aroused the natural desire which every magician seems to possess—the desire to prove that any supposedly genuine medium, spiritualist or clairvoyant is a fake.

They passed a parked car. A drunk slumbered in the machine. Gull grunted softly in the darkness, went back and shook the soak. The fellow only mumbled. He was about Gull's height, but thicker.

Gull began undressing him.

He took off his own coarse garments and put on those of the inebriate.

"What's the idea?" Spook muttered.

"I'm going to test out this mind-reading stuff," Gull said grimly.

"That is very foolish!" Columbus warned. "It is only delaying our search for Cass and my adopted daughter."

"I may spot Cass inside," Gull said.

He finished dressing in the borrowed garments, and applied a match to the cork out of the liquor bottle, crouching inside the car. He had Spook Davis apply the burnt-cork blacking to his spectacular cotton-colored hair. This took some time—they finally had to empty grease cups on the car front wheels and mix grease with their improvised blacking. The coloring of the hair was finally completed, and Gull left Spook and Columbus.

He warned them to remain in the trailer, which belonged to the Silent Saints, if not Ivan Cass himself, lest their presence arouse curiosity.

Gull sauntered into the great white temple-like revival tent and found himself a seat.

At least two thousand persons were present. A large crowd for this part of Missouri. It was not long before he began to understand what drew them.

A Silent Saint took the rostrum, and the tent was darkened, except for where he stood. He began talking in a rather solemn voice. "Welcome all who seek the truth. By truth, I do not mean the humble truths of life, but the hidden truths of the unknown, which men have formerly called the unknowable. Through diligent efforts, we of the Silent Saints have seized this hazy veil that has long obscured mankind's combined vision, sweeping it away as ye would cast aside a dirty old cobweb."

Gull realized he was subtly setting the mood of the crowd for what was to come.

The speaker understood crowds. In short order, he had done an excellent job of driving home the point he was trying to make—he sold them on the idea that there might actually be supernatural powers which men do not understand.

Next, he convinced them—he *was* convincing them, Gull could tell from the faces around him—that such supernatural powers might be bestowed by a supreme force upon those who believed strongly enough in that force. It was the belief of the jungle native that his witch doctor could perform miracles, dressed up in a new guise for an audience who considered themselves civilized.

The man was explaining about the Silent Saints—they numbered thousands, and were to be found in all parts of the nation, spreading their particular philosophy.

That interested Gulliver.

"Five years ago, brethren, this great philosophy of the Silent Saints was inspired," declared the speaker. "The founder was a woman, that amazing leader who has come to be known as Saint Pete."

Electricity, or whatever nervous shock was composed of, turned Gull Greene over inside. It stopped his breathing.

Saint Pete—the Silent Saints' leader! The entrancing young woman whom Gull considered the maximum in desirability. He was stunned, but with the next thought told himself there was no reason why he should be so flabbergasted—at no time had Pete seemed an ordinary girl. She frankly hadn't told him the truth about herself, although it was a tribute to her honesty that she had advised him in so many words that she wasn't telling him anything. A strange girl, yes.

The speaker grew more feverish, more convincing. Then he announced that he would proceed to prove that the faith of peace and docility of the Silent Saints actually gave his followers something in spiritual power which others did not have. He called for a volunteer.

GULLIVER GREENE had waited for this. So had the crowd. And both got their money's worth.

Three minutes later, Gull had left his back seat and sidled up front, the better to see. He was baffled. The subject—a well-dressed man—was told, as preliminary, his name, his address, his wife's name, the names of his parents. All old mind-reader stuff. But what followed was not. The subject was told what he had in his pockets. He was told the make of his watch, where he had bought it, and what he had paid for it. He was informed that, long before leaving his seat, he had agreed with his wife to think of the movie he had liked best during the last year. He was told its name. He was told the joke he liked and remembered from the movie. He was told other things.

He looked dazed when he sat down.

The speaker called for another skeptic.

Gull advanced. He did not believe he was taking a chance, because the main lights were out, and there was only faint illumination on the speaker.

A moment of tension, while the Silent Saint looked at Gull. The fellow closed his eyes, seemed to muse.

"My brother, your last initial occurs near the center of the alphabet," he said.

"Huh?" Gull said, sounding surprised deliberately. This was an old gag.

"The name," said the Saint, "is an old American name."

That was safe enough; this country was full of old American names. "Right," Gull said loudly.

Without moving his lips, the Saint whispered, "Don't spoil the show, buddy. Give me your name. Whisper it and collect five bucks after the show."

"Johnson," Gull said, secretly elated. "Jim Johnson."

The Silent Saint announced the name loudly.

They got along very well after that. Gulliver whispered imaginary facts and the Silent Saint announced them loudly. The first subject, Gull thought, had been a stooge for the house. It had been arranged in advance.

The Saint dismissed Gull and he went back and sat down, turning his attention to looking for Ivan Cass.

THE SAINT who had been speaking now announced that one of his brothers would take over the show. He left the rostrum, quitted the temple by the rear door, crept through the darkness and tapped on a trailer door, then entered.

Ivan Cass, his stony-featured face looking more grim than usual, sat in the trailer. He compressed his lipless mouth expectantly at the Silent Saint. Beside Cass, standing, but so short he seemed seated, was the little man with the big voice, Cass' broken-nosed first assistant.

"What's wrong?" Cass asked.

"Gulliver Greene is in the audience," said the late speaker. "He came up to test my ability of extrasensory perception. I gave him a stall, made him think it was a fake."

Ivan Cass jammed his fists in his pockets and swore feelingly, then began to glower thoughtfully.

The Saint added, "Spook Davis and Christopher Columbus are probably with Greene, but waiting outside somewhere. It's a sure bet that they are in your missing trailer. And not very far from here, either."

Cass leered. "Good!"

"What do you want me to do?"

"Get our boys together," Cass said. "Take these three troublemakers. Take them quietly if you can. We don't want anything to happen around the Promised Land that might draw the law's attention."

"There is nothing here in case the place is searched?"

"Only some, ah—tools," Cass said, "I'll take that stuff away later. Everything else is up on the island. We'll take the prisoners there—along with the girl—and dispose of them."

The Silent Saint nodded and left the trailer.

Cass grinned at the midget. "It looks like we're coming out of this all right after all, little stupid."

The small man scowled darkly. "It's about time, big brain."

"You should be happy, small-and-dumb."

They left the trailer arm-in-arm, smiling in the friendliest fashion at each other.

SPOOK DAVIS stood beside the trailer containing Christopher Columbus. He had come outside to watch, lest someone approach. Spook had become a little uneasy in the darkness. Once he whirled—he knew very well nothing was behind him, that his mind only created fear, and he gave way to the impulse to spin, for it was in his makeup, to obey impulse. He had been trying to figure out what Cass was engaged in doing. He felt confused. As Spook himself freely admitted, he was easily upset. His was a delicate sensitiveness where trouble was concerned. He much preferred peace, and he must have felt at the present moment a strong return of an idea he had entertained off and on during the last day or two, the idea being: Why didn't they chuck this whole thing and skip the country?

When again came the thought that something was behind him—he refused to whirl. Nothing! Just his mind creating....

This time he was wrong. Hands took hold of him, several of them, so he knew he was wrong after it was too late. His mouth opened to free a yell. Cloth crushed against his lips, was shoved in his mouth, stopping the noise.

A voice growled, "Silence is golden, brother."

"Let not the evil beast of thy rage urge thy flesh into rash motion," added another.

Possibly good advice, but not taken. Spook kicked. Arms banded his feet. He was heaved off the ground. Absence of that solid surface made him feel grotesquely helpless. The assailants were too many for him, anyway, and it had been done silently.

The burlap-suited attackers entered the trailer and took Christopher Columbus. He cried out once, but not loudly enough to get attention.

Ivan Cass came up, trailed by the little man with the much-battered features.

"Take both of them to the trailer," Cass grated. "We'll get Greene next. Then we'll bring him and the girl to the island."

GULLIVER GREENE seized his first opportunity to get out

of the temple-like great tent. He could find no trace of Ivan Cass inside. He had convinced himself there was nothing to the mind-reading, and he was anxious to be about his other business.

He went straight to the trailer which he had, during the day, seen Cass enter and leave. It was unlocked. He clambered inside, after listening, and began to feel around. He came across a flashlight, and used it, covering most of the lens with a hand.

When he found a radio set, he failed at first to recognize what it was.

It was portable, and not exclusively a receiving set, he comprehended, after thinking at first that it was. It was both transmitter and receiver, one of the all-wave outfits used for long-distance telephonic conversations. They were effective over immense distances, capable of communicating with other continents, he remembered reading.

The cameras interested him, too. Particularly intriguing was the fact that they were the most expensive of miniatures, the type which, with the kind of lenses these had, cost as much as a small automobile.

There were two extremely powerful and compact monocular-type telescopes. Also, a surveyor's transit.

There was a box. In this box were five glass vials, and Gull uncorked one with particularly dirty looking liquid contents. He put the cork back with wild haste, then sat on his heels and breathed heavily. "Holy murder!" he gasped. He felt of his forehead and it had become wet with sudden sweat of fear. Magicians are confirmed experimenters with chemicals, so he'd been able to recognize the vial as hydrocyanic, one of the deadliest of poisons.*

The box also held several common pins—uncommon pins, rather. For closer inspection showed their points were daubed

---

* *Magicians use many effects of chemical nature. Commonest of these probably, are the tricks where the magician takes a pitcher of water, and pours from it different colored drinks, various liquors, etc. The chemicals are usually concealed in the glasses or in pellets in the magician's palm, or elsewhere.* —KENNETH ROBESON.

with something. He decided it was poison, although he had no proof, and no desire to experiment.

As if to drive home the point, three triangular-bladed daggers of the type that had been used to knife the telegrapher up in La Plata were in evidence. They appeared to be wickedly sharp.

Convinced it was a box of death, Gull closed the lid and got away from it. He would have been hard put to describe his reaction to what he had found. He did know that his skin felt as if small things were crawling on it.

He got out of the trailer more cautiously than he entered it. A feeling kept growing inside him, a feeling he did not like. For he recognized it as terror. Some of it must be the thing the dictionary called horror. He had never practiced reducing his inner sensations to such realities as words. But it was appalling to come upon such concrete evidence of evil and death and mystery....

Spook Davis would have to be warned—told that there was more than the incredible in this affair. Such seeming impossibilities as Christopher Columbus being alive and a girl who claimed to be a genuine mind-reader and a great deal of desperate maneuvering to keep something a secret—all that was puzzling. But that box in the trailer was death. More than death—it indicated something hideous and not quite understandable. The irrepressible Spook should be made to understand that, in order that sobriety might keep them out of trouble, if possible.

He bumped into someone.

Gull made his voice deep, like Cass' own voice. He had decided to do that if he was found.

"Why the hell not look where you're going?" he growled.

"Anybody find Greene yet?" the other asked, deceived.

GULLIVER struck with a fist. A man went down, cursing. A flashlight ray popped on. Gull socked it. The beam became a corkscrewing comet in the dark. The owner howled for help.

He got yelling response.

Gull ran.

Powder flame began working out of the gun behind him. The lead missed, which was understandable in the darkness. More men began arriving.

"Clear out! Get the girl! Clear out quick!"

That was Ivan Cass.

Gull angled for the voice. He ran more silently, straining his eyes, and shortly he saw a burlap-clad figure—it was a large man—hauling a bound figure out of a trailer. The trussed one's face became visible. A flashlight showed this briefly. Christopher Columbus, his longish hair askew.

"Take him ahead," Cass' voice ordered. "We'll follow if we can't get that damned magician."

"Douse that damn light!" someone ordered.

Darkness descended over the confusion of struggling forms.

The revival meeting audience was jamming out of the great tent to see what it was all about, bringing more noise and confusion.

Gull jumped into the crowd, mingling with it, trying to blend in. He succeeded, thanks to his disguised hair.

Not far away, a man suddenly sneezed. Then, he sneezed again. Or was it a different man sneezing?

Soon, there was an epidemic of sneezing, coming from different compass points.

"Spook!" Gull murmured to himself. "That old trickster!"

Placing two fingers into his generous mouth, Gull produced a piercing whistle, which he blew one long, then two short. It was a signal they used.

An answering whistle came through the darkness. Two long. That meant Spook was free!

Gull threw out another whistle, and broke away from the milling confusion, leaving the Promised Land behind.

Chapter XXVIII

PREDICAMENT UNPARALLELED

DOC SAVAGE'S MEN were ferried to shore and driven at gunpoint to what looked from the outside to be a small aircraft hangar.

A door in the blind side was opened and they were shoved in, and out of the blinding rain.

Once inside, there was no question of the building's purpose.

There were faint zones of light here and there. Lightbulbs of modest wattage hung from cords in all four corners of the barn-like interior and these showed an aircraft sitting idle, propellers still. It boasted three motors, an egg set into each wing, and one in the nose.

Renny appraised this with the canny eye of an airman.

"Foreign job," he thumped.

"Yeah," muttered Monk. "This is gettin' interestin'."

"It is about to become more interesting," said the thick-bodied man who seemed to be in charge of the proceedings. They noticed for the first time that he had a trace of an accent. Only a trace, however. European.

"Parle-vous Francais?" inquired Ham.

"Nein," the other retorted.

"I didn't think so," said Ham thinly.

"You men are to sit on the floor with your hands over your heads until it can be decided what to do with you," the soaked straw boss directed.

"Doc Savage isn't going to like this," bluffed Renny.

The other stepped up and stared at Renny for a very long interval.

At length, he grunted, "It does not matter. Doc Savage is dead, never to return."

"Holy cow!" boomed Renny. "What makes you say that?"

"Your thoughts tell me this, large ox."

Renny, Ham, Monk and Johnny all swapped uneasy looks in the gloomy hangar.

"You sound rather confident of your facts," challenged Ham.

The other sneered. "Thoughts do not lie. You four will remain here under guard while a consultation over your fate takes place."

They sat down. Ham began peering about for a spot that was not speckled with motor oil. Finding none, he pulled out a monogrammed handkerchief and sat upon that.

They were obliged to keep their hands clapped over their heads.

Twenty minutes passed and the straw boss who seemed to possess an abundance of knowledge he shouldn't own came back and made an announcement.

"They are to be taken to the island, with the others."

"What island?" asked Ham.

"What others?" wondered Renny.

"Why don't you read my mind and find out?" countered the straw boss coolly.

And for some reason, their captors began laughing among themselves.

Monk watched them enjoy themselves and picked his moment. He sprang for the straw boss—for his rifle, rather.

Hairy hands seized the long barrel, yanked hard.

The rifle swapped ends and Monk trained it on the stunned man.

"Guess you kinda forgot to read my mind," he gritted.

From behind him, a disembodied voice came gutturally.

"He did, ape man. But I did not. Give him back his weapon or I will shatter your spinal column with a single bullet. It is a dum-dum."

The hard roundness of a gun barrel prodded Monk's lower back, grinding painfully into his vertebrae.

"Where'd you come from?" grunted the hairy chemist.

"I sensed your intent, ape."

"You a mind-reader, too?"

"Most of us that you see here are."

Renny rumbled, "I'm beginning to think they aren't tellin' tall tales."

Reluctantly, Monk Mayfair handed the straw boss back his weapon.

The other examined it, as if looking for damage. While Monk watched this operation, the rifle butt was suddenly thrusting in and slamming against his ridiculously small forehead.

Monk went down, landing flat on his back. All breath was consequently knocked out of him. His eyes bugged out.

Renny lunged for the weapon, but another man got between them, blocking roughly.

The straw boss growled, "Place this man-monkey in the plane first. The rest of them must be trussed before they can be loaded. Then we will wait for the others."

Everyone wondered what others, but they were not mind-readers and so remained in the dark.

Outside, the thundering rainstorm did not contribute to their peace of mind.

IT was less than a hour later, when a new prisoner was brought in at gunpoint.

He was tall, easily six feet in height, wore his hair long and full after the style of the old-time Quakers. The new arrival looked as dejected as a church deacon in a pool hall.

The quaint-looking man was loaded into the aircraft, also bound hand and foot.

Doc's men regarded him at great length until Ham Brooks inquired, "Who are you?"

"I was born Christoforo Columbo," he said flatly. "I am known to the court of her majesty, Queen Isabella, as Don Cristóbal Colon. History remembers me as Christopher Columbus."

A chilly silence filled the plane interior.

Renny breathed "Holy cow!" in a voice so uncharacteristically soft that it might have been a prayer.

Johnny Littlejohn sidled over to the new arrival by inching along on the seat of his pants—the only way the gangling geologist could move, tied as he was.

"In what year were you born?"

The man hesitated.

"1451?" prompted Johnny.

"Yes. How did you know?"

"Did you know Francisco de Bobadilla?" Johnny asked sharply.

"I did, the scheming dog. But forgive me, for I speak ill of the dead. Don Francisco was appointed governor of New Spain in the year 1500. He perished after refusing to heed my warnings not to sail to Spain at a time when I recognized the sea air was heavy with impending storm. A hurricane swamped his fleet of caravels, but a lesser ship carrying my personal gold survived the disaster, for which I was accused of sorcery by some. Wrongfully, I might add."*

---

* *Christopher Columbus, discoverer of America, during later life was schemed against by jealous enemies. A particularly zealous schemer was the then governor of a Cuban colony, Francisco de Bobadilla. Word of his finagling got to the King and Queen of Spain, and they became a bit wrathy. They sent word for the governor of Cuba to come home and explain. Customs of the day being what they were, the governor had a hunch he would be minus one head upon reaching Spain, unless he had a good story. In order to appease them, Bobadilla had all the gold in sight cast into a gift in the form of a great table. A flotilla was organized, but Christopher Columbus somehow sensed an approaching storm. He was ignored. In the Mona Passage between Puerto Rico and Hispaniola, a powerful hurricane descended upon the exposed ships, destroying all but one. The alleged gold table was either heaved over the side or went down with the galleon. Miraculously, the sole survivor was a small ship, said to be the weakest in the fleet, carrying Christopher Columbus' personal fortune in gold. The* Aguja *weathered the gale and safely reached Spain. This astonishing fact, combined with the unheeded warning of an approaching blow, caused some to accuse the Great Navigator of being in league with the Devil. —KENNETH ROBESON.*

"In what year did Queen Isabella die?"

"I did not live to see that year," Columbus returned softly.

"What was the last year that you recall?"

"That was two years ago by my recollection—1503. My crew and myself were shipwrecked on the island of Santiago."

"That is what the Spanish called Jamaica," Johnny mused. "His story lines up with what Herman Bunderson told us."

Renny demanded, "What year is this?"

"I am reliably told that it is the Year of Our Lord,1937," Columbus imparted. "How I came to be here is a miracle, although a fearful one. I merely entered a strange house that appeared on the island one day. I entered. Then I lost my senses."

"Miracle!" boomed Renny. "Sounds like a durn nightmare to me!"

His voice rising, Johnny put other questions to the weird stranger.

"One of the great mysteries of the life of Christopher Columbus," he began, "was his almost supernatural ability to unerringly navigate great tracts of ocean. How was this accomplished?"

Christopher Columbus hesitated. "In my day," he said quietly, "I was a very prayerful man."

"That fails to explain the uncanny success of Columbus as a seaman," Johnny pointed out.

"Today, moderns would credit my navigational prowess to what is called extrasensory perception."

They took in that remarkable statement without utterance. It floored them.

Ham Brooks was eyeing the purported Christopher Columbus skeptically.

"This man," he sniffed at last, "does rather resemble in a general way, portraits of the Great Navigator I have seen. Yet you say that there are no authentic likenesses of Christopher Columbus in existence. Every one was painted without reference to the living man. Then how is it this person resembles those portraits?"

"That discrepancy is easily elucidated," remarked Johnny in his best professorial voice, not taking his eyes off Columbus.

"Yes?"

Johnny made baffled faces. "But I fail to conceive how that might be," he confessed at last.

"Then this man is an impostor, passing himself off as a likeness to someone whom history cannot describe," spat Ham.

But Johnny Littlejohn was not convinced. At length, he said, "Tell me, what caused your ships to be wrecked upon Santiago island?"

The long-haired man answered without hesitation, "Shipworms."

"Correct. What is your actual birthdate, which history does not record?"

"October the twelfth," replied the man without hesitation.

Johnny did not react to that. Addressing the captive, he drew himself up and said, "It is a distinct pleasure to meet with your excellency, the Great Admiral of the Ocean Sea, Christoforo Columbo."

"Holy cow!" rumbled Renny. "You mean this is the character we've been searching for?"

"I am virtually certain of it. My own researches, which have never been published, arrived at that exact birth date."

"A lot of good it does us now," said Renny miserably, straining at his bonds.

Christopher Columbus hung his head heavily.

"What do they want with you?" asked Johnny.

"They thought I knew the location of a certain treasure. A solid gold table was lost when the galleon captained by de Bobadilla went down in the savage storm about which I earlier spoke. This sinking took place in the year of Our Lord, 1502, in the Mona Passage."

Johnny nodded thoughtfully. "Yes, I know of that treasure. Some say it was a gold table, others that it was a great gold nugget, in either case weighing over three thousand pounds. If it could be raised today, it would be worth a young fortune."

"I did not sail with that fleet," related Columbus, "so I could not help my captors. Then they began questioning me about the whereabouts of the sorcerous house that had plucked me out of my rightful century. But I had no idea where it now stands, either. Now that they know I am of no use to them, I believe they intend to slay me."

"Holy cow!" boomed Renny. "These guys mean to murder Columbus. *The* Columbus."

The thought made their heads swim.

Johnny pondered this. "I do not think that they will succeed."

Everyone looked at him.

"What makes you say that?" demanded Ham Brooks.

"If Christopher Columbus were to be murdered out of his time before the events of his later life took place, how could history have recorded those happenings? They could not—would not—have taken place."

Renny made a mournful face. "Makes sense when you put it that way. But what if they do manage to murder him before he can get back to 1503?"

"I do not know," admitted Johnny. "Perhaps time will be irrevocably altered. Perhaps not. It cannot be known with any certainty because there has never in the history of the human race been a predicament such as this one."

As the bony archeologist's words sank in, a fresh round of thunder and lightning made the commodious aircraft hangar rattle and tremble, while the sound of rain, which had been a steady patter on the metal roof and sides, now became a fierce drumming that further depressed their spirits.

Chapter XXIX

MISDIRECTION

GULLIVER GREENE RAN fingers through his upstanding pile of blackened hair. The weirdly colorless coif, the theatrical shock of it, belonged to the character of The Great Gulliver, magician, and not to Gulliver Greene, who had a snub nose, freckles, pleasant features, emerald green eyes and a large mouth. Gull Greene called himself The Great Gulliver for stage reasons, and had assumed a showy personality, likewise for professional reasons. But Gull, underneath, was an ordinary young man in that he had the average person's capacity for wishing to high Heaven that he had taken an easy job, such as loading anvils, or a comparatively safe one—parachute jumping for instance—instead of letting himself be sucked into a dark mystery.

Disapproval of his own gumption was uppermost in his mind. Even after Gull found out he was barging into a queer mystery and plenty of trouble, there had been an opportunity to withdraw in safety and betake himself and his assistant, Spook, to healthier far-away places. But he'd passed up the chance. He'd plunged ahead, like Sir Galahad, filled with grand visions of helping a pretty girl. When he should've known such stuff went out of style with iron pants and broadswords. He was only a few hundred years too late. That was all.

In total, as a knight errant, modern style, he'd staged a swell flop. It was almost funny. So funny they'd probably finish hanging him. Or did they electrocute you in Missouri? He'd been trying to remember which it was and couldn't; this happened to be the first time he had been greatly interested in the point.

Gull was most of the way out of the Promised Land campground when Spook Davis came trotting up, as scary as a rabbit in a lettuce patch.

"That black pepper I filched out of the trailer just saved my bacon," puffed Spook. "I pretended to pull out a handkerchief to blow my nose, but I blew the stuff into their faces instead. That fixed them! I got away."

"I thought you were guarding—" Gull began hotly.

"Those men were dressed like gunnysacks, Gull. What does that tell you?"

"Silent Saints."

"They nabbed Columbus!" Spook blurted out.

"But not you, eh? Spill it!"

Spook took a moment to recapture his breath. He had been running, it was plain to see.

"I was outside the trailer, watching," Spook fibbed. "Watching for you. I spotted what I thought was Ivan Cass peering from behind a tree. I decided to investigate."

Gull bent a skeptical eye at his stooge. "Did you now?"

"Long enough to be half-sure it was him. Then I skedaddled. But they surrounded me. That's when I pulled out the old pepper-in-the-face gag, and got away."

"You left old Columbus to fend for himself!"

Spook said wildly, "I saw a gun in Cass' hand! Honest. And I knew I'd better warn you, or all three of us were going to end up in scalding water."

Gulliver turned that over in his mind. It made half-sense, putting aside Spook's overwhelming instinct for self-preservation, not to mention his yen for prevarications.

But Spook wasn't done explaining. "They glommed Columbus, Gull. I heard the struggle. But there was nothing I could do. There was a gaggle of them. They had gug-guns!"

"Let it ride," Gull said softly, looking about. He mentally cursed himself for not returning to the trailer right away. But he had wandered about, hoping to run into Saint Pete. Now his disappointment had doubled.

Gull took hold of Spook's arm and sought words that could convey the horror he felt. He didn't need them. Something about his tense grip must have conveyed his concern.

"What happened?" Spook breathed. "What'd you learn?"

"It's bad, this thing we're in," Gull said grimly.

"You're telling me? Brother, if them cops ever catch us—"

"It is more than that, Spook. In one of those trailers is something, well, hideous."

Spook Davis' swallow was audible. He did not say anything. His silence was proof that he was impressed, for his words were rarely taken from him.

Circumstances seemed to be tumbling through The Great Gulliver's brain with the demolishing effect of trains of brickbats. "Things are in a devil of a mess," he said at last.

"South America is a thought," suggested Spook hopefully.

Gull ignored the hint. The quicksand wasn't yet up to their necks, but it would take a lot more than jackrabbiting south of the border to extricate them.

A fresh storm was coming up. Thunder had started whooping hollowly in the west and there was a little splintery lightning, while the night was becoming unnaturally still, as it does before storms in the middle west.

Over the grove of the Promised Land camp lay black silence, except when the glow of distant lightning licked faintly red over the great hump of the tent where the evangelists held their revivals. Of the smaller tents—the cook tent, the dining tent—nothing could be distinguished, nor were the several trailers and small trucks of the Silent Saints discernible, except as the vaguest shapes.

Then, the headlights of an automobile appeared on the road, coming from the south. The machine was a gray roadster, and it pulled a house trailer of identical hue—a mud-gray monster rumbling and splashing in the receding lightning.

Gulliver Greene and Spook Davis, walking down the road, bounded off the pavement and landed among weeds in the grader ditch before the lights of the approaching car whitened them. They lay hidden as the roadster and trailer passed. Trailers were plentiful on roads at this Autumn season; they would have given the incident no notice, except that the trailer was the one they had driven to Lake of the Ozarks only hours before!

After thunder had finished muttering in the west, Gull said, "Let's see where that roadster and trailer go."

Standing erect, he watched the roadster pull the jouncing trailer down the road perhaps half a mile beyond the camp, where it turned sharply to the right. Gull recalled that there was a small pasture at that point. The roadster entered the pasture, stopped, and its lights went off.

"We'll keep an eye on that outfit," Gull decided.

"Could be a trap," cautioned Spook. "To smoke us out of hiding."

They crept onward, and on the chance that someone might come from the direction of the distant roadster and trailer, they went beyond the Promised Land grove. Off to the left, across the road, lay a pile of field stones—evidently the chimney remains of an old house or cabin that had burned down long ago. Gull scavenged a pair. Spook Davis copied the action.

"Now I feel fit for battle!" Spook said vehemently.

They went back to the road where Gull sat down on the edge of the grader ditch.

Hunkering down beside him, Spook asked, "Plan?"

"Wait a while and let's see if anybody comes from that trailer."

They sat there for a long time while the thunderstorm pushed up out of the west, brighter and noisier by the minute, attention riveted patiently in the direction of the distant trailer.

This concentration on the trailer was nearly their undoing.

A foot scuff, the leap of a flashlight beam, jerked their eyes toward the Silent Saints' camp.

"There!" Gull breathed suddenly. "Two of them!"

Two figures—distinguishable as two forms but little else—were approaching from the grove. Then the flashlight came on, and its backglow disclosed only one of the pair....

"Cass!" Gull hissed. "I'll take him. You get the other one."

Spook gripped one rock tight, held it cocked.

THE TWO nocturnal strollers came on. Gull, remembering the distinct feeling of dread the last time he had wielded a brickbat, considered dropping the heavy thing and using his fists. What made him hesitate was the realization that if he injured his hands, his magician's dexterity could be impaired. Perhaps, seriously.

Gull crouched there, sampling the horns of a dilemma—a tall young man whose muscles were not especially bulky, but instead were rather amazingly like wire. He waited, listening so hard that he could feel the muscular tension around his ears.

A roll of thunder kept Gull from hearing the conversation of the approaching pair.

Rising from the ditch, he impulsively left the stones behind anyway.

Almost at once, Gulliver had Ivan Cass by the neck.

The throat is no place to grab an opponent. All bloodthirsty stories of strangling to the contrary, men do not choke easily, as Gull now discovered. Moreover, a neck hold leaves both opponent's hands free.

Gulliver got a slam alongside the head. Again. He dodged; a thumb nearly got his eye. Oof! A fist struck his stomach, hard. It stopped his breathing. A toe peeled his shins. Knuckles hit his ribs with drum sounds. All this, and he was having no luck with his throttling.

He let go the neck and the fight complexion changed. Gull began pummeling with his own knuckles. In a moment, the foe was down. On him, Gull ground with his knees, punched with his fists. His fists were dynamite.

The air should have turned blue with his foe's profane shrieking. "Oh—Oh—"

Ivan Cass fainted.

At this point, Gull looked around.

The other one—Spook's intended victim—was dodging wildly.

"Missed!" howled Spook.

He sounded horrified. He jumped around, hunting. Spook continued to stumble in the dark. Wind and trees made convulsive sounds. Then a small, scared voice put a hesitant question.

"W-Who?"

Spook echoed the inquiry. "Who?"

Two owls might have been calling.

Gull rushed in and batted the stones from Spook's upraised hands.

The surprised stooge came stumbling toward Gull.

"Who—what?"

Gull said, "Relax."

They were all still until lightning came—a long lurid brightness—and Gull could see the girl, her wealth of cinnamon hair awry from rough handling, her exquisite lips drawn, blue eyes wide, straining. Saint Pete was in one of the Silent Saints' frocks of dark burlap which Gull had always thought looked fetching on her well-rounded form.

Ivan Cass lay on his sour, puritanical face, long arms outflung senselessly, a fallen crow in his dark burlap suit.

"Oh," gasped Saint Pete. "I thought you were in jail!"

"I would be," Gull grunted, "if I depended on you to get me out."

HE was irked. Not at her personally, he believed, but at the unreasoning fear which he could discern on her face. It was terror, it had been there during all the time that he had known her, a grim strain that never relaxed, and he had struggled to penetrate this silence that fright forced upon her, but never had success been satisfactory; this aggravated him, because it defeated him.

"Where was Cass taking you?" Gull demanded.

She did not answer.

"Look, Pete," Gull said grimly. "You've got to talk to me. You've got to go to the police with your story. That's the only thing that will clear me. Tell them that Cass has been threatening you."

But her silence continued.

Gull asked, "What has Cass got against you that is so terrible you won't talk?"

Again, no response.

As her unanswering stubbornness continued, and the storm noises seemed to get louder, as though mounting with her determination not to reply.

"She ain't learned any conversational habits since last time," Spook Davis remarked.

Gull held both the girl's arms, and felt them quivering under his fingers. She was terrified, all right. It made him angry. He had, to a degree, a masculine impatience with abject fear, although perhaps not being impervious to it himself. But it was so important to him that she talk, but she wouldn't. So it made his temper mount.

The lightning, fortunately, still splashed red. He could see whenever the incandescent forks flashed. Rain began to fall in big cold drops, promising more misery.

"Give me your belt," Gull grunted at Spook. But they had taken Spook's belt from him at the police station, a precaution usually taken to prevent prisoners hanging themselves.

With Spook's tie, Gull strapped the girl's wrists together. He used Cass' belt to fasten her ankles.

Meantime, Spook Davis searched Ivan Cass. He found a roll

of greenbacks, very fat around, and remarked, "Boy, some profit, huh?" Gull glowered at him. Spook hastily restored the bankroll, then palmed it after Gull looked away. When his fingers encountered a revolver, Spook jerked them away as if stung, gasping, "Whew! Another gun! Cass must collect them."

Gull quickly appropriated the weapon, muttering, "Magician's luck! Twice in a row."

More drops of rain fell on them, large drops for a while; then they commenced getting smaller. Soon, they were immersed in a misery-inducing Missouri downpour.

Gull shouted over the storm, "Can you pop Cass with your rock if he wakes up?"

"I'll kiss him with the greatest pleasure," Spook hollered.

"Then you stay here and watch Saint Pete and Cass."

"But what—?"

"I'm going to have a look at that roadster and trailer up the road," Gull bellowed.

"You may get into trouble!"

"That," Gull yelled, "is probably an understatement."

GULLIVER strode off, hunched against the rain, and left the road. There was a field of tall corn through which he moved—evidently these were crops the Silent Saints grew for food. They provided good cover through which to pick his way, but rich loose soil made footing tough until he broke free of the waving green stalks.

The pasture which the roadster and trailer had entered was rapidly filling with dancing rainwater. Gull's shoes began to fill, soaking his socks.

Light came from the trailer windows. Gull waited for a time, but no one moved outside the trailer, so he crept forward, a watery shadow pelted by the ceaseless torrent. He held Cass' revolver inside his coat to keep it dry.

Gull's intent listening netted no sound from the trailer. Windows of the trailer were closed, water sheeting over them made it impossible to see inside, although he stood on tiptoes and tried. Then, the revolver in hand, he sidled toward the door.

A fiddle string seemed to break against his right ear.

It was exactly like that. He'd never heard a bullet at inches range before; when they glanced off rocks, they went *pin-n-g!* or made a singing noise. This was a report! And it was a bullet, because the gun noise came after it with a big bump. From the roadster.

Gull went down. Not hit. Not scared, either, surprisingly enough. Suddenly, he felt as calm as a carpenter opening a keg of nails. Lifting his own gun, he aimed deliberately, fired. A man leaning out of the roadster door, plainly distinguishable in the lightning blaze, suddenly lost his grip; he fell to the ground, making a splash.

A man opened the trailer door. Gull fired. The man jumped back into the trailer.

Then that man shot off a gun. Several times. The bullets came through the trailer sides, popping into water and mud near Gull. He rolled. Then he put two lead blobs into the thin hide of the trailer. Someone bawled.

Suddenly, it sunk in to Gull that Christopher Columbus might be in that trailer, a helpless prisoner.

Gulliver Greene did not often obey a wild impulse. But he made an exception now. It seemed like a good time for a falsehood.

"It's the G-Men!" Gull yelled. "Throw your guns out of there!"

The results were not overly satisfying. Lead came out of the trailer in quantity. Shots bumped dully inside, but the bullets, once outside, made about the noises that a man with pneumonia makes coughing.

"It's the United States government out here!" Gull yelled.

Technically, it was only a hundred and twenty millionth part of the republic, but the words had the desired effect this time. They struck terror into the trailer. The door popped open, men bounded out and ran.

"Stop! Get your hands up!"

Gull yelled more orders. They were ignored. He fired off the gun. Rain roared down. Water blinded the men. Thunder whooped, cackled, seemed to slam great portals among the clouds. Lightning flashes stabbed eyes. Result was general bedlam, confusion. The men from the trailer ran away. Probably they did think it was a federal raid. The man Gull had winged in the roadster got up and loped lopsidedly with them.

It was the midget with the outsized vocal cords.

They all ran down the road in the direction of the Silent Saints camp which took them toward where Spook Davis was holding the girl and Ivan Cass. Before long, guns began making noise again, then Spook let out a series of squawling sounds.

Chapter XXX

FREEDOM IN BRONZE

LONG TOM ROBERTS was an inveterate tinkerer. He could take apart anything from a radial aircraft engine to an all-wave radio sending and receiving set and restore it to better condition than it had been when he started.

The mechanical brain that governed what old Method Gibbs had dubbed the Chronodomus was a different matter. Aside from not resembling anything he had ever encountered, much of its profuse wiring had melted and fused.

As a first step, Long Tom had pulled out the bad wiring. It was strange stuff. Some of it was the old loom-cord type. But it could be replaced with modern material.

Herman Bunderson paced around nervously.

"Can you make yourself useful?" Long Tom snapped peevishly.

"All I know about electricity, " Bunderson admitted meekly, "is that you hook dry cells up by connecting the inside post of one to the outside post of the next one, and that when they run down, you could get some more juice out of them by poking holes in their zinc skins and sitting them in a fruit jar of vinegar or sal ammoniac."

Long Tom frowned. "Are there any spare parts to this contraption?"

"The closets are full of electrical junk, but I don't know how much of it will help."

"Gather up everything and dump it out in the hall," instructed Long Tom.

Bunderson galloped off. Long Tom continued picking apart the damaged wiring, face a knot of concentration.

An hour of so later, Bunderson dropped the last of the extra material at the foot of the tower room staircase and called up.

"This is all of it."

Reluctantly, Long Tom pried himself from his work and came down to examine the litter of electrical components and other items. Among the debris were replacement wires and vacuum tubes. The latter looked handmade. His sour face began to brighten.

Lugging armfuls of the stuff upstairs, Long Tom set about replacing the useless wiring.

"This is going to be like stuffing an old horse-hair armchair," he grumbled.

Deep into the day, the electrical wizard toiled. Ordinarily, he relished such challenges. But the thought of Doc Savage trapped in the Nineteenth Century made him rush through it—this despite the undeniable fact that if the renowned electrical genius could get the mechanism to work again, time and distance might not matter.

On the other hand, it might be of tremendous import.

Long he labored, and when Long Tom finished rewiring the device, the slender electrical wizard stepped back and called Herman Bunderson up.

The inheritor of the Chronodomus examined the mechanism from all angles and finally said, "It looks pretty much like it did before."

"But will it work? That's the question."

"I don't know," confessed Bunderson, eyeing the concentric and interlocking calibrated rings of brass that resembled an old astrolabe. "Some of these governors appear to be out of kilter."

"Figured that. The question is—how far out of kilter?"

"I wish I knew," confessed the other.

"Never mind the electric-eye timer, can you set the controls to send this thing back?"

"Yes."

"Start it up. Let's see if it works."

"The only way to know if it works is to try to go back."

"That's the idea. We are going back to get Doc Savage. Set the controls to land on January 1, 1830. Never mind why."

"But-but if it doesn't operate properly, we could land anywhere. Anywhere at all. With disastrous consequences."

Long Tom's pale eyes challenged those of the other man. "We'll risk that," he stated grimly.

Herman Bunderson looked contrite. "I guess after all the damage I have done, I will risk it, too."

He went to the main controls, began adjusting them, carefully setting and resetting elements until he was satisfied. He consulted an old leather-bound journal, evidently the manual handwritten by his grandfather, the inventor of the temporal displacer.

Finally, Bunderson called out, "Say when ready."

Long Tom did not hesitate. "Ready."

A knife switch was thrown and the house lights flickered. Magnetic forces plucked at Long Tom's wrist watch. He slapped a hand down to hold it in place.

A sensation of dislocation began immediately. It was a downward jolt. The house seemed to rise off its foundation, and before he could find his balance, Long Tom Roberts was swimming in a gray haze in which his vision no longer operated.

This went on for some while. Bringing his watch against one ear, the electrical wizard listened for its ticking. He grunted. The works were running normally. He had wondered if it would function.

The sensation of coming to rest coincided with the return of normal vision.

Long Tom rushed to the tower window.

Where before it was light, now it was dark. Moonlight flooded the landscape outside the window pane. The forest below was spectral with a coating of ice and snow.

Long Tom muttered, "We've landed smack in the dead of winter. No telling what year it is, either."

Taking Herman Bunderson by the collar, he snapped, "Let's reconnoiter." Long Tom had to rough the man down the stairs. Bunderson was not eager to encounter any more Indians.

They stepped out onto the railed porch. A bitter snap plucked at their exposed skins. Bunderson began to shiver.

"This looks like the forest by the Chariton," he decided.

"Right. But *when* is it? That's what I want to know."

Stepping off the porch, Long Tom began to stalk around the property. The scorched maroon sides still stank of smoke. Some of the ornamentation that so brought to mind angular spider-webs had been charred black. The hideousness of the old manse were never more appalling.

He soon found himself ankle-deep in snow. The bitter cold had formed a crust and this rime squeaked when stepped on, breaking easily.

Long Tom produced a flashlight and began investigating the immediate vicinity.

"What are you looking for?" Bunderson asked, excited breath producing cold clouds.

"Signs. Now be still."

Long Tom was very methodical in his searching. He began with the trees nearest to the house and gave them a good once-over with the thin beam of the generator flashlight, winding it often to resupply juice.

His painstaking effort was rewarded when the glowing dime of light touched a raw cut in the side of an old hickory tree.

Long Tom whistled, once. It was a musical exclamation of pure pleasure.

"Doc made that," he said, indicating with a pointing finger.

"How long ago?"

"Months. But the arrow points in a specific direction. We

will follow that trail."

"What about the house?"

Long Tom hesitated. "Stay behind and guard it."

"What if you don't come back?" asked Bunderson.

"I will come back. And I won't be alone, either."

With that, the pallid electrical wizard marched purpose-fully into the woods.

LONG TOM walked for over an hour by moonlight, but found nothing. These woods appeared untrammeled. He found tracks of bear, squirrel and other woodland creatures.

No human footprints did he uncover.

The night moved farther along and discouragement caused his lean shoulders to sag like rotting timbers.

From time to time, Long Tom ventured a bird call. It sounded like a bobwhite, but the spacing of the piping constituted a code. If Doc Savage heard it, he would reply in kind.

But Doc Savage evidently did not hear it, for no answering call came to Long Tom's oversized ears.

Finally, compelled by sheer frustration, the puny electrical expert removed his supermachine pistol from his inner holster and pointed it at the night sky. Finger on the firing lever, he pulled back.

The superfirer unleashed a brilliant burst of noisy reports, gun-powder flashes painting the surrounding trees. The blending per-cussions produced the unique bullfiddle roar the compact weapon made in operation. There was no other sound like it on earth.

Long Tom let the compact drum run empty. Then he lowered the smoking muzzle.

Patiently, he listened.

The snow cover was such that if a man approached from any direction, the creaking and snapping of the crushed hoarfrost cover would warn of it.

Long Tom heard nothing of the kind. Superfirer smoking,

dejection settling over his unhealthy looking features, he turned to retrace his steps.

Long Tom covered some leagues south when above his head, tree branches began to spill powdery snow.

He looked up.

And from a branch directly overhead, a startling figure dropped.

An uncouth giant stood before him. Towering, dressed in buckskins with windburned face obscured by a plump beard the color of copper wiring. He might have been an old frontiersman of Daniel Boone's day, living rough.

Golden eyes burned into his own with an almost feral light. "Doc?"

"Long Tom," returned the voice of Doc Savage.

"Doc! You're alive!"

"Later. Let's get to the Victorian."

"We haven't much time," Long Tom warned. "I left that Bunderson guy in charge of the works. If anything spooks him, he might take off on us."

Suddenly, Doc Savage grabbed Long Tom and lifted him off his feet.

"Hey!"

"Hold on," warned Doc.

Suddenly they were in the trees with the bronze man rushing along branches, leaping from springy bough to bough and covering yawning space so rapidly that the pale electrical wizard had to close his eyes to keep from becoming dizzy.

In his heart, a strange joy danced.

Doc Savage paused only once, and that was to stop at a tree house where he gathered up two items—Habeas Corpus and a makeshift sack which rattled and jingled metallically. It was obvious that the bronze giant had been living in the tree house, awaiting relief.

Chapter XXXI

THE FRONT

GULLIVER GREENE, RUNNING in the direction of Spook Davis' outcries, felt drained of whatever it was that had made him go through the gunfight with the reckless calmness of a veteran. The aftermath was sudden unpleasant nervous convulsions. A few minutes ago, The Great Gulliver had been as calm as a combination of David with the slingshot, but whatever juice had given him that Penthesilean moment had leaked; the rod had gone limp. Every bullet of the fight was being shot once more in his brain, with disconcerting effects on what he had always considered to be an average amount of bravery.

He continued running toward Spook Davis, but it took more sheer forcing than anything he had ever done. His legs felt about as efficient as rubber hoses full of milk; marvel of it was that they carried him at all. The rain roared and threshed. He couldn't see, but his dull heavy-feeling feet telegraphed faint jars, so he knew he was still going down the highway pavement. He carried Cass' revolver. It felt as though it weighed a ton, and it was useless, because it was now empty. If anybody shot at him, two things could happen; either the bullet would kill him instantly, or he'd turn, and not stop running for hours.

It seemed like a devil of a lot of emotion to feel over something that characters in fiction and actors in movies typically took in stride—these actors were shot at, they shot back, and that was that. But The Great Gulliver, having been shot at for the second time in as many days, was having a case of compound jitters as a result.

Lightning ran a grizzled streak of flame in front of his face; thunder seemed to knock the level of the earth down several feet. In the scarlet roaring moment, Gull saw that he was abreast with the spot where he had left Spook Davis, Saint Pete and Ivan Cass.

None of the three were there.

"Gull!" a voice piped up tremulously.

Spook's voice! It was off to the left, in a grove of maples. Gull slogged down into the roadside ditch, tossing handfuls of water, dug mud up the other side, took hold of a barbed wire fence thinking what would happen if lightning struck the fence just then, got over it, and reached Spook's side.

Spook Davis hugged close to a tree and gurgled noises which he finally made turn into words. "Are they guh-guh-gone?" he wanted to know.

"Where's Pete?"

Spook winced from a particularly bright lightning burst. "They tuh-took her."

"Cass?"

"Him tuh-too. They took 'em both." Spook grabbed Gull's soggy coat with both hands. He seemed to have a grievance. "Why in huh-huh-hell did the G-Men run them guys in this direction?"

"G-Men?"

"They kuh-kept yuh-yelling that the G-Men were after them," quavered Spook.

The rain seemed to suddenly slacken and the thunder went cackling away in the night. Water fell out of the trees in thinning dribbles, but gurgled and rushed over the ground in volume.

"You better tell the G-Men to chuh-chase them birds!" Spook yelled.

"I was the G-Men," Gull explained.

GROWING calmer, Spook Davis advised that Ivan Cass' men, after they had rescued their chief and abducted the girl, had continued on toward the Promised Land. Gull then realized that it might be a good idea if Spook and he were not to be found in the vicinity. Also, it occurred to him they might find weapons around the roadster and the trailer. He put that thought into words.

"I don't want any guh-gun," Spook explained. "What I want is to get out of this mess."

However, they ran back to the trailer, hurried feet knocking up sheets of water. The pasture was like a lake, across which they waded into the trailer. On the chance that there might be an enemy lurking inside the trailer, Gull shouted, "This is Cass! Come on out!" But no one appeared, and the interior was dark; someone had turned out the trailer light during the gunfight, an incident which had gone unnoticed in the fracas. Gull felt inside the door, presuming the light switch would be located where light switches are to be found in houses, and sure enough it was, so he brightened the interior.

Gull looked inside the trailer. No one here. But—his gaze became fixed. His whole long body grew tense. His face must have showed concern, too, for Spook Davis pushed in beside him, looked, then snorted.

"Huh!" said Spook deprecatingly. "Just a box."

To Spook Davis, it would seem to be just a box, for Spook hadn't seen it before. He didn't know that this box of wood, about four feet square, height two and a half feet, with a hinged lid, held grisly death. Obviously, it had been conveyed here for some reason.

Lifting the lid, Gull let Spook have a look inside the disquieting box.

Now it was Spook's turn to register astonishment. He did so most effectively. Spook's eyes popped.

"Suffering Robinson," he breathed, dazed by the vicious-looking three-edged daggers he saw within.

"It's a murder box," explained Gull quietly.

"I can see that. But what—?"

"Take a gander at the rest of stuff," suggested Gull.

Spook peered about, and began noticing the expensive cameras, and other unusual optical instruments.

"I think," Gulliver Greene said grimly, "Cass and his men are high-class crooks."

Spook's eyes grew wide. "You mean—?"

Gull nodded. "The Silent Saints are a front for a roving murder gang."

Gulliver Greene frowned as he carefully lowered the box lid. Good grief! Reading about such things in the newspapers, it always sounded sort of impersonal, like the Coronation. But now it was real enough. And clear? Well, reasonably. Ivan Cass and some of the others must be traveling with the Silent Saints' mobile units, doing their dirty work—whatever it was. Evidently, they were assassins of some secretive kind. This must be what Saint Pete had learned, so that Cass had found it necessary to do something to keep her silent.

"What should we do, Gull?"

"If we weren't wanted by the law, I would give all this evidence to the nearest State Highway Patrol barracks."

"Maybe we should do that anyway," Spook suggested.

"Are you growing horns, like a bull?" Gull asked.

Spook shook his head vigorously. "I'm thinking we can swap these mugs for a ticket home."

Gull's freckled features gathered thoughtfully.

"It's an idea," he drawled.

"We could borrow this rig while we're thinking about it," Spook offered hopefully.

"Even better," said Gull suddenly.

SPOOK DAVIS remained in the trailer and Gull got in the roadster, belatedly wondering if the key would be in the ignition lock; the key was there. Rain had turned the pasture soft, and it was a small miracle when he got the rig onto the highway. He drove north. Rain stringing down kept wipers going *click-cluck* on the windshield for a while, then the rain thinned out entirely, after which driving was easier and Gull had some attention to spare for thinking. He seemed to be able to think quite clearly now that they had captured the death box. That surprised him, yet everything about the affair did align itself in his mind with something closer to approaching order. The reason this surprised him was because there seemed to be as much mystery as ever; the only thing that had been cleared up was that Ivan Cass was the leader of a gang of assassins traveling around the country ostensibly as members of the Silent Saints.

This did not mean all the Silent Saints were rascals—far from it; Gull was convinced that the majority of the evangelists were sincere men, earnestly endeavoring to spread the doctrine of simple living, moral restraint, and honesty—all qualities which it certainly wouldn't hurt the country to possess in greater quantity.

Unfortunately, what the situation now possessed in clarity was completely overwhelmed by the additional trouble it contained. Gull twisted lean lips thoughtfully. Let's see—he was wanted for murder, jailbreak, robbery, and for all he knew, kidnapping. Violent acts of lesser importance included shooting one or more of Cass' men, assaulting Cass and robbing him, stealing this car and trailer, and possession of the deadly devices in the wooden box. It seemed a sizable array of charges to have collected just because Gull had innocently received a telegram from his long-absent Uncle Box.

In the middle of his troubles, Gull found time to sympathize with the girl. And to puzzle, as well, about her connection to the odd duck, Christopher Columbus.

Blast women, anyhow; particularly the pretty ones. They had no business up against the realities of life of the grimmer kind, such as the present situation. Their places were in the home; they belonged across from a fellow's breakfast table. Pete did, at least. He was irked at her, rather than appalled, for not telling the police the truth. He understood exactly why she had not told the officers what he knew, that she had learned Ivan Cass was traveling with her Saints and doing dirty work.

Alternately, Gull wanted to wring Pete's shapely neck, or take his sword and go forth and slay the dragon that was menacing her. She was sweet; she was honest. He'd lay his bets on that. The trouble was that she could be terrified into silence. This was an entirely human failing, Gull realized in more restrained moments. He might even be scared into silence himself, under the proper circumstances. But none of this contemplating of spilled milk was getting him out of the shadow of the gallows.

But if bringing evidence of a murder gang to the authorities would convince them to begin a search for Ivan Cass, he hoped that hunt would lead them to Saint Pete, in time.

The roaring violence of the wind was easing, but even more rain was coming down; it rushed through the headlight beams in squirming curtains. The road was surfaced with what the natives called blacktop; it was exceedingly slick. Gull gave his driving close attention. Lucky, so far, that they had encountered no State Highway Patrolmen. If fortune only persisted....

A small black coupé whipped past the roadster and trailer, continued down the road a hundred yards, and suddenly slowed. The driver threw the car into an expert skid. It stopped broadside of the road, making a blockade. A man jumped out of the far door of the machine. He leveled a revolver over the hood, and the gun muzzle began sticking out a red tongue.

THERE seemed to be only one man in the coupé. He was shooting, not directly at Gull's approaching roadster and trailer, but in the air. A warning, obviously, to stop. Gull came down hard on the foot brake, yanked the hand brake back, and was promptly slammed forward against steering wheel and windshield. Brakes in car and trailer seemed to be very efficient.

After the caravan stopped precipitously, Gull pushed himself back from the wheel and pulled breath back into his lungs.

"Braggs!" he yelled.

"Get outta there with your arms up!" Harvell Braggs roared.

There was no doubt about it being Braggs who had stopped them. The man's head, beginning modestly at the top and widening out in innumerable amazing chins, was unmistakable. It was Braggs, the collector of Columbus artifacts. The black coupé was the machine Braggs had fled in, not many hours before. Gull recognized it now.

"It's that damned magician," Braggs gritted fiercely.

The roadster lights, shining on the mountainous man, disclosed that he was wearing a strained, fatigued expression, as well as grimness. He started when Spook Davis popped out of the trailer and took to his heels. Spook did not bother to look to see who it was. Braggs was just a shadowy figure with a gun that had stopped them, and Spook wanted to be far away quickly.

After Harvell Braggs fired in the air, he roared, "Stop!"

Spook Davis stopped, came back, pale and shaking, ogling Braggs' gun.

"Raise your hands," commanded Braggs.

Gull and Spook silently complied.

"Now call Christopher Columbus out of that trailer," instructed the fat man.

"He's not—" Spook started to say.

With a surreptitious foot, Gull kicked his mirror-image stooge in one ankle. Spook subsided, offered a shaky grin.

Gulliver called over his shoulder, "Come on out, Columbus!"

But Columbus did not come out, of course.

"He's asleep," Spook fibbed earnestly.

"Call him again," Braggs insisted.

Gull and Spook took turns demanding that the unresponsive Christopher Columbus exit the trailer. They expended all their lung power in the fruitless effort.

"Must be a deep slumberer," Gull said sheepishly.

"Or drunk maybe," suggested Spook innocently.

Seeing no result, Harvell Braggs strode forward like a quivering mountain on teetering legs. He used the muzzle of his gun to prod Gull and Spook into opening the trailer door.

"He's not really Columbus, you know," Gull said as he turned the chromium door handle.

"That's what you think!" snarled Braggs.

"Now, who's the inebriated one," Spook muttered to himself.

GULLIVER GREENE had no plan. He was just going to throw the door open and see what Harvell Braggs did. Maybe a safe opportunity to seize the gun would present itself.

It was just as well that The Great Gulliver had wasted no thought on planning.

For up the road came the bouncing headlights of another machine. The sound of it braking came, accompanied by the squeaking of springs.

A door opened. Out of the vehicle came an angular form, which stepped into the headlights and became recognizable.

"Cass!" shouted Harvell Braggs. "Just in time. I have cornered Christopher Columbus in this trailer!"

Cass snarled out an epithet. "You fat fool! We have Columbus. Now get in the back seat with the girl."

A flash of scarlet lightning blinded everyone just then. Spook thought it was Braggs' gun going off. He slammed himself on the ground, where he hoped no bullets would fly.

Ivan Cass threw an arm across his startled optics.

While everyone else was reacting, Gulliver Greene grabbed for Braggs' pistol and got hold of it.

Lifting the muzzle to the sky, he began discharging the weapon in rapid succession.

This created further consternation. Braggs flattened. Cass threw himself to one side. Curses were hurled about.

While everyone was ducking and trying to get out of the way of imaginary lead, Gulliver sprinted for the Cass car, managed to avoid Cass himself, and fumbled for the man's waiting machine.

Finding a door handle, he twisted, flung himself inside.

A deep voice like a hound dog baying began expostulating.

Reaching out with his free hand, Gull found a floundering figure that was about the size of a small boy. He applied the butt of the now-empty gun to the midget's head repeatedly until the person ceased fighting back.

"Pete!" hissed Gull.

A muffled voice tried to say something. It was coming from the rear seat, so Gulliver got out and began rooting around in the back.

His clutching hands liked what they encountered, so he pulled what he fervently hoped was Saint Pete from the vehicle and bore her away as fast as his soggy feet could carry him.

Behind him, a rumbling commenced like a bowling ball careening down the road until a barrage of thundercracks re-mindful of monster tenpins scattering noisily smashed against his eardrums. He could not tell over the atmospheric detonations if Spook was following behind....

Chapter XXXII

TINY TRAIL

DOC SAVAGE EXAMINED the complicated gyroscopic astrolabe mechanism in the tower room of the strange old Victorian house in the Missouri wilderness.

"You did a credible job of restoring this," he told Long Tom.

"It was mostly a rewiring job." The puny electrical wizard kept staring at the bronze giant. He was garbed like an Indian, and his bronze hair, normally laying across his scalp like a skullcap, was longer than normal, showing signs of having been cut with a sharp tool by hand. But it was the beard that kept holding Long Tom's gaze. He had seen Doc Savage unshaven before, but never with such a luxurious growth of beard. It was disconcerting.

Doc asked, "Are you certain that the temporal device will take us back to 1937?"

"The timer was engaged to land six months after our last visit, but there's no telling about the return."

Doc nodded. "We will chance it," he said.

They called Herman Bunderson up to the tower. Doc conferred with the man, and the temporal return mechanism was reset and activated.

They waited. The mechanism kicked in and the familiar if distressing sensations of dislocation and visual impairment returned.

When their senses cleared up, an intense darkness filled the space—so black they might have landed in a void, and the fear that they had not returned to their rightful time fell over them like a frost.

Doc hurried down and stepped out onto the porch, seemed satisfied by what he beheld.

Long Tom joined him, and let out a sigh of relief. The familiar Missouri wilderness surrounded them. The air was cool, but not cold. The absence of snow was a welcome sight.

The moon-dusted sides of Doc Savage's small airship tethered to a tree was the most welcome sight of all.

Doc said to Long Tom, "The others?"

"Gone searching for Christopher Columbus."

Doc turned to Herman Bunderson. "Details, please."

Bunderson again unburdened himself of the story he had earlier told Doc's men. He included everything, from the accidental and unfortunate relocation of Christopher Columbus to the present, and the vain search for the missing discoverer of America.

At the end of it, Doc Savage was very quiet.

"Our problems seem to have multiplied," he offered at last.

"We have to fetch Columbus back to his own time," Long Tom stated.

"Without delay," agreed Doc.

Doc gathered up the two things he had carried back from the year 1830, Habeas Corpus and the rough sack of heavy items.

"Take care of this until our return," he instructed, handing the sack to Herman Bunderson.

The man blinked. "What is in this?"

"You might call it a downpayment of sorts."

Bunderson looked momentarily blank. Doc Savage left him without elaborating.

"The gasbag looks to be in airworthy shape," Long Tom remarked.

"What we need is an automobile," said Doc.

After replenishing their supplies from the dirigible's stores, Doc and Long Tom started off into the woods, seeking a way to reach the outside world, Habeas Corpus trotting happily after them.

Eventually, he found U.S. Highway 63, and for lack of a better plan, Doc Savage attempted to interest a motorist in picking them up.

However, the sight of his great buckskin-clad form and hirsute face caused all passersby to press harder on their gas pedals and accelerate away with alacrity.

"Maybe I had better stick my thumb out while you go hide behind something," suggested Long Tom.

"Good thinking." Doc slipped behind a shagbark hickory tree.

"What happened to your clothes?" asked Long Tom, as he listened for approaching traffic.

"Burned them, along with everything else. I lived off the land and stayed strictly away from people so as not to contaminate the era with my presence."

"Makes sense," grunted Long Tom, as a sedan blew by without stopping. "Ham found the message you carved in the rock."

"I did that only last week, when I concluded that rescue was unlikely," related the bronze man without emotion.

"That was why I had the timer set for January of 1830. I figured that was the safest way to go about it since your message said you'd already passed so much time in 1829."

"There is no telling what would have resulted had you arrived before I carved that message," Doc said quietly.

As luck would have it, the next vehicle to speed into view was a Missouri State Highway Patrol car.

Long Tom retracted his thumb and waved his thin arms wildly.

The car pulled over and a uniformed officer stepped out.

"What's the matter, buddy?"

"I'm Long Tom Roberts, and this is Doc Savage. We need a lift, pronto."

The bronze man stepped from behind his tree, looking like a forest wild man, Habeas the pig cradled in one mighty arm.

The uncouth sight caused the trooper to instinctively grab for his service pistol.

"It's O.K.," Long Tom interjected. "That is Doc. He's been out camping." Which was no lie—if one left out the year.

"Since when—January?" barked the trooper.

Long Tom produced his driver's license, which settled part of it. Doc had no identity cards, but the trooper agreed to transport them to his barracks.

There, Doc Savage was fingerprinted and given use of a shower and a shaving kit while his prints were wirefotoed to Washington, D.C.

When he re-emerged, refreshed and close-shaven, wearing clothes Long Tom had gotten from a hunting store, he looked like Doc Savage once again.

The attitudes of the local minions of the law underwent a remarkable transformation. They all but asked the bronze man for his autograph.

"Anything we can do for you?" asked the Macon patrol officer in charge of the barracks. He had introduced himself as Captain Chase.

"The use of an automobile to start with."

"Done. You know, we've been trying to reach you since the other day. There's a body in the morgue that has a medallion on it, giving your name and telephone number. We left a telephone message on some funny contraption at your headquarters, in New York."

"Who is the deceased?" asked Doc, interested.

"Box Daniels. Know him?"

"Yes. What happened to Box?"

"Someone bludgeoned him to death with a heavy shoe. We

thought it was the handiwork of a woman known as Saint Pete, but as it turned out the finger of suspicion pointed to an out-of-work magician named Gulliver Greene, also called The Great Gulliver. I don't suppose you know him as well?"

Doc Savage did not reply to that directly. Instead, he asked, "Have there been any other unusual events recently?"

The captain did not have to think long about that one.

"As a matter of fact, there is an unsolved killing in La Plata. The railroad depot telegraph operator up there was stabbed. We kinda have Gulliver figured for that as well."

"Let's start there."

SOON, Doc Savage was at the scene of the first crime, the telegraph office in La Plata's rail station. Fat Smith, now in charge of the railroad depot, told his side of the story, which amounted to less than nothing. He had missed the killer by several minutes.

The bronze man examined the tiger-cage office where the poor telegrapher had been working when stabbed to death.

Doc put his first question to Fat Smith.

"Was anything different when you returned that night of the slaying?"

"Yeah, poor Les was lying there with a knife wound in his ticker."

"Beside that."

Fat considered.

"Yeah. That stool over there was here instead."

"Was it the operator's habit to move the stool about?" asked Doc.

"It was nobody's habit. I put it back to where it belonged."

Those who worked with Doc Savage grew accustomed to the bronze man pulling any number of unexpected items from his equipment vest. These ranged from a fingerprint kit to a surgeon's scalpel. The contents of this vest were often changed, depending upon the circumstances Doc expected to encounter. As it happened, he was temporarily embarrassed. He packed no fingerprint kit.

Doc took a mechanical pencil from a holder, removed the thin lead, and crushed it to a powder on the counter. Scooping up the resultant dust onto a sheet of paper, the bronze man sprinkled these grains over the stool. Then he blew away the powder, leaving a grayish residue.

The Highway Patrol captain peered down at two blurry marks.

"Looks as if a child stood there," he commented.

"We don't allow no children into the place," insisted Fat Smith.

Captain Chase inserted, "There was talk of a dwarf mixed up in it somehow. But we never found any dwarf, so we figured it was a story made up to throw us off the scent."

"Was any motive for the killing established?" asked Doc Savage.

"This is where the two killings seem to tie in together," reported the captain. "A telegram addressed to this Gulliver Greene went missing. It was from Box Daniels, who is supposed to be Greene's uncle."

"Was the telegram recovered?" asked Doc.

"Not that we ever heard. This Gulliver claimed that he saw part of it, but that it didn't make any sense whatsoever. Seems the wire contained some wild talk about Christopher Columbus still being alive and kicking."

Doc Savage got his trilling under control before much sound escaped his firm lips, but it was a near thing. Long Tom made a growling noise, which he covered by patting his stomach, as if famished.

"We figured that was a story the killer concocted on the fly," continued Captain Chase. "Nervous crooks often grab at the first thing that comes into their mind, and with the new federal holiday and all just around the corner— Well, it made him sound guilty as hell."

Doc regarded the State Highway Patrol officer steadily. "I would like to see the bodies."

"Of course, Mr. Savage."

THE COUNTY MORTUARY in Macon was not a cheery place. Too, it smelled of sanitized death. They rolled out the body of old Box Daniels first, which rested on a porcelain drawer. Doc examined the head wound and found nothing of special interest.

Next, the steel-faced drawer housing the late telegraph operator came sliding out, revealing the man's still, pale features.

Doc stripped open the corpse's shirt and examined the wound carefully.

"A three-cornered knife did this."

The captain nodded. "Yeah. We have the knife. That Gulliver tried to hide it in a tree by the gas station where he worked, but one of my men discovered it. Had his fingerprints on it."

"The angle of the entry wound is unusual."

"Unusual how?"

"An average-sized man will bring a knife downward or plunge it straight into the heart. This wound shows an upward thrust."

"Meaning what?"

"A very small man committed this murder."

"You saying this Greene fellow is innocent?"

"From what I know of Gulliver Greene," insisted Doc, "he could not have possibly committed this or any other crime."

The captain went out and made a telephone call. Coming back, he said, "Fingerprint expert tells me that they found a few prints that they figured came off a child, so these were ignored."

"Those prints unquestionably belonged to the killer. Let me examine them."

This took them to another place, and the prints—which had

been lifted using graphite fingerprint powder and tape—were laid before Doc Savage.

His golden eyes came to rest on them. They had been very still up to this point. Now they began to whirl strangely.

From his parted lips came the trilling sound that marked his emotional state when agitated, or interested, or fascinated by something.

Doc was all three now.

Long Tom alone understood the significance of that sound. "What did you learn, Doc?"

"The identity of the killer."

AN urgency seized Doc Savage then. Turning to Long Tom, he said, "Many things are tied together that did not seem so when we first came to Missouri."

"Right," said Long Tom, who didn't actually follow the bronze man's trend of thought at all.

Addressing the captain, Doc asked, "Know anything of a midget in these parts? I do not mean a dwarf, but a true midget—a miniature man standing about three feet tall."

Rubbing his jaw, Captain Chase considered.

"About a year ago, we picked up a petty thief going by the name of Daniel Dill. We thought the name was funny."

"How so?"

"Well, he was so small he reminded us of a dill pickle. That was the joke we all told."

"This is no joke," said Doc grimly. "Where is Dill now?"

"Served thirty days in the county cooler for lifting Judge Lambert's wallet, then released. Haven't seen or heard of him since."

"We must find Daniel Dill," Doc told Long Tom.

Bafflement twisted Long Tom's features. "What about the other fellow—you know, that missing seaman we've been hearing stories about?" he asked, picking his words carefully.

Some of his natural bronze coloring seemed to have gone out of the bronze man's rugged features. It could not be said that Doc grew pale, but the loss of healthy hue was noticeable.

"It is difficult," he said, "to tell which trail is more urgent."

A slow light of understanding came into Long Tom's pale eyes. He started to whistle, low and amazed, but at a sharp look from Doc, he cut himself off. Obviously, Doc did not wish to rouse Captain Chase's curiosity in the matter of the missing Christopher Columbus.

Doc addressed Captain Chase, "Flash the surrounding towns," he instructed. "See if you can find any record of Daniel Dill, or someone matching his description."

The captain all but saluted. He came back with a simple typed report.

"A midget fitting that description was pulled over for—you won't believe this—driving without a license over in Elmer. He gave a story and was released when a friend came and bailed him out. This midget skipped out on his bail and hasn't been seen since."

"What was this midget's name?"

"Called himself Monzingo Baldwin. Think they are the same midget?"

"I know they are the same midget," replied Doc.

"Bad actor?"

"The very worst," said Long Tom, who now had a good idea who the murderous midget was.

Chapter XXXIII

THE SCARED SAINT

SOME TIME LATER, Gulliver Greene lowered Saint Pete beside a willow tree at the edge of the valley, then removed her gag. She told him that Spook Davis and Christopher Columbus were probably going to be taken away to a secret hideout by Cass' men.

The remaining rain made some sound; the water running in a nearby ditch was more noisy. The thunder seemed very far away now, and no lightning of consequence had happened for some minutes.

They were hunkered down under a group of sheltering willows. Pete was still bound.

"You might free me," the girl suggested.

Gull untied her. Her cinnamon-colored tresses were all fluffy, as naturally curling hair becomes when the weather is damp. They talked in low voices, pausing often to listen intently for danger, and Gull gave her a brief synopsis of what had happened, touching particularly on one point that mystified him—how had he been discovered?

Saint Pete clarified that.

"The Saint you tried to deceive at the speakers' stand has extrasensory perception," the girl said calmly.

Gull crouched on his heels, and his fingers found a blade of grass in the darkness and slowly picked it into pieces, rolled the fragments into little lumps and flipped them away. He ran his fingers through his hair, got them greasy with the mess of burnt cork and grease, wiped them thoughtfully on the grass, then shook his head. He was not going to surrender his convictions that there was no such thing as a genuine mind-reader.

The girl rested a hand on his arm. "I'm sorry," she said slowly. "I should have told you the truth, as much as I knew, when we met last night. But they had promised to kill Chris—my adopted father—if I went to the police, or talked to anyone about it."

"What are Cass and his gang doing with these traveling units of the Silent Saints?" Gull asked quickly.

Pete said she did not know. The only information she had in addition to what Christopher Columbus had known was that one of the units had returned today, and one of the Cass men had brought a small package for his chief. She had no idea of the contents. This verified what Gull had surmised from observation during the day.

By now, the hubbub around the Promised Land had died down. Once, Gull heard a searching party go prowling near, but it was dark in the woods. And they were not found.

"They got away with Spook," Gull said. There was not much of anything in his voice. "I looked over the crowd but Braggs—Spook—none of them were there."

After that, Gull announced his determination to rescue Spook. Saint Pete thought Spook Davis and Christopher Columbus would be kept alive, although she was not sure. Her reason for thinking they might be was simply that Cass might try to use their safety as a threat to keep Gull and Pete from going to the police.

"Then we'll go to the police right now!" Gull said abruptly.

Pete spoke softly, explaining something else. Cass had not been idle, but had perfected his murder frame against Gull—two of Cass' men stood ready to take the witness stand and swear they had seen Gull knife the telegraph operator, and had heard him threaten to kill old Box Daniels.

Gull, thinking that over, decided to risk it. He planned at first to go alone, and try to free Spook and Columbus. Saint

Pete dissented. They argued at some length, and the girl flatly refused to be left behind. She showed more determination than Gull cared for.

During their wait, the doors of the big white hangar opened, and out trundled a very large tri-motor seaplane, under power.

It slid into the water, pulled a wake behind it, and took to the sky, bawling over the steady rain.

"What do you want to bet that Spook and the others are on that thing?" gulped Gull.

"I know they are," sobbed Saint Pete. "And I know where they are going."

Gull could see from her wracking shoulders the truth of the girl's words.

"I've been wrong before," Gull said at last. "But I'm a hunch player. My hunch right now is that you are all right, but somebody happens to hold the means of making you do what they order." He paused, then added more earnestly. "How about a little ball playing? I've got to find old Spook—if it isn't too late."

"Ball playing it is," the girl said suddenly, wildly. Then both her small arms were fastened tightly upon his arm. "We've got to secure a plane, to get to where they'll take our friends."

"Plane?"

"I'll explain while we're flying. It will be a long trip."

"Where can we get a plane?" asked Gull.

"You are wanted in Missouri, but they may not be looking for you over in Illinois. We might get one there."

Gulliver eyed her. "But what will we use for money?"

"Dollars. They didn't rob me."

As proof, she produced a plump wad of greenbacks from somewhere in her coarse burlap frock.

Seeing this, Gull whistled low and slow.

THE MOON peeked a silver eye between two close-packed clouds. It was the first time Gulliver Greene had ever noticed any malevolent quality about the lunar sphere which is supposed to mean so much to lovers and superstitious farmers who plant their potatoes in its dark or its light.

They moved to the lake shore, discovered there was enough moonlight to make it impossible to escape the area unobserved, and waited, hoping the clouds would thicken. There was nothing else to do.

Eventually, a storm front rolled in and darkness swallowed everything.

They made one short foray and discovered a canoe in a rough boathouse, which belonged to the Promised Land property.

They used this to paddle away through the sprawl of water that was Lake of the Ozarks. They failed to see the abandoned amphibian plane that lay anchored some miles distant in another neck of water, never imagining a second plane being present, for the noise of its landing had been swallowed by the elemental storm.

Reaching land, they made their way to a small town, where they secured a lift to a larger town over in Illinois, where it was possible to rent a small plane. They did so.

There ensued a small argument over who would fly the plane. As it turned out, they were both licensed pilots, but Saint Pete had racked up more hours in the air, so that won her the argument. Gull had only fooled around with flying during his palmier days.

She sent the neat yellow crate scooting along the runway and into the air as sweet as any man.

Gull relaxed. After some time, he went into the mind-reading subject again. It bothered him. Being a professional magician who dealt in fakery, he could not credit mind-reading as being anything but fakery. As a matter of fact, he could do an excellent job of it himself, beginning with the old trick of divining questions which the audience wrote and sealed in envelopes.[*]

---

[*] *This "psychic" trick of reading messages inside sealed envelopes is one of the oldest tricks.*

He assured Pete as such, and reminded her that Christopher Columbus had stated she had extrasensory perception to some extent. She astonished him by quietly admitting that she did.

"Now listen," Gull said doubtfully. "Are you trying to tell me you can sense what I am thinking?"

"To some extent. I haven't the ability of some of Cass' men."

Gulliver fell silent.

There really isn't any such thing as a genuine mind-reader, Gull assured himself. The next instant the doubt he had pushed out of his mind jumped back and slapped him with what had happened in the past, proving with almost undeniable certainty that this girl could tell exactly what he was thinking.

But I'm certainly wacky about her in spite of it all, Gulliver thought.

"*Oh!*" said Saint Pete.

Blast the luck, Gull reflected. *She can tell what I'm thinking. Her tone when she said, "Oh," showed she could.*

"Hadn't you better get your mind on our troubles?" Saint Pete suggested.

"Uh—maybe so," Gull agreed sheepishly. "Say—*our* troubles! What do you mean—"

"Why do you think they were holding me a prisoner?" the young woman countered.

"That has me baffled, like a lot of things."

They were out of the rain now, and effulgent moonlight turned the wings silver. It was still very dark. Neither of them seemed to have much appetite for conversation until Saint Pete

---

The gag is this: The audience writes their questions and seals them. The envelopes are brought to the stage. The performer, without touching the basket containing the envelopes, dramatically recites a question aloud, then picks up an envelope at random, tears it open, drops the message on his table, then picks it up and passes it out to the audience that they may read it and see it is the message he just read. The trick is done thus: Actually, the performer has a stooge in the audience, and the stooge's question is not in the basket, but is placed beforehand on the tabletop, which the audience cannot see. This is the first one read. The performer then takes a genuine message from the basket, tears it open, drops it on the table, picks up the one he just read—thus making a switch—and passes it out to the amazed audience. He simply repeats this operation from then on, but of course the switch has now put a genuine message in front of him, concealed on the tabletop. —KENNETH ROBESON.

began speaking.

"I founded the Silent Saints five years ago. I intended it to be a small group. But Cass joined. Ivan Cass—and he had plenty of money. He seemed sincere. We expanded. Now the Silent Saints are all over the country. And now—now they're not—spreading our belief. I mean—that is not our real purpose."

Gull watched her. She was speaking jerkily.

"Go on," he said.

"Cass introduced many new Silent Saints. They are his men. I did not know what was going on. I never knew until—well—"

"Well? What went on until which happened?"

She skipped that. "Your Uncle Box Daniels worked for us," she said. "He was in the tent business. We rented or bought our tents from him. Sometimes he traveled with us, for he dabbled in mind-reading. He found out, shortly after I myself learned of it."

"Found out what?"

The plane sank on a down current, dipped a wing, and the girl moved the stick a little to level them out. The plane was a cabin job with a body like a barrel, low monoplane wing, and a big gas-eating motor. Pete did not answer Gull's question directly.

"Poor Box Daniels was terrified," she said. "He came to me. He wanted to go to Doc Savage."

"Don't mention that name to me," muttered Gull, running agitated fingers through his greasy mess of hair.

"Whatever do you mean?"

"He's the reason my hair turned white," groused Gull.

Saint Pete stared at him, possibly searching for signs of insanity.

"Long story," grumbled Gull. "Never mind."

Saint Pete looked at him a long time as if trying to penetrate his thinking, then gave it up as a bad job. "I wouldn't—couldn't—let Box go to Doc Savage," she continued quietly. "I couldn't go to the police myself, for the same reason I couldn't tell anyone. You think I'm crazy?"

"Sure," Gull grinned. "Anybody does crazy things when they are made to do them against their will."

She looked at him. "Thank you," she said. And his heart turned over.

THEY gave attention to the compass and the dark earth below—it was still night. The line of beacons—the government lighted airline route between Chicago and Kansas City—became visible, and they followed these.

"Your Uncle Box thought of you," Pete continued. "He had never met you, but he knew all about you. He said you were one of the cleverest living magicians. He'd heard others say that."

She sighed. "Well, Box Daniels decided to come to you for help. He sent a telegram. But Cass overheard us. He must have had a dictograph planted—well, they stopped the telegram, killing the depot agent in doing so. Then they—murdered your uncle before he could talk to you. The telegram is destroyed by now, of course."

Gulliver growled, "Cass showed me a telegram from Uncle Box, asking Cass to act as his bodyguard when he joined up with me in La Plata."

"A fake, obviously. Designed to make you think Cass was a friend of your uncle."

Gull made a face. "That means the anonymous note to Braggs was another fake, contrived to trick me into concluding that Uncle Box sent that one, too. They sure tried to surround me with hokum."

"Evidently," murmured Pete.

"I remember when I first met you," Gull said, making it a question.

"I was trying to stop your Uncle Box Daniels from getting to you," she explained. "I had to knock him out in the darkness

in the filling station where you were working. You almost caught
me then. Unfortunately, the little man who works with Cass
took that opportunity to slay him."

Gull nodded, for he had guessed that the midget was Cass'
main assassin. He asked, "What are the Silent Saints engaged
in pulling?"

She only shook her head and after that remained silent,
answering no more questions. But nearing Chicago, she said
Ivan Cass wanted to take Christopher Columbus to a spot
where he could be questioned at length, no doubt to the very
spot for which she and Gull were headed. They would take
Spook Davis there, too, from what she had heard.

"They'll kill Spook," Gull said with horrible conviction.

"No. Not as long as you are alive. After you told the police
what had happened, they planned to threaten to kill Spook if
you did not inform the police you had lied, and steer suspicion
from the Silent Saints."

"Oh," Gull said, enlightened. "What about Harvell Braggs?"

"I never saw him until he turned up in La Plata. I don't know
much about him. But I can tell you that his story about Christopher Columbus stealing his property is a lie."

"How do you know that?"

"I know it because the supposed theft occurred at Braggs'
island home in the Caribbean," Pete said firmly. "And Christopher Columbus has not been in the Caribbean in a long time.
A very, very long time," she emphasized.

Gull looked at her, but her face was very vague in the tiny
glow from the instruments. "That mind-reading of yours doesn't
hold all the way, does it?"

"Isn't this what you mean—how did Cass deceive me?"

"Maybe." He felt uncomfortable. But he wanted to know.

"It's extrasensory perception, not mind-reading," Saint Pete
corrected.

"Oh. I thought they were the same thing."

"They're—not." Gull was near enough to feel her shudder. She added, "Whatever ability I have is subconscious, beyond my control, and does not always work. It's just that sometimes I seem to be able to tell exactly what people have on their minds."

They landed at Chicago and ate in the lunchroom. While the plane was being refueled, Gull Greene was thoughtful.

The stock in trade of most mind-readers, he knew, was a bag of tested tricks to impress, a keen judgment of human nature, common horse sense and observation. To say nothing of luck, and a quick hand at making the other fellow fail to notice any mistakes. But this remarkable girl....

"The spot we are going to is out on one of the Great Lakes," the girl revealed. "A seaplane should be much better."

They rented one from the airport. By that time, it was almost dawn. They took off.

Gull shouted, "I wish you'd clear up that Christopher Columbus mystery. Who is he? What is Cass trying to get out of him? Why don't you want to tell me?"

The expression which whipped the girl's face shocked him, it was so agonized.

"The truth is too dreadful to impart," she said at last.

Gull didn't know what to say to that.

"You'll be surprised," Saint Pete added, "when we reach the island we are headed for."

"Island?"

"They call it Rat Island."

Chapter XXXIV

DEAD MAN ALIVE

DOC SAVAGE USED a State Highway Patrol police radio to contact Renny's plane.

"Doc Savage calling RR-1," he called into the microphone. He repeated this for over twenty minutes. RR-1 was the radio designation for Renny's ship.

The thumping of far thunder in Missouri's warm night was making it hard to hear over the static and carrier-wave hiss coming out of the radio loudspeaker. It caused Habeas Corpus to seek shelter under a desk.

There was no answer.

Long Tom Roberts stood by, his concerned face ashen where it was not the hue of a cellar mushroom. He worried an oversized ear while pacing.

Doc snapped off switches.

"They do not answer," he said.

"One of them should have stayed with the plane."

Doc shook his bronze head. "Not if they have scattered in the search for Christopher Columbus."

"It's a safe bet that they do not know about the other problem."

"It is," Doc Savage said slowly, "difficult to know which situation is more grave."

Long Tom gathered his high smooth brow into corrugations.

"You don't suppose that all these peculiar doings could be connected, do you?"

"So far it has not seemed so. But this has turned into a complicated matter."

"Box Daniels was an operative of yours," suggested the pale electrical wizard.

"A graduate of our college, who was sent to St. Louis to be on the watch for trouble worth our interest," admitted Doc. "Hence the medallion he wore and the instructions thereon."

A trooper barged into the radio room.

"A two-motored plane answering the description you gave us has gone down in the Missouri Ozarks, during a bad storm. It landed on Lake of the Ozarks."

Doc Savage was so stunned by that pronouncement that he actually repeated the statement.

"Did you say Lake of the Ozarks?"

"Damn!" said Long Tom. "That's where—"

"That's where what?" asked the trooper, frowning.

"Never mind," interrupted Doc. "Did the plane sink?"

"No. It's just sitting in the middle of the lake, hatch open and cabin empty."

"What portion of Lake of the Ozarks?" asked Doc.

"The northern arm, near where those Silent Saints have their main camp and headquarters."

"What do you know of the Silent Saints?" asked Doc Savage.

"A group of itinerant evangelists," reported the trooper. "As I say, they got their headquarters there, but they send out groups all around, preaching the faith and doing good deeds when they don't pass the hat for donations."

"Of good reputation?" asked Doc.

"A woman runs it. They call her Saint Pete. Seems honest, and there haven't been any complaints about the outfit."

"May we borrow an official car?"

The man nodded. "You can run the siren all you want, too."

"Thank you," said Doc.

290 / A DOC SAVAGE ADVENTURE

DOC SAVAGE drove south at a high rate of speed. He used the siren from time to time, but only to clear a path. His metallic face was very grim.

"We thought he was long dead," Long Tom was saying. "Drowned in the ocean before we could catch up with him."

Doc did not reply at first.

"You will recall, Long Tom, that we never found a body."

"Sure. But I never paid that any particular mind. He was so small, like a ten year old boy, but built like a miniature adult man. I always figured his body was washed out to sea, or he went down a shark's gullet."

"He is calling himself Monzingo Baldwin now."

"Baldwin," mused Long Tom. "That was the name of that brother and sister pair that worked with him, Buddy and Bess Baldwin. You put them through the college and straightened out their crooked thinking for good."

"Cadwiller Olden has taken their last name for an alias, possibly as a sly jest."

"Some joke," grunted Long Tom. His mind went back to a time nearly a year ago when they were caught up in an incredible adventure surrounding a weird rock that a South Seas volcano had coughed up. This was no ordinary stone, for it contained an element hitherto unknown on Earth, which Doc had dubbed Repel. It had the uncanny property of hurling objects as large as ocean liners great distances. It was unbelievable stuff.

Unfortunately, a criminal genius named Cadwiller Olden had acquired a covetous interest in the Repel substance. Doc Savage and his men had trailed Olden from the South Seas to Lake of the Ozarks, Missouri, where a portion of the expelled Repel rock had landed. There they had tangled, with the result that the ambitious little man had successfully carried off the powerful substance.

The mite commenced a reign of terror never before witnessed. Olden began loading Repel fragments into weapons with which his criminal army went on a campaign of wholesale crime and pillaging. One thing was certain—the very small man thought big. Doc tracked the foe down to a yacht anchored off the waters of Long Island. Olden had presumably drowned during a fierce battle. But no body had ever been recovered. Doc Savage and his men had loitered in the vicinity for several weeks, seeking the mortal remains.*

Coast Guard and Harbor police had been alerted to keep a weather eye out for any sighting of a midget—any midget—should they encounter one.

Doc Savage had received no such report.

Tooling the patrol car south, weaving around blacktopped turns in farmland where dull red barns showed from time to time, Doc Savage rolled grim thoughts around in his head. In the back seat, Habeas Corpus slept.

After a time, the bronze man broke the silence.

"One aspect of Olden's subsequent behavior puzzles me. He goes in for operations on a grandiose scale. But he has kept very quiet for almost a year."

"I'll admit it's not like him," Long Tom said. "You gave him a rough time over that Repel element. Could be he doesn't want to tangle with you again."

"It is a possibility," admitted Doc.

"At least the little devil doesn't suspect we know he isn't pushing up daisies. It will make it that much easier to sneak up on him."

Doc rarely used the word "I" in speech. But he did now.

"I am not proud of my record in dealing with Cadwiller Olden," he said.

"Record?"

"For better than two years, I had been assembling data on a mysterious master criminal," Doc said quietly. "A crook so subtle and so merciless that he was only a name. For a long time in

---

* Repel.

my investigation, he was only a name."

"You're thinking that if you were more aggressive in the beginning, we might not have had all this trouble."

Doc nodded. "And had I been more diligent last time, this present complication could have been avoided."

"We'll get him this time," Long Tom said firmly. "Now that we know he is alive."

"There is no telling what deviltry Olden may be engaged in."

"Well, we haven't received any reports about any phenomenal crime sprees in this area."

"Olden appears to have been laying low for months," Doc said. "Yet he murdered that depot agent in order to intercept the telegram from Box Daniels to Gulliver Greene, warning that Christopher Columbus is alive. This ties him into the Columbus mystery somehow."

"What does a flop magician have to do with anything?"

Doc Savage seemed not to hear. He went on speaking, however.

"It all hooks together, but as yet the connecting skeins are unclear."

"Herman Bunderson never said anything about any midget," Long Tom murmured. "Just some talk about a fat collector of Columbus items who was mixed up in it all, Harvell Braggs, and another guy, a shady private detective named Ivan Cass. They were searching for Columbus, who was supposed to have stolen so me stuff from Braggs' collection."

Doc Savage said, "We are looking for five individuals: Harvell Braggs, Ivan Cass, Gulliver Greene, Cadwiller Olden, and as fantastic as it may seem, Christopher Columbus. Should we find any one of them, there is every reason to believe he will lead us to the others."

Long Tom grabbed fistfuls of pale hair. "My skull aches just thinking about it all," he complained.

Ahead, faraway lightning danced soundlessly on the horizon.

Doc Savage gave the engine more gasoline.

Chapter XXXV
WOMAN'S INTUITION

THE LONELY ISLAND might have been a nodular gray whale floating on the largest of the Great Lakes, not many miles from the Canadian shore—or so it appeared when they first sighted it from an altitude of ten thousand feet.

They could not see the water, for it was early dawn, and a fog, very thick and probably no more than a hundred feet deep, lay over the lake. A coating of milky lather, it covered the island entirely at times. It seemed to be boiling, stirring.

Gull—he was flying the seaplane now—idled the motor and slanted down gently. It was a quiet motor. They could hear the wind singing in the wing struts.

He asked, "Sure that is it?"

Petella van Astor nodded at his side. "Positive. I have never been there, but I overheard Cass giving exact instructions on how to reach the place to the pilot who was to take Christopher Columbus—here."

Gull glanced at her intently. She had not told him more than she had earlier, and he was accepting her reticence because there was nothing else to do. Many things about her puzzled him, but most of all the strain that came into her voice when she mentioned Christopher Columbus.

He decided to test her reaction. "Your long-haired friend claims to be the discoverer of America. Claims his name really is Christopher Columbus. *The* Christopher Columbus."

"Have you ever heard of any *other* Christopher Columbus?"

the girl asked without much emotion.

"Columbus called you his adopted daughter," Gull pointed out. "Explain that."

"That is how we refer to one another. But you misunderstand, Columbus did not adopt me. Rather, it was the other way around. You see, he is a kind of a castaway, shipwrecked in a land that is unfamiliar to him. When I found him, I took pity upon the poor man, and took him in."

Gulliver didn't know what to say to that. It—this whole thing—is an impossibility, he kept telling himself.

He decided to try her again. Yes, and he'd fool her. He'd think of some utterly irrelevant question and learn if—

"You needn't go to all of that trouble," Saint Pete said thinly. "It is not necessary."

Gulliver sat perfectly still, feeling as if ice water was trickling down his backbone. Up until this moment, he had been trying to convince himself that Saint Pete had been reading his facial expressions and body gestures. But now—

Profoundly disturbed, anxious to do something to take his mind out of its present channel, Gull concentrated on his flying.

"We're getting a break," he said with an effort. "That fog will keep them from seeing us. Notice how the fog is boiling? There's wind down there. Wind that will keep them from hearing our motor."

She asked, "How do you want to work this?"

"I've got to know what we're tackling."

"I do not know what is on the island." She looked at him levelly. "That is the truth. I suspect it is Cass' headquarters. I'm certain Cass and Christopher Columbus and Spook Davis—as well as Harvell Braggs—are there. I believe the false Silent Saints will be guarding them. If they get us, they will slay you and Spook, and perhaps others—"

Gulliver waited. She did not continue, did not say who the others were. He believed she meant one of them would be herself.

"You wouldn't tell me where we were going," he said suddenly, "because you were afraid I would take this whole impossible story to the police on the chance that they might clear me of those murder accusations."

"Yes," she admitted. "You remember that my shoe was used to slay your Uncle Box? And my fingerprints were found on the knife that murdered the poor depot agent?"

Gull remembered that very well.

"Cass did that to terrify you further," he suggested.

"I'm sorry," Pete said. "I—I wanted to tell you."

A protracted silence followed that admission.

GULL considered. If he cut power, it might be possible to glide down to the lake surface. It was not calm, as he could spy through occasional breaks in the boiling mass of condensation, the wind whipping it into a driving chop. But neither was the surface dangerously turbulent. Landing under power should be comparatively safe. But without it, should the pontoons stub against a wave, the result would be a crack-up on water.

"We'll make another pass before we decide," he said finally.

As he took the seaplane around, Gull's thoughts drifted back to the matter of the Silent Saints and their queer mind-reading ways.

By now, Gulliver was convinced that the majority of the Silent Saints were fine men, genuine evangelists. He had realized, too, as he listened to the sermon which one of the Saints delivered to a large crowd in the great tent earlier in the evening, that they were engaged in a good work. Possibly they were accomplishing more in their way than the average church. Where Sunday school and church attendance had decreased generally, these evangelists were drawing huge crowds, simply because they tacked some interesting and mystifying mind-reading on the end of their sermon. They sugarcoated the familiar pill of a sermon with entertainment. Gull wondered, entirely aside from his other troubles, if the system the Silent

Saints were using wasn't the answer to the problem of decreasing church attendance. At first, the idea seemed like a desecration of religion. But in practice, it worked out much differently.

Saint Pete seemed to be reading his thoughts again.

"You do not entirely approve of the work that we do, do you?"

Gull assembled his words carefully.

"Preachers come in all varieties, I guess. Nine out of ten are earnest and really pay their way by persuading people not to be so danged ornery. But the tenth, a fake, comes along claiming to be God or somebody, makes a lot of susceptible people believe him, then takes advantage of them."

"The Silent Saints are a good, wholesome organization," Pete insisted. "Or they were until Ivan Cass came along."

A thought struck Gull. He put it into words.

"Why do you call yourselves the Silent Saints?"

"We believe in a time to come where men and women will communicate without sinful words, as we do. By telepathy."

Gull frowned. "What's so sinful about words?"

"Words can be used to hurt, confuse and deceive," Pete said firmly. "Thought is pure. Silence is golden. We are the Silent Saints who embody the Golden Rule."

Gull didn't know what to make of all that, so he fell into a pensive silence.

Completing a second pass, Gulliver saw that the lake chop remained rugged—too rugged for any but a powered landing.

"We'll have to chance they don't hear our motor," he said at last.

The girl nodded. Her knuckles were turning white.

Gull shut off the plane motor and turned the craft into the wind. He pulled two life preservers out of their clips and had the girl put one on, donned one himself. His lips were thin. He didn't like a landing on the lake; it would be rough, judging from the way the wind was rolling the fog along. But their safest procedure was to land two or three miles to the windward side of the island and let the wind blow them down silently to it in the fog. Uneasy, he worked the self-starter, thankful the motor had one, and got the propeller turning over slowly. The advantage of the motor power was worth the small chance that the noise of the exhaust might be heard. They were in the fog now. He set himself. His teeth felt like steel ball bearings against each other. If they cracked up in the waves....

They didn't.

GULLIVER shut off the motor and they removed the life preservers when Saint Pete told him quietly that she could swim. The girl was sober, thoughtful. He thought she was getting scared.

"It could get pretty rough," he said. "Maybe I better land you on the Canada shore and come back alone."

She looked at him, then away, and her small white teeth worried at her lips. "That isn't it. I was just thinking how low I have been."

"Low?"

The waves tossed the plane, making them sway and hang onto things.

"Of course," Pete said. "You trusted me, and I have not trusted you, nor given any definite explanations of why I am acting this way."

Gull suggested, "What you are trying to say is that I'm a sap for going it blind, for trusting you."

"Something like that." She was not looking at him. "I do not understand it."

"Want me to explain?" he asked.

"I wish you would explain," she said.

He took her in his arms then. He thought he would do it quickly, confidently, but found himself doing it slowly. She did not pull away, nor did her lips. The results were startling and wonderful....

The pitching of the plane unbalanced them in time, and Gull braced himself with his feet, held her more tightly.

"That's the explanation," he said huskily. "I wish you had asked for it a long time ago."

"Dear... I've been reading your thoughts all night...."

Gull, after he had sampled her delicious lips a second time, murmured, "This mind-reading is really something...."

Waves smashing on the plane's pontoons tore him out of his pink cloud. Gull hurriedly opened the plane door, got out on the wing. If it was a stony shore, they had an anchor—and it was. Working with frenzied haste, he rigged the tiny anchor. It seemed inadequate, but when he got it over the side, it dragged only a short distance—over rock, he could tell by the feel—then caught and held securely.

Gull paid out the line until the tail of the plane was only a few yards from shore, then made it fast to a pontoon strut.

Listening, he heard nothing. The water was no more than waist deep, he found, and they waded cautiously ashore. The stone was rat-colored, the rocks the same hue. Surf piling in made a great deal of noise, but he still heard nothing—at least no sound of danger.

The island lunged up steeply and was a labyrinth of brush and trees, with frequently a jutting rock ledge or a boulder as large as a house. A wild place, Gull reflected, but excellent concealment.

Still, its sheer desolation made him wonder if Pete could have made a mistake.

As if in answer to his doubts, Saint Pete suddenly said, "This is the place. I am certain of it."

"Want to stay in the plane?" he asked.

"I want to go with you," Pete said gently.

Gull started to climb, but the going was so awkward that he concluded to follow the beach around. If there was anything here, they would find signs of it near the water.

As they walked along, Gulliver decided to test the girl's

extrasensory faculties.

"Tell me what I am thinking about right now," asked Gulliver firmly, mentally picturing a juicy orange.

The girl closed her eyes. Her pretty brow furrowed.

"I am seeing a color," she began.

Gull said nothing. He did not wish to provide her help in any way. He knew that mentalists employed subtle clues to gain knowledge in situations such as this, often producing astounding, even uncanny, results.

Saint Pete's next measured words stripped the composed look off Gull's regular features and made the short hairs at the back of his neck stand up.

"You are thinking of a tangerine."

Gull swallowed his exclamation of surprise. Taking hold of himself, he said flatly, "Wrong."

The girl looked honestly chagrined. "I am sometimes wrong. Especially when I am nervous. Like now."

"Well, you were completely wrong this time," he said curtly.

"Let me try again," Pete implored.

"Don't bother. We have more serious stuff in front of us."

"Well, *I* like that!" she huffed.

Taking her firmly in hand, Gulliver led Saint Pete into the underbrush. His palms were moist with perspiration and his mouth felt dry. It was not only the peril of the situation that made them so, he reflected. The girl had been half correct. It had rattled him. Contrarily, he did not want her to try again. What if she perceived completely correctly this time? A tangerine is not an orange, but it was uncomfortably close to one.

Inching forward, they moved along, eyes searching, heads swiveling in all directions, lest they be ambushed.

So when a pair of long gun barrels poked blunt snouts out of the brush at them from opposite directions, they were caught entirely unaware. Gull found himself looking at the cold dark eye of a Winchester rifle. Pointing at Saint Pete was a double-barreled shotgun.

"No movements, please," a voice warned. "You are prisoners."

"Can I say something?" Gulliver asked.

"Speak!"

Turning to Saint Pete, Gulliver demanded, "What happened to your extrasensory perception?"

Petella van Astor turned a shade of crimson and her blue eyes darted away, refusing his gaze.

"I was not in a receptive frame of mind," she murmured defensively. "It doesn't always work."

"Excuses," snapped Gulliver as he began to march toward the inland direction the two men were pointing out with their weapons.

Chapter XXXVI

AMNESIA

THE MISSOURI NIGHT sky looked like an avalanche as Doc Savage wheeled into the picturesque Ozark leg of the sprawling dragon of water created by the damming of the Osage River, known as Lake of the Ozarks.

Colossal storm clouds paraded across the sky like boulders cascading along in defiance of gravity. Blinding sheets of rain drummed across the roof and hood of the borrowed State Police machine. Windshield wipers worked valiantly, but visibility was a humorless jest.

Doc Savage had recovered his many-pocketed gadget vest back at the strange Victorian house and Long Tom took out his compact but complicated supermachine pistol to check the magazine indicator. Both men were reviewing their store of gadgets and ammunition.

Plainly, they believed a fight was in the offing.

Forked lightning bolts made a hot glare against the sky, died away, leaving only a reverberant rumble. Then the long stretch of thunder and lightning finally abated. This caused Habeas Corpus to climb out from under the back seat, where he had been hiding. His long ears were very sensitive, and loud noises naturally bothered him.

Doc climbed out of the vehicle, was immediately drenched, but had time to employ a collapsible monocular of his own devising. He trained the tiny telescope-like instrument upon the pontoon plane resting on the rain-worried water.

301

Doc sank back behind the wheel. "Renny's plane," he said.

"Any sign of our group?" asked Long Tom.

"None. And the door is ajar."

"Renny and the others would never leave the door open—not in rain or any other kind of weather. That means they didn't leave under their own power."

"Precisely," said Doc Savage.

"Secure the plane first?"

Doc considered. "No. It would give away our presence. We will attempt to infiltrate the Silent Saints. There is an excellent chance that our friends are being held captive there."

"But where? Looks like it's a regular circus campground."

"That long structure has the look of an airplane hangar," indicated Doc. "We will begin our reconnoiter there."

The pounding, driving, slashing rain made it easier than it should have been. Easier from a standpoint of stealth, of course. Creeping into the encampment was simply a matter of braving the elements. All sensible inhabitants were indoors.

On the other hand, by the time Doc and Long Tom reached the hangar, their clothes were plastered to their bodies and they could barely see. Both men had whipped out protective gas-proof goggles to spare their eyes from the merciless precipitation, but the lenses had become so coated with water, visibility was difficult at best.

Reaching the door, Doc Savage paused.

He was an excellent reader of sign, but such clues required a better working environment than they had. Doc had looked for indications of men entering and leaving the hangar in recent hours, but the puddling rain defeated his scrutiny.

At the side door, he paused and sniffed at the air.

Even Long Tom smelled it.

"Airplane engine exhaust," muttered Long Tom. "A plane took off from here in the last hour or so."

Doc nodded. He had already spotted what appeared to be

big hangar-type doors at the seaward end, cleverly constructed so as not to be detectable except under close inspection. The bronze man had his monocular out and manipulated the instrument until it was in the form of a small black periscope. This he used to peer into the hangar confines through a small crack in big lake-facing door.

"Empty," he said.

They went in.

Lights were on—what few existed.

Doc moved around the interior, golden eyes roving, seeking all, missing nothing.

He stopped in a spot where the floor was spotted with machine oil.

There lay a silk handkerchief. Doc picked it up. It was monogrammed in fine stitching, *T.M.B.*

"Theodore Marley Brooks," Long Tom breathed, giving Ham Brooks' full name.

Doc nodded. "No doubt Ham and the others were held here for a time, before being flown to another location."

"But where?" asked Long Tom, looking around.

"We will endeavor to locate someone who knows," Doc said grimly.

They pushed out into the rain. Lightning popped very close; they could almost hear its eerie sizzle, as if a bullwhip had coiled past and cracked.

It was very late and few lights were showing among the trailers and tents. No doubt the inhabitants of the evangelical group had turned in for the night, there being nothing better for them to do on such an elemental evening.

One rain-smothered light did call out to them.

It was a gray trailer parked a ways from the rest, unhitched from an automobile. They made a beeline for that, which exposed them to danger, but since no shelter existed in the sodden pasture, there was no avoiding it.

Stealing up on the metallic rump of the trailer, Doc got his periscope out again and used it to check the interior, moving from window to window.

There appeared to be no one inside, but it was difficult to be certain. The interior was broken into compartments, at least one portion of which had curtains drawn over its window.

Going to the door, Doc tested the latch. It surrendered. Long Tom thumbed off the safety of his supermachine pistol.

Easing the door open, Doc let Long Tom go first, since he could more effectively confront danger with his tiny rapid-firing pistol.

The puny electrical expert crept in, then looked around. Light showed camera equipment and other paraphernalia.

Doc was soon beside him. Employing the special finger sign language they all knew, they conversed.

E-x-p-e-n-s-i-v-e s-t-u-f-f, signed Long Tom.

T-h-e-r-e i-s m-o-r-e h-e-r-e t-h-a-n m-e-e-t-s t-h-e e-y-e, returned Doc.

A wooden box invited their inspection. Doc lifted the lid, and for the briefest moment his eerie trilling was an ethereal sound under the sound of drumming rain.

M-u-r-d-e-r! Long Tom signaled.

Doc glanced around, indicated the camera and transit equipment. S-p-y r-i-n-g.

M-y i-d-e-a t-o-o.

They were still taking it all in when from behind them a deep croaking voice warned:

"This cannon is full of bullets and if you don't freeze in your tracks, you will be, too."

They turned only their heads, so as not to invite any lead.

Doc's trilling became a wild thing then.

FOR standing in the doorway to what appeared to be a small compartment—they could now see had a tiny cot—stood a most remarkable man.

He stood approximately three feet tall and could not have weighed one hundred pounds. He was no misshapen dwarf, however. He appeared perfect in his proportions. They were adult proportions, too. The man sported a day-old growth of beard.

In both tiny hands he gripped one of Doc Savage's super-machine pistols and had the spike-snouted muzzle trained on Doc and Long Tom.

"We will not move," Doc assured him.

"Drop that gun!" the midget ordered Long Tom.

The superfirer fell to the floor.

"Dandy. Now who are you birds?"

Doc Savage was so taken aback by the question he did not immediately answer.

Long Tom had no such inhibition.

"Don't you recognize us?"

"Why would I? Never saw you two mugs in my life."

Doc found speech. "I am Doc Savage. Does the name refresh your recollection?"

The tiny man eyed them narrowly. "Sure. A big shot from back east. I read about you. They say you're bronze-plated poison, especially to crooks."

"Crooks like you," Long Tom said pointedly.

"Maybe," the little man said, moving to slam the lid down on the wooden box of murder implements.

"What is your name?" asked Doc.

"What's it to you?" snarled the other.

"You look familiar."

"Baldwin. Monzingo Baldwin."

"Did you ever have a brother?"

The other shook his head. "No. Not that I remember."

Doc Savage said strangely, "If you ever had a brother, surely you would remember that?"

"Yeah. Sure I would. So I guess I don't have no brother. What's it to you, tall, brassy and nosey?"

"Have you ever heard of a man named Cadwiller Olden?" asked Doc.

"Never. Say, who's got the drop on who here? Stop asking dumb questions and keep still. I guess you barged in here to find your friends."

"Do you know where they are now?"

"Sure," chuckled the midget. "They're being ferried up north for the funeral."

"Whose funeral?" asked Long Tom, suspecting the answer.

The tiny little man offered a perfect pearly smile. "Theirs."

Doc Savage had been watching the weapon in Monzingo Baldwin's double fist.

"Do you happen to know whether that weapon is charged with lead, or mercy bullets?" he casually inquired.

"What's the difference?" croaked the other in his bullfrog voice. "If I pull the trigger, you're going to get a belly full."

"Some of my men carry drums of demolition shells," advised Doc. "Each one is packed with sufficient concentrated explosive that it would demolish an automobile."

"So?"

"If that is an explosive drum, and you pull back on the trigger, a single round would rip this trailer apart."

The midget teetered on his tiny heels. "I'll take my chances."

"On the other hand," continued the bronze man in a steady tone, "if it is set on continuous fire, the result will be horrific. There will be no survivors."

For the first time a lack of confidence crawled across the midget's scarred features.

"Is that so? How do I tell?"

"There will be a spot of red paint on the drum, signifying explosive shells. You may want to inspect it."

Monzingo Baldwin thought that was very sound advice, so

he raised the weapon in order to inspect it.

Doc got a better view of the condition of the superfirer. What he saw made him lunge for the tiny man like a streak of bronze lightning.

It felt like a thunderbolt descending upon the midget, too. For a crack of thunder picked that precise moment to detonate and, combined with the terrible metallic fingers that snatched the pistol out of his diminutive hands and lifted him to the ceiling, Monzingo Baldwin momentarily thought he had been struck by a sudden electrical bolt.

Outside, lightning drove an incandescent devil's pitchfork into the ground, adding to that unnerving impression.

Doc Savage pressed the midget against the ceiling of the trailer, where the latter bawled and flapped helpless hands.

"Leggo! Let me down, you big brass lummox!" he bleated.

Doc made his voice as hard as metal. "The truth now."

"Anything! Just put me down."

"Your real name?"

"Monzingo Baldwin!"

"Alias?"

"Danny—Danny Dill. But I'm really Monzingo Baldwin. Honest."

"Give him to me," gritted Long Tom. "I'll wring the truth out of him."

Doc Savage suddenly noticed a leakage of scarlet fluid dripping down from Monzingo Baldwin's left arm.

He lowered the man and, without setting him on his kicking feet, managed a thorough examination of his person. The midget wore a peculiar suit tailored out of burlap and heavy, old-fashioned shoes.

"You have a bullet wound, freshly dressed," Doc pointed out.

"Yeah. Damn that magician, Gulliver."

"Gulliver Greene shot you?"

"Yeah. He was trying to kill me, I think."

Monzingo Baldwin abruptly sealed his narrow lips.

Doc held the midget's face up to his own. Now he scrutinized the tiny features. He saw scars, the remnants of a broken nose, and other signs of facial injuries, both recent and healed, the former consistent with a through pistol-whipping.

"What has happened to your face?" inquired Doc.

"I lead an active life," the other sneered.

Doc regarded him steadily. "You do not know if you have a brother, nor how your face became so scathed?"

"That," snarled the scrappy little man, "comes under the heading of my personal business."

Long Tom grunted, "I can guess how you collected that broken nose."

"Set me down and I'll be glad to pop you one in the snoot, sourpuss."

"Any day of the week, small fry," retorted Long Tom.

"Go curdle milk, sourpuss!"

Doc Savage asked, "Does the name Cadwiller Olden mean anything to you?"

"No, why should it?"

"Merely asking," said Doc. "How far back do your memories go?"

"None of your damned business."

Long Tom had collected both superfirers and clucked, "Amnesia."

Doc nodded. "Almost certainly. His face, even his pattern of speech, are different from before."

"Different from what?" demanded the mite.

Instead of replying, Doc Savage asked, "Where is this spot up north you mentioned?"

"I'm no rodent. I'll never squeal."

Doc Savage was a master at self-control. He had been schooled to keep his emotions in check. But Cadwiller Olden, alias Monzingo Baldwin, had been the source of terrible tragedy in the past and was connected with equally dire doings now.

Doc Savage placed one iron-fingered hand over the midget's diminutive face as if to suffocate him.

The midget did not like that. Not one bit. He struggled, got his mouth free.

"Great Lakes! Up in the Great Lakes!"

"Which lake?" asked Doc, removing his hand.

"The big one. What's it called?"

"Superior," supplied Doc. "Lake Superior."

"Yeah," rasped the other. "That one. They're all on Rat Island. I stayed behind because I got shot. Now set me down before I get rough!"

Instead, Doc Savage shifted his fingers to the midget's small neck and exerted careful pressure. He was searching for the sensitive nerves that enabled him to render a foe insensate.

The problem was that in this case, the nerves were so small in contrast to the bronze giant's digits that applying the correct pressure to the appropriate spot proved elusive.

"Want me to put him to sleep?" Long Tom asked casually, rapping the tiny squawling man on the head with his super-machine pistol's hard muzzle.

It proved unnecessary. Perhaps it was the nervous strain of helplessness, combined with blood loss, but Monzingo Baldwin gave out a strange drawn-out sound and promptly fainted in Doc Savage's cabled hands.

"What do we do with him?" asked Long Tom.

"We will take him to Rat Island," decided Doc. "There is no time to make other arrangements."

They went out into the howling, lashing, rain-driven night.

Chapter XXXVII
A TRICK WITH DEATH

GULLIVER GREENE AND Petella van Astor were marched inland for a time.

There were rats on the island—Gull stepped close to one and it shot away with an abruptness which made him jump wildly; for some reason, this small incident cracked his shell of brittle desperation and he began to feel the aftereffects of the excitement. He grew almost limp, and sweat came out on his body. He grimaced and gnawed at his lower lip. It seemed that there was something very awry in his makeup; he got scared at the wrong times. Gull had discovered that he apparently could go through hell and bullets with the greatest of mental ease, but as soon as it was over, he had jitters with compound interest. A few minutes ago, he had been in imminent danger of getting killed. He'd been as calm as could be. Now, he was comparatively safe—for a while at least—but he was scared. His own psychological makeup aggravated him.

"They are going to separate us," Saint Pete undertoned at one point.

Gull looked at her. Their captors, prodding from behind, did not appear to have heard the whispered warning above the steady wind whipping over the rocks.

"They think it will be easier to manage us," she added firmly.

While Gull was wondering if this was another example of mind-reading, one of the captors abruptly said, "Separate them. Throw that damn magician in with the other one."

Gull decided that he had nothing to lose by resisting. But before he could formulate a course of action, a rifle butt caught him at the back of his skull.

Gulliver saw stars, reeled, went down on the rocks.

"Did you forget that some of us can read the mind?" a harsh voice inquired.

As Saint Pete was dragged away, her voice came floating back to him.

"Try to stay alive until Doc Savage arrives."

Cass' remaining man laughed recklessly. "Doc Savage has been dead longer than we have been alive."

As he pulled himself to his feet, Gulliver wondered what possessed the man to say such a crazy thing. For that matter, what had made Saint Pete offer hope in the form of a man who had no idea any of them existed?

He crept forward, finding it necessary to force each step, for he was not able to drive the unwelcome jitters out of his system.

Gull heard, before long, a series of faint outcries. They seemed to be shrieks, but they were muffled, unnatural, something like a cat meowing under a house. Gull hesitated, but the sounds aroused his curiosity. He was herded toward them, while his captor pushed bushes aside with his shotgun barrels, as he was marched across the rocky, brush-tangled island. The sounds ceased for a time.

An idea formed in his mind. If these people could read minds, perhaps he could turn that against them somehow....

"Go ahead, buddy," the shotgun wielder growled. "Try something, and we'll all see how it works out."

Gooseflesh began crawling over his forearms, which were already clammy from the lake fog. *His mind was being read like a book!*

In his career as The Great Gulliver, Gull Greene had learned to think on his feet. He had developed great presence of mind. He applied some of that now.

Pretending to start, Gull peered through the rolling fog.

In his mind, he made a mental image. A Herculean giant of bronze moving stealthily through the pale murk, slipping up from the shore, golden eyes seeking.

Doc Savage! Gull thought. He put all the force of his magician's powers of concentration into the imaginary figment.

It worked. Cursing, the shotgun man wheeled, swinging the double-barreled muzzle of his weapon around with the intention of unloading on the imaginary Doc Savage. Squinting through the fog, he groped for the double trigger.

They were among high rocks now. Gull made his mind a blank, and applied one well-worn shoe sole to the seat of the man's pants. The fellow toppled, struck rocks below and did not stir again.

Scrambling down, Gull heard a groan issue from the stunned individual's mouth. He used his fist to crack him on the jaw. Gull snatched the scattergun out of clutching hands. He did not have to strike again. The man stayed down.

"Whew!" Gull breathed. "That was close."

A new sound smote his ears then.

"Lemme ou-u-u-t!" came from nearby.

Gull wheeled, trying to fix the source. Such unexpectedness threatened to demolish his already badly mistreated nervous system.

Then he realized it was Spook Davis' voice! He whirled completely around, but did not see anything but rocks and boulders.

"Spook!" he called softly.

"Sh-h-h!" Spook gasped. "I'm in this ruh-rock."

It was a ledge of rat-colored island stone. In it, a door of wood, painted to fairly imitate the rock. Gull tested it, discovering that it pivoted and let him into a small stone chamber, the walls of which were painted deep black. There were shelves also painted black, and a sepia workbench. Interesting also was an array of mechanical gadgets—dark lamps, enlargers, projectors, splicers, retouching brushes, bottle after bottle of photographic chemicals. A secret darkroom, obviously where Cass' men developed photographs. But—photographs of what?

Gull pushed out his lips thoughtfully. It began to dawn on him that his previous theory that Cass was operating a murder ring under cover of the Silent Saints was not a complete picture....

Spook Davis wailed sarcastically, "We've got all day, of course!"

Gull took his gaze off the place and leaped to Spook's side. Ropes bound Spook, and he must have been tugging at the knots to get them so tight and tangled. Scooping a film-cutting knife off the bench, Gull cut the ropes, then lifted Spook erect. Spook was very scared, pale.

"The others?" Gull asked.

"What? Oh—Braggs and Columbus?" Spook rubbed his trembling wrists. "They're here, but somewhere else."

"They've got Saint Pete, too," Gull said, and wheeled for the door. "We've got to—"

Spook took one step and fell down. "Oo-o-o!" he gasped. "Golly!" He beat his own legs.

"Charley horse?"

"Herds!" Spook tried to get up, couldn't. "I've been tied all night," he moaned. Gull helped him, and they got outside.

No one was in sight, and they shuffled hurriedly into concealing brush.

"Don't go in this direction!" Spook gulped. "The rest of their layout is down there. Couple of bungalows and some shacks. A fake fishing camp. That's where I was being held."

They changed their course and traveled in silence, mounting a short distance, then descending the opposite side of the small island, and shortly they were on a beach, not a very wide beach, but one that was smoothly packed, level, and rather long.

"Their flying field," Spook said, indicating the graded beach.

Gull was astonished. "What? They have a plane here?"

"Sure. Two. Down this way. I hope to tell you to Merlin, this thing isn't small. I think they keep the planes for a getaway."

"Any idea exactly what Cass is up to?"

"Not yet. But it must be profitable."

Gull examined Spook Davis and he had the feeling that he was staring in a mirror at himself, because of their nearly identical features and physical build, and due also to the twin uneasiness which each of them was registering. Like Gull, Spook was pale, bruised, and carried strain on his features.

"Want to try something with the planes?"

"Guess so," Spook quavered. "It's about time we did something."

THE PLANES were not hidden, but stood on the beach openly. A man on guard with a rifle loafed beside one of them, and Gulliver and Spook held a whispered conference in the nearby brush, while the fog rolled about them, and the wind shook the underbrush.

"Guns!" Spook muttered, squinting. "Here's where I go back."

Gull caught him. "Take it easy. I don't like guns any better than you do."

"You've been acting," Spook accused, "as if you loved to be shot at. I personally am not an odds fighter. I will go farther and say I am no fighter at all."

"Let it slide." Gull suggested a plan, and ended, "…and it's the old conjuror's trick of misdirection. Want to take a chance?"

"No," Spook said shakily. "But I will."

Spook crept away. A few minutes later, he appeared in the lake, drawing near the shore where the plane stood; he waded in and held his hands high in the air. The guard, seeing him, raised his rifle. Spook stopped, paralyzed by fright. He was supposed—according to Gull's plan—to walk on out of the water, keeping the guard's attention while Gull crept up behind the fellow. Spook couldn't. He stood and shook; the shaking grew violent, his knees began to hinge so that he rose up and down foolishly, hunkering, a little lower each time, nearing a collapse.... Then Gull got close enough to hit the guard with the hard butt of his captured shotgun.

Spook came out of the water.

"Kuk-kill him?" he asked, so weakly he could hardly be understood.

Gull checked, said, "Out cold," tightly, and seized upon the fallen man's rifle. "Here," he added, and offered the rifle to Spook.

Spook took the gun, but immediately began to shake and grow pale. He handed it back wildly. "You carry it!" he gulped.

Gull kept the weapon, then ran to the planes. They were big crafts, with three motors apiece, he noted. The motors were canvassed against the fog. Gull got the covers off one craft's engines, then climbed into the cabin.

Spook started to get in after him.

"No!" Gull said sharply.

"Huh?" Then Spook understood. "Holy Houdini! If you think—I've had enough of this! I've had enough before it ever started. I won't—"

Gull said, "Save it!" and began starting the motors. They caught readily, to his immense relief.

Spook grew frantic.

"There's over a hundred of Cass' men here!" he screamed. "They've got machine guns—bloodhounds—poison gas! They'll kill us! Murder us! We can't do anything against them!" He got more desperate. "We can't—it's suicide—no! *No!*"

Gull yanked the throttles wide. He'd already set the controls and wedged them somewhat with cushions. The rest would have to be luck. He dived out of the plane and fell hard, for it was already traveling fast.

Spook Davis was running after the plane, still yelling. He stopped disgustedly when he reached Gull.

"If I get killed, it's your fault," he groaned.

"It's the brush for us," Gull said.

They ran into the brush.

The plane went booming down the beach, dragging its tail, bouncing and swaying and changing its direction a little; it hit a larger bump, jumped into the air, did not come down—it had taken off, no hand at the controls.

"Darn!" Gull breathed, realizing the craft was climbing too fast. It was sure to get out over the lake, nose up into a stall and crash—which was exactly what it did. But by that time, Ivan Cass and his men were on the beach. They had not been there, though, when Spook Davis said they were.

Gull eyed Spook where they crouched.

"I'm suh-sorry," Spook whispered contritely.

Gull Greene sighed like a black cat at Halloween.

"Let's just hope that Pete's eerie intuition was correct and by some miracle Doc Savage finds his way to this miserable rock before it's too late for us," he said.

"Amen to that," chattered Spook Davis, nervously counting the assortment of revolvers and rifles gripped in the hands of Cass' men.

Chapter XXVIII

FEAR FLIGHT

THEY REACHED THE Lake of the Ozarks shore without complication, other than the discouraging feeling that they were melting in the clammy rain.

Doc carried Cadwiller Olden under one arm, as if he were a limp bundle of clothes. His tiny pink tongue protruded like a viper's organ of taste.

They found a canoe upended on the beach, and tipped it upright, whereupon it began filling with rainwater.

Reaching the empty plane was a matter of rapid paddling before the rain swamped them. It was a near thing, however. They had to do some bailing with Long Tom's hat.

Doc got on the wing, accepted Olden from Long Tom, and they entered, examining the cabin with their eyes.

The controls had not been damaged. Indeed, the plane showed no sign of having been rifled, other than the fact that there were no spare drums for supermachine pistols. That by itself might or might not be significant. The others were in the habit of filling their pockets with extra ammunition.

Still, a thought troubled them. Long Tom put it into words.

"If Monk and the rest ran afoul of a spy ring, that means a bunch of our unique machine pistols might have fallen into unfriendly hands."

"Dictators in certain foreign capitals," Doc Savage said, "have told their spy chiefs that acquiring one would be their greatest dream."

Doc dropped into the control bucket while Long Tom went in search of dry clothes. He returned a moment later, wearing spare stuff that belonged to Renny Renwick, which swam on his undersized frame.

"Just until my own duds dry," Long Tom assured Doc, settling into the co-pilot seat.

There was only one problem. No Rat Island could be found on any map or marine chart of the Great Lakes.

Doc Savage was not greatly surprised, for his astonishing memory had offered up no such place. If it could be found on a map, the bronze man knew where it lay.

"Think the little gink was lying through his teeth?" wondered Long Tom, jerking a thumb back at the cabin where Cadwiller Olden slept in a seat too big for him.

"Doubtful. He was very frightened."

Doc Savage got on the radio and began contacting the local aviation authorities. To Long Tom's surprise, he described a large three-engine aircraft of European manufacture, a bird unlikely to be seen in American skies.

"I wish any and all reports of such a craft," requested the bronze man as he engaged the electro-inertia starters. The motors crashed into life, exhausts coughing noisily.

"How do you know they're flying one of those crates?" wondered Long Tom.

"Back at the hangar, I noted spare parts that could only fit a seaplane of that type."

Doc Savage got their plane rushing across the water, and up on step. Getting off the lake was problematic. The combined wind and downpour tended to push the fuselage down. Then there was the problem of water suction holding the pontoons down.

They solved the latter by rocking in their seats, which broke the suction seal, freeing the craft for flight.

Finally, the bronze giant got her aloft. Motors bawling, the plane turned north.

They flew across the Missouri State line and into Illinois. The foul weather was falling behind them, but it was not exactly a night for smooth air.

Before long, they received the requested report.

"No such plane sighted," Doc was told.

"Any unusual aerial activities tonight?"

"Yes. A man and a woman rented a crop-dusting crate in Quincy."

"Quincy, Missouri, or Quincy, Illinois?" asked Doc.

"They rented one plane in Quincy, Illinois, and in Chicago acquired a larger seaplane. Said they were flying up to the Great Lakes."

"Their names?"

"The renter said she was Petella van Astor. The man gave the name of Rico Verde."

Doc thanked the official and signed off.

"Who are they?" asked Long Tom.

"Unless I miss my guess," returned Doc Savage, "that is the evangelist known as Saint Pete and the other is an alias of Gulliver Greene, otherwise The Great Gulliver."

"How do you know so much about that guy?"

"I have been following The Great Gulliver's career for some time," replied Doc. "It seems very likely that they are also headed for Rat Island."

Long Tom grunted. Turning to look back at Cadwiller Olden sprawled wet and bedraggled on a seat, he said, "What do you think he is doing way out here? Looking for more of that Repel stuff?"

"Possibly. But it may be that in his amnesiac state, Olden wandered back to Missouri because he still possessed a fragmentary memory of this location."

"What about the new name?"

"That same disordered thinking could have dredged up the last name of Baldwin from his subconscious. I do not think Cadwiller Olden remembers anything of what happened before he was supposed to have expired."

"They never found that big black bodyguard of his, either."

"Nero undoubtedly perished, otherwise he would be at Olden's side."

Long Tom said, "I wouldn't want to encounter him again. He was a devil. Say, do you suppose Nero's other name was Monzingo?"

Doc Savage said nothing. After an hour, he turned the controls over to his aide. For Cadwiller Olden was stirring.

Doc checked the midget's wound, saw that the dressing was intact, and brought out an ampule of the chemical stimulant that never failed to rouse a person to wakefulness, broke it under his tiny nostrils.

Olden snapped awake as if shot a second time.

"Where—where am I?"

"En route to Rat Island," advised Doc.

The midget licked his pink cupid lips. His eyes narrowed. Olden bared tiny teeth in what passed for a wolfish smile. "You'll never get there in time."

"The exact location of the island, if you please."

"You think I would tell you that? In a pig's eye!"

"The lives of my friends are at stake," Doc said firmly.

The other made a swift motion as if zipping his mouth shut. "My lips are sealed."

"Last chance," warned Doc.

Olden pushed out his petulant lower lip and crossed both arms before his chest in the manner of a sulky toddler in a high chair refusing his creamed spinach.

Calmly, Doc Savage picked him up and carried the tiny man over to the cabin door, which he threw open.

Slipstream began howling. Cadwiller Olden matched it in intensity. His eyes became like round marbles.

"What are you doing, you brass-faced galoot?"

"Disposing of a useless nuisance," said Doc, thrusting the miniature man out the door.

Tiny fingers clutched and clawed air. Cadwiller Olden let out a screech longer than he.

"I'll tell! I'll tell!" he bleated.

"Thank you," said Doc, retracting the flailing midget and closing the door against the wind scream.

"You were going to hurl me to my death," the other accused after Doc had dropped him into his seat.

"Possibly," admitted Doc, who had no such intention.

Taking a seat, Doc began interrogating the amazingly small man.

IN very short order, Cadwiller Olden told of waking up all alone, having been washed up on a lonely Long Island beach, with no clear memory of who he was or what he was doing, many months ago.

"A lady took pity on me, took me in, fed me good," he related. "As soon as I felt better, I robbed her and ran away."

"How did you reach Lake of the Ozarks?" asked Doc.

Olden upended a minute thumb. "Hitchhiked, rode the rails, lived in hobo camps. Did anything I could."

"Why Missouri?"

Olden made faces, as if struggling to cudgel memories out of his brain. "I remembered it for some reason. It seemed important. I think I might have grown up there."

"You did not grow up in the Ozark Mountains," corrected Doc Savage.

"No? Then why did I—"

"Continue with your account."

"Got in a few scrapes with the law there," Olden admitted. "Then I hooked up with the Silent Saints. They took me in. I sold pamphlets for a while."

"Pocketing money on the side when you could," suggested Doc.

"Say, are you a mind-reader, too?"

"Too?"

"Yeah. Some of the Saints can read minds. That's where Ivan Cass came in. Cass was a local detective, strictly on the shady side of the street, you understand. He and I became pals. He caught me pilfering and decided I was a right guy. So he let me in on his racket."

"Which was?" prompted Doc.

"Is," corrected Olden. "Cass runs a high-class spy operation. We steal secrets, selling them to the highest bidder."

"Doubtful," countered Doc. "All signs indicate otherwise. Cass appeared to be in the pay of a certain foreign nation."

"Well, he tells it different," stated the midget.

"What do you know of a man going by the name of Christopher Columbus?"

The midget nodded. "They took him up to that island, too. Along with that fat fool, Harvell Braggs."

"How all this fits together is difficult to reconcile."

"It's complicated," admitted the little man. He examined his shirt sleeves and frowned at their soggy condition. "I could die of a cold after what you just put me through."

"Unlikely," returned Doc.

"I think I have told you everything worth telling," Olden suddenly said.

Habeas Corpus trotted up at that point, having been napping. He sat down and began staring at Cadwiller Olden.

"Is that your pig?" Olden asked Doc.

"What pig is that?" returned the bronze man.

"The one looking at me like I was a freak."

Doc Savage called up to Long Tom in the cockpit. "He says a pig is staring at him. Do you see a pig?"

Long Tom scoffed back, "That's rich. A pig on a plane!"

Doc said, "Long Tom sees no pig, either."

"Well, I sure see one," said Olden, not very confidently.

"Psychologists say that a man's conscience can begin to act

up over a lifetime of wrongdoing," suggested Doc. "Could it be that your conscience has taken the form of a pig and is haunting you?"

Olden bent a gimlet eye on the porker. "If that's my conscience, it sure is scrawny."

"That sounds about right," said Doc.

Cadwiller Olden tore his gaze from the steadily staring pig to Doc Savage and decided that reticence was not in his best interest. He began reciting more facts.

"Harvell Braggs went to Cass in his front as a private detective. He wanted Braggs to locate a man who stole some of his private collection of Christopher Columbus junk. Talk was the thief looked like Columbus himself. It was wacky, but when Braggs described this thief, Cass already knew who he was. Saint Pete had taken him in, just as she did me."

"Why did Cass not turn Columbus over to Braggs?"

"He was milking the thing. Braggs had a lot of dough, and he didn't want the theft to get into the papers for some reason. So Cass began stringing him along. But then that Box palooka stuck his nose in. He had joined the Silent Saints, too. We suspected him of being a spy for someone, but didn't know who or why."

"Box Daniels worked for me," said Doc.

"Oh." When this had sunk in, Olden added, "Box brought Gulliver into it for some reason."

"You killed the telegrapher at La Plata to stop Gulliver from entering the picture," said Doc.

A stab of fear stung the midget's face. "I am saying nothing more about anything."

"There is no use denying it. I recognized your fingerprints at the murder scene."

"You must have good eyes, or something."

"You also framed Gulliver Greene for the murder of Box Daniels."

"You'll have to prove that in a court of law," snarled Cadwiller Olden.

"A court of law," said Doc Savage, "is not your ultimate destination."

Rising from his seat, Doc Savage left the midget to digest those foreboding words.

Habeas Corpus continued sitting and staring with beady eyes that never seemed to blink.

"Shoo, you ugly conscience," the midget snarled.

The porker pointedly declined the invitation. His staring continued unabated.

Cadwiller Olden sat quietly, looking out the window with sunken eyes. Remembering that Missouri hanged its convicted murderers, he began feeling of his slender throat, whose injured larynx accounted for the midget's hoarse speech.

Chapter XXXIX

BAD MOVE

SPOOK DAVIS WAS invariably sorry after he had told a lie, and genuinely so, but contrition never deterred him from telling a falsehood freely when the next urge presented. He was normal in most respects, although the lying was not the only trait that made him a pleasant screwball. In the face of his fixation—his subconscious urge for exaggerating—Spook Davis was without resistance; he was as powerless as is a child when faced with the opportunity to steal a piece of cherry pie. Spook had lied about the Cass crew being so close, Gull knew; Spook had been scared and had wanted to frighten him into fleeing from the island. So when it occurred to Spook that he might tell a whopper and scare Gull into departing from the isle in haste, he hadn't hesitated. Fortunately, Spook was in too much of a dither to do very convincing lying. He could tell the most believable fibs when he was in proper form.

Gull whispered, "How many of Cass' men did you say are on the island?"

"A hun—"

"Whoa!"

"Aw—maybe a dozen and a half, all told," Spook amended.

"What about machine guns, bloodhounds and poison gas?"

"Uh—rifles, anyway. And revolvers."

"Better," Gull said. "Now let's turn into observers."

What they saw seemed to promise a more peaceful future, for Cass was obviously convinced that Gulliver and Spook had

325

been in the plane when it crashed out in the lake. That was good, Gull thought. Swell! The ship had hit the water with enough force to smash it, and being a metal plane, it would surely have sunk. Therefore, Cass would never know he was wrong.

Cass' men brought a speedboat which must have been hidden along the stony shore somewhere, and they went out to inspect the lake where the plane had hit. When they came back, they seemed much happier, and yelled to those who had remained ashore that the plane had sunk, carrying Gulliver Greene and Spook Davis to their deaths.

"We fooled 'em!" Spook breathed proudly.

Gull Greene remained crouched where he was, it being unlikely that they could find a clump of brush that would be better for concealment. Also, he had no idea what their next move had better be. The fundamental thing to be done was plain, of course—get Saint Pete and Columbus out of Cass' hands, then get Cass arrested in some fashion. There were complications, not the least being more than a dozen men which Cass seemed to have on the island, and the demonstrated willingness of these gentlemen to take the life of anyone who threatened their activities.

Gull forced his mind to take hold of the future as reasonably as it would approach the preparation of a magical effect. Before presentation to an audience, each step in a magic trick was carefully worked out, with consideration given each word and each small gesture, so that the effect of the whole trick would be smoothly successful. He had gone through the planning process with magic tricks a thousand times; it seemed logical that he should consider the present situation with an attitude as cool—but he found it a great deal more difficult. His thoughts even seemed to shy off from the unpromising future; he found them repeatedly summarizing what had gone on in the past, beginning with the unfortunate moment when he had learned of the mysterious telegram sent by Box Daniels, which had been the fuse to the entire package of perpetually exploding dynamite.

The thing to be regretted was that no more progress had been made getting clear of the mess, and yanking Saint Pete out of it.

Pete, Gull realized with increasing horror, would not be safe any longer. Gull moistened his lips. He had, he knew beyond any shadow of doubt, fallen heavily for the girl. He didn't regret it, particularly since, on their way to the island, the young woman had given some indication that his prospects were good.

Gull chewed his lips as he considered. It would be insanity to delay their efforts to free Pete, Christopher Columbus, and Harvell Braggs. There were many reasons for haste, not the least being that the fog which afforded concealment now would probably lift when the sun got a little higher. Likewise, the wind, now making a little noise which covered their movements, might drop later in the day.

"Was there anything worth looking at in that secret photographic darkroom?" Gull asked.

"No," Spook muttered. "Otherwise, they wouldn't have put me in there."

"Just why did they separate you from Columbus and Braggs?"

Spook shrugged. "Search me. Maybe it was because I kept slipping out of their knots all the time." He cracked a weak grin. "Guess that they had never tied up a magician's assistant before."

Gull rubbed his jaw thoughtfully, then announced that they had better proceed at once with the polecat hunt.

"But how are you going to do it?" Spook asked uneasily.

"The only way we can."

"Huh?"

Gulliver clicked the barrels of his captured weapons together. "Pick them off one at a time."

Spook began to muss his hair with his fingers and squirm as if his clothes were too tight. "Pick them off one at time, eh? Well—ah—whew! I don't think we'd better try that, Gull."

Gulliver eyed his nervous stooge. "You want to try to make it to shore for help?"

"You know I can't swim so good!" Spook hardened his jaw.

Gulliver stared at him. Suddenly, he reached out and took Spook by the throat. He said, "For a long time, I've wondered if this wasn't the cure for your lying!"

"Hey—wait!" Spook gasped. "I'm not lying!"

"Then why don't you think we better try to get these phony saints the only way we can—one at a time?"

"Well—" Spook registered discomfort. "Dang it, Gull, I think some of them are mind-readers."

Gulliver asked, "Why not come out with it, if that's what you think?"

"Because you know darn well there ain't no such thing as a mind-reader," Spook mumbled. "But I tell you, them birds just come close to me and look at me and tell me exactly what I'm thinking about." He squinted at Gull. "Your girl does that, too, according to what Christopher Columbus told us. Remember?"

"Pete!" Gull sighed. "You know what? I think I may get some place with her."

"You're welcome," Spook groaned. "Go ahead and marry the source of all our troubles."

Gull said, "I think I'll take the chance, if I can."

THEY were taking a chance some time later when they lurked near the crest of the rocky, brush-covered island. Gull stared, amazed, and pointed.

"Radio," he breathed.

Object of his astonishment was a pair of tall telescoping masts which had appeared from a cleverly camouflaged conceal-ment. Gull did not happen to be posted on the latest short-wave wrinkles in aerials, but this one looked efficient as it stood coppery and bright between the masts.

"Cass must keep in touch with his men by radio," he said. "I found a portable set in Cass' trailer. Wonder what they're really up to?"

Spook scratched his head. "They're sure organized."

Gull gripped Spook's arm and pointed. A figure was moving through the smothering fog, but that glimpse was enough to assure them that the moving shape was only one person, alone.

"There goes our first victim," Gull breathed.

Gull handed Spook the Winchester. Spook immediately began to tremble, and they had not crept far before Gull discovered the rifle was missing. Gull looked at one of his own fists meaningly.

"A-w-w!" Spook went back and got the rifle where he had left it. He returned carrying it as if it were a snake capable of biting him.

Gull hefted his shotgun. They couldn't shoot the prowler, of course, even if they were so inclined. The noise would be heard. What he was trying to figure out was the best way to hold the weapon to knock a man senseless, and still not kill him; it had never before occurred to him that this would be any problem, but now that the necessity confronted him, it was something to think about.

"You get behind him," Gull breathed. "If I miss him, he'll turn to run. You get him."

Spook put down his rifle and picked up a rock.

"I'm scared enough without handicapping myself with that firearm," he said determinedly.

Gull sighed and gave up trying to make Spook Davis rely on the rifle. They separated. Gull circled, and by listening intently, got an idea of the course of the lone stroller, then posted himself ahead of the fellow. It turned out to be simple—he glimpsed a head over a rock and gave it a whack with the scattergun's heavy barrels. That was all.

Gull was standing over the prize muttering, "Whoever said to look before you leap knew what he was talking about!" as Spook Davis came up.

Spook popped his eyes at the victim, who was swimming in

clothing several sizes too large for his slender frame.

"I recognize this guy from the newsreels," he exploded. "They call him the wizard of the juice. Long Tom Roberts!"

"Yeah," Gull agreed lugubriously. "One of Doc Savage's assistants. What in Cagliostro's name is he doing here?"

"Probably looking for his friends," Spook muttered absently.

"What friends?" asked Gulliver suspiciously.

"I clean forgot to tell you, Gull. But when Cass and his boys ferried us up here, they also dragged along a bunch of Doc Savage's boys."

Gulliver swallowed his rebuke with difficulty. "How did this one slip free, I wonder?"

"He didn't," Spook admitted. "He wasn't one of the bananas in that bunch."

Gull's green eyes flashed like hard emeralds. "And exactly when were you planning to reveal this deep, dark secret to me?"

"I was kinda hoping that Doc Savage would show up and pull their sorry souls out of the fire," Spook admitted sheepishly.

"I wouldn't be at all surprised," mused Gulliver Greene, peering around the foggy surroundings, "if Doc Savage wasn't on this island right now."

"What makes you say that?"

"Saint Pete warned me he was coming."

Spook grunted, "How would *she* know?"

"The things Saint Pete knows," returned Gulliver grimly, "would surprise a crystal gazer."

Chapter XL

SINISTER CACHE

DOC SAVAGE *WAS* on Rat Island.

The bronze man had found the island in the fog and overflew it once, at a high altitude, where their plane was unlikely to be seen. The super-silenced motors of Renny's plane, combined with the milky fog, kept the aircraft from being heard.

Anchored a fair distance from the southern shore was the small seaplane rented in Chicago by Petella van Astor, so they knew they had found the correct island. Long Tom employed a special pair of mechanical goggles combined with the plane's infra-red lamps to pierce the fog and make out the bobbing craft.

Doc had set down on Lake Superior a good distance from the leeward shore of the islet, where the fog would keep them smothered in concealment.

There was a pneumatic raft stowed on board. Doc inflated it and he and Long Tom used it to paddle close to the island, under the cover of the turbulent wind-driven fog bank. Long Tom still wore Renny's oversized clothes, his own not having dried sufficiently. This did not improve his commonly sour mood.

They had left Cadwiller Olden behind in the cabin, along with Habeas Corpus, the pig. It was perhaps the least desirable alternative, but absolutely necessary given that they planned to scout an unmapped island held by enemies. Experience had already shown that Doc Savage would be unable to render the tiny man unconscious through chiropractic manipulation of his spinal nerves, and after going through his carry-all vest, the bronze man failed to discover an alternative. He would probably need all of his gas-producing gadgets for the battle ahead, and the vest lacked a hypodermic needle or sedative.

"I'll fix his little wagon," Long Tom had fumed, taking great pains to lash Olden to a seat. After Doc tested his bonds, they disembarked, leaving Habeas Corpus to stare accusingly at the miniature man like a guardian Cerberus.

As they approached the rocky isle, Doc Savage and Long Tom saw a big foreign airplane come ripping along the lake surface and vault into the sky, only to do a nose-over and crash into the water, then sink from sight.

They elected to avoid the wreck when they heard the sound of a speedboat motor starting up.

"What about survivors?" breathed Long Tom.

"There was no one at the controls," said Doc. "So it is improbable that anyone was on board."

Long Tom did not question that. The bronze man possessed the penetrating vision of an eagle.

Landing on the leeward side of the island, they concealed their raft in the scrubby brush and split up, deciding that way they could cover more ground during their search.

Thus it was that the bronze man was entirely unaware of the misadventure into which Long Tom Roberts had stumbled.

Moving like a wraith through the milky murk, Doc made virtually no noise and encountered nothing more than scuttling rats. Obviously, the island had gotten its name from the local rodent population, which appeared unchecked. Bushes twitched and moved unexpectedly, indicating their furtive movements.

As a hideout, Rat Island was very clever. Boaters landing on its uninviting shores were unlikely to tarry for very long.

Doc Savage discovered the hidden workroom almost as soon as he noticed the ledge that concealed it. His alert eyes perceived the faint difference between the gray of the rock and the paint-camouflaged door.

Ground disturbance told him that there was a pivoting entrance, and he listened for only a moment before testing it with his weight. He cracked it, then hooked the tiny grappling hook he always carried to the edge, paid out line, and retreated to the shelter of a large boulder. As an extra precaution, Doc donned a gas-proof hood. Pulling steadily, he got the door open. No explosion or squirt of gas greeted this operation, so the bronze man reclaimed his hook and entered confidently.

The interior proved to be a fully-equipped photographic darkroom. Doc prowled among the equipment for some minutes, but discovered nothing more enlightening than the existence of the workroom itself. He did not remove his gas-proof hood until his examination was complete.

Cautiously, the bronze man exited and re-closed the pivoting door, rolling a large rock in place to keep it from being used by anyone without a pry bar and a strong back.

Doc moved on.

AMONG the senses which Doc Savage had perfected over a lifetime of diligent exercise was that of smell. His olfactory awareness was as keen as those of many animals.

The smells of the island were limited to its rough foliage and the odors associated with rats. There were seagulls, too, but these were not aloft in the fog.

The harsh tang of fresh blood came to Doc's nostrils. It might mean anything, but the bronze man immediately veered toward the scent.

So it was that he came upon two men standing over a third. They were unusually similar in size and build, the greatest different between them being their hair. One was carrot-topped, while the other displayed a shock of premature white that had gotten very dirty. They were armed with a Winchester rifle and a double-barreled shotgun. The third lay on the ground, unmoving. He appeared to be wearing clothing several sizes too large for his undersized frame.

The bronze giant swept in like a fog-shrouded spectre of flexible metal, so utterly soundless that the two armed men failed to detect his approach. They were not very cognizant of their surroundings, anyway, being immersed in discussing the prone person.

Doc was upon them before they detected metallic hands emerging from the grayness to snatch their rifles from their grip.

Both men let out howls of unbridled astonishment and whirled, empty hands clutching helplessly.

"Sh-h-h!" Doc Savage told them.

Seeing the bronze giant, they subsided.

"What happened here?" Doc demanded.

"I didn't look close enough before I swung that rifle," the white-haired one complained.

"It was foggy," seconded the other, who so greatly resembled the first that they might have been twins, or at least brothers, except for their hair. "We're suh-sorry," he added.

On the ground, Long Tom Roberts groaned weakly. His thin lips were drawn back off his teeth, and a few drops of scarlet crawled like red bugs where the rifle barrel had hit.

The white-haired individual started to say, "My name is—"

"I know your name," said Doc Savage, bending down to examine Long Tom's scalp.

"You do!" gulped Gulliver, greatly surprised.

Taking from his clothing a small first-aid kit, Doc Savage ministered to Long Tom Roberts' scalp. An ampule of chemical stimulant placed under his nose brought him around.

"What happened?" Long Tom moaned, looking about with slightly dazed eyes. Sitting up, he clamped both hands tightly to the top of his head as if to squeeze the confusion out.

"I made a mistake with that," Gulliver said, pointing to the rifle which lay on the ground.

Face reddening, Long Tom sprang to his feet and made hard

fists. "I'm going to turn your face into a mistake!"

Doc Savage said calmly, "It was an accident. Let it go, Long Tom."

The pallid electrical wizard, who looked as if he was about to take on all comers, reluctantly subsided, although his face remained flushed with fury. He gathered himself together, seemed annoyed at rediscovering that he wore—or swam in, rather—Renny Renwick's colossal clothes.

Spook Davis volunteered, "Mr. Savage, your men are being held prisoner on the other side of this island, along with some friends of ours, Petella van Astor and a man who calls himself Christopher Columbus."

"Are they alive?"

"I confess I have only a grisly fear on that point," Gulliver said, somewhat formally. The sudden arrival of Doc Savage had impressed him deeply.

"They—they're down in the fishing camp," added Spook. "Or they were until they kicked me out for being too good for their knots. They were to be killed, I think. But Ivan Cass—he's their leader—was holding off."

"For what reason?" demanded Doc.

"They took these special pistols off your men," said Spook. "They seemed to think they were real prizes, or something. But they couldn't get them to work. Cass was trying to pry the secret out of your men. When I was dragged out, they were beating one of them something terrible."

Long Tom growled, "For now, the safeties on our supermachine pistols have them baffled. But we can't let them get out of the country with the weapons. They would be worth a fortune to a foreign war department."

"Cass is some kind of master spy," inserted Gulliver. "There is a photographic darkroom hidden in a ledge near here, and a radio rig for long-distance communicating. They have been using the Silent Saints as a cover for their espionage operations. I finally figured it all out."

Doc Savage took this in with no flicker of expression. It was as if all were known to him. Then the bronze man asked a question that showed this was not entirely true.

"A large foreign aircraft went down not long ago. What do you know about that?"

"I did that," Gull admitted. "I set the controls and let her rip, hoping Cass and his gang would think we were dead. From the sound of their cheering, it worked out just that way."

"Stay here," Doc said.

"Eh?"

"You, too," Doc told Long Tom Roberts. "Keep an eye on them."

Gulliver asked uneasily, "What are you planning on pulling?"

"Just taking a look around," Doc explained.

DOC SAVAGE left Gulliver and Spook with Long Tom Roberts, who took charge of the weapons. The bronze giant crept cautiously up the hill, then down the other side. He located the fishing camp. As Spook Davis had said, it consisted of two bungalows and a few shacks, apparently an island fishing camp; a perfectly innocent looking place.

There were a few of Cass' men around. Doc lay in concealment and watched, occasionally flicking away a foraging rat. The place abounded with them.

Cass' men began to enter the farthest bungalow. Soon, they were all out of sight. Doc hesitated, decided to take a long chance, and eased to the nearest shack. Listening, he heard nothing, then entered.

First object he saw was a large metal box. Recalling the deadly box back at the Silent Saints encampment and being wary of booby-traps, the bronze man left it strictly alone. He peered about the place, inspecting its other contents.

This was a workshop. Whatever objects manufactured here were small, judging from the equipment. Doc moved about, taking an inventory. The remains of a tiny lady's wristwatch got his attention. The mechanism had been removed, and two electrical contacts soldered, one to the hour hand, the other two to a movable disc which had been substituted for the dial. The wires from the contacts ran to the smallest dry-cell battery he had ever seen, an equally minute coil, and into what seemed to be a tiny steel rod—the latter a tube which had been filled with dark composition at each end. All this apparently was destined to go into an ordinary man-sized fountain pen.

Doc scrutinized the pen; it was European manufactured, a popular one. Another bomb close by was apparently designed to explode when the filling lever was raised preparatory to charging with ink.

There was a regular chemical laboratory, the contents labelled. Doc examined some of the bottles and recognized the contents—he'd had a bit of experience concocting invisible inks. He went back to the fountain-pen-infernal-machines, then cast about in search of the stock of explosive from which they had been charged. No luck. He pocketed one. About to leave, Doc's interest became riveted on an incredibly tiny camera which was being built into a cigar. A very nice bit of work.

Rat Island, obviously, was the source of various devices espionage agents might use.

Doc left the building furtively, was not observed, and went back to where he left Gulliver Greene, Spook Davis, and Long Tom Roberts.

"We have the advantage of Ivan Cass and his group not knowing that we are at liberty," Doc told them. "It may be possible to work out a plan to free the prisoners."

"Don't be so sure of that," said Gulliver.

"What do you mean?"

Gull looked sheepish and seemed to have trouble forming words.

"Out with it," prodded Long Tom.

"Well, I–I'm a professional magician and I'd sooner eat my rabbit than admit this—since before today I never believed in this crazy stuff—but some of Cass' men can read minds."

Doc Savage looked at Gulliver with steady golden eyes. "Read minds?"

"They call it extrasensory perception," added Gull. "Saint Pete has it, too. She told me to try to stay alive until you got here—although some of Cass' men were saying that you were already dead and had been longer than we had lived. Whatever that means."

"It means," said Doc Savage grimly, "that this spy ring may be the most dangerous of its kind ever formed."

Chapter XLI

EXECUTION PARTY

IT WAS THE morning of what promised to be a difficult day. The sun had arisen with plenty of light but not much warmth.

Doc Savage was saying, "An espionage ring whose members possess extrasensory skills would have the ability to acquire the deepest secrets of other nations without those governments being aware of any loss."

"You don't believe in that malarkey, do you?" Spook Davis inserted with a trace of indignation.

"We have encountered this phenomenon before," Doc replied gravely.*

"Really?" said Gulliver. "Where and when?"

"None of your business, bushwhacker," Long Tom said sourly.

Doc Savage did not elaborate, other than to say, "Make no mistake, extrasensory perception may be rare, but it is very real. And there is no known defense against a skilled practitioner. Hence, we must move swiftly to rescue the others before Cass and his group suspect or sense our presence on this island."

"If they haven't already," muttered Spook.

"Can we storm the big bungalow cabin?" Gulliver wondered.

---

*During previous adventures, Doc Savage has come to grips with the eerie force called, variously, extrasensory perception, telepathy, along with similar strange mental powers, sometimes of a mechanical nature, but on other occasions naturally possessed by humans. While he has never unraveled its mysteries, the bronze man has acquired a healthy respect for the phenomenon—whatever it is. See The Midas Man, The Mental Wizard and Ost. —KENNETH ROBESON.

"Better to attempt to smoke them out," returned Doc. Reaching into his carry-all equipment vest, he began producing grenades of different types. Some were metallic cartridges.

With the natural curiosity of a magician toward unfamiliar gimmicks, Gulliver Greene observed these carefully. Tiny timers on the sides showed how they were actuated.

"Smoke?"

Doc nodded.

"I call them 'dragon eggs'," Long To said grimly. "When they hatch, everything turns black as Erebus."

"Once they are flushed from shelter," said Doc, "we will employ anesthetic grenades to overcome them."

"We'll have to work mighty fast," warned Gull.

"We will," said Doc.

But they were already too late on that score.

As they crept toward the mock fishing camp, the fog had begun lifting and men became visible gathering before the main bungalow cabin.

"That's our group!" muttered Long Tom, recognizing Ham, Johnny and the others. All had their hands tied behind their backs.

"Where's Pete and Chris Columbus?" asked Gull, searching with anxious emerald eyes. "I don't see them."

Activity had come over the Cass menage; more than a dozen men were in view. That, as far as they knew, comprised the total of Cass' men on the island. They wore dark Silent Saints garb, as befitted their role of sinister corruption in what was otherwise an honest organization. In their strange suits of burlap, they looked like crows whose color had faded.

The men were strapping on revolvers, opening cartridge boxes and stuffing shells into the pockets of their dark suits. Rifles were to be seen in numbers.

A man came out of a hut, staggering under a ponderous—for hand transportation—machine gun of the type used for mounting on Scarff rings in airplane cockpits. A drum of ammunition was in place on the weapon, and the man was trying to manage two more ammo drums.

Cass snapped, "Don't bother with that. Too bulky for what we're going to do."

"Sure." The man dropped the machine gun on the ground, obviously glad to get rid of its weight, and left it lying there with the ammo drums.

As Doc and the others watched, Ham, Renny and Johnny were marched off at rifle point. Two men dragged Monk Mayfair by his heels. His simian face was purple from numerous beatings.

"That was the poor fellow they were pounding on," offered Spook.

Doc Savage said nothing. He was observing the behavior of the captors.

Voices began booming and echoing among the rocks. They seemed unnecessarily loud.

"We don't need these snoopers anymore," Ivan Cass was saying. "So we'll administer a strong dose of lead sleeping tonic and roll rocks over them."

"They're going to be executed," Long Tom said tightly.

"What about the one in the hidden darkroom?" a Cass underling demanded.

"That magician's fool assistant?" barked Cass, driving his words through his teeth. "With Greene dead, we don't need him anymore. We'll collect him along the way."

All of Cass' men then crept away, Cass leading, and the brush swallowed them. They were being very quiet now.

Doc tracked the execution party with his eerie eyes. "They are being taken away from the others," he intoned, "evidently to be shot at a spot where their bodies can be best disposed of."

"We can circle around and ambush them!" Gulliver suggested.

Doc shook his head. "Long Tom and I will take care of the

ambushing. You and Spook wait until they are out of sight, and attempt to free the other prisoners. Get them away from the cabin. We will join you by the beach once we have succeeded with our part of it."

"What if you don't?" Spook asked anxiously.

Doc did not reply to that. His mental machinery did not factor failure into his operations. The bronze man had supreme confidence in his physical and mental powers.

"It is our policy to refrain from killing," Doc said, handing them the captured weapons. "If you must fire, shoot to intimidate or, at worst, to wound."

Gulliver accepted both, explaining, "Spook is afraid of guns. And I'm not keen on flinging lead indiscriminately."

That settled, Doc and Long Tom took their departure, merging into the scrub and rocks like expert woodsmen.

AFTER they were gone, Gulliver turned to Spook and said, "I hope you have some of that black pepper left. Might come in handy."

Grinning sheepishly, Spook turned his pockets inside out, demonstrating their forlorn emptiness.

Gull frowned. "Well, stick close. We may not have to fire a shot."

They began working their way to the fishing camp.

There was no outward sign of human activity when they came upon the camp. Only a number of buildings, camouflaged so as to escape discovery by a casual aerial flyover. They were clustered close together. The largest was a log cabin—not genuine logs, but the trick things that are turned out by lumber mills, a lap-board siding that resembled genuine logs, but without the bark.

It did not seem such a dangerous job to crawl to one of the structures and enter, but Gull and Spook lay in concealment and perspired for some time trying to get up the nerve. Spook felt tempted to go back, try to steal the other plane, and really fly away from the island this time. Gull thought of Daniel Boone and the other Indian fighters, hoping their feats would reassure him. They didn't. It did give him a healthy respect for Indian fighters.

Gulliver waited until he believed the Cass organization could no longer be heard tramping away, then ran forward to begin searching. He scuttled to the nearest building, listened, heard nothing, and entered. He looked around the shack, saw nothing but bunks—and when he came out, the machine gun attracted his eye. He tried another shack, saw more bunks. One structure remained, in addition to the log bungalow. Gull cast glances at the rapid-firer, for the deadly weapon fascinated him. He peered into the remaining shack and relief flooded him.

"My luck has changed at last," Gull breathed. "It couldn't go on the way it was."

Saint Pete stood against the single pole which supported the roof of the hut, being held there by encircling ropes.

She gasped, "Oh—be careful! They just left!"

Christopher Columbus was likewise trussed on the floor, looking grimly helpless. Next to him sat ponderous Harvell Braggs, eyes squeezed tight, his heavy features the unforgettable beet red of frustration. He bore some startling resemblance to a pile of blubber confined only by a tight brown skin and some rather immaculate clothing. The human whale had been trying to exert pressure on the heavy ropes winding about his bulk. The ropes holding him were tight, sunken almost out of sight in his fat at points.

"You're here too, eh?" Gull commented.

"He was a prisoner like myself!" Spook whispered.

"Fat chance," retorted Gull. "He's in league with Cass and the others."

Two or three ripplings stirred in Braggs' fat. He opened his eyes, mumbled, "Let me state for the record, gentlemen, that the reasons for my unwilling incarceration here are a complete mystery to me, for as I have explained several times, my only interest is to secure my very dear Columbus collection which was stolen from me."

"Gosh, that was a windy sentence," Spook muttered.

"—stolen from me at my island home in the Caribbean Sea—" the fat man continued "—and therefore you should be kind enough to permit me my liberty. Indeed, I do fervently wish I were back in my West Indies island home."

"What about Cass?" demanded Gull.

"A crooked man. I have never met one more crooked. I paid him handsomely to assist me in my quest, and you can see what has become my unjust reward."

Pete gasped again, "They just left—Cass—someone told them you were alive— They also know that Doc Savage has arrived on this island. Do you understand what that means?"

"I know," Gulliver said grimly.

Spook said, "Somebody has been mind-reading—"

"Yes," Gull agreed. "Somebody has been mind-reading all right. And that execution party was a ruse staged to lure Doc Savage into an ambush."

Gull began freeing the prisoners. He took the girl first. And his eyes, searching anxiously, discovered with relief that she had not been harmed physically. Her exquisite features showed to some extent the strain she had been under, but it occurred to him that if anything she was more exquisite now. Her command of courage was remarkable; he freely admitted that it exceeded his own, although he had been surprising himself considerably during the last few days. Like most men who go through the world in this life trying to make a living and at the same time sandwich in a little enjoyment, Gull had never been for any protracted time up against a danger that demanded bravery. He had supposed courage was something you were born with. But he had changed his mind about that. Conditions governed your courage. If you were in a jam, and there was a way out, you took it. If somebody shot at you, you ran. Maybe that wasn't courage. But it was sensible. On the other hand, if somebody shot at you, and you couldn't run, you fought back. That seemed to be the sense of the thing about which the historians, poets and songwriters had so much to say. Perhaps it was a grubby way of looking at it, but Gulliver believed that was what it amounted to.

He got the prisoners all untied. The girl moved about readily. But Braggs roused his blubbery hulk laboriously, began stamping his feet to get the blood circulating again. He had been a prisoner all night, much longer than Saint Pete, and he was stiff.

"I'll have to carry Columbus," Gull advised. "We have no time to waste."

"You've got a plan?" Braggs asked, grimacing.

"A kind of a one. We need to warn Doc Savage that he's walking into a trapper trap."

Braggs took a careful step on wobbly legs. "I can feel my feet again."

Gull asked, "Have you secured any idea of what is behind the Silent Saints devilment?"

Harvell Braggs shook his head, showed his teeth in pain. "I confess I have not, nor can I imagine what my collection of Columbus relics, which you will recall my telling you were stolen, have to do with this present mystery, neither can I suggest an explanation for that strange creature called Christopher Columbus—"

"Is Chris in another trance?" Spook asked, indicating the unmoving Columbus.

Harvell Braggs looked to see if Spook Davis was being funny, and saw he wasn't. "Christopher Columbus has not moved a muscle," Braggs said. "But he is alive, as I'm quite sure, for I saw Cass feed him, just as one would feed a helpless baby or a—"

He named several other things which Christopher Columbus had been forcibly fed, including milk being poured into a milk bottle.

Pete put in, "There was something in that milk, for after

giving it to him, he seemed to become dazed, then they asked him all manner of questions."

"About what?" asked Gull.

"A gold table that was lost in the Caribbean long ago."

"A myth!" Braggs said quickly. "There is no such treasure. You can take my word on it as an authority on the Great Navigator's life and fortunes."

"They also wanted to locate a strange old house on the Missouri woods," added Saint Pete. "They seemed to believe that it was very important in some way."

No one contributed anything to that latter assertion, but the expressions on the faces of Saint Pete and Harvell Braggs were uncomfortable. Both seemed to know more than they were letting on.

Gull tousled his soiled white locks thoughtfully. "Do you want to help us?"

Harvell Braggs' jaw rose and sunk in his many chins as he nodded vehemently. "I most assuredly do wish to contribute in any way possible to such measures as you may care to take and I will say further that my willingness cannot be overestimated, for I have suffered—"

"Right," Gull said. "Got any idea of how their establishment here was laid out?"

"I arrived by night," Braggs stated. "All was dark. I saw nothing useful."

At the bungalow door, Spook hissed, "All clear!"

Gulliver hefted limp and loose-limbed Christopher Columbus over one muscular shoulder and they started out into the thinning fog.

Braggs took one of the rifles; Saint Pete clutched the shotgun.

Stepping off the porch, Gulliver's emerald gaze swept the area. He suddenly stopped, took on the immobility of stone and his mouth did not loosen nor his eyes move from straight ahead.

Gull cleared his throat, swallowed. "Spook," he hissed. "I thought you were watching."

"I was."

"What happened to that machine gun?"

The perforated snout of the weapon in question suddenly protruded from a jumble of boulders off to the right and a nasty voice called out, "There is more than one trap being laid today."

The underbrush shook on all sides, and other men emerged, weapons in hand.

"I'm suh-so suh-sorry, Gull," Spook Davis mumbled.

"Not as sorry as we're about to become," Gull said grimly.

Chapter XLII

CURTAINS

DOC SAVAGE DID not follow the execution party down to the beach.

Instead, he broke off his trailing and gestured for Long Tom to follow him to higher ground. Puzzled, the slender electrical genius changed course, taking care not to tread dry brush under his feet. For his part, Doc moved with the soundless stealth of a phantom. Even the ever-active island rats failed to perceive his passing until he was almost atop them. Once, a jackrabbit bounded out of the way, startled. Doc was forced to make slight noises of warning after that, lest frightened animals give away his presence.

The bronze giant soon led him to the rock ledge that concealed a well-equipped photographic darkroom. It was still blocked by the large stone Doc had earlier placed there.

"Why are we stopping here?" Long Tom wanted to know. "What about the others?"

"Trap," said Doc, wrapping corded arms around the boulder and moving it to one side. It made a distinct sound dropping into place, indicating its extreme weight. The bronze man had handled it easily, however.

Long Tom tugged at an oversized ear. "What makes you say that?"

"Did you hear what Cass and the others were saying they intended to do as they were organizing?"

"Every word."

"Exactly."

Long Tom's eyes grew crafty. "They were talking loudly so that we would be sure to hear every word."

"Baiting a trap," said Doc. "Therefore, we must bait a better one."

Doc placed his weight against the false door painted to look like natural stone. It pivoted, disclosing the gloomy interior.

"What if they decide to kill Monk and the others?" asked Long Tom.

"They will refrain from doing so until they are certain that they have snared us, too. They know we are on Rat Island. They will also assume that we are armed."

"I get it. They want the secret of our supermachine pistols. If everyone ends up dead, they might never figure them out."

"That is my hope," said Doc.

They were inside the darkroom now. Doc employed his spring-generator flashlight for illumination. Long Tom produced his, gave it a vigorous winding to get it going.

Two thin beams swept around the dim interior. They examined the camera equipment carefully.

"Not much to work with here," Long Tom muttered.

"The contrary. There is just enough."

"Enough for what?"

Doc began to take his flashlight apart.

"How did the spider catch his dinner?" he asked.

Tiny lights of understanding came into Long Tom Roberts' eyes. He smiled thinly. Then he began to disassemble his flashlight as well....

MONK MAYFAIR was coming to. His gimlet eyes jumped open. He peered around warily.

"What in blazes?" he muttered through crushed lips.

Johnny Littlejohn offered, "As a thespian might say, the superultimate act is commencing."

"Johnny means that it's curtains," Renny said dryly. "These mutts are about to execute us."

Ivan Cass strode up to the hairy chemist and gave him a fearful kick in the ribs.

"One last chance before lead slugs dash out your brains," he snarled. "What is the secret of unlocking these weapons?"

"I don't think I should tell you," Monk mumbled vaguely. The hairy chemist appeared dazed. He glanced toward Ham Brooks. "What do you say, shyster?"

Ham Brooks made a thoughtful mouth.

"They say they'll let us live if we talk," he ventured.

"Do we believe them?" mumbled Monk painfully.

"Hard to tell," rumbled Renny, shrugging giant shoulders.

"It is a foregone conclusion that our utility will prove of diminutive duration," offered Johnny.

Monk gave his bullet head a shake, as if to clear his mental machinery. He winced in pain.

This byplay seemed to bring out the innate impatience of Ivan Cass. He lifted his voice.

"Form the execution squad." He said it much louder than necessary. Everyone noticed that.

Men assembled themselves into a line and raised their rifles. A few leveled revolvers.

"Ready!" shouted Cass, hard eyes ranging the rocks above the beach. They stood not far from the surviving tri-motor plane.

Monk clambered to his feet. He looked shaky from the beatings he had endured. One eye was turning purple, while the other showed a greenish discoloration. He spat out a loose tooth. It clicked against one of Cass' shoes.

Monk growled. "I don't know about the rest of you, but I've had a bellyful of all this."

Ham glared at him. "You don't mean—"

"You wanna know how to operate these hoot guns," the apish

chemist said defiantly. "There's a trick to it, and I know the trick."

Cass stepped forward. "What is the trick?"

Monk opened his wide mouth to speak.

Ham and Renny and Johnny started to object loudly.

"Don't listen to him," roared Renny. "He's punch drunk!"

Cass silenced them with a dark glare.

"Let this ape speak his mind," he ground out.

Monk struggled for words, made simian faces, but finally said, "I—I can't do it. I can't betray Doc's memory."

Cass leaned in, as if to peer into Monk's homely features. He was very silent as he did so. No one spoke. It became very quiet.

"I have it!" crowed Cass. "I have the secret."

"Blazes!" said Monk, jaw dropping.

"He read your mind!" thumped Renny. "Now we're in for it."

Seizing one of the compact superfirers from an underling, Ivan Cass took it in both hands.

"According to this dull ape's mental pictures," the spymaster stated, "one merely has to press this stub and slide this hornlike projection forward." Cass did so. Distinct clicks came. Taking the weapon properly in hand, Ivan Cass wrapped his trigger finger around the firing lever. He aimed the weapon's snout at the prisoners. Into his crow-black eyes came a wicked gleam.

"I will now demonstrate the proficiency of this remarkable weapon," he announced.

Instead, Ivan Cass began howling and hopping in circles as the supermachine pistol suddenly began to smoke and grow hot. Soon, it was incandescent. The barrel drooped, falling off like ashes from a long-burning cigar. It sizzled when it struck sand.

Moaning in pain, Cass dropped the weapon, where it commenced melting into liquid slag.

"Thermite!" grinned Monk. "Burns, huh?"

"Nice bit of acting, you misbegotten tree-dweller," Ham undertoned.

The others kept straight faces. Built into these intricate pistols were two small charges of the chemicals which, when combined, constitute thermite. When two studs were simultaneously engaged, the incendiary substances—iron oxide and aluminum powder—mingled and were ignited, producing terrific heat, melting the weapon in a matter of moments, as they all witnessed.

Enraged, Cass barked, "You tricked me!"

"Guess you read my mind wrong," countered Monk, displaying missing teeth in a wide grin.

Cass seemed not to know what to say to that. His dark eyes kept searching the surrounding rocks, as if he expected visitors.

But Doc Savage did not show himself.

"We will shoot one as an example to the others," Cass decided at last.

Monk, Ham, Johnny and Renny all rushed to volunteer to be the one shot. Ham took up a position before the much-battered Monk, protecting him. Johnny leaped in front of Ham. Then Renny stepped before all three of the others, making hard blocks of his bound fists behind his back and growling, "Do your dead-level worst."

This astounded Ivan Cass, who did not know what to do then. He ground his teeth in impotent rage.

The problem was solved when one of his men approached and whispered in Cass' ear.

"One of the men senses that Doc Savage has entered our secret darkroom."

Cass grinned. "Send three to seize him. Now!"

This was done.

Addressing the prisoners, Cass announced, "We will see how brave you are when we stand Doc Savage before the rocks and shoot his eyes out."

The others said nothing. They stood stunned. This was the first glimmering they had that their bronze chief was alive and active in the Twentieth Century. Fighting back wild hope, keeping their demeanors subdued, their thoughts churned.

Doc Savage was no man's prisoner until he was produced in chains. They did not think for a moment that Doc Savage would be captured by a mere trio of men—even if some of them were sneaky mind-readers.

THE THREE Ivan Cass underlings moved up to high ground, seeking the rock ledge that concealed the darkroom cave.

They slipped up to it, saw that the door was ajar, but could not see in, the pivoting panel having nearly closed tight.

Cautiously, they approached.

The man in the lead paused, and seemed to be concentrating.

"I am sensing the bronze man's brain waves. He has entered the darkroom, and has concealed himself there in order to ambush us."

As if to confirm that, their alert ears picked up the muffled sounds of a man's voice coming from within the hollow ledge.

Although pitched low, it had the unmistakable ring of Doc Savage's outstanding voice. Another voice, less powerful and more querulous, joined in from time to time. The Cass crew did not recognize those sour tones as belonging to Long Tom Roberts, but they did not need to know the identity of the second man, only the first.

Carefully, they crept up to the ledge.

One man set himself on the rock-sheltered side of the pivoting door, while the leader—the one who claimed to sense the bronze man's mind—put his weight against the portal. With a gritty grinding, it turned ponderously.

All together, they rushed into the hollow work space.

From his prone position atop the ledge, Doc Savage leaped down and slammed the door shut, then rolled the huge rock into place, blocking egress.

Muffled shouting came from within the darkroom. The trio was trapped, and they knew it. Fists pounded futilely. Profanity crackled.

Long Tom emerged from the prickly concealment of the

brush. He was grinning so hard his gold front teeth gleamed.

"Your ventriloquism fooled them good. They were dead sure you were inside."

Doc nodded. "They may also have perceived the false mental pictures I endeavored to create that illusion."

"Next move?" asked Long Tom.

"If any of those men is a mind-reader, he will soon settle down and summon the others telepathically."

"We want that?"

"Very much," replied Doc.

Retreating to the underbrush on either side of the narrow upward path, they took out their dismantled spring–generator flashlights and a great deal of wire harvested from a tool box, and got to work.

IVAN CASS was not a patient man. He waited, paced and fretted, his rock-like face working darkly. From time to time, he unleashed a stream of fluent profanity.

"What is keeping them?" he raged.

Cass glanced toward one of the others.

The man closed his eyes and seemed to go into a reverie. When they snapped open, his face was unpleasant.

"Doc Savage has trapped our men in the darkroom."

Cass ground his molars as he spoke. "Take four men. Release them. Locate Doc Savage! And be sure to shoot him very dead!"

Monk, Ham and the others saw that the ranks of Ivan Cass' operatives were growing thin. They exchanged glances.

"Still too many to rush," Renny muttered.

"You will rush no one," Ivan Cass snapped. "Soon you will all be kaput."

"Don't count your corpses just yet," returned Monk.

THE FOUR Ivan Cass operatives worked their way along the narrow path with their weapons held before them. Their gaze grew very sharp. They meant business. Rats raced to get out of their way.

They were so concentrated upon the possibility of ambush from either side that they failed to notice the snare lying across the way.

This was understandable. The snare was all but invisible.

As they walked into it, utterly oblivious to the danger, the cautious quartet heard around them a whizzing or whining sound that might have been produced by drowsing insects. They halted, then advanced more slowly.

Thus it was that they blundered into a haze of unseen stinging things that made them believe they had stumbled upon a wasp's nest.

The first man encountered something thready but unyielding with his pistol barrel.

He received a shock from his own weapon, and doubled over in agony. The revolver fell.

The others, right behind him, slammed into the same strange stinging phenomenon.

Soon, all four were twitching and contorting and moaning as pain shot through every atom of their paralyzed bodies. Weapons hung frozen in their fingers, which began clutching spasmodically.

Crouched on either side, Doc Savage and Long Tom continued winding their spring-generator flashlights, out of which tiny wires trailed.

After a bit, Doc said, "Enough."

Long Tom stopped, leaped up and socked a man in the jaw. He went down.

Emerging from concealment, Doc Savage wrapped massive fingers around the heads of two stunned foes and brought them together with an audible *bonk!* The pair collapsed into a pile of loose burlap gunnysacks.

That left one foe remaining. He was still recovering from his shocking experience.

Doc Savage took him by the back of the neck and made kneading motions that rendered him unable to move a muscle. Eyes remained open, able to see, but not to move.

"How many men does Cass have left?" demanded Doc.

The man stuttered out a number in his thick voice.

"Call for help," directed Doc Savage.

The man made strangling sounds, indicating he had little control over his vocal apparatus.

Doc kneaded spinal nerve centers some more, permitting movement above the neck.

The man found his tongue, and started howling his head off.

"Cass! Come quickly! Hurry!"

At a nod from Doc Savage, Long Tom returned to his station in the tangled underbrush. Doc bundled his hapless prisoner under a massive arm and sank from sight. The man went silent, a victim of the bronze man's surgical touch.

There, they checked the wire connections between the spring-generator flashlights and the web of tiny superfine wires they had strung across the trail, spider-web fashion.

"More flies for the web," Long Tom murmured as the tramp of footsteps came near.

But the puny electrical expert was overconfident. For the footsteps, they soon recognized, were not coming up from the beach, but from inland.

Doc Savage realized this first, and a flicker of concern animated his flake-gold eyes.

A moment later appeared a contingent of Ivan Cass' men, driving Gulliver Greene, Spook Davis, and Saint Pete before them by gunpoint. Gulliver was packing Christopher Columbus over one shoulder. Leading the group was whale-like Harvell Braggs, his big stomach swinging from side to side.

Chapter XLIII

TABLES TURN TWICE

DOC SAVAGE, MAN OF BRONZE, took in the unexpected and unwelcome sight of the procession of captors and prisoners coming down the path without a change of expression.

His flake-gold eyes read the situation in flash parts of a second. Gulliver Greene had been seized in the act of freeing the prisoners, or shortly thereafter. This complicated an already involved picture.

Long Tom Roberts yanked his supermachine pistol from its underarm holster, trained the muzzle upon the oncoming parade, and awaited word from his bronze chief.

A rat scampered across the path, looking almost as large as an alley cat. Another followed it. They were foraging for food.

The group drew near.

Doc Savage told Long Tom, "Hold your fire, unless you obtain a clear shot at Cass' men."

"Right," said Long Tom, who had no such luxury at the moment. The prisoners would catch most of the mercy slugs he sent their way. Although they would not prove fatal, the bullfiddle roar of the tiny superfirer would attract Cass and his men, who would no doubt execute the helpless prisoners if he lost the upper hand.

Motioning for Long Tom to fade back into the underbrush, Doc Savage stepped into view, revealing himself.

Doc Savage had once been described by a journalist with a

flair for a colorful turn of phrase as resembling a well-oiled machine of muscles, sinew and cables. In the mid-morning sunlight, he perfectly fit that description. Caught unprepared, Cass' men froze.

In that breathless moment before his foes could get themselves organized, the bronze man extracted from a pocket the trick fountain pen he had earlier purloined from the cache of espionage tools.

Holding it high, he let the others see it clearly. Like a conjuror attempting a trick, Doc made certain they got a good look at it.

Then, making a show of tripping in the ink-charging lever, he let fly.

The celluloid pen turned end over end as it covered the intervening space. Eyes popped. Jaws sagged. Instinct and reflexes took over.

The first person to dash madly for cover was balloon-bodied Harvell Braggs. He literally careened into the brush, body parts seeming to fly every which way, as if his overstuffed arms and legs were all seeking shelter at different compass points.

The others, alarmed by Braggs' wild action, quickly followed suit. Gulliver Greene urged Saint Pete into some nettles.

Amid the frantic scramble for cover, the bronze giant made his move.

Pitching forward, he surged for the Ivan Cass confederates. Every one was armed, but shooting was the last thing on their minds. Their feet all but struck sparks as they flung themselves into the hard rocks, seeking protection from the innocent-looking infernal device.

In his wild haste, one dropped the heavy machine gun he had been toting.

Doc Savage moved like a thunderbolt unleashed, but the Cass operatives were no sloths. Their skins were at stake.

Doc Savage managed to seize one of them by the collar. The man gave out a sheep-like bleat, and tore away. Simultaneously, the bronze man seized the wrist back of the man's revolver, then grasped the weapon by its cylinder, his steel-strong grip preventing it from turning, effectively paralyzing the pistol.

As a result, Doc found himself holding the gun and the man's burlap garment. The frightened individual had literally ripped free of his coat, so great was his fear of the impending explosion.

From prone positions all around—everyone understood that flight from shrapnel was futile—men plugged their ears to protect sensitive eardrums from concussion and held their breaths.

But no detonation came.

"Now, Long Tom," rapped Doc.

The slender electrical expert popped up and began hosing the underbrush with mercy bullets. The hollow capsules—for that was what they were—began worrying nettles, splashed chemical contents harmlessly against gray rock.

Very quickly, Long Tom's drum ran empty.

"I think I got one over there," he called to Doc, pointing west.

The bronze man surged in that direction, but discovered that Long Tom had managed to bag an overfed island rat, not a man.

From the beach came angry shouting and commotion.

"Cass will investigate without delay," warned Doc.

Clipping a fresh drum into the superfirer receiver, Long Tom said, "I'll pick them off when they do."

Brave words. But at that moment, the Cass operatives lying flat in the surrounding brush realized that the devilish pen gadget was not about to detonate.

Two of them jumped up, looked about like upset gophers. Each had Winchesters.

One drew a bead on the big bronze man. The other picked Long Tom as his target.

Both rifles emitted sharp reports. Their noise blended into

one spiteful snarl of sound. The riflemen displayed a precision that spoke of military training.

Almost together, Doc Savage and Long Tom Roberts toppled off their feet and lay still.

Letting out a yell of victory, one of the Cass agents called upon the others to investigate the result of their marksmanship.

It was a tribute to the bronze giant's reputation that there was some considerable hesitation before nerves were summoned up.

In that brief interval, a coiling dragon of black smoke erupted in the vicinity of Doc Savage.

"Trick!" yelled a man.

Winchester rifle barrels trained toward the smoke. Levers worked. Bullets began lacerating it.

It was impossible to say what, if anything, those pellets struck.

For the black pall began swirling as if alive—or something was disturbing it from within.

Down at the beach, the sounds of combat had reached Ivan Cass' ears.

"Leave the prisoners here!" He charged up the path, his men following.

IN the squirming ball of chemical smoke, Doc Savage used his ears. Sounds bounced off the surrounding rocks. A shotgun blatted. Buckshot punctuated the roiling blackness, whizzing close by.

Doc kept low. His chainmesh undergarment would turn most anything a shotgun could hurl at him, but his head was unprotected except for the bulletproof skullcap he wore over his natural hair like a helmet of hammered metal.

The bronze giant cut through a brushy tangle, feeling his way. His plan to overcome his foes with various gas bombs had been thwarted by the confusion created by the arrival of the new prisoners, and the scattering of forces that resulted. He paused only once, crouched behind a large bush. What he did there was obscured by the smoke.

Doc Savage soon found Long Tom in the sepia swirl. The puny electrical wizard was coughing violently—the result of a lead slug catching him in his chest.

Doc sank at his side. "Hurt?"

"No," wracked out Long Tom. "But my ribs ache like blazes."

Doc helped Long Tom to his feet and urged him in the direction of the camouflaged photographic darkroom—the only high ground, as well as the best shelter on the island.

"Cass is on his way here," Doc undertoned. "He told his men to leave the prisoners behind, so they are unguarded. Work around and free Monk and the others."

"What about Gulliver and his group?"

"They have scattered. Collecting them would be like going after stray cows. Dispersed, they will present less tempting targets."

"In other words, they're on their own."

"In other words," Doc clarified, "they can fend for themselves until you organize Monk and the rest of our friends."

"You going to create a distraction?" asked Long Tom.

"If possible. But it is imperative that Christopher Columbus be conveyed to safety. His demise could irrevocably alter human events leading up to the present day. That single fact may well be more important than the lives of anyone on this island."

With that disquieting statement, the bronze man melted into the swirling smoke, seeking the unconscious Columbus.

GULLIVER GREENE was crawling through the blackest smoke he had ever breathed. It made his lungs feel scratchy, but the ebony stuff didn't seem to be poisonous. He had attempted to carry Christopher Columbus to safety, but in the darksome miasma that had proven too risky, so he had deposited the unconscious man in a cluster of rocks, trusting to fortune that he would be safe there.

Gull called out Spook Davis' name, low and urgent, but this produced no response. Likely Spook had fled.

In the brush, he discovered Harvell Braggs, also crawling.

"I think Doc Savage was shot," Gull breathed.

Harvell Braggs was too busy trying to climb to his feet to comment on that announcement. He was so ponderous, his wide body such a linkage of loose, teetering balloons, that he had to struggle to get all of his component parts organized.

Finally, he found his feet.

"I believe I can navigate," Braggs allowed.

"Know how to work an airplane-type machine gun?" Gulliver asked. "They dropped the big one when Doc Savage spooked them."

"During the late war," Braggs said bombastically, "I did my share of shooting."

Picking up the machine gun, the mechanism of which was completely a mystery as far as he was concerned, Gull said, "I'll carry this piece of artillery. You better stick close to me and be ready to pull the trigger, or whatever it is you pull to make it talk."

Saint Pete came over, offered, "I'll carry the ammun—"

"No," Gull interrupted hastily. "There's another job for you. Cass has a speedboat on the island. You must get to the boat, and be ready to get the motor going. We'll make our getaway in the speedboat if we have to."

The girl hesitated. "But—"

"Please," Gull urged. "To make a go of this, we've each got to do a separate part. Won't you cooperate on yours?"

"Well," she said, "I—yes."

Pete went away toward the beach to the speedboat Gulliver had conjured up in her mind, casting anxious glances over her shoulder until she was out of sight.

Gull and Braggs crept up toward the ridge of the island. Gull did not head for the plane, but led the way cautiously up the steep slope toward the hidden darkroom.

"Good idea to get the girl away from the trouble," Braggs

breathed softly.

"Thanks," Gulliver whispered.

"Look, Greene, I've been plenty rough on you two magicians a time or two. Forget it, eh?"

"Sure," Gulliver said. "Let's keep our eyes open for Doc Savage and his men."

They stepped in carefully selected spots to avoid cracking twigs, and finally Gull pointed at the newly-arrived Cass reinforcements, who were gathered around the ledge which contained the secret door. The men were arranged in a semicircle, guns trained on the concealed portal. It looked as though they had been there for some time. Furthermore, they seemed to be getting impatient.

The reason for their interest was plain to behold. The pivoting door was closed, but in closing, it had clamped on a fragment of someone's shirt, which hung like a limp rag. From within, increasingly weak voices called out, so muffled they could not be distinguished.

"Looks like Doc Savage or Long Tom ducked into that darkroom," breathed Gull.

Braggs nodded vehemently. "Cass has no intentions of taking the bronze man alive, I will wager."

"We have to do something."

An argument was taking place. The reinforcements were insisting that Doc Savage was inside the darkroom, while others were equally insistent—apparently based on their extrasensory perception—that he was not.

The shirt sleeve fragment flapped in the breeze, taunting both sides. It was one of Long Tom's.

Cass, dark rage on his hard face, suddenly made a number of imperative gestures for his men to charge the darkroom. He stood back, rifle ready for anyone who might come out of the hideaway.

Three men strained mightily, and muscled the rock aside. The door received encouragement to open in the form of prodding rifle stocks. The portal swung on its pivot, revealing the cave-like interior.

Out stumbled the Cass men Doc Savage had earlier imprisoned. They emerged with their hands raised high. Consternation followed. Someone belatedly realized that Doc Savage could not have rolled the rock into place after he had secreted himself within. It was an impossibility.

Gulliver got set.

"Cass! Lay down your arms!" he roared.

Cass was the only one who dropped his weapon. He was so startled that he lost his rifle. All his men jerked about, seeking the author of the command.

"Shoot over their heads, Braggs," urged Gull.

When no racket came, he spun.

Lying there was the big machine gun—but Harvell Braggs was gone!

"Vamoosed!" gritted Gull. Seizing the cumbersome weapon, he found the firing trips, opened up, shooting over their heads. The machine gun blared intermittently. Then it went silent.

"Surrender!" Gulliver yelled again, blindly. Gun smoke was a haze before his vision, defeating it.

Answer was a sharp bark from a Winchester rifle. Gull returned fire ten-fold.

Then Gull swiped powder fumes out of his eyes, peered, and was astonished at his success.

One Cass man was down, somehow shot through the legs. The others had flung away their weapons and uplifted their arms.

"Stay still!" Gulliver roared.

They became as rigid as trees. They didn't much resemble vicious killers who had terrorized Gull's existence for some days. They were just men at the end of the rope, and scared of death. A machine gun will do that.

Ivan Cass' wrath seemed to foam up within him until no

room remained for words; at any rate, he fell into an about-to-burst silence.

Gulliver worked his way down and collected their weapons, which he tossed into the unoccupied photographic darkroom. He searched the prisoners for concealed weapons, which he also flung into the darkroom. He then closed the darkroom door and rolled the convenient rock in front of it so that it could not be pivoted open in a hurry. The captives glared, some sullenly, and Cass did some of his best swearing. Gull thought stagehands in the theaters where he had played as a magician were the only real masters of profanity, but that was an error. Cass had them stopped.

"You want to keep your teeth?" Gulliver asked.

Ivan Cass went silent. His stony countenance burned whitely.

Then Spook Davis came stumbling sheepishly out of the underbrush.

"I THOUGHT I'd wait until you got all those guns put away," Spook exclaimed, then grinned vaguely. "I don't lay any claims to being a brave man," he added needlessly.

Spook was disheveled, and seemed unsteady on his feet. He kept pressing his fingers over his forehead, snapping crimson drops off on the surrounding leaves.

"Wounded?" Gulliver asked.

"Almost annihilated," Spook groaned. "Listen, do you know what happened to me after you left me to—"

Leaping, Gulliver caught Spook by the arm, rushed him to a nearby bush, and shoved him down in its concealment.

"Stay there a minute!" Gulliver hissed.

A crashing of the brush that Gull had heard now came closer, and as he waited for the maker of the noises to appear, Gull gripped a revolver he had collected.

Harvell Braggs came out of the brush. His eyes seemed about to fall out when he saw the situation. He stopped. His mouth opened and shut. Sheepishly, he managed a grin while he fumbled with a Winchester rifle he had discovered somewhere.

"I thought I was ready for anything," he grunted uncertainly. "That is, my spirit was ready. But my poor body was—Well, I heard shots."

"Yes," Gulliver agreed. "There was some more shooting. It's all over."

Braggs made a wan smile. "That's—that's—"

"We seem to have everybody," Gulliver said flatly.

"Uh—well—that's wonderful," Braggs muttered. "You were doubtless wondering where I had gotten to."

"Exactly. Spill."

"You see," stammered Braggs, "I was circling around in order to—"

"You turned tail. Why?"

Harvell Braggs swallowed several times. "I fear—that is, I am afraid that all that talk of machine guns and proficiency with them was just that—talk. I am ashamed to admit that I am, in total, a terrible coward."

Spook Davis came out of his bush wearing the expression of a man about to swat a dining mosquito.

"I ain't a fighting man." Spook began rolling up his sleeves. "But—" He glared at Harvell Braggs.

Braggs gulped, "Ah—"

"You're in cahoots with Cass!" Spook gritted.

Braggs said, "Now—"

"You're the guy who kayoed me after I flopped to the ground—" Spook said. "You hit me when I wasn't looking, and carried me off into the bushes. You must have thought I was dead. You know what I'm going to do? I'm going to take you apart!"

Braggs gasped, "Why—awful lies—"

Gulliver put in, "No, Braggs. You're with Cass in this. Way back, you go way back with him."

Spook danced about, pointed at the quaking cone of flesh

that was Harvell Braggs, and howled, "Come on and fight like a man!"

Gulliver took a step forward and threw his words. "When Doc Savage flung that fountain pen, you showed your true colors. You knew it was a grenade."

Braggs bellowed, "That's not true!" But his wild tone and his desperate expression showed it was true. "Yes, we were allies at one time. But Cass turned against me, making me his captive, as you witnessed with your own eyes."

Gulliver said, "You can't talk your way out of it. I just remembered that Saint Pete told me that your story of Columbus stealing your collection couldn't be true, because he hadn't been anywhere near your Caribbean island in years."

"You have me there," Braggs admitted grudgingly. "The truth is Columbus wanted to wrest back from me a blunderbuss belonging to him. And I wished to add the illustrious Columbus himself to my collection. For that is what the man is—the one true discoverer of the New World."

"You're crazy!" Gull exploded. "Why would you tell everyone you met that a guy looking like Columbus stole your collection? It doesn't make sense."

Braggs emitted a windy sigh. "How best to locate Columbus, who was at large in the world, was a conundrum. Yes, it was. But every schoolboy has seen his portrait, and would know him by sight. Especially with the new holiday in the news. By telling all I met that my quarry resembled the great admiral, I did not expect to be believed. Indeed, I did not wish to be taken literally. But who would believe that Christopher Columbus was still living, having not aged a day since the year 1503? No one. Therefore, I was safe in broadcasting his description. It was my misfortune to fall in with Ivan Cass and his disreputable crew, whom I believed were working on my behalf, but who turned against me so viciously and, well, you know what the evidence of your senses tell you—"

Spook yelled, "I'm going to kick your ribs in, you windy whale—"

Spook sprang forward.

Harvell Braggs lifted his Winchester rifle, jammed it against Spook's chest. Spook apparently hadn't noticed the rifle in his mad excitement. He turned paper white in an incredible instant.

Braggs pulled the rifle trigger. The rifle hammer made some noise as it fell, but there was no other result.

Spook reacted in unexpected fashion when the weapon missed fire. He knocked the weapon aside, grabbed it, jerked it out of Braggs' hands, reversed it, and did his best to shoot Braggs. He jacked the lever and snapped the hammer several times before he realized the weapon was empty. Then he clubbed it and struck Braggs a glancing blow. Braggs rolled back among Cass' men, upsetting several. Thus disturbed, Cass' group tried to renew the fight. There was a mad scramble for the darkroom and its confiscated weapons.

Cass himself came at Gulliver feet first, and Gull got aside, hit him, tripped another man, used his fists on the third. Then he himself got knocked down. Dazed, he realized a man was trying to wrench the gun out of his fingers. They rolled over and over. Another man joined the fight for the gun. It was Harvell Braggs.

Seconds later, a supermachine pistol hooted briefly.

Monk Mayfair howled, "Get clear! Make room so I can use this gobbler on 'em!"

Nobody paid him heed. Gull pulled hair out of a head, got a firmer grip, knocked the head against a rock. He did that with his left hand. His right held the revolver. Then it didn't hold the revolver. The weapon had been taken from him. Braggs had gotten it. He jumped clear, as the fat man tried to draw a hasty bead.

Monk's machine pistol rattled. A peppering of tiny holes appeared along the front of Harvell Braggs' well-tailored coat. His eyes got strange. He sagged like a deflating balloon, and promptly went to sleep on his broad back. His pursy pink mouth made the same shapes as does a fish when it breathes.

Gulliver got up and looked around. All over.

RENNY RENWICK hove into view, appearing disappointed at missing out on the action. Ham Brooks and Johnny Littlejohn soon appeared, fists squared.

Last to arrive was Long Tom Roberts, looking tigerish.

He marched up to Monk Mayfair and began making accusations.

"A fine thing!" he raged. "I bust you loose and the minute my back is turned, untying the others, you up and make off with my superfirer!"

"I was spoilin' for a fight from being tied up so long," Monk countered.

Long Tom rolled up one shirt sleeve and then did the same to the other.

"Now I am the one spoiling for a fight," he gritted fiercely.

Monk Mayfair outweighed the puny electrical expert by well over a hundred pounds. Moreover, the hairy chemist had been known to bend horseshoes in his bare hands and fold silver dollars between fingers and thumb.

Yet Monk actually turned pale when he saw how Long Tom had his dander up. For it was rumored that Long Tom could lick his own weight in wildcats. So when his ire was openly displayed, even Monk Mayfair was a little bit afraid of him.

Erecting white-knuckled fists, Long Tom squared off, began circling the apish chemist, oversized sleeves flapping. Reluctantly, Monk put up his hairy fists, blocked them. Fisticuffs impended.

Ham whispered to Renny. "My money's on Monk."

"Long Tom will whip him in two shakes of a monkey's tail," the big-fisted engineer scoffed.

"I will wager that Monk is about to learn a great lesson," confided Johnny.

What would next have transpired was never known.

Up from the beach came Petella van Astor, otherwise Saint Pete, looking rather dejected. She was very pale in her otherwise becoming burlap frock.

For walking behind her was an unexpected figure of a man.

It was the midget who had been calling himself Monzingo Baldwin—otherwise Cadwiller Olden.

He had a revolver. It looked ludicrously big in his small fingers. But it was trained on the girl's back, which took away some of the ridiculousness of the way he gripped it in both hands.

"Don't think I have any scruples about shooting a frail, because I don't," croaked the tiny man in his comical hound-dog voice.

Chapter XLIV

RAT ISLAND RIOT

IVAN CASS TOOK immediate charge. He seized a Winchester and cocked the lever unnecessarily. An unfired shell popped out. Casually, he reached down to recover it and fed the cartridge back into the receiver.

Weapons were hastily recovered from the blocked darkroom. Soon, Cass' agents were bristling with rifles and revolvers. Their expressions portended violence.

Cass' voice became as if a frozen Satan were speaking. "Now," he growled, "where did we leave off?"

No one answered. The reinstated prisoners were forced to drop their captured weapons. Thinking fast, Monk Mayfair manipulated his empty supermachine pistol, and tossed it away, where it was promptly reduced to smoking slag.

The prisoners were collected—all but Doc Savage and Christopher Columbus, who had not been seen since the mad scramble to avoid the fountain-pen bomb which had failed to detonate. Harvell Braggs lay snoring in the brush, out cold as a result of the potent dose of mercy bullets Monk had inflicted upon him.

Cass counted noses, then looked around angrily.

"Find Doc Savage! Get Columbus, too. We're gonna stage a kill party. We'll just have to forget about those fancy pistols."

There was a commotion in the brush and all eyes shifted in that direction.

The sun was climbing toward the noon hour, so sunlight

splintered down in shafts of strangely chill brilliance.

One of those shafts showed the metallic top of Doc Savage's head. The bronze man appeared to be lying in wait behind a very large bush. The bush was wonderfully still and unmoving.

Ivan Cass himself took a bead on that unmistakable target. He made careful aim.

Monk, Renny and Long Tom all attempted to rush him. They were clubbed to their knees with lavish viciousness.

Cass called out, "Savage, surrender!"

No response was forthcoming. So Ivan Cass unleashed a bullet and the shimmering skullcap gave a jump.

Gulliver Greene gave out a groan when he saw it. Saint Pete moaned. Doc Savage's men turned their heads from the awful sight.

To all appearances, it looked as if the top of Doc Savage's head had been shot off!

A realistic sprinkling of scarlet accompanied the gory display. Droplets made a red rain in the vicinity, falling with a soft but grisly pattering.

"Let there be no doubt," intoned Ivan Cass grimly, "that Doc Savage is now dead."

There seemed to be no argument on that score. Not even a moan of mortal pain emerged from the bush that was now spattered with what appeared to be the bronze giant's life fluid.

Cass turned to the little runt that had been his second in command.

"We were about to execute the prisoners. Care to join us in the festivities?"

"Swell," said Monzingo Baldwin. "But what about Columbus?"

"Later!" Cass rapped. He turned to a confederate. "You with the new rifle. Give it to the little numbskull here."

"Sure. But it's only charged with rat-shot, on account the rodents have been getting brave lately."

Cass' crow-black eyes suddenly narrowed. "On second

thought, anybody got a knife?"

A man produced one of the three-cornered blades that had been the midget's favorite tool for murder. He tossed it, saying, "This do?"

"Swell," said Cadwiller Olden, catching the dagger by its bone handle. "Keep the rifle."

The assembled Cass men faced their helpless captives.

One of them—one who had evidently picked up a colorful way of assembling his words during his stint as a Silent Saint— remarked in a hollow and piously eloquent tone, "A thorny path is the lot of the transgressor, and his just lot, too. So let it be said that no mortal man should stand forth to say it shall not be."

A trifle obscure, but enlightenment was not delayed. Another fellow in tattered burlap spoke up.

"As just men of peace," he intoned, "it is our bounden duty to leave you in fit circumstances such that the rodents partake of your bones."

No clarity lacking in that, certainly.

Then matters took a very strange turn.

"Stand them up against the darkroom ledge," ordered Ivan Cass. "It will make a swell bullet stop for the firing squad."

Doc Savage's stunned men were kicked to their feet, made to join the others. The prisoners were prodded in the high ledge's direction.

Cadwiller Olden assisted by poking Gulliver Greene with his triangular blade.

"I ain't forgot that you winged me back in Missouri," he grated. "I think I will use you for target practice. I'm pretty handy at knife throwing."

"Hey, runt," asked Cass suddenly.

"Yeah? What is it, stone-face?"

"One of the machine pistols we took off Savage's men back in Missouri went missing. Know anything about that?"

Olden grinned. "Sure, I filched it for myself. Ain't I entitled to my rightful share?"

"Thought so. Where is it now?"

"Savage snatched it back," the midget admitted.

"In other words," Cass said darkly, "you lost a piece of armament worth maybe fifty thousand bucks."

The little man's eyebrows shot up. "That much?"

Cass nodded stonily. "That much. Why don't you join the rest of the rodent bait at the ledge?"

The runt looked injured. His miniature eyes popped in horror. A tiny viper-like tongue emerged to lick drying lips.

"You're funning me, right?" Olden croaked.

Cass laughed. It sounded as if his throat was full of blood lust.

"Snappy now! Don't want to keep the hungry rats waiting, little morsel."

Cadwiller Olden found himself looking at a dozen dark eyes that were gun barrels suddenly directed his way. He swallowed twice, wordless for once, continued trudging.

They were nearly to the makeshift execution wall now.

Raising his voice, Ivan Cass all but yelled, "Once we shoot dead these Doc Savage assistants, we'll go looking for any stragglers."

If Cass thought that shout would bring Christopher Columbus out of hiding, he was very much disappointed.

The only sound was a vague one—a songbird seemed to call out in a melodious voice.

"That don't sound like no seagull," a man muttered.

"Never mind!" Cass snarled. "Firing squad assemble."

Saint Pete looked desperate, began pleading—she was trying to kill time, hoping for something to turn up.

She cried, "But my adopted father—what about him? What about Columbus—"

"Shut up!" Cass snarled.

The girl stepped back, shrugging. It was very convincing acting, for she got behind a Cass man who held a rifle. She pushed him.

Gulliver Greene was ready and grabbed the rifle as the man fell toward him.

The fellow fell on Gulliver, trying to keep a grip on his rifle. They wrestled; Gull's finger found the trigger and made the rifle blast. Cass, dodging, was not where Gull hoped he would be when the bullet arrived.

Gull got the rifle, jacked the lever, fired. A miss. It started Cass' men dodging, though. Gulliver dived behind the big boulder. He really ran after he had this shelter.

Pete was likewise disappearing into the brush and rocks to the left.

Behind him, Gull could hear the thundering voice of Renny Renwick. "Every man for himself!"

"Ye-e-ow!" howled Monk Mayfair. "Free-for-all!"

Fists began colliding with jaws, from the sounds which followed.

GULLIVER GREENE flopped behind a large stone, jammed the rifle stock to his shoulder and waited. He'd never killed a man, but he was convinced he was going to do so now. But when a man leaped into view, something happened to Gulliver's viciousness, and he lowered the rifle muzzle, broke the men's legs betwixt knee and thigh. Strangely enough, the man fell flat on his back, the way the dead are supposed to fall. A red fountain came out of his leg; he began to scream and writhe, then to pile sand on the wound and to beat the leg with his hands, screeching all the while.

Gull went on. "Pete!" he called. He couldn't hear her running.

"Here!" She was ahead, to the left.

Veering for her voice, Gulliver heard crashing behind him and drove a random bullet backward, barely slackening his flight; when he was about to shoot again, he remembered re-

peating rifles of this type—with a so-called two-thirds magazine—held five cartridges in the magazine and one in the barrel.
He'd shot four times already—two shells left, so it was no time
for extravagance with lead.

Then he forgot that, for Pete began crying out, staccato
sounds of surprise, then words that warned, "Go back! More
of them are over here!"

Gulliver did not go back, although it might have been better
if he had, or at least better if he had changed his course, for he
saw that several of Cass' men had seized Pete. She must've come
upon them unawares, as they hurried about in the general confusion. The men shot repeatedly at Gulliver, so that he had to veer
off to the right to avoid their lead, leaving Pete in their possession.

MEANWHILE, Doc Savage's men had not been idle. At the
beginning of the mêlée, they had shrugged off their grief-
stricken gloom and gone into action.

Renny was the first to strike. He possessed fists as massive
as coconuts, and twice as hard. They turned into pumping
pistons, rocking heads backward, sending jaws askew.

One man came at him feet first. Renny got aside, hit him
hard. He tripped another man, used his fist on a third.

Monk was not far behind him. He didn't bother to hit anyone.
He was too busy yanking weapons out of hands that lacked the
strength to hold onto them. When he had two fistfuls, he flung
them in the faces of two Cass confederates, who went flying
backwards.

Monk rushed in and began hopping up and down atop their
ribcages, which commenced making distressing noises like
crunching glass. Monk seemed to be enjoying himself immensely.

Johnny Littlejohn ducked behind a spindly tree that would
have afforded no individual other than the skeletal archeologist
any shelter, just ahead of a flurry of lead. It peppered the tree
harmlessly, proving that it was mere rat-shot.

A Cass man happened by, unaware of the lurking Johnny. The latter detached himself from the tree, and wrapped his elongated arms and legs around the man, who was trying to shoot Long Tom's head off, with the result that the fellow felt as if he had been attacked by a giant granddaddy longlegs spider. They rolled around on the ground, the Cass cohort seizing Johnny by his longish hair and attempted to smash his skull against convenient rocks.

After socking a few eyes and jaws, Long Tom stepped in and applied his well-skinned knuckles to the nose of Johnny's assailant. This drew blood, and the man went tumbling backward, arms windmilling. After his head struck a stone, he shook feebly, then subsided.

Long Tom helped Johnny find his feet. Then he backed into Renny, who was busy pummeling a face into red ruin. The big engineer wheeled, knobby fists ready to fly.

Renny's eyes narrowed suspiciously. "Are those my duds?"

"Borrowed them," returned Long Tom, waving a sleeveless arm.

Renny grunted, "Ruined 'em is more like it. I'll send you a bill."

They went back to fighting.

Bony fists flying, Johnny was now trying to whip two men at once, not succeeding very well. He finally disposed of one, was smashed down by someone who leaped upon him. They fought. The leaper had a rock. The rock changed hands and the foe went to sleep.

At a temporary loss due to the lack of his sword cane, Ham Brooks found a Winchester and began drilling assorted arms and legs, causing his foes to bleat in pain and drop their weapons. The dapper lawyer did not miss once.

The air was full of the sounds of combatants grunting and hitting and getting hit in turn.

In the middle of all this uproar, no one noticed Cadwiller Olden, still clutching his vicious-looking triangular dagger, sneak up on his erstwhile leader, spymaster Ivan Cass. The midget jumped up onto a clump of stones, the better to slip the sharp blade into his boss' ribs. It went in smoothly.

Cass let out a short gasp of pain, and immediately began struggling for breath. A lung had been punctured. The little man bared a fierce set of miniature teeth and jerked out his knife. This time he squinted one eye shut, and said, "I've been meaning to do this for a good long time."

With that, Olden drove the triangular blade into the center of Ivan Cass' chest, directly into the man's pounding heart. With a last leaky sigh, the spymaster rolled up his dark eyes and released all animation. A pinkish froth began foaming on his thin lips. From one set of fingers, a fountain pen dropped. The man had been about to settle the situation by flinging one of the powerful disguised bombs into the thick of his foes.

After Cass fell, the diminutive murderer retrieved his knife, and went looking for more scores to settle.

In the beginning of the battle, the close quarters made it difficult for Cass' men to bring their unwieldy rifles to bear, for fear of shooting their comrades. But now, as their numbers began to dwindle, they got themselves organized.

Someone found the machine gun that Gulliver had employed to good effect up in the rocks, trained it downward.

He let out a short burping burst. That got everyone's attention.

"Everyone not with Cass, raise your hands," he ripped out.

Ham Brooks was the quickest to react. He raised his Winchester and plugged the man's right shoulder with a bullet. It was a good shot, but deliberately not fatal.

The man managed to squeeze off another burst, this one very wild.

That set everyone to scattering.

Now the shape of the battle became different, with men ducking into brush or behind boulders, seeking shelter or a safe place of ambush.

It promised to become a bloody massacre.

GULLIVER GREENE was circling around in a determined effort to get ahead of the Cass contingent who had made off with Saint Pete. His heart pounded. His mouth was dry as a bone. He felt as if he was trying to swallow a toy balloon.

Creeping along, he did not sense anyone looming up behind him.

A hand vised his mouth shut, another pinioned his wrists, wrenched, forcing the Winchester to the ground. Gull struggled mightily. He was strong, but this individual who had seized him was stronger still. So strong that he felt like a helpless child in the other's grasp.

His captor spun him around without effort.

Gull looked up. He had to. The man towered over him.

There stood Doc Savage, golden eyes vital.

Admonishing silence, the bronze man released his grip.

"H-how?" sputtered Gull. "You're dead."

Doc explained, "Ruse. Cass shot at a protective skullcap I wear, to which was affixed with gum arabic a vial of Mercurochrome, rigged on a bush in order to draw his attention while I moved Christopher Columbus out of harm's way."

"Sure made a realistic effect," grinned Gull with the admiration of one illusionist for another. "You fooled everyone."

Doc acknowledged the compliment with a modest nod.

Gulliver's face suddenly clouded. "They nabbed Saint Pete."

"No longer. I came upon them and flung several anesthetic grenades in their direction. They are quietly slumbering now, as is Saint Pete."

Gull let out a gusty sigh of tension release. "Then it's finally over."

"Not quite," said Doc.

Sounds of battle began assaulting their eardrums.

Doc Savage reached into his equipment vest and carefully

removed a case containing metallic grenades no larger than robin's eggs.

"Explosive?" asked Gull.

By way of replying, Doc began arming the tiny devices and pegged them in the general direction of battle, seeming not to aim. Then he pushed Gull to the dirt, directly behind substantial boulders.

The bombs detonated well short of the zone of combat.

Gull had recovered his Winchester rifle. "Want me to pitch in?"

"No," said Doc, who hurled more of the grenades. He threw them seemingly every which way, and the resulting explosions were entirely random.

They did, however, produce an interesting reaction.

A straggly bush quivered. Another gave a jerk, as if trying to leap off the ground. Nettles everywhere stirred. That was just the beginning.

All around commenced a skittering and scampering in the underbrush, which began to twitch and jitter as if phantom feet were racing through them.

Gulliver scratched at his dirty white hair. Fleet forms were darting, close to the ground, almost too fast for the eye to follow. They had tails.

Then he got it.

"Rats?"

"Rats," said Doc Savage.

THE STAMPEDE of rodents charged in the direction of the ledge, the vicinity about which men crawled and fought and took pot shots at one another.

The arrival of the rodents altered the character of that combat. They flowed like a river with many branches, surging toward the sea. They swarmed over everyone and everything, climbing brush, rock, even screeching men, tiny teeth biting wildly in their frenzy. There seemed to be hundreds of them. It was too much to bear.

There was a frantic exodus from the battlefield. Even Doc's men sought relief from the fast-spreading swarms. Ham rushed them to the darkroom, and they got the pivoting door slammed ahead of frantic gray rivulets.

The Cass operatives plunged toward the beach, which they imagined was the safest place to go, since the maddened rodents were unlikely to follow them into the surf.

Doc Savage watched this spectacle and his lips parted.

From his mouth came the melody that had earlier been mistaken for a songbird. This time it rose, assuming greater volume. It made a weird music, as if the Pied Piper of medieval legend had emerged from antiquity to summon Rat Island's rodent population to do his bidding. It was the herald-call of Doc Savage!

Below, Doc's men heard their leader's uncanny trilling and understood that it signaled victory was at hand.

The thrilling sound trailed off. A silence descended. The day had seemed several years long.

Doc Savage turned to Gulliver. "Go back and collect Saint Pete. You will find Christopher Columbus in a safe place—the bungalow. Await us there."

"Right," said Gull, taking off.

Doc Savage took charge of the bullet-scarred area around the ledge. There had been casualties, but only a few dead. All were Cass' men.

His own aides emerged from concealment and took inventory. Harvell Braggs was still dead to the world. They had to kick scurrying rats off his bloated form. A few had taken nips from his sausage-plump fingers.

Renny Renwick came upon a body, called out, "Hey, Brother Cass is dead!"

They gathered around the deceased spymaster, whose eyes stared upward in mortal agony. Rats had gotten to him, too. They were sampling his blood, not his flesh. The bronze man chased them away by snapping his coat at them.

Doc knelt, examined the stab wound and abruptly came erect, his vibrant voice brittle. "Find Olden."

His men scattered to search. Their joy at being reunited with their leader was subordinate to the desperate situation at hand.

Monk Mayfair found Cadwiller Olden high up in the rocks, where he was using his bloody blade to fend off a number of voracious rats.

Doc discouraged the rats by pegging unerring stones at them. They fled.

Looking up, he asked, "How did you escape our plane?"

Cadwiller Olden peered down, croaked, "One of Cass' boys read the mind of your man, Long Tom, and learned I was on the plane. He took a rowboat out to the plane and cut me loose. When we got to the beach, I found that girl prowling around and took her hostage."

Doc Savage said nothing to that.

Then, "You slew Ivan Cass." It was not a question.

"Guilty. I've been wanting to stick a shiv into that skunk for a long time. Imagine his starch, belittling me every chance he got. It stuck in my craw, it did."

Wordlessly, Doc Savage reached up and extracted the deadly blade from the midget's powerless fingers, and with his other hand removed Cadwiller Olden from his precarious perch.

"Guess I'll fry for this, huh?" gulped the miniature man.

Doc Savage said a grim nothing. He handed the midget over to Long Tom Roberts with instructions to ferry him back to the airplane before anyone could see that Olden had survived.

The men clustered on the beach were another matter. They had splashed into the surf and were working their way around to their big plane, with the idea of fleeing now that their leader, spymaster Ivan Cass, had perished.

They managed to clamber aboard, although a brief fight broke out in which two men were pitched overboard, for fear they would overload the aircraft. When one attempted to leap back aboard, he was shot between the eyes, discouraging the other.

One man planted himself in the control bucket and began snapping starter switches.

Nothing much happened.

"When they realize that their motors lack distributor caps for the carburetors," said the bronze man, "they will have no choice but to surrender. Take them into custody."

It was easier said than done. They surrounded the disabled craft, calling for its passengers to exit. A hatch popped and a fusillade of bullets came rushing out. The besieged men were unpleasantly generous with their lead.

Doc Savage discouraged their defiance by the simple expedient of entering the surf out of range of their vision and swimming submerged until he was under the aircraft.

There, the bronze man began introducing an assortment of the tiny grenades he carried into the open cabin. These included tear gas cartridges and smokers. For good measure, he added the fountain-pen bomb, which did not detonate because it had contained no explosive charge in the first place. But it added to the psychological effect.

Those who were not immediately overcome came tumbling out of the ship, appropriately enough, like rats from a disturbed nest. Doc fell upon these men, his terrible bronze hands knocking heads together and depriving them of their senses in other ways. He was so efficient at this he suddenly had to suspend operations, and grab for collars, collecting bunches of heads in either hand. Otherwise, his defeated foes would have drowned.

Doc's men plunged down from the rocks to take charge of the demoralized prisoners, dragging the incapacitated ones bodily onto the sand. They had no fight left in them.

"Quite a haul," Renny boomed, flexing his battle-scarred fists.

"How are we gonna get all them babies to our college?" Monk wondered.

"They are not going to the college," replied Doc gravely. "This affair is too serious for that remedy."

Chapter XLV

TROUBLE, INTERNATIONAL

AT A LATE hour that afternoon, everything was fairly settled. The Coast Guard and certain grim federal government men had come and gone with the surviving prisoners. Notably absent was the wounded Cadwiller Olden, and unconscious Harvell Braggs. Doc Savage had placed the latter aboard his plane before the arrival of the federals. Both men were going to Doc's Crime College. They had also taken along the thing which, indirectly, had been a cause of much of the trouble—the ingenious spy devices that were being manufactured on Rat Island. The newspaper press association wires would carry the story of the trapping of a gang of thieves who were responsible for the killing of several people. Thieves! That took Gulliver by surprise. So far as the newspapers and the public were to know, it appeared Ivan Cass had been running a nest of thieves from his St. Louis detective office. No mention was made of any devices of military value, such as fountain-pen grenades and camera-equipped cigars. No hint breathed of espionage. Not a word. Nor were the Silent Saints implicated.

Gulliver Greene was somewhat astonished at the subtlety of his own national government; his idle thoughts had always consigned such stuff to the pages of fiction, or international intrigue. This was his first contact with it, and he began to acquire an infinite respect for Uncle Sam. Apparently, the old boy wasn't the gullible oaf he seemed to be. It was a very smooth bit of diplomacy, and doubly satisfying because Gulliver and Spook discovered they weren't even to stand trial for the curious killings. This was avoided simply. The fingerprints of the missing midget showed that he had been the killer of the depot agent and old Box Daniels. So Gull and Spook were clear.

A hasty grave had been dug, and marked with the name MONZINGO BALDWIN. It was very small. The federals left it alone. That seemed to satisfy them.

The future looked rather rosy around five o'clock when Gull and the entrancing Petella van Astor came to a mutually delightful understanding over on the beach beside the big tri-motor plane. Pete had recovered from the shock of their ordeal; it was, on top of all that had happened, not so overpoweringly terrible.

"I can read your mind easily, dear," Pete assured Gulliver. "You won't stand a chance of fooling me with your magic tricks, once we're married."

"I'll bet it'll be tough," grinned Gull. "But I'll just have to make adjustments."

They were adjusting to being in one another's arms when Spook Davis trotted up. Spook's arms were filled with rifles and revolvers.

"What on earth!" Gulliver exploded. "What happened to your phobia?"

"I've decided to start collecting 'em!" Spook grinned wisely. "You know when Cass poked his rifle in my tummy and pulled the trigger and a miracle happened and—"

Gulliver corrected the miracle impression. "Doc Savage had unloaded the rifle previously. Took it behind a rock and removed the cartridges before leaving it for Braggs to find."

"Well, it didn't go off," Spook amended. "But boy, I went through the motions of dying anyway." He tossed his guns into the rented seaplane. "When it didn't go off," he added, "I decided guns were my friends."

Gull looked to Pete.

"You better go get the rest of your guns," he suggested to Spook.

Gulliver embraced Pete again. She returned this gesture warmly.

Spook began to retreat, but hesitated just before he vanished.

"Engaged yet?"

"Who said anything about—? Mind your own magic," growled Gull.

"Saint Pete ain't the only mind reader on this island," Spook reminded knowingly.

Not long after, the chief special agent was reminding Gulliver that all that had transpired on Rat Island was to remain a secret, not to be divulged or repeated. And certainly not something fit for newspaper copy.

"Doc Savage has vouched for you," said the federal man. "That's good enough for me."

Gulliver asked, "What country is Cass doing espionage for?"

The federal agent looked at Gull. "We're in a peculiar position about that," he said.

"How come?"

"This country is not at war."

"Of course not."

"It's getting to be a custom for nations to conduct espionage on each other during times of peace," the other advised.

"Not this country."

"Don't fool yourself— Well, we won't go into that." The agent shrugged his shoulders. "Here's the point. To avoid friction, there's sort of an unwritten agreement between nations to mention no names in a matter like this. Once in a while, the dope slips out. Take those Japanese spy cases we've had during the last year. Newspapers happened to get hold of them. They caused a lot of international embarrassment, when, if the truth were known, nations besides Japan were doing just as much espionage over here."

Gull frowned, "What are you getting at?"

"We have a clear idea of who employed Ivan Cass," the agent

replied. "Their tri-motor gives it away. I'm going to tell you. But you are not to repeat this. It wouldn't do any good. Cass' surviving men will be tried and executed for their killings. But there will be no international repercussions. It's not good for peace."

"I see," Gull said.

"Promise to keep it under your hat?"

"Yeah—reluctantly."

"You must never repeat this name in this connection," the agent cautioned.

The federal gave the name.

Gull swallowed. He rubbed at his jaw. He shrugged. "You read about such stuff as this in the newspapers," he remarked dully.

A year or so ago, Gull suddenly recalled, they had tried some fellow for selling U.S. military secrets, and he had followed the accounts as printed. However, he had read the stories with the same impartial feeling that digested the revolution in Spain, or a Soviet purge. It hadn't seemed very close to home. That made it hard to credit what he was hearing now. Gulliver was floored. But then international finagling always surprised him, and often seemed quite foolish. This seemed foolish now. But he decided to drop the subject forever.

A LITTLE while later, as Doc Savage was loading up his plane to depart, Gulliver approached him.

"What's going to happen to Columbus?"

"Do not worry about him," advised Doc Savage. "He is going back where he came from."

"I guess he and Pete are in there saying their goodbyes now. Say, that bunk about him being the real Christopher Columbus—"

"Bunk," said Doc, "sounds like a fair description of it, don't you agree?"

Gulliver nodded. He scrutinized the bronze giant with undisguised admiration. "I feel as if I know you, somehow," he began awkwardly.

The bronze man regarded him without much expression.

"You would remember if we had met, would you not?" Doc asked.

"Well, sure. Sure I would. That's not what I meant to say."

"What is it, then?"

"Well, I've been an admirer of yours for a long time. In fact, it's because of you that my hair turned white. You see, I'm a magician, strictly professional, you understand, and as part of my act I used to impersonate you, doing a strongman routine."

Doc Savage looked interested. "Why did you stop?"

Gull patted his unruly mop of hair. "I was smearing this infernal theatrical bronze greasepaint on my body, so that I shone like a man of bronze under the spotlights, but the stuff caused a reaction, and turned my hair white. So I had to stop."

"Regrettable," commented Doc.

"For a while I kinda blamed you," Gull muttered vaguely. "You know, I just can't shake the feeling that we met somewhere along the way. But ever since that auto accident a few years back, my memory's been pretty punk."

"You were in an automobile accident?"

"That's right. Me and my stooge, Spook. We woke up in the same hospital room together, as a matter of fact. The doctors told us we piled into a tree and were lucky to be alive. They fixed us up good, helped us to remember who we were, and got us started in life all over again. Never charged us a dime, either."

"There are many excellent charity hospitals doing good work," the bronze man reminded.

Gull was rubbing the back of his neck thoughtfully. "One thing that still bothers me: What about that midget with the bullfrog vocal cords? I noticed that you did not turn him over to the federal men."

"Better not to mention him, either."

"I never did catch his name...."

"Forget that you ever saw him," asserted Doc, "and his name won't matter to you."

"But—"

At that point, Petella van Astor came out of the aircraft and laid a calming hand on Gulliver's agitated arm.

"What Mr. Savage is trying to say," she soothed, "is that the matter is in good hands."

"If you say so, honey," said Gull, scratching his ivory locks.

Doc Savage addressed Petella van Astor. "What can you reveal about the cell of spies which had infiltrated your group?"

"Some of the Silent Saints—and certain of Cass' men—have an uncanny ability to tell exactly what a person is thinking," Pete supplied calmly. "As you now know, I can do it to a certain extent—as nearly the real thing as there is."

"Not all of Cass' men are genuine telepaths?" queried Doc.

"I do not know whether all of it is mind-reading, or also good character judging and guesswork," she admitted. "Some are ex-fortunetellers, mediums, and so on."

"Experts at getting information out of other people—whether they are genuine mind-readers or not, eh?"

Pete nodded. "Yes."

"They probably made swell spies," grunted Gulliver.

"They worked for whatever country paid them," supplied Pete. "They have traveled all over the world, gathering military information, committing political assassinations—everything terrible that such an organization might do."

"Sounds like they should have called themselves Trouble, International," Gulliver remarked. "They probably had plenty of work, with things as they are in Europe now."

Changing the subject, Doc Savage asked him, "Are you still interested in that engagement in New York—the one you declined?"

Gull brightened. "I'm getting married, so it would be a big boost."

"It happens that the manager involved is an acquaintance of mine. This can be resolved, but at your old salary."

"My old salary sounds great!" Gulliver enthused. "Thanks!"

"It will be arranged upon my return to New York," promised the bronze man.

They shook hands, and Doc Savage climbed into his plane and closed the cabin door.

Gulliver and Pete stepped back as the propellers began turning over.

"Strange," said Gull, plucking at his bruised lower lip.

"What is?"

"Everything. But it's like I know him, even though we've never met."

Pete gave his arm an affectionate squeeze. "He is the greatest man who ever lived, and that is all you need to know."

"I'm going to miss old Columbus," mused Gulliver.

"That, too, is something we had better forget," said Saint Pete, squeezing his arm again.

They watched the Doc Savage plane depart. It pushed off the island and began scooting along Lake Superior's wind-rippled surface.

Gulliver Greene suddenly had a thought.

"Heck, how did he know about that?"

Petella looked at him with melting azure eyes.

"About your New York connection?"

"Yeah, how— Hey, how did *you* know? I never mentioned it to you, either!"

"Telepathy."

"Is that like mind-reading?"

"Exactly like it."

"Guess I'm going to have to take your word for it from now on. But that doesn't explain how Doc Savage knew about it. Think he's a mind-reader, too?"

"I wouldn't be at all surprised," said the soon-to-be Mrs. Gulliver Greene. And suddenly she laughed merrily.

"What's so funny?" Gull demanded.

"Your hair. I was just thinking—what if our future children are born with white hair?"

At that ridiculous thought, Gulliver Greene began laughing, too.

As the Doc Savage plane vaulted into the air, it banked, waggling a silvery wing in farewell.

They were too busy with one another to notice.

Chapter XLVI

MIRACLE BY SAVAGE

HOURS LATER, DOC SAVAGE had landed at the emergency government air field in Millard, Missouri and secured an automobile for the drive to the weird Victorian house in the woods that had lured them all to what was probably, if not definitely, the most bizarre adventure of their hectic careers.

They drove as close to the house as they could, got out, and proceeded on foot through the cool forest.

By this time, Monk Mayfair was feeling well enough to start ragging on Ham Brooks, who was still bereft of walking stick, and not liking it one whit.

"Maybe you should get yourself a pair of crutches to go with that patch of ice you call your hair," Monk jeered.

"Once we are back in New York," Ham said waspishly, "I fully intend to whet my best blade against those hideous hog bristles sprouting from your simian skull!"

The apish chemist smoothed the top of his rusty head and remarked, "You're just jealous because I still got the hair color I was born with."

Ham sputtered, chiseled face turning a crimson that verged on purple. It was a hue the hairy chemist rarely roused in his nemesis, but one he relished.

They found Herman Bunderson puttering around the rambling old place, looking drawn and emaciated.

"I have been expecting you," he said quietly.

"Have you looked into the bag left in your keeping?" asked Doc.

Bunderson nodded.

"What did you find?"

"The Fox tribe gold lost back in 1832. It's all there."

"All but the thousand dollars which I left behind to be found by the boys in 1870," corrected Doc.

Bunderson managed a shaky grin. "My grandfather spent a lifetime looking for that trove."

"If you wish, you may have it."

Bunderson looked startled. His bobbing Adam's apple seemed to rise with some unexpressed emotion.

"We desire to purchase this property," added Doc.

"It's worth more than that bag of gold, I would think."

"The land you may keep. We only want the building. It's too dangerous to be left in unscientific hands," countered Doc. "And perhaps too dangerous to ever use again."

Johnny Littlejohn had a question.

"Tell me, can the house travel into the future?"

Bunderson shook his head vigorously. "No. Not our future. Only the future of the past, once the house lands back in a previous era. Every time my grandfather attempted to progress forward in time, the house refused to budge from its foundation."

"Intriguing," remarked Ham Brooks.

Doc Savage said, "The house cannot leap into the future for a simple and logical reason."

"Which is?"

"Such a future is simply not there, because it has not yet been created," explained Doc. "Therefore, there is no solid reality for the house to alight on."

It made sense after they reflected on the bronze man's words.

Herman Bunderson had been considering Doc's proposition.

"There are other treasures I might seek if I hold onto the old place," he mused.

"You failed to find the one most close at hand," Doc pointed out.

That decided the man. He said, "Have your attorney write up a bill of sale. There is no deed to the place."

To his astonishment, Ham Brooks pulled out a bill of sale he had drawn up during the plane trip.

After Herman Bunderson got over his dumbfoundment, he signed the document and the bag of gold coins was ceremoniously handed over to him.

Doc Savage said, "As our first act as owner, we must return this unfortunate man to his rightful era."

Christopher Columbus was brought forward for the first time. Renny packed Cadwiller Olden under one arm. The midget flailed a little, but became passive after the big engineer clamped a massive paw over his battered face, grunting, "Pipe down, peanut!"

Habeas Corpus leapt from Monk Mayfair's apish arms, squealing with glee and frolicking about, happy to be on solid ground once more. After he had settled down, the shoat trained his beady eyes on Olden, who glared back with deep resentment.

Columbus studied the faded Victorian dwelling with troubled eyes.

"I rue the day I entered that temple of black sorcery," he said thickly.

"I will need a few minutes alone with Don Christopher," said Doc.

The others stayed put as the bronze man escorted the renowned Admiral of the Ocean Sea into the Victorian house. The door closed behind them.

In the octagonal parlor of thick walls, Doc faced Columbus.

"You cannot be restored to your own time with your memories intact," Doc Savage explained quietly. He spoke Spanish, the tongue in which he had questioned Columbus during the flight, putting to him many inquiries, satisfying himself that this indeed was the historical Columbus.

A momentary start shook Christopher Columbus' large frame.

Doc reassured him, "There are safe ways of seeing that you no longer remember any of the events experienced since you first entered this dwelling back in 1503."

Christopher Columbus regarded the towering bronze man without words for a long interval.

At last, he bowed and said, "I am in your power."

Doc sat the man down on the inner staircase. He took from his pocket vest a shiny coin. It was Monk Mayfair's buffalo-head nickel. This the bronze man passed from hand to hand until the object had Columbus' undivided attention. The latter started tracking it with his dark eyes.

Doc Savage began speaking in a steady tone and soon had the mesmeric effect he sought.

"I will count to ten. You will fall asleep when you hear the word ten. You will slumber peacefully. You are not to rise until an hour passes. Upon awakening, you will remember nothing of what has transpired in the last several months since you first entered this house. You will not remember anything of the Twentieth Century. Nor will you ever be able to summon up any names or faces belonging to our present time. Instead, you will awaken thinking you had fallen asleep in this house for only an hour or so. Then you will leave this house, not to return."

Doc paused. "Do you understand?"

"I understand," intoned Christopher Columbus. His voice was already drowsy, having succumbed to the bronze man's hypnotic influence.

Doc began counting. As he began, Columbus' dark orbs grew heavy of lid, and by the time the bronze man reached the number five, the Great Navigator could barely keep his eyes open.

At the sound of the word ten, he slumped forward, fast asleep.

Doc Savage caught him before Columbus landed on the floor.

Then the bronze man called in Herman Bunderson.

They conferred over the tower-room controls, consulting the notebook of hermit inventor Method Gibbs. After many minutes, they had the mechanical astrolabe set to what they fervently hoped was the original time-and-location the house had first visited back in 1503. The hour was set forward, of course, so that the house did not land upon itself with calamitous results.

That accomplished, they retreated from the weird dwelling. Doc Savage gave a last look at the slumbering form of the Discoverer of America. His normally expressionless face for once was very strange.

"Everything is set," he told his men. Together, they retreated beyond the perimeter controlled by the electric eye and waited.

They did not have to wait very many minutes. The house simply winked out of existence. They stood firm against the sudden inrush of air created by the resulting vacuum.

"How long must we wait?" wondered Ham.

"Not long," Doc told him.

The house returned within twenty minutes. Doc Savage mounted the porch and entered alone.

When he returned, his bronze features looked distinctly relieved.

"The house is empty." That was all anyone said about it. Christopher Columbus had been returned to his proper place in the orderly history of the world.

There remained the matter of Cadwiller Olden, who did not seem very much of a threat tucked under Renny's right arm, like a football equipped with arms and legs.

"What about him?" asked Long Tom, cocking a surreptitious thumb in the midget's direction.

"Cadwiller Olden is a special case," Doc avowed. "He must never be permitted his freedom under any circumstances. The same treatment I gave Columbus can be used to suppress recent memories."

"Why not give him the full treatment?" rumbled Renny, referring to the delicate brain operation that wiped out all criminal memories.

"Too risky in his present mental condition," said Doc. "Nor would I consider releasing him back into society. He will remain at the college to the end of his days."

"Which I hope will be around Halloween," grunted Monk. "That guy don't belong with normal folks. Right, Habeas?"

The porker grunted as if in acquiescence.

Cadwiller Olden, entirely unaware that he was the subject of these discussions, at that point inserted himself into the conversation.

"That scrawny pig ain't my conscience. He's real! And never mind talking about other mugs, what about me?"

"You," said Doc Savage, "are going for a ride on our dirigible, along with Harvell Braggs."

The little man noticed the airship anchored to a nearby tree.

"I don't want to," Olden sulked.

"Pipe down," said Monk, "or I'll tie a balloon to you and pull you along like a kite."

"You wouldn't dare!"

Doc Savage instructed, "Long Tom, you and Renny will remain behind. You are to supervise the dismantling of this structure. Pack up all the electronic parts for transport to our headquarters. We will study them at a later time."

Johnny regarded the faded structure wistfully, asked, "Think we might take her out for a spin some time?"

Doc Savage considered this at great length.

"It is very tempting. But also very doubtful. There is no telling what misfortune may occur while navigating blindly through time."

THEY received a partial answer to that a few days later when Doc Savage was supervising the arrival of the sections of the

Chronodomus that had been salvaged from the razed Victorian house. This work was being done in the impressive experimental laboratory that occupied the greater portion of the bronze man's skyscraper headquarters in midtown Manhattan.

Johnny Littlejohn came bustling in from the vast library that adjoined the laboratory, flourishing a book.

"I have been going through every historical tome relating to the Big Neck Indian War I could find in our library," he announced.

Doc Savage looked up from his work.

"According to every account," continued Johnny, "Big Neck did not simply vanish, never to be heard of again. He was arrested, and tried, along with two others, Red Snake and another brave named Swift Turtle. All were acquitted."

Doc Savage's trilling piped up, very faint and fluid.

"You and I distinctly recall that these same books recorded a fate consistent with his vanishing from history," concluded the long-worded archeologist.

Doc took the offered book and purused the open pages. His trilling sound, low and ethereal, wandered about the laboratory like a curious insect seeking understanding.

"This book," he said slowly, "does not reflect the same history that it did before we set out on our investigation of the vanishing Victorian house."

"In other words," said Johnny, voice quivering with excitement, "when we returned Big Neck to his rightful era, we rewrote history."

"So it would seem," admitted Doc. "Have you looked into the record pertaining to Christopher Columbus?"

"I have. Nothing appears to have been changed. Columbus went to his grave never suspecting that he had discovered a new continent."

"All the more reason never to employ this time-deflating device again," Doc said gravely.

"It is a shame not to," Johnny said wistfully.

"It would be a greater shame if we altered the trend of human events in a way that was irreconcilable with our present."

Thoughtfully, Johnny put the book aside.

"There is another puzzle I have been wondering about."

"Gulliver Greene?"

"Yes. Some of the others thought he looked familiar, but cannot place him."

"That is not his original name," stated Doc. "Do you recall the adventure in which we encountered the criminal master mind who called himself 'The Crime Annihilist'?"*

"Vividly. We shipped a lot of people to the college at the conclusion of that affair."

Johnny suddenly reached for his monocle. "Gulliver is a graduate!"

"A former pickpocket and confidence man, along with his brother, the man now known as Drury 'Spook' Davis."

Johnny gave vent to a decidedly unscholarly whistle. "So they *were* brothers, after all...."

Doc nodded. "But they do not know that, thanks to the brain surgery that wiped out all recollection of their troubled pasts. In selecting a skill with which the two could make their way in society, the specialists at the college decided that they would make very good magicians, once they were taught the requisite skills. I placed them in the hands of a very famous illusionist, now retired, who was happy to coach them in his craft."

"Remarkable! But how was he drawn into the affair in the first place?"

"Through his uncle, Box Daniels, another graduate," related Doc. "Box was investigating reports that the Silent Saints were practicing a credible form of mind-reading. Since this is a subject that interested us, and we were too busy to look into it ourselves, I gave him that assignment. His instructions were to bring Gulliver Greene and his brother into it if he discovered anything useful."

---

* The Annihilist.

Johnny's smooth brow puckered. "Why Greene?"

"Gulliver Greene was well versed in the ways of mental-ists—fake mind-readers. If he looked into the matter and found the Silent Saints were merely clever fakers, there would be no need for our involvement."

"I see. But the Christopher Columbus complication threw all that into a cocked chapeau."

"It did not help matters that Box Daniels had a weakness for the bottle, which clouded his judgment," Doc admitted. "He should have communicated with us once the matter promised to turn deadly. As it happened, we landed in the vicinity looking into the vanishing Victorian house. One thing led to another. But it has all worked out now."

"This," said Johnny ruminatively, "has to be one of the most complicated cases we have ever gotten embroiled in."

"That," admitted Doc Savage, "is putting it mildly."

Johnny took out his monocle magnifier and began polishing it thoughtfully. He frowned.

"Something bothering you?" queried Doc.

"Indubitably. How is it that Christopher Columbus so closely resembled the portraits every school boy knows, when no one painted him when he was alive?"

"Not everyone saw it that way," reminded Doc.

"The subjective nature of the human mind, plus faulty memory," Johnny said loftily.

"Care to hear some conjecture?" asked the bronze man.

"Certainly."

"Consider that Columbus' fame was not achieved until long after his death. He thought he had found a new route to Cathay, instead of a hitherto-undiscovered New World."

Johnny tapped the lens of his magnifier against his front teeth. "What does that have to do with the mystery?"

"Columbus had two sons, Diego and Fernando. Would it not be reasonable, once men began painting posthumous portraits of the Great Navigator, to have one of his own descendants sit for those portraits?"

Johnny brightened. "Producing a familial resemblance! Supermalagorgeous! I must write up that theory." The gaunt geologist started. "Er-r-r, I cannot very well do that, now can I?"

"Not without revealing the unprovable story of your having met Columbus in the flesh," reminded Doc.

Johnny's frown grew deeper. "I take it back."

"Take what back?"

"This was not the most complicated adventure we have ever had. It is the most confoundedly frustrating!"

With that, the lanky archeologist pocketed his magnifying monocle and stalked off, leaving Doc Savage immersed in his work.

Entering the library, Johnny noticed that the calendar read October 12, and that it was now officially Columbus Day—the day on which, over four hundred year ago, a new continent was discovered. The fact that it had been established to be the Great Navigator's actual birthday, as confirmed by his very lips, was an historical truth Johnny Littlejohn would never breathe to a living soul—no matter how much it pained him to keep silent.

About the Author
LESTER DENT

LESTER DENT WAS born in the tiny agricultural community of La Plata, Missouri, on October 12, 1904. His roots there were deep. The Dent farm had been in the family since before the Civil War. There is a Dent County in central Missouri.

Although Lester spent his formative years in Wyoming, Nebraska and Oklahoma, the family returned to La Plata, where his parents, Alice and Bernard, took over the family farm in 1918 upon the death of Bernard's father. Lester began attending La Plata High School the following year. Upon graduation in 1923, he relocated to Oklahoma. After quitting his job as an Associated Press telegrapher in Tulsa to become a pulp writer for Dell Publications in 1930, it was to La Plata that Lester retreated when the Great Depression crushed Dell's pulp line, and with it Dent's first flyer at living in New York City.

After writing Doc Savage for two years, Lester and wife Norma began summering in La Plata in between periods in Manhattan and wintering in Miami on his schooner, the *Albatross*. There, he became involved in local affairs, lecturing on writing and showing home movies of his Caribbean treasure hunts, proceeds from which went to buying educational materials for needy school children. He also staged popular amateur boxing matches in the community. He did his writing in the local bank, from which he rented office space.

Tiring of the nomadic lifestyle, in 1939 the Dents relocated to La Plata year round, first renting a home, then finally building their famous House of Gadgets in 1942. There, Lester lived out the remainder of his days, writing Doc Savage, hardcover novels and making his first slick magazine sales. He became even more involved in community affairs, volunteering as a Boy Scout scoutmaster, and joining the Masons, eventually becoming a 32nd degree Mason of the Scottish Rite. During World War Two, Lester took up light-plane flying, becoming acting commander, Civil Air Patrol, Kirksville Squadron.

Lester Dent was given the Missouri Writers Guild Award in 1946. In 1948, he launched Airviews, an aerial photography service which grew so rapidly that he opened up a storefront photography studio in downtown La Plata, housing his fleet of five camera-equipped airplanes in the nearby Kirksville Municipal Airport.

With the death of his parents in the early 1950s, Lester reluctantly took over his father's dairy farm and went into this full force, modernizing the operation. Dent brought Grade A milk to his part of Missouri for the first time, launched a successful fertilizer operation, The La Plata Chemical Company, and wrote the La Plata Centennial pageant program, "Centorama," in 1955. That year, he also organized The La Plata Rural Fire Association to raise funds for a modern fire truck for the town. As a Ham radio operator, Lester became director of La Plata Civil Defense activities, participating in RACES—the Radio Amateur Civil Emergency Service. He was once asked to run for Mayor of La Plata, but declined the invitation.

When Lester Dent died in 1959, he was buried in the La Plata cemetery, where he rests today. His House of Gadgets was later placed on the National Register of Historic Places.

In the 1970s, the La Plata town government erected signs on the north and south approaches of U.S. 63, proclaiming the tiny village of about 2,000 residents to be the birthplace of Lester Dent, Creator of Doc Savage. Although those signs were later removed, new ones were put in place in 2013, the eightieth anniversary year of the beginning of Doc Savage.

About the Author
WILL MURRAY

WILL MURRAY WAS born in Massachusetts in 1953, and is the author of some sixty books, including forty novels in the Destroyer paperback series, thirteen Doc Savage novels, and a well-received history of the Western pulp magazines, *Wordslingers, An Epitaph for the Western.*

Twenty years ago, Murray wrote the Doc Savage novels released during the 60th anniversary of the character's beginnings. With the Man of Bronze turning 80 in 2013, he has again collaborated with the late Lester Dent to produce additional adventures in this legendary and influential pulp series.

Murray has visited Missouri only three times in his life, but each time was very special. On the first occasion, he attended Pulpcon in St. Louis. The year was 1977. Murray recalls dining in the hotel restaurant with Ryerson Johnson, one of Lester Dent's best friends and ghostwriters, when Mrs. Lester Dent walked in. That was their first meeting.

Out of that wonderful weekend convention came the beginnings of a long-term working relationship. By the end of the convention, Norma Dent had decided to permit Murray to market the Lester Dent literary properties, which he does to this day.

A year later in October, 1978, Murray made the pilgrimage to La Plata, Missouri, where the entirety of Lester's files, papers, and manuscripts were made available to him. There, he discovered the complete outline to "Python Isle," which subsequently triggered his novel writing career when he was granted permission to transform the document into the first authorized Doc Savage adventure since the original series ended in 1949.

Two years later in June, 1980, Murray again returned to La Plata to do further work. By that time, he had written *Python Isle* and sitting in Lester Dent's study, making notes on Lester's typewriter, Murray felt very comfortable indeed.

Norma Dent passed away in 1995, and Will Murray has not been back to La Plata, Missouri, since. But he recalls it fondly as a magical place in which miracles happened. He is delighted to have co-authored *The Miracle Menace*, which evokes the La Plata of the mid-1930s.

About the Artist
JOE DeVITO

OVER THE PAST thirty years Joe DeVito has illustrated, sculpted and designed hundreds of book and
magazine covers, posters, trading cards, collectibles, toys and
just about everything else in a variety of genres. He is especially known for classic depictions in both painting and sculp-
ture of many of Pop Culture's most recognizable icons. These
include King Kong, Tarzan, Doc Savage and super heroes such
as Superman, Batman, Wonder Woman, Spider-man, and *MAD*
magazine's Alfred E. Neuman (a super hero to some). He
sculpted the award trophy for the highly influential art annual
Spectrum and his poster painting has become their logo.

Deeply rooted in the fine arts, he has sculpted two monu-
mental statues of the Madonna and Child, one of which is
placed in Domus Pacis at the Our Lady of Fatima Shrine, in
Portugal. The other resides at the World Apostolate of Fatima
Shrine in Washington, NJ, where several of his original Fatima-
themed oil paintings hang in the shrine's gallery. Joe also restores
historic icons and statues, such as the Odessa Madonna, now
in Kazan, Russia. Joe is usually working on several large painting and sculpting commissions in the fine arts concurrently
with his illustration work.

An avid writer, Joe has co-authored (with Brad Strickland)
and illustrated two novels. The first is *KONG: King of Skull
Island* (DH Press, 2004). The second book, *Merian C. Cooper's
King Kong,* was published by St. Martin's Griffin, in 2005. He

has also written many essays and articles including *Do Android Artists Paint In Oils When They Dream?* for *Pixel or Paint: The Digital Divide in Illustration Art.* He has recently finished the screenplay for his "faction" world of truly epic proportions tentatively titled *The Primordials,* now in early movie development.

In the past year, DeVito finished sculpting the official 100th Anniversary statue of Tarzan for the Edgar Rice Burroughs Estate, is painting covers for *The All New Wild Adventures of Doc Savage* written by Will Murray, is participating in the development of *KONG: King of Skull Island* in various media, with cutting edge app versions of the book already available. He is also planning a new YA *King Kong* book series with Brad Strickland.

www.jdevito.com
www.kongskullisland.com
www.novenaart.com

About the Patron
BOB GASPARINI

LIKE MANY OF you, I was first introduced to Doc Savage and his five aides by reading the Bantam Book reprints that ran from 1964-1990. But whether you became a Doc fan from the original pulps, the Bantam reprints, Will Murray's 1991-93 series or more recently through Will's new Wild Adventures of Doc Savage, all of us who read Doc share a love of adventure, science fiction, suspense and American heroes. The Doc Savage covers have also enjoyed an amazing evolution over the last 80 years featuring a select number of very talented artists including Walter Baumhofer in the '30s, James Bama in the '60s Bob Larkin in the '80s and Joe DeVito since the '90s.

An opportunity to collaborate on a classic Doc Savage 80th anniversary cover with both Will Murray and Joe DeVito was a once-in-a-lifetime opportunity for me. Both Joe and Will brought so much to the table during the discussion and planning phase, it was an absolute pleasure for this Doc fan to work alongside them. Pouring over the details and nuances of the poses, the settings, the backgrounds, the lighting and then watching Joe bring all of our ideas to life made for a wonderful experience, and for this I am thankful and appreciative to both Will and Joe.

I also want to thank my wife Carlita who has patiently stood by and supported my Doc Savage collecting over the last 35 years. I know it was not always easy. I sincerely hope that you and all who are reading this enjoy a classic Doc Savage 80th Anniversary cover painting and adventure.

Bob Gasparini
August 18, 2013
Sharon Springs, NY

Bob Gasparini is a cancer geneticist who is President and Chief Scientific Officer of NeoGenomics Laboratories, a NASDAQ-listed cancer genetics laboratory headquartered in Ft. Myers, Florida. Bob lives most of the year in Ft. Myers with his high school sweetheart and wife of 38 years. They have three grown children, Scott, Lindsey & Connor and four other "kids" with fur including a Golden Retriever, a Yellow Lab and two Siamese cats. When not in Florida, Bob & Carlita can be found in the small town of Sharon Springs, NY where they enjoy life and the outdoors in a rural American community. Bob can be reached anytime of the year at bgasparini@ neogenomics.com

WORDSLINGERS

AN EPITAPH FOR THE WESTERN

☞ WILL MURRAY ☜

Will Murray's *Wordslingers* is not only the first in-depth history of the Western pulps, it's one of the best and most important books on the pulps ever written, perfectly capturing the era, the magazines, and the writers, editors, and agents who helped fill their pages. Pulp fans will be fascinated by the rich background provided by hundreds of quotes from the people involved in producing the Western pulps, while writers will benefit from the discussions of characterization and storytelling that prove to be both universal and timeless.

—*James Reasoner*

$29.95 softcover
$39.95 hardcover
$8.99 ebook

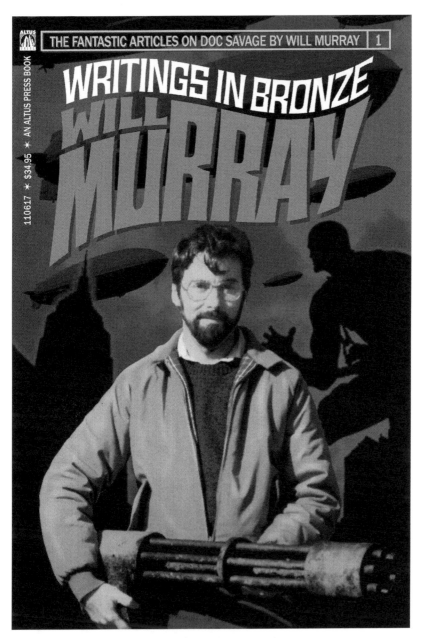

Really.
Totally.
Awesome.
—Book Nut

To the world at large, Doc Wilde and his family are an amazing team of golden-skinned adventurers, born to daring escapades and globetrotting excitement! Join them as they crisscross the Earth on a constant quest for new knowledge, incredible 21st-century thrills, and good old-fashioned adventure!

Now in deluxe illustrated editions, Tim Byrd's Doc Wilde novels recapture the magic of classic pulp cliffhangers for readers of all ages.

"Doc Wilde swings in on a jungle vine to raise the flag high for adventure. Infused with pace, fun, and all the two-fisted action a reader could ask for... "
—**Zack Stentz, screenwriter, 'Thor', 'X-Men: First Class'**

"Written in fast-paced, intelligent prose laced with humor and literary allusions ranging from Dante to Dr. Seuss, the story has all of the fun of old-fashioned pulp adventures."
—**Kirkus Reviews**

OUTLAW MOON

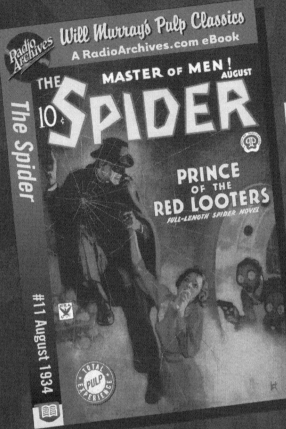

Made in the USA
Lexington, KY
27 November 2013